Oriana Oakleigh

and the Primrose Path

W.R. COOPER

Oriana Oakleigh

and the Primrose Path

TATE PUBLISHING & Enterprises

Published by Tate Publishing & Enterprises, LLC
127 E. Trade Center Terrace | Mustang, Oklahoma 73064 USA
1.888.361.9473 | www.tatepublishing.com

Tate Publishing is committed to excellence in the publishing industry. The company reflects the philosophy established by the founders, based on Psalm 68:11,
"The Lord gave the word and great was the company of those who published it."

Book design copyright © 2010 by Tate Publishing, LLC. All rights reserved.
Cover design by Kandi Evans
Interior design by Chris Webb
Illustrations by Robert Pendergast

Published in the United States of America

ISBN: 978-1-61663-267-0
1. Fiction / Fantasy / Epic   2. Fiction / Fantasy / Historical
10.12.27

For my children,
Phillip, Audrey, and Cedric

Acknowledgments

foremost, I wish to thank my wife, Dawn, without whose untiring patience whilst I remained cloistered in my study and my madness for months on end, this book could not have been written. She has been, and continues to be, my toughest critic and most ardent supporter.

A special thanks to my brother, Seth, for his literary, epistemological, and metaphysical critiques. Having a philosopher in the family is a good thing.

To my mother, Mary Lynne, and son, Phillip, who read some of the earliest and ghastliest drafts, and yet offered nothing but encouragement, my deepest gratitude.

I am especially grateful to Mr. Robert Pendergast for his life-giving illustrations and Ms. Kaitlyn Wright for her fine reproduction of the runic-border on the front cover.

To my friend and colleague Ms. Susan Nolan and my gifted student Ms. Megan DeWitt, who provided extensive editing and analysis, my sincerest thank you.

To my editor, Ms. Briana Johnson, though we had our disagreements, I am indebted to her vastly improving my story. A special thanks to Ms. Carmen Walsh of Walsh Writing for her superb post-production editing.

Finally, to my many college and high school students who have read snippets in various states of completion and opined most freely and frankly whether solicited or not—cheers!

"[K]eep this great wonder of nature as it now is … You can not improve on it. The ages have been at work on it, and man can only mar it."

—President Theodore Roosevelt

"[I]t is well known that the little creatures commonly called fairies, though there are many different kinds of fairies in Fairyland, have an exceeding dislike to untidiness. Indeed, they are quite spiteful to slovenly people. Being used to all the lovely ways of the trees and flowers, and to the neatness of the birds and all woodland creatures, it makes them feel miserable, even in their deep woods and on their grassy carpets, to think that within the same moonlight lies a dirty, uncomfortable, slovenly house. And this makes them angry with the people that live in it, and they would gladly drive them from the world if they could. They want the whole earth nice and clean."

—George MacDonald

Table of Contents

Part Two
The Dragaica Bride

Lay of Ethélfleda

Ethélfleda, O fair maiden,
Bright song in darkest fen;
Ethélfleda, sweet Faërie queen,
Restore primrose; we wait.

In sable sky five shall appear,
Stars yellow, blue, and red;
Soon all will join in vastness cold
With young suns of silver, gold.

Prepare wise men, whose beards yet grow
With cloaks red, shimmering,
To summon folk from Faërie land
Down silver lane, babe in hand.

Ethélfleda, dear Swan Maiden,
Green eyes are meadows sown.
Ethélfleda, the forests sing
To one who shares their fate.

Great sacrifice high elves shall make
When hawthorn tree is found.
In sunderance last hope be hid;
Elven child, farewell is bid.

O hoary head, tall points so keen,
Grim tidings you must give
To purest heart, then make haste,
By wood and wash and fens of waste.

Dragaica Bride! O Litha maid!
Solestitia Eve!
Guide and thee in Seed of Life,
Atone for others' ruin rife.

Twice doomed, alas, thy course is set;
In caverns pitch, beware.
Dread Fáfnirson is lurking low
To slay hope his mortal foe.

Ethélfleda, great golden name,
In whom the world's returned
Ethélfleda, the hills remain
Lest song is sung too late.

In dark shadows, the old wyrm's lair,
Elf lady may be freed,
By gentle girl and kingly lance
To mend, love, and heal with dance.

When hope shall flee take heart, unite,
Quintessence and quintet.
With Faërie song and weapons old
Send fell beast to yonder, cold.

Next bride be wed to Saxon king,
A union meant to join,
The fate of worlds both Faërie old
And troubled men, reckless, bold.

Year and a day, O Faërie queen,
Thy union must endure,
Or woe to thee!
Cross with tears by silver road
To Faërie kin, far abode.

Ethélfleda, white citadel,
Thou nourish primrose wine.
Ethélfleda, warm sun in spring,
Doomed brook and vale await.

Prologue:
A Bitter Sacrifice

In a glade of oaks, ancient and secret, there stood an old man, a boy, and a tall faërie king. Yet three they were not, for the king was holding close to his bosom a baby girl. A half moon looked down curiously; beyond him, stars beyond measure sparkled cold, winking with anticipation. And from long silver chains, high in the boughs, lamps swung yellow and red through a crisp autumn air.

Babe, boy, old man, and king were not alone. In the centre of the glade rose a single tree; yet no oak was he, but an immense hawthorn rather, easily thrice the girth and height of the nearest tree. A terrific cleft gaped wide down his long, hollow trunk.

The king had just arrived.

"King Gwyn ap Nudd!" said the wizened old man with a reverent bow. "We are honoured, Your Majesty." The old man had warm blue eyes and a long, curly white beard flecked with brown, which he was just now tucking in behind his wide black belt. His tall, pointed hat matched perfectly the red of his robes.

"Melchior," replied the king with a cordial nod. And as the tall king drew near he seemed to shimmer as though possessing an inner radiance of young starlight. "Liu Shang also sends his greetings."

"You have been to the Eastern Guild?"

"I have."

The king was a sight to behold—a radiant being in white cambric, girded by a gold-leaf belt. A broad sword set in a purple scabbard of crystallized foxgloves hung long at his side. He wore a crown too, not of gold or silver or anything ordinarily thought precious, but a tall, wooden crown rather. Indeed it did not, on the whole, accord with the kind of crown one would suppose a king to possess. For one thing, it was very tall—nearly half as tall as he, with eleven slender points round the top. For another, each tip was capped by a most unexpected thing. They weren't diamonds or rubies or anything of that sort, but unexceptional and altogether ugly-looking black rocks the size of a small fist, balanced perfectly atop its fine wooden spire.

"And the Sun Brooch?" asked the old man nervously. "Is it—"

"Safe? Yes," returned the king quickly, "as safe as may be in such times. Liu Shang has kept its secret well these many years. This too he sends with his blessings."

At this happy news the old man's gaze fell on the baby girl in the king's arms. She yawned and smiled at him. His eyes went suddenly sad.

He then noticed the child's swaddling cloth. How unusual it was; it looked nothing short of woven gossamer. Though it was impossible to say for certain, owing to its many folds and tucks around the child, it appeared to have a strange landscape embroidered on one side.

"And who is our young friend here?" asked the king, gesturing to the youth by the old man's side. The blond-haired boy blushed in return, excitement glinting in his wide eyes. "I understood your guild was not to admit pupils before early adulthood," he added with a perplexed air.

"It is so, Your Majesty," returned the old man directly, straightening his back with the aid of his staff. He smiled down at the boy, clapping his hand gently on his shoulder. "But we thought it prudent to relax our custom for this one exception. Already have we seen extraordinary song in him."

"Really?" replied the tall king of Faërie, raising his silvery eyebrows intrigued.

"Allow me to introduce, Dunstan, son of Heorstan of the house of Baltonsborough," said the old man eagerly.

"Hail and good fortune I extend to thee, Dunstan, son of Heorstan, from me and all free folk of Danuvia—Faërie, so I believe your kindred call it," the tall king said brightly. "Greetings, I say."

"I—I," sputtered the boy in reply, falling to his knees. "I am overwhelmed, Your Majesty. This is an honour beyond that which words can convey. I am at your service, O great king of unwithering lands."

"Are you?" replied the king, fixing the boy with his fierce eyes. "Then I shall take that as an oath. Rise, young mage, and be a friend to Faërie. Indeed, I fear the hour draws nigh when Danuvia shall require your service, yours and all the guilds'."

The boy rose without a word, staring back in a worried way. He nodded mildly to the king.

"But alas, Sire," resumed the old man with a troubled voice, his shoulders slouching again, heavy with the weight of many years. "We cannot offer what you seek—"

The king yet had his eyes riveted on the boy.

"Long have we of the Crimson Guild wondered when this day might finally come," the old man went on. "Yet in all those nine hundred years, we have been unable to locate the twin hawthorn for you, Sire."

"Eight hundred and seventy-two years in the mortal realm, to be precise," returned the king, smiling. "Be at peace, good druid."

With these words, the king gave a hearty tug at the old man's beard, putting to flight two small grey wrens nesting within.

Intrigued or amused or both, the baby lifted her head from the king's arms and followed the birds' path with smiling eyes.

Looking down, the old man began tugging at his beard himself as if half expecting to discover other vagrants lodging within. The boy glanced sideways at his master and put his hand to his face, forcing back a quiet laugh.

"Truly have many winters passed since your kinsmen journeyed from the east," observed the king. "Now is the day come at long last."

"We are eager to begin, Sire," continued the old man, still examining his beard. "Long ago did our first master, Joseph, sunder his staff for this very moment, indeed for this very purpose—one to give and one to receive, so he instructed."

"Yes, Melchior. That is what I seek—the staff buried to blossom anew in the Tree of Reception."

"It grieves me that we can be of no assistance to Your Majesty in this matter," returned the old man, shaking his head frustratingly at the enormous hawthorn ahead. "In all those years, never have we been able to unlock its enchantment."

On hearing this, the tall king bent his eyes kindly on the boy who had been listening ever intently. "Master Dunstan, if you would be good enough to excuse us for a moment. I should like to have a private word with your master."

"Of … of course, Your Majesty," muttered the boy, gawking still at the ethereal king and small, emerald-eyed bundle in his arms. It was then, in the moon's faint light, that the boy seemed to notice the baby had the king's eyes, surveying her curiously, then glancing up at the king and back down again at the child.

"Yes, I think it's high time you were scooting along, Dunstan," agreed the old man with a wink. "Tell the others that I'll rejoin them shortly."

At once, the boy turned on his heel, taking his departure in the direction of a lamp-lit lane through the forest enclosure, saying over his shoulder as he sped, "O great king, I say again, I am ever at your disposal." Waving, he disappeared into the ancient wood.

The king smiled and turned to the old man. "Take heart, Melchior. I am not troubled by your tidings. Nay, rather it is well that the tree's whereabouts should have remained hidden."

"And so it has, lord." The old man's voice went suddenly dark and low. "Our master insisted he set out alone on his final pilgrimage. He … he never returned to us." The druid coughed twice and cleared his throat to compose himself. "As it is, we have never known where he chose to inter its severed half."

"Be comforted, my friend," said the king reassuringly. "Here, at least I may be able to help. Behold! For the king of Danuvia shall he point the way to his sibling."

So saying, the king handed the babe to the old man and darted forward with long strides to the hawthorn, which both had been eyeing. The old man followed, shambling behind, leaning on his staff as he came. Once there, the king removed his towering wooden crown, knelt, and placed it inside the hollow trunk. He closed his eyes.

Neither spoke. The air was tense, rife with anxiety. Suddenly, the crown began to glow as crystal, then spin, slowly at first, but then ever rapidly till its speed lent the appearance of a child's whirling top, only much taller. Gusts of air flew from the spinning crown like a seaward gale, waving and snapping the king's hair behind him in a silvery sheet.

And there was another sight too. Moments after the king's crown began to spin, there came a dazzle of yellow-green light, singing and dancing. It at once surrounded them, circling wide around the tree, ruffling the tall grasses and wild daisies in its dance. Then, just as the crown brightened and quickened, so the curious wreath of light changed with it. Delicate, amorphous shapes, clasped hand in hand, emerged steadily from the chartreuse glow, swaying side to side, gay and lilting in their song.

"The Gandharvas!" gasped the old man, his eyes sparkling as he marveled at the light-maidens and their singing.

Gradually, the crown slowed and came to a halt. It looked of wood once more, and as it resumed its form, the wide faërie ring, merrily singing and dancing, vanished too in an instant.

The king stared hard at the crown as though analyzing its new position. He reached inside and set it back upon his long silvern locks.

"I have it," said the king blissfully, casting his starry gaze to the east. "He has sung of his twin's abode."

"Mother Danu be praised!" returned the old man, marveling still. "Well done, Sire!"

"Yes, I have it. But it is not for me to say if the tree is near or far. It awaits the child! I must away at once."

The druid looked down at the precious bundle in his arms. She was smiling back at him.

"What a beautiful child, Your Grace. Have you ever looked upon anything prettier?" The baby girl seemed also to have taken an interest in the old man, to his long white whiskers particularly.

"She is a miracle of beauty, yes," agreed the tall king, nodding. "Yet once you beheld a greater child, did you not, Melchior?" he asked with sudden reverence.

"Indeed, Sire, many years ago—before our journey into the west."

"And so did it begin," added the king, looking as if he were reflecting on something very important.

"This deed is unthinkable, Your Majesty," the old man grumbled lamentably, his head shaking with disfavour. He went suddenly dull-eyed, reluctant to hand the child over to the king. "Are you sure there is no other way?"

The king nodded with equal ruth, smiling sadly. "I am afraid so." He then paused as if in thought and asked, "Has the guild prepared the hope chest according to Whitethorn's design?"

"It is done."

King and druid now turned and strode briskly toward the entrance of the winding forest lane.

"The casket has been etched with the Saxons' own sacred writing along with the borrowed tongue of Danuvia," said the old man, now obliged to scuffle in quick strides just to keep up with the much taller king. "The carvings too foretell of the coming of the Swan Maiden and her expected place among the Magi Order. Our artisans have been diligent in their strokes. Through their careful marks is the Great Reconciliation between the wielders of Worldsong and the new faith duly honoured."

"Fine!" said the king in a pleased way, staring over his shoulder. The druid was starting to fall behind. "And what of man's sin, his dominion—is it depicted?"

The sage nodded. "That too is carved in deep relief as an exhortation to those who would believe."

"The guild has done well," replied the king sincerely. "The power of the casket should serve to conceal the Sun Brooch until the time is ripe."

"But, Sire," said the old man, looking down at the baby's unusual swaddling as he lumbered after the king, "what of the cloth? Does it also bear the writing as was foretold?"

"Yes, Melchior, I have seen to it, personally."

"The Lay of Ethélfleda, Sire?"

"Verily!" returned the king. "The rejoinder of hope—the very answer to the Lay of Dread. The verses are scored with sprite dust into the back of the cloth."

"Then may we now … may we now know the answer?" asked the old man, puffing in his difficulty to keep up. "Surely we are to prepare the lady's return to her rightful place beneath the moon."

"Those preparations are for another to make," insisted the king, stopping at last at the forest entrance several strides before the old man. "The Lay of Ethélfleda is intended for her. Only through her own deciphering shall she be able to embrace her true destiny and free the Faërie Queen. And so, in the meantime, I must ask the patience of the Order once again. Yet the hour will not be long in coming, I deem. Soon will the five stars be joined, and hence the hour the hidden amulets must be rejoined. It is written that by the queen's hands alone shall the Hawthorn Disk be restored—*should* she ever be freed in Malgorod! For this is of course the great gambit we make, Melchior. Should the child survive to womanhood she will require the aid of all the Order, even your warlock friend of old, that recluse of the northern Winter Guild—his wisdom too will be required.

"Yet," he said with a pause, peering ahead through the forest,

"I expect you are right. Much may depend on one who has all but begun his studies."

"The boy, Your Majesty?" inquired the old man, releasing his staff to stroke the full length of his beard. And as he pondered, his beard began to glow just as crimson and sorcerous as his fine robes.

The king nodded. "I sense your appraisal is an apt one. I too heard Worldsong waxing strong within him."

The old man said nothing. He had a troubled look in his eyes. He continued stroking his beard till it turned white once more.

"Take heed to my counsel, Melchior," cautioned the king finally. "I must stress upon you one last time; only through the combined efforts of the *entire* Order can our worlds be permanently bridged and ruinous deeds set to rights! But I can say no more, my friend. I have foreseen no more."

The king stretched out his hands to the druid. The time had come.

"It is then a grave choice, Your Majesty," said the old man with a deep measure of pathos in his voice. And wrapt in these reflections, he gently prized the child's grip from his beard.

The druid's eyes went suddenly misty as he handed the baby girl back to the king. "What a bitter sacrifice. Abraham of old could himself have known no greater sorrow."

"Come now, my friend, no tears," said the king delicately. "Be of good hope, for hope there is still! Have your guild bring forth the chest—Liu Shang's gift awaits it. By Idun's grace, may it protect her from unfriendly eyes."

The druid wiped his eyes on his palms.

"Now is the hour come! Now for abandonment and doom—and for hope! Indeed she is our only hope."

Part One
Lord Whitethorn

CHAPTER I

Of Woe and Linens

It was a grand day for most who attended and most unusual for one. The early morning sky promised ample sun with just the right amount of silvery clouds—the fun, fluffy sort easily shaped to suit the fancy of one's imagination. Concerns of yet another unwelcome rainstorm passed and were replaced with a collective relief that today's feast would be just as splendid and pleasantly dry as the last. Villager and noble alike agreed if Oakleigh Manor[1] were to be punished with yet another day of showers, having already endured more than a fortnight of the unforgiving damp, the cereals of the east field would surely begin to rot. And then of course, and perhaps worse, they would have faced the very disagreeable prospect of the second annual Brunanburh Victory Feast being canceled altogether—no one wanted that!

Indeed, of all feast-days in Wessex, Brunanburh Day had quickly risen to become the most anticipated summer festival. No self-respecting Saxon—lord, yeoman, or otherwise—would dare miss it. Now, happily, with the obliging change of weather, none would.

---

[1] The word "manor" does not enter the Old English tongue spoken in Oriana's time until after the arrival of the Normans in 1066. Though in practice, the form and function of manors do begin to emerge in the late-Saxon period, even if the word itself was not present. The work, thoughts, and leisure of peasants, their intimacy with the land and obligations to their lord, and the relationship of their lord to his lord, often the king, differed very little whether one calls this agrarian structure a village, hamlet, manor, or multiple-estate.

"Nothin' but gossipmongerin's all that rot is," said a man behind a wheelbarrow filled with awning poles and braces. "You mark my words, you won't be seein' no cottagers 'ere from Shaftesbury, not a one; that's a fact, that is."

"Maybe, but wot they got planned fer the second day—now that ain't no rumor, to be sure," said a second man, a short man, as he drove his last tent peg into the soil. "There's to be a tournament—a contest of arms—'eard it from Lord Elgar's own lips, did I, before 'e set off."

"Aye, an' falconry, from wot I've 'eard," said the first man's wife, as she began removing the wooden poles one by one from her husband's barrow. "Scores of mewed peregrines and—and Welsh 'awks too, they'll be bringin'."

"An' an archery competition, wot's more," added the second man eagerly.

"Well I can't speak to no archery match," said the first man gruffly, putting down his barrow with a wet thud, "but if there is I shouldn't go gettin' drummed up over it if I was you."

"Why not?" asked the second man defensively. "I'm as good a shot as any in our shire, 'cept for Lord Éthelhelm, maybe."

"What of that? They won't let no ox-herd like you nowhere near their private contests."

"Yeah, well that just shews wot little you know, now don't it?" scoffed the second man. "I've already 'ad a word with the lady 'bout it last week, I 'ave."

"With Lady Mildreth? Are you daft? Surprized you didn't get double duty as a reward just for speakin' to her highness."

"Why don't yeh put that there gimlet in yer apron to good purpose an' bore through them waxy ears. Yeh 'aven't 'eard me proper. I said I spoke with the *lady*, the *true* lady of Oakleigh, Lady Oriana. She's seen m' fletchin' an' says m' skill with a bow is the best around—said so 'erself many times, she 'as. Told me I'm welcome ter try me hand against the nobles."

"Ah, Lady Oriana! I should've guessed your meanin' from the start," said the first man, nodding and grinning in a way that marked his favour most decidedly. "Has there ever been a maid so fair, so sweet-tempered? As gentle a maid as ever lived!"

"If you'd said that 'bout anyone else," returned the wife sternly, shaking her finger warningly at her husband, "you'd be findin' yerself polin' these 'ere tents without my aid I can tell yeh sure as spit in a sty. But who can deny the truth of it? Lady Oriana is the flower of Selwood."

So had their kind words reached her ears just the day before. She hadn't tried to eavesdrop, but it couldn't be helped. She had walked right by them while inspecting the party grounds, and as she had been cloaked and hooded to shed the noon's drizzle, none had recognised her as she passed.

And just who is she? She is Miss Oriana, daughter of the steward of the house of Oakleigh, the flower of Selwood in the opinion of nearly all in the village.

◇◇◇◇◇◇◇◇◇◇◇◇◇◇◇◇◇◇◇◇◇◇◇◇◇◇◇◇◇◇◇◇◇◇◇◇◇◇◇

Oriana woke from a fitful sleep. She had scarce slept a wink all night. In that hazy twilight between sleep and wakefulness, she recalled this very conversation between the village peasants—it lightened her heart. Indeed, they were not to blame for her restless night. Something else was agitating her mind.

As Oriana made to get out of bed, she found herself in a sullen mood despite the fine spring morning, the sixteenth of Plough Month to be precise—you probably call this month June. Typically, Oriana was as far from gloomy as one could ever hope to be. But this could not be said of her today. Today was different!

"Come on, Oriana," she said to herself languidly. "Let's have it over with."

Sulking, Oriana dragged herself out of bed, rubbed the sleep from her eyes, and bent to her toes with three quick stretches. She went to her window. It was framed on each side by ivy, tall climbing roses, and bryony tendrils all wonderfully intertwined. There, she knelt on a low trestle bench richly engraved, planted her elbows on the open sill, and rested her chin in her palms.

She sniffed one of the dew-beaded roses and then gazed up at the clearing skies. Part of her was hoping for more rain.

"How will I ever manage to get through the day?" she said wistfully. "My nerves are one thing, but my grief! O how it oppresses on this day."

As she surveyed the lazy clouds, she thought one began to take the shape of a bear with donkey ears. She attempted a smile. None came.

Oriana was in the bloom of youth, half a score and seven in years, and uncommonly handsome. Her emerald eyes shone like the bright of day and her blonde hair was as the sun, reaching with thick waves down to the fold of her lower back. She was slender and tallest of her peers but in no respect ungainly. She had a disciplined mind and a body that did exactly as she told it. In fact, Oriana was so agile her friends often looked on in envy when she took exercise. And when it came to archery or riding—riding in particular—Oriana had not her equal in the whole of Selwoodshire. She preferred riding bareback—that is, when she could get away with it—but such fun could only be had when her father or Governess Bathilda were not in close attendance, and that occasion was not readily got. Both considered this an unnecessary hazard to rider and steed alike despite Oriana's repeated professions to the contrary.

Though Oriana was strong of body and certainly attractive, she never regarded herself as a great beauty. But truth be told, this mattered little to her. In the main, she was really quite content with her appearance—an uncommon and fortunate attribute for any young lady, then or now. Oriana was blessed with a pretty face, a sound mind, and good health.

"That alone should be enough to content any young girl," so Governess Bathilda took care to instill in her from a young age. Oriana never could find fault with this simple aphorism.

Nevertheless, Oriana did, on occasion, compare herself with others her age. She could no more help thinking she would never rival the poise and grace of Lady Elenoora of Frome, who was her friend, than believing she hadn't the beauty or beguiling charms of Lady Edgira of Shaftsbury, who was most decidedly and happily *not* her friend. Indeed, when it came to Lady Edgira, it was widely voiced that she and Oriana had agreed in disliking one another these past three years. Both made it plain enough through their words and conduct that there would never be any love lost between them come what may. Nothing was likely to change this.

So, Oriana was satisfied with her looks as far as it went. However, there were her eyes. Green and warm they were to be sure, but there was no getting round it, they were different. Her eyes were in fact one degree oversized and half a degree and one again, too wide-set. Oriana never really believed the size and placement of her eyes dimmed her appearance, though it did lend her the look of an outsider in her opinion. As it was, she usually gave little attention to this oddity (as she viewed it) except when mentioned in silly conversations with some of her more officious girlfriends.

Now apart from her fine looks, her governess would be proud to tell you Oriana had been high spirited and gregarious almost from birth. Yet she would be quick to point out that her *pretty darling* had never inclined toward childish frivolity, so enriched she was with more noble virtues. Always did Oriana give her preference to deeper, more philosophical exchanges over superficial chatter or threadbare subjects.

Still, Oriana was a teenager! And as might be expected of most girls her age she looked forward to the excitement of feast-days, saints' days, and market fairs. And when unexpected messengers arrived at Oakleigh Manor to announce a royal visit from His Majesty, King Athelstan, well, let us just say she was positively a portrait of impatient expectancy. But this day, this Brunanburh Feast day, was not like those days.

From her window high atop the mighty bluestone escarpment of Oakleigh ridge, Oriana fixed her eyes upon the gentle contours of the green glade beneath. O how her window admitted a most delightful view! Oriana's chamber was one of several such buildings of the Great House, but hers commanded a perspective not to be matched anywhere on Lord Elgar's manor, or for that matter, the whole of Selwoodshire itself—or such was her opinion at any rate.

Within the outer ward grew a pleasance of vegetable and herb gardens, orchards, and wild berry patches that encircled Oakleigh ridge in sloping, concentric rings. The grounds were beautifully kept and well defended behind a stout, wooden bailey wall painted white.

Presently, Oriana looked beyond the outer ward for signs of early guests, and, she had to confess, was enjoying the nearly forgotten delight of the sun's warmth on her cheeks.

"I suppose I really ought to view things in their proper perspective—as they really are," she said pensively, twirling the ends of her hair round her finger.

"After all," she went on, "had the rain and cold continued much longer, wonder knows what would've become of the villagers' crops and haymaking, not to mention our own storehouses. The farmers have had such a horrid time of it. I know it's entirely selfish of me to pray for another day of rain for my sole benefit. I really oughtn't to set the welfare of so many against my own wish to avoid the memory of his loss."

At this thought, Oriana suddenly caught sight of something small off in the distance flying straight for her. Intrigued, she blinked and narrowed her focus. But to her astonishment, it was no longer there.

"That's odd," she said quizzically. "What can it have been?"

She rubbed her eyes thinking perhaps the morning drowse was affecting her vision. Yet whatever it was she had just seen was now gone.

She returned to her musing over the festival.

"Oh, but why delude myself? If I know Lord Elgar and Lady Mildreth aright, another day of showers would alter nothing in the end anyway. I expect the heavens could hurl brimstone, and still they would not cancel today's feast—certainly not after more than a week of preparations, preparations left almost entirely to my care. And, besides, today's celebration is a directive from the king, after all."

Just then, an ugly grey and white-speckled moth nearly the size of Oriana's hand flew swiftly toward her, stopping within feet of her nose. It appeared, seemingly, from out of nowhere.

"This must be that tiny speck I just saw," she remarked of the peculiar sight.

And it was peculiar; she did not like the look of this moth at all. For reasons she could not give, it gave her a dreadful chill that ran throughout the whole of her body—yet she did not, or could not, recoil from it. Minute after minute the moth hovered directly in front of her. In fact, had Oriana not possessed such rational sensibilities, she would have actually thought it to be watching her—indeed, to be studying her!

Eventually, the moth slowly fluttered away north. Oriana looked on, still curious over the frost-like sensation it effected.

Oriana lost sight of the moth and, giving no further thought to it, turned her attention to the southern reaches of Oakleigh Manor. She could just see a narrow sliver of the old cobbled lane.

It was a skilled patchwork of white and reddish stones, running from the western bend of Feldway Lane right the way up to the outer gatehouse then straight on through the encircling gardens of the outer-ward and coming to rest at the foot of Oakleigh Ridge's grand staircase.

What a stairway! It had been hewn directly into the southern face of Oakleigh Ridge by skilled masons of old and lifted impressively from the end of the cobbled lane in a terrific height up to the flattened summit of Oakleigh Ridge. Visitors to Oakleigh Manor always complimented Lord Elgar on its beauty, for the interlace and zoomorphic carvings fretted on its treads and risers, landings, and rails were ornate beyond any of its kind in the whole of Wessex.

There, at the steps' uppermost landing was a timber-colonnaded portico with oaken, double-hung doors poised at the far end. With their wide iron hinges and pointed bronze studs, these trusty doors granted limited admittance to the inner ward—or the "house," as it was simply called. Long had these stout oaken doors been celebrated in song for their power to invite guests or deny trouble.

Oriana wished she could spend the whole day alone, enjoying the honeysuckle aroma now rising up to her window. She watched the shadow of a swift-moving cloud sail southeast past the walls of the outer ward, over Willowrun Creek then down to the peasant village, a cluster of cottages and workshops, barns and stables. There also, were the village mill and smithy, oven and smokehouse, and the small parish church—the Church of St. Cuthbert.

Even more than the village, the ancient forest of Selwood, which encircled the manor on all sides like a wide, green belt, was easily Oriana's favourite haunt. Oh, she simply adored it! She had passed the greater part of her youth exploring its mysteries. Oriana could wish for nothing better than to run and sing and dance amongst the attentive beeches, elms, oaks, ashes, and firs of Selwood Forest. Lately, she was spending just as much of her leisure time there as could be got—much more often, in fact, than her governess approved. But it just couldn't be helped; the forest called to her, and she couldn't disappoint it.

Oriana got to her feet, stretched her back, and, looking out on Selwood's southern entrance, said, "Ah, that must be Cadwallon with his household from Shaftesbury. They certainly are arrived early. I wonder if he's brought the pigeon loaves and rashers of bacon as I requested? I'll bet a mancus[2] of his own Shaftesbury pennies that he hasn't."

Oriana, being keen-sighted, could just make out their caravan of six wagons racing up Feldway Lane. Lord Elgar and Lady Mildreth were among the company, returning home in time to commence the victory feast. Over the past week, Lord Elgar had been attending Cadwallon's court to take up matters Oriana could only guess. She wondered if their counsels concerned the rumoured regrouping of the northern foes or maybe King Athelstan's reported illness.

Four of the approaching wagons belonged to the lord and lady of Oakleigh and were mostly filled with empty barrels, their contents apparently consumed the previous week. As for Cadwallon himself, it appeared he was bringing only two wagons, and from what Oriana could see, they had no barrels, empty or brimming.

That Cadwallon was bringing nothing to share at the festival was little surprize to Oriana. The lord of Shaftesbury was widely regarded as a detestable man who was not at all gentle or generous with his peasants. And his treatment of his few slaves was yet another matter entirely. Oriana thought that if Cadwallon

---

[2] A mancus is a weight measurement equal to thirty silver pennies. It was used to assess the value of gold armlets, rings, or necklaces. Under the directives of King Athelstan, two mints were recently established in the village of Shaftesbury.

had but one redeeming quality it resided in his cordial, though rarely pleasant, exchanges with her father.

"Oh, Father, why?" she said to herself, shaking her head in a despondent way. She gazed out on the swelling number of villagers gathering below in the west meadow. "When shall you return to me?"

It was her father, Phillip, high steward of Oakleigh and royal tutor to King Athelstan's court, who was the source of Oriana's sullen mood this morning. Rather, it was his absence that was to blame. For on this very day, two years ago, her father had vanished during King Athelstan's campaign against the northern-allied foes. The morning of his departure to help lead Selwood-shire's fyrd[3] was the last she ever saw of him.

It was odd—odd and incensing. A great buzz over her father's whereabouts spread as wildfire when he failed to return from Brunanburh with the others. Several of the valiant men of Oakleigh had, of course, fallen that fateful day, never to return home. But unlike they, what befell Phillip was very mysterious indeed!

Almost no one agreed on what had happened to the learned steward of Oakleigh. Some claimed he had been slain on the field of battle and, for reasons never mentioned, left where he had fallen. Others reported he had been betrayed by one of his closest squires, bound, and taken by the enemy. And there were yet still more who whispered, at one time or another, that he had been seized by a sudden madness during the thick of battle, running off to a wooded glen screaming, "Black hiise! Black hiise! Beardless gnomes and darkest elves! Our doom is near!"

It was this last rumour that infuriated Oriana the most. Naturally, she regarded such hackneyed gossip, such fanciful hearsay, as sheer lie, knowing her father to be neither cowardly nor mad. She resented, quite rightly, any fantasy that did little to

---

[3] Saxon militia

explain her father's actual disappearance and much only to fuel local superstitions.

His loss afflicted Oriana most severely. For Oriana was an only child, and as her mother, Ariánrod, had died bringing her into the world, the bond between father and daughter had grown all the stronger thereby. So sorely did she now grieve for him. Oriana missed her father, by the very hour she missed him.

Presently, Oriana's thoughts began to stray back to her father reclining alongside a cheering fire, wrapt in his travel worn cloak. It was a lovely memory; it had been a lovely spring evening. A sickle moon hung crisp and bright, and fireflies by the hundreds twinkled about, aiding the stars above.

◇◇◇◇◇◇◇◇◇◇◇◇◇◇◇◇◇◇◇◇◇◇◇◇◇◇◇◇◇◇◇◇◇◇◇◇

"Oriana, my dear golden-haired child, delight of my heart," he said, stoking the bottom embers with his walking stick. "How is it that I should be so fortunate?"

Lord Phillip was tall with curly, brown hair, his face smooth and the colour of olives ripening. He possessed a slightly aquiline nose and deep brown eyes closely set. Needless to say, he did not have the look, or accent for that matter, of your typical West Saxon.

He went on thoughtfully, "To have so lovely a daughter is rare enough. But to have one both fair and full of thought is *quite* a rare thing, a singular gift indeed. How special you are, and how lucky I am."

"Now. Father, really!" pled Oriana sheepishly, letting her eyes drop from his.

"No, no, you heed what I'm saying, Orie," he said firmly. "You are an extraordinary young woman."

Oriana could feel her cheeks blushing. She shook her head mildly at her father.

"You don't believe me, huh? Well, consider this for start," he continued, poking the fire again as he spoke, his talk turning to philosophy as it ever did. "When I make the effort to listen to others your age—boys and girls alike, mind you—all I hear talk of is events, events, simple self-centered concerns, such is how they spend their hours; they speak of little else. Never do they discuss ideas—ideas in the abstract; never do they talk of possibilities beyond the confines of their own, narrowly-circumscribed world. All I hear is, 'Did you hear who Ine fancies? When shall the workday end? Who will be invited to tomorrow's hunt? I thought it was Hilda's turn for the winnowing and thrashing this week? You reckon there'll be tales in the mead hall tonight? Did you notice how soiled Wulfric's tunic was at Martinmass?' On and on they drone—typical vanities, simple occupancies of the mind, never a meaningful thought in effect."

Phillip sat up and leant closer to where the then fifteen-year-old Oriana sat, knees thrust upward in locked arms.

"You do understand me, don't you, daughter?" asked Phillip with a warm smile.

Oriana had got to expect such lectures on their outings. But she really didn't mind. On the contrary, finding occasion to further plumb the depths of her father's wisdom was one of the things she loved best. Oriana valued his opinion in everything.

"Yes, I think so," she replied, peering with soft, unfocused eyes into the yellow-red flames. "People my age, and I daresay even a good many of yours as well, Father, often dwell only on—well, superficial matters to put it bluntly. Their thoughts run no deeper. Yes, I think I understand," she added confidently. "When you say events you might well be saying gossip. You're right, I think. My acquaintances, and even some I regard as close friends, rarely discuss ideas not—uh, *centered round the self*, as you so often remark."

There was a silence as both sat peering into the orange flicker, listening to the night's unseen stirrings.

After a pause Oriana continued. "Though for my part, I confess I sometimes find myself engaging in conversations similar to those you just disparaged. After all, Father, I may be different, as you say, but I am not unique."

"Ah! but we were discussing typical concerns and those are not yours … not *typically* nor even *topically*." This he said with a grin as if pleased with his little word play. "It is a comfort to me, daughter, to know your disposition does not allow for such hubris. You haven't the capacity to conceive just how special you might be. But trust me, Oriana, when I say you are unique, and, yes, I do say this with full acknowledgment of my own partiality," he added with a wink. "Never was there a daughter of such consequence to a father—never. Yes, you are unique, child. I promise you this: you will discover this truth ere long."

"No, Father," rebuked Oriana as she started to her feet. She bent to the fire's edge and scooped up one of the fireflies she thought had landed just a bit too near the blaze. "There I must disagree with you," she went on reflectively. "I still insist there is nothing extraordinary about me at all, though indeed I thank you for the pleasantry. And as to my mind, well, I'm afraid it may not be as open to as many possibilities as you would wish."

"I'm sure this is no shortcoming. But tell me, to what exactly do you suppose your mind shut?"

She paused. "Well … if I may speak plainly."

"Of course. Always."

"It's like this." She set loose her firefly and reseated herself comfortably on the ground beside her father. She began picking off the small briar seeds clinging to the bottom of his cloak.

"What if I were to tell you," she went on, flinging the tiny green seeds into the fire, one by one, "that, while I am quite willing to accept your assertion of other realities—other worlds even—I still argue, as I have often observed, that a generous dose of skepticism is a more sensible tonic than misplaced hopes in that which cannot be experienced, just imagined."

"Then I would say in return that you are wise, daughter," he answered, now himself removing the briars. "For it is skepticism in the end that allows us to separate fact from fancy. Yet I ask you, are ideas that may never be experienced truly misplaced? Do not be overconfident in your senses or in that which experience has taught. Forget not the lessons of our good friend Plato, my love."

At this, he reached inside his cloak and withdrew a small circlet of interwoven primrose petals and hazel twigs concealed within. He bent toward his daughter and gently positioned the fresh anademe on her head.

Oriana had never seen the headpiece before that moment nor did she know how long her father had laboured in secret on the adornment. It was lovely. A tiny expression of his much greater love.

"There, now," he said with great gentleness, "a sweet crown for a noble mind. Happy birthday!" And with that he kissed his daughter affectionately on her brow.

"Oh, Father! How lovely it is. I shall treasure it always."

Many such displays of tenderness lived in her memory; she could easily recall them and often did, especially of late. Oriana stretched her arms out the window and closed the shutters, securing their bronze clasp. Now was her room illuminated by candlelight alone.

Shuffling her feet, she crossed the room to the dressing table in the far corner where still she kept her father's gift locked in a small whalebone casket. She seated herself near her polished looking glass and picked up the small chest.

This she valued above all her possessions, though in truth,

it probably wasn't hers at all really. She had no memory of the casket being given to her. As it was, it had been in her room for as long as she could remember and probably had been there well before she was born.

It was indeed a curious thing. Round all its surfaces were inscriptions in ancient runes and a strange, confused type of Latin script. And carved in deep relief were images from the old pagan beliefs and an especially exquisite scene depicting the magi at the nativity. But its most interesting feature by far lay inside— a small, irregularly shaped keyhole in the centre of the bottom panel. While Oriana always kept the key to the outer lid near to hand on her dressing table, she had never seen the one that unlocked the bottom. She sometimes doubted such a key ever existed or that it could even be opened in the first place as there were no bottom hinges. Even if the panel could be unlocked it would probably only make the bottom drop out. Silly.

Oriana placed the casket back on the dressing table, slid her chair closer, and stared at the somber eyes gazing back at her from the looking glass. She doubted anything would assuage her loneliness on this day.

"How can I hope to be gay on this of all days?" She began to brush the morning tangles from her hair. "While everyone is celebrating our great victory, feasting, merry making, and praising our visitors from Malmesbury, I alone, I'm sure, will be the only one grieving his loss. The irony of it all! The one feast out of the whole year I could well do without, and it's the very one left in my charge."

Just then, Oriana had a queer feeling. Something was wrong. She put down her brush at once. It felt as though—as though someone were staring at her! She spun with a start. But there was no one there. In fact, she saw little of anything save what the dim candlelight could reveal. And that was as it always looked. Or was it? All about her, light from the many winking, yellow points seemed to be swaying the timbered walls, and their fine tapestries as partners joined during a slow waltz. In that light, wall and hangings actually seemed to be alive!

But there was nothing else to be seen. No one was there! No one was watching! Perhaps her nerves were more strained than she had supposed.

Despite the obvious fact that she was alone, the feeling of being watched lingered. She sat gazing at the wall and at her tapestries in particular. Oriana was nearly as fond of these as her casket. Of the three, two had been woven by her hands. But the third halling was most peculiar and not of her make. And again, like the casket, it had always been in her room, so far as she was aware.

Oriana couldn't stop gazing at it. For it was this tapestry, above the other two, that looked alive indeed in the flickering candlelight. On its left side and occupying much of its foreground was an ancient hawthorn with a wide crack in its curving trunk. To the right of the tree, a white stag with oversized antlers rested on a green knoll in the distance. In the middle of the scene, a long silver road or bridge (it was difficult to tell which) was suspended in mid-air, arching downward to touch the grassy sward below, just several paces away from the hawthorn's wizened trunk.

You, no doubt, would have thought this tapestry unusual had you seen it. The scene alone made it a curiosity in its own right. But it was further mysterious in that there were no stitches anywhere to be seen. And you probably would have thought it altogether magickal had you felt the fabric. What exactly was it? Oriana never could guess. It was a bit like pearl to the touch yet as supple as the finest silk. In spite of its mystery, or maybe because of it, this tapestry was Oriana's favourite, and it hung squarely over her bed.

Oriana started to her feet to have a closer look at the stag tapestry, when loud came a knock to the door at the far end of her room.

"Yes?" said Oriana, a bit softer than she intended. She continued to stare transfixed at the unusual tapestry. There was silence then three more knocks in quick succession.

"Yes? I say, who is it?" she said a little louder this time.

"Sorry, wasn't sure if I heard you that first time," said a high-pitched, crackled voice through the door. "It's me. I mean it's I. Well anyhow, by Welund, it's definitely one of us."

"Ah, Penda, but you never said … half a moment."

Oriana grabbed her embroidered robe hanging beside the dressing mirror and wrapt it hastily over her linen undergarment. She rushed to the door, slid back its bolt, and welcomed her guest.

A lanky, brown-haired boy, shorter than Oriana by a head at least, stood swaying at the threshold. He was drest in a worn green tunic with a brown mantle and dull black boots that laced up just below his bony knees. The moss-coloured trim round the hem of his tunic was fraying in several places.

"I say, Penda, this *is* a pleasant surprise," she said gaily, embracing her friend in a warm hug. "I never expected you to call so early, or for that matter, at all today, come to that."

"Yeah, I thought you might do with a bit of cheering up this morning," he returned with a wide, fiendish grin, exposing as many teeth as he could manage. "So here I am with enough cheer to make even an old weather-beaten Dane laugh at Alfred's sword."

Her unexpected guest was a witty, and often mischievous, fifteen-year-old boy who, beneath the surface of his irreverent exterior, was really quite a man of sentiment, though he wouldn't care for that to get round. He had large brown, rather cow-like eyes—that is, when they could be seen at all on account of his neglected bangs. A fine-looking boy he was to be sure, only he possessed a rather restive nature that made him appear awkward at times. For one thing, he had a fixed habit of swaying side to side when he spoke, while simultaneously, and repeatedly, flicking his right thumb from under his forefinger. His fidgeting used to annoy Oriana, but now she gave little notice to it at all.

Truly, they were the best of friends despite their different stations in life, not that this mattered to Oriana in the slightest. Penda was baseborn, a ceorl,[4] while she, on the other hand, was a gentle lady of the house of Oakleigh. Four years ago Oakleigh's chamberlain had engaged Penda to assist him in maintaining the house. Master Cerdic, as Penda was always to address him, supervised the furnishing, sorting, scrubbing, and mending of the personal quarters and effects of Lord Elgar and Lady Mildreth, as well as those of their steward, Phillip, and his daughter,

---

[4] In days prior, the word ceorl described a peasant freeman under Wessex law. But by the tenth century, however, ceorls were losing much of their earlier autonomy to become increasingly tied to the soil and will of their lords.

Oriana. The duty of scrubbing and mending invariably fell to Penda, the honour of supervising to Cerdic. Yes, in those four years Oriana had grown particularly attached to Oakleigh's houseboy—she couldn't imagine life at Oakliegh Manor without him.

"I certainly hope I won't need that much encouragement," observed Oriana, smiling. She could feel her morose humour taking a decided turn for the better. "Honestly, do I look as melancholy as all that?"

"Hmm," he sighed, as if giving the question very serious consideration. "Shall I answer merely as an honest man or as your humble and obedient servant?"

"Well, given that you are neither of these, your opinion will do just fine, thanks."

"In that case, my lady ... you look for all the world every bit a catastrophe, if I'm any judge," he blurted out, bowing deeply until the ends of his shaggy, brown hair swept the turf. "Might want to smartin' yourself up a little," he added comically with upraised eyes before straightening himself.

"Cheers, Penda," she said, not entirely sure if she should be smiling at that remark. "I can always count on you to pay a compliment."

He bowed again with an impish grin.

"Incidentally, how ever did you manage it?" she asked seriously.

"Manage what?"

Oriana tilted her head. One eyebrow was raised.

"Oh ... right—well, I suppose you mean, how was I able to slip past the watchful eye of the outer gatehouse, evade Master Bardulf—our esteemed doorward and trusted protector of the house—and cross the full breadth of the exposed courtyard undetected to arrive safely and unmolested at your doorstep?" He was gesticulating as if in a performance before the king and all his aldermen. It was far more than his usual swaying to and fro.

"Not at all," returned Oriana with a tight grin. "What I meant was, how did you manage to persuade Master Cerdic to give you leave from a day of obligation? Or are you playing the truant again?"

"Since you evidently refuse to believe in my powers of stealth and cunning, in a word—I lied. Yesterday I told Chamberlain ..."

"Don't you mean *Master* Cerdic," interrupted Oriana, now repressing the desire to laugh out loud.

"The very same, yes; well, yesterday as I was makin' ready to return home, I told Chamberlain—*Master Cerdic*—that you had some special linens that wanted washin' before the lord and lady returned home. I told 'im you'd grant me liberty of the stables on Sunday next if I saw to 'em straightaway."

Oriana took her friend by the arm. "Here, in you come. We can continue your fib inside. The ground outside is yet damp. Ah, here! Let's sit by the hearth. Give me a hand with this bench, will you?"

They grasped a high-back double seat with worn, purple cushions and carried it away from the wall, sometimes lifting, sometimes sliding, positioned it alongside the central hearth, and sank comfortably into its soft padding. What little smoke was rising from the hearth's cooling embers trailed up to the thatched roof and out through the open-air gables at either end of the room.

"Now, you were saying," resumed Oriana, folding her hands across her lap, "that Cerdic gave you the day off from today's feast duties *just* to help you earn special favours from me, with nothing in it for himself at all? Are we talking about the same Cerdic?"

"Well ... not exactly *nothing* to gain, no," said Penda as he unlaced his boots, slipped them off, and began drying his feet by the coals. "There was also the secondary issue of the riddle. I promised I'd finally give 'im the answer to one of the riddles your father brought with him out of the east—been a right frustrating poser for our good Chamberlain for ages—told 'im I've known the answer for years. Know the one I mean?"

"Wait, don't tell me! The long Byzantine riddle, right? The one by—let me see now—who did compose that?" Oriana thought for a moment, she too now warming her toes by the hearth.

"Pisides. Yes, I believe that's it. But I never knew you worked out the answer to that one—at least … I mean—well Father never mentioned to me you had," she said glumly, lightly crossing her legs and looking down suddenly at the folds in her robe.

"Oh come on, Orie you know I haven't. Blimey, a fella'd have to be a genius, a right Venerable Bede, to sort that one out," cried Penda as he lifted Oriana's chin, searching for some efficacy of his humour. "I haven't the faintest idea what the answer is. But did old Chamberlain know this? No. That's what made it such a lark, you see. I just spat out the first image that jumped into my head as it were."

"Well, what did you tell him?"

"A cat."

"A cat?" she repeated.

"That's right," he said nodding. "One grey cat in a cleric's smart pouch."

"You mean to say you made that up—just then … on the spot in front of him?" she asked admiringly.

"Yeah, pretty good, huh?" he said, now waggling back and forth in his seat with noticeable energy.

"That's more than good, it's brilliant actually—deceitful, but brilliant."

"You think?" he asked, scratching his chin, apparently reassessing the merit of the glib answer he had given his master.

"Certainly I do," returned Oriana. "Especially if you pair it with the first two stanzas—it does work in its own comical sort of way."

"Say, maybe there's a bit of old Bede in me after all," he replied in a tone of feigned smugness.

"My friend, mender, and lore master."

"Well at any rate, it accomplished the purpose I set for it, as I am now sitting comfortably next to you on these fine cushions and enjoying this increasingly pathetic fire," he said in an appraising tone. He got to his feet, grabbed a small billet from the hearthrug, and eased it into the bed of coals. He reseated himself next to Oriana, rubbing his hands over the heat.

Instantly the hearth rekindled to life as the red cinders fell to dancing with new yellow tongues.

Just then, Oriana jerked her head in a startled way and glared straight ahead at the far wall.

"What's the matter? What's wrong?" Penda asked worriedly.

"Nothing," returned Oriana unconvincingly, still staring forward. "I just thought I saw—I mean it looked like—Oh never mind, Penda. It was just my imagination."

"Come on Orie, give—what is it?"

"No chance, you'll only laugh," she said, unable to remove her gaze from the tapestry.

"Now would I *ever* do a thing like that?" returned Penda, his hand upon his breast with the pretence of indignation.

"No—not you, Penda, surely."

"Well?"

"Oh very well then. From the corner of my eye, I thought … that is, I thought I saw the white stag move."

"Huh?"

"In my tapestry—over there above my—"

"Yeah, I know, I know—I hate that thing. It gives me the creeps."

"I thought I saw him lower his antlers to the ground. It looked like—well, like he nodded at me." Oriana squinted as she studied the image.

Penda shot Oriana a bewildered look. "Orie, you sure you're feelin' all right? Haven't been nipping at the mead have you— still pretty early, you know?"

"What do you think? I told you it was nothing," snapped Oriana, her eyes now wide and unblinking as she continued staring ahead. "The flames were playing pranks with my eyes— that's all."

Now were both scrutinizing the tapestry with strained eyes as if half expecting to see the stag jump to his hind legs and dance a Scottish reel at any moment. They stared and they stared, and then—nothing happened of course.

By-and-by, Penda turned to study Oriana as she continued studying the stag. Neither one spoke. It was Penda who broke the awkward silence.

"So, have you seen Cerdic this morning?" he asked, apparently trying to force the conversation in a new direction. "The whole house is a desolate bore, if you don't count Bardulf and Bathilda menacing the place."

"What! Bathilda?" cried Oriana, jumping up from her seat. She was no longer thinking of the stag. "When did you see her?" she asked quickly.

"Not fifteen minutes since."

"But I thought she was down in the south meadow helping Garrick with the pavilions. I'll catch it hot for sure if she sees you in here with me alone." And under that apprehension she darted over to the door. "Brilliant!" she exclaimed, looking out nervously onto the courtyard. "The last thing I need today is another telling off from her."

"'Settin' to fix another scandal in there, m' love,'" croaked Penda, mimicking the governess's howl and looking thoroughly tickled with himself. "First it's that no account coxcomb, that … that Leofa the lay about—now Penda, is it? I'll soon put a stop to this!"

"This isn't funny, Penda," returned Oriana, but she was laughing a little. "I may be the daughter of the steward, but the fact remains until I come of age next spring, Bathilda is *still* my mistress."

"Relax Orie, for Frige's sake," cried Penda, pulling his boots back on. "I've already seen to her—"

"Oh no. What've you done this time?" she asked acrimoniously.

"What's the difference?" he said, walking cautiously to her side as though fearing she might give his ear a proper yank till he offered full confessions. "I got 'er out of your hair for a while, that's all that counts."

"Penda?" she said sternly, elevating one eyebrow again.

"All right, all right—don't get in a flap!" he droned after a quick, sideways glance out the door. "As soon as Bardulf let me inside, there was the governess headin' straight for me. I knew what was on her mind, sure enough. So I thought up a good one, right quick."

"Another flash of brilliance, huh—as good as the last?"

"Good enough, I'll warrant," he said coolly. "I knew she was goin' to ask me what I thought I was doin' headin' to your room *so* early and *so* unannounced. So before she could bellow at me, I told 'er I'd already seen you on my way up here, just as you were passin' through the outer gatehouse. I said you told me your head ached and were off for a short walk-about in the forest to clear your mind."

"Well if she believed that, why didn't she question why you were heading to my room in the first place?"

"She did," returned Penda, nodding. "I told her the same thing I told Chamberlain."

"Not the cat again?"

"No—that you had linens for me to wash."

"And that satisfied her?"

"Well you don't see her peerin' round the corner poised to pounce at any moment, now do yeh?"

"I'm half afraid to look," said Oriana, smiling once again, her worried expression softening.

"The thought of you spoiling your new kirtle in the forest sent her off. 'Won't be fit to be seen,' I heard 'er yell—flew past ol' Bardulf and down the Great Stairs like a bolt of blue blaze. She'll be reachin' the forest right about now, I'm thinkin', all puffed and red with running."

"And I was worried her being cross with me," laughed Oriana, shaking her head at him. "You realize, Penda, she'll have your guts for garters over this, you know that don't you? It's a good thing you have the favour of Lord Elgar ... as you once had of Father."

At this last point, a second awkward silence descended on the room like a heavy fog, neither knowing what to say to the other. Thumbs were twiddled, earlobes scratched, and fingernails chewed.

Eventually, Oriana took Penda's hand in hers.

"Look, Penda, I really do appreciate your visit. You're probably the only other person who mourns his loss nearly as I, and you haven't mentioned a word of his ... his absence. You've been very clever in trying to keep my mind off it. Thanks." She kissed his shaggy head. "Father always did say you were one of his more promising pupils."

"What d'you mean *one* of them. I was *the* most promising, thank you very much," he insisted, tilting his head back in a profound sort of way.

"*I don't know,*" she said, trying to sound very serious. "I'm not so sure you may claim that distinction. I seem to remember Father once said ... now what was it? Oh yes. He said when it came to grammar and rhetoric you couldn't hold a candle to his students at the king's court in Cheddar; said you've no head for figures either."

"He said nothing of the kind," accused Penda, appearing relieved that Oriana's mood was ever improving.

She laughed. "You're right; he didn't."

"All kidding aside, you'll be just fine today, really."

"Thanks, I hope so."

"I imagine folk from all around will start pourin' in any time now."

"They already have," said Oriana with a slight frown, "and more every moment. I saw Cadwallon's caravan coming out of Selwood just moments before you knocked. He only brought two wagons with him, and they looked empty. You know what that means."

"No bacon burnish delights, yeah?"

"Exactly," said Oriana grumpily. "We'll just have to make the best of it."

"And the lord and lady?"

"Yes, they were with him. The whole lot was coming up Feldway at an impressive rate."

"So Cadwallon's already here, huh?" sighed Penda. "That unaccountable, crusty, old bird. I'll never forget what he did to my friend Éthelric last winter—gee, I just thought of something."

A sinister look flashed suddenly in his eyes.

"What is it this time?" drawled Oriana rather flaggingly.

"Bathilda—she was headin' for the forest. I certainly hope they didn't run down the old girl. That'd be a terrible shame, that would," he chortled.

"You're monstrous!" returned Oriana, scathingly. "Besides, you know what that would bring, don't you?"

"Oh yeah, I follow you—Lady Mildreth. I reckon she'd step in wouldn't she—play the part of the spiteful stepmother, or is it the wicked foster mother in all the old faërie tales?" He gave a final tug to his bootlaces. "Yeah, she and Cadwallon got on famously last week, I'll bet."

"How would you like to have daily run-ins with *her* imperious ladyship in Bathilda's stead?"

"Speaking of things monstrous you mean?"

"Penda," laughed Oriana "But you must own this scenario certainly paints the governess in a better light, now doesn't it?"

"That goes without saying. Bathilda may be nosy and ancient as old Roman ruins, but she's ten times better than that bloated, overbearing wit—"

"Penda," interrupted Oriana abruptly, smiling all the while. "I'll thank you to mind your tongue, lest I forget the privileges granted to ambassadors and . . . and serving boys." This she said in her best imitation of courtly protocol.

"Well, my lady," he said with a pretentious bow, "I shall be about the grounds today if you are in want of anything—someone to sample the primrose wine, or look after the roasting partridge, or any such unenviable task that might come to your mind."

"I'll let you know," she said, patting him on his shoulder.

"Oh, by the way, Penda. Before you go," she said, sweeping over to a cedar chest at the foot of her bed. "I suppose it's up to me to keep you an honest man."

Oriana reached down to the bottom of the chest and quickly returned with a wrapt bundle in her arms. She handed it to her friend.

"Since you are not otherwise engaged—there you are, some nice dirty linens that want washing."

Oriana sent her friend on his way, stomping across the courtyard gibbering half-discernable expletives under his breath. Oriana waved good-bye laughing to herself over his sudden misfortune. And as Penda exited through the double doors of the inner-ward, Oriana's mind raced back to an earlier thought. This time, however, she was not thinking of her beloved father. She was thinking of her tapestry. She was thinking of the white stag.

CHAPTER 2

From Peasants...

Penda's antics hadn't been in vain. Now was Oriana in a much-improved humour, though puzzling still over her tapestry.

She was drest and off to the festival.

Under skies crisp blue and a hastening sun, Oriana could be seen flying from one corner of the party grounds to another, greeting the new arrivals, and seating them according to their families and station. So attentive was she to her guests, one might have easily mistaken her for one of the serving maids were it not for her genteel manners and attire. Only the previous evening, in fact, Governess Bathilda had sponged, pressed, and beautifully goffered Oriana's best satin kirtle just for the occasion—the white fussy one with thread lace and gold braid trim embroidered on the sleeves and neckline. Oriana would have much preferred wearing her simple peasant gown, but in light of Penda's little prank, she thought it best not to try her mistress's patience any further.

Now Oriana understood as well as anyone else that, as acting stewardess, her only real responsibility was to supervise the nearly two dozen villagers who had drawn duty to cook, serve, and clean for the two-day celebration. But it was not in Oriana's nature to delegate work and leave matters at that. O no! Supervision without participation was a philosophy Oriana never held for herself nor respected in others.

To see Lady Oriana balancing stacks of dirty dishes on her

way to the scrubbing bins or donning a gravy-stained apron while tending steaming pots of rabbit stew was shocking to some of the nobles from the bordering villages. Given Lady Mildreth's icy stares, it was obvious she too regarded Oriana's behaviour as wonton meddling with the servants and altogether disgraceful. But for the free peasants of Oakleigh, long accustomed to the lady's humility, there was nothing unusual or even unexpected in her conduct. For the better part of the afternoon, Oriana worked just as hard as any one of her ceorl servants, and they loved her all the more for it.

The Brunanburh Victory Feast was held in the south meadow near the village pond. Lord Elgar personally chose this site before departing on his sojourn to Shaftsbury. For one thing, it afforded the most convenient access from Feldway Lane. For another, it was large enough to accommodate the two hundred and thirty-four guests who were invited and the dozens more who, with much pleasure, would arrive just the same. And happily, it was dry.

Lord Elgar had always taken a keen turn in the management of his farm, when he was about the place, that is, and knew the properties of all his fields, pastures, and meadows. The soil of the south meadow possessed the least amount of the dense-grey clay that the village potters valued and the greatest quantity of dark, loamy silt that the winter rye favoured. The net result was a well-drained, dry bit of ground fit for a gathering of free Saxon countrymen.

"Good afternoon, Freydis," said Oriana, stopping near the edge of Oakleigh's fish pond, its surface glistening silvery-blue in the sun. Purple irises and yellow-orange marigolds rose cheerfully along its slanting banks. Bluebottles and dragonflies buzzed from one petal to the next. Four rabbits there were too, nibbling on young dandelions just at the marshy edge while two grey dabchicks took to courting one another with fresh weeds in their tiny bills.

"Hullo, Miss Oriana. Good afternoon ter yeh as well: weather's certainly taken a turn for the bet'er, 'asn't it?" said the woman from under the shade of a great mulberry tree. She was busily working on an unfinished wicker hanaper gript between her knees.

"Indeed it has. We've been blessed today," returned Oriana, admiring the woman's skill at twining such thin osier willows. "That is a very handsome basket you have there, Freydis."

"Thank you, ma'am. Though I daresay it isn't 'alf so fine as me gran used to make. Still, it should hold a fair store of pixie pears. I'm 'tendin' to finish gatherin' this afternoon. A most worthwhile occupation, collectin' pixie pears is in my view. Care for one?" she asked, handing Oriana a tiny red fruit.

But as it happened, the woman's fruit was lost upon Oriana as she suddenly caught sight of a small boy struggling with a large fish on the end of his line. Dozens of floating white lilies and yellow crowsfoot were bobbing in the wake of the boy's tugging. A brood of ducklings and their mother quaked and paddled off in a startled display from all the splashing.

"What did she say? A pixie pair? What quaint fancies our peasants do have," said Oriana inwardly still gazing ahead and instead said only, "No thank you, Freydis."

The woman ate one of the miniature apple-like fruits and closed the lid.

"Are your children enjoying themselves today?" Oriana asked as the boy finally flung his sparkling catch up on the bank.

"I'll say they are, m' lady. Me youngest boy there, Offa," she said, pointing, "as already caught two perch an' a trout. Looks as though 'e's got 'imself another perch. No ... pike—no ... Careful, boy," she called to her son, "that's a stickleback, is that. Come an' 'ave a look, m' lady."

The woman got to her feet, shook clean her blanket, which sent rather a frowsty smell as she waved it, and crossed to the pond, beckoning Oriana to the water's edge. Out of the water she pulled a line strung with three plump fish, the end of which had been girded round the trunk of an old willow.

"Well I must say, *that is* a very nice catch. Your Offa's quite the fisherman."

"Caught 'em with switch and line 'e did, every last one of 'em," she said proudly. "No weirs for 'im. Cheatin' that is, or so me 'usband always says."

"I envy your son, his patience," said Oriana heavily with a sigh. "I pray I may have such forbearance today."

"Wha' you, Miss Orie?" returned Freydis, dropping her son's fish back in the water with a *pla-blump*. "You needn't trouble yer head about that, I shouldn' think. Why, you're as patient as the day is long. And this ain't lookin' to be no short day, as the sayin' goes."

"Thank you, Freydis," returned Oriana warmly.

"Can you sit for a short space?" she asked, smoothing her blanket flat over a patch of soggy darnels and settling herself cross-legged. "It seems such a time since we've visited."

"Indeed, it's been a very great while. But I'm afraid I haven't leisure enough for such pleasant conversation at the moment. As it is, there're still some things in the noble quarter I have to manage. More candles are needed for one thing, so I've been told—perhaps later."

"Oh pray forgive me!" said Fredyis, wringing her hands. "I can't begin to imagine 'ow busy yeh must be today. But before yeh set off—that is, I'd be so very much obliged ... well, if I may take the liberty of yeh—"

"It's all right, Freydis," laughed Oriana lightly, noticing that the woman's sudden embarrassment seemed to be choking her words. "Say on."

"I'd ... I'd like ter request a small favour of yeh."

"Why, certainly. Just name it."

"It's me 'usband, that's what it is. Wine and watchin'—always wine and watchin'," she then muttered almost imperceptibly, shaking her head. "If you should happen across 'im," she went on in a more audible tone, "could yeh tell 'im I've been lookin' high and low fer 'im. Can't find 'im nowhere. And Offa 'ere wants to show 'im 'is fine catch. Wants to do a bit o' braggin' to the ol' buffer, 'e does."

"Of course, I'd be happy to. Happy Brunanburh Day, Freydis," she said over her shoulder.

Oriana trotted over a low rising hill toward the village and repaired directly to the candlestick maker's workshop.

Earlier that afternoon, all the wagons and gigs, stuffed haversacks, and panniers slung from the backs of shaggy Ponies, had been unloaded of their party provisions by stocky lads from the village anxious to catch the first glimpse at the delights lying within. From the good men and women of Warminster, crates of fresh fish, dried meats, and barrels brimming with cherries, apples, pears, and plums were donated with their compliments. Ready-made mulberry pies, fig cakes, gooseberry fools, and all manner of other delightful confections neatly wrapt in yellow cloth were the gifts from the generous butteries of Frome. Even the guests of honour, the warden and freemen of Malmesbury, brought a dozen roast grouses, twenty smoked hams, and twice as many spiced pork pies. Lord Cadwallon of Shaftsbury brought nothing; that is to say, nothing apart from his less-than-modest appetite and more-than-moderate disdain for the peasants disgracing their celebration—or so his infatigable scowling suggested most decidedly that day.

Once the last of the crates and barrels had been unloaded, Oriana sent two stable boys to lead the ponies to the village corrals for a sound currying and well deserved lunch of oats, mash, and apple cores. Brond, the stable master and aspiring marshal to Lord Elgar's house, personally saw to the nobles' horses, wagons, and carts, proudly driving each in turn off Feldway Lane, across the meadow, and up to the broad, yellow and white striped pavilions erected the previous day as temporary garages. Brond was particularly cautious with Lord Cadwallon's carriage. It was the finest of the nineteen such transports to arrive that morning—as fine a coach as its owner was foppish and foul.

Scores of brightly coloured pavilions, plank tables of alderwood, oak benches, and faldstools were scattered over a wide section of the south meadow in no particular arrangement. And in the east corner of the field near Willowrun Creek, a large area was given over to an even greater quantity of tents newly pitched by the peasants arriving from the far reaches of Selwoodshire. The nobles, of course, would be enjoying more commodious lodgings in Lord Elgar's mead hall within the inner ward.

All that day peasants from Oakleigh Manor mingled and laughed with the other villagers from Frome and Warminster. There were no peasants from Shaftsbury; Lord Cadwallon simply would not stand for feasting and dissipation by his own peasants when there was plenty of plowing to be done at home.

But those who did attend, upon the whole, spoke of the day's mirth and merriment for many moons hence. The festival grounds simply bustled with mothers bragging over the cleverness of their children and fathers spinning exaggerated tales of cabbages and pigs that they were proud to call their own. Some of the ceorl men could be seen sitting, others reclining, still more dancing as they might, but none without a full tankard in hand.

Queues of thirsty farmers had begun forming early that afternoon round the freshly tapped barrels of Welsh ale, mild ale, mead, and magnificent mulberry morat. And for every thirsty farmer there was an attentive farmer's wife to tally the exact number of drained libations, hoping the barrels might soon run to dry or dregs. Burnstan, a tolerable beekeeper from Warminster, enjoyed honey sweet-barley bread with his wife and five children. Sidrac, Oakleigh's own swineherd, parceled out sizable chunks of goat's cheese and ripe bullace plums to his brothers and cousins gathered round a long table well out of earshot of their wives. And all these treats were rendered even more delightful when it was remembered this was only the light fare—mere morsels before the afternoon feast commenced in earnest. Betwixt the midday snacking and continual joke cracking, wives caught up on the latest gossip from their distant relations in the bordering villages, as their husbands—in between relays to the ale tents—fished, bowled, and gambled with dice as they pleased.

Yet the nobles little noticed these things. They celebrated chiefly amongst themselves. It was a longstanding tradition in the southerly shires of Wessex to reserve exclusively the finest and most private acres for the nobles during high feasts. Of course, Sycamore Henge was the natural choice.

Sycamore Henge, or the "ring of white fathers" as it was sometimes called, was a flat, six-acre dingle in the most westerly rim of the south meadow. In some ways, this circular grove, enclosing a lush nook of grasses and wildflowers, called to mind the more famous druid-henge of giant blue stones five leagues to the southeast. Sycamore Henge was actually more a circular tree line, or ring, than a true grove. Though perhaps not a perfectly apt name, as it had no surrounding embankment or fosse typical of most henges, the name Sycamore Henge had been decided long ago, and there seemed no reason to change it now. The trees were magnificent, full-limbed, and pearly white, strong, and in some intangible way, even wise.

Each tree was equally spaced with just enough room for the passage of a single mounted thegn or two lovers walking hand in hand. Their canopy was dense and uninterrupted, casting the illusion of an emerald crown set upon a kingly head of snowy-

white locks. Despite the belief of many in the village, Oriana
thought it entirely unlikely the trees had naturally grown in that
pattern. There were no trees in the interior and none nearer than
a furlong beyond. Trees of any variety, as far as Oriana was aware,
never grew in perfectly circular groves. Obviously the trees had
been intentionally planted that way or else the interior trees had
been felled and uprooted. Either way, each was a more satisfac-
tory explanation than a "faërie ring in wooded guise" as she was
meant to believe as a child.

Presently, Oriana was hurrying toward Sycamore Henge with
two wooden pails filled to the top with yellow beeswax candles—
yet another detail overlooked by one of the servants. Hence, she
had taken it into her head to check if the other servants had
things well in hand before the guests of honour were seated.
Always was there the discomforting worry that the cheeses and
bread might run short, to say nothing of the ale and wine. Candles were her present concern.

Oriana reached the shade of a large elm, seated herself, and
began counting the contents of her buckets. She had a sneak-
ing suspicion that the candles were not going to total half a
gross as Finwine had promised. And what was more, it appeared
that nearly half of the half gross were going to be too short. Oh
bother!

Just then as she was counting, Oriana felt something splash
down the front of her dress.

"What on earth?" she cried, rising to her feet. She pulled out
her dress to see what had spattered. Her first instinct imagined a
hapless and very badly timed bird dropping. Fortunately, it was
not this. Rather, there were two red, finger-length streaks soak-
ing into her beautiful white dress just above the top of her apron.

"What could it be?" she wondered. It was obviously not
blood, so there was no cause for alarm. It actually looked more
like ... like—

"Welund smash m' tongs!" shouted a deep slurred voice from high above. Oriana looked up.

"I'm awful sorry 'bout that, Miss Orie. Didn' see yeh down there, I didn'," said a strong-limbed, middle-aged man perched nearly fifteen feet above in the best climbing tree in the south meadow. He was tall and rather bull-necked, and, except on the top of his head that was greying, had long black hair and matching curly moustaches. "Can yeh ever fergive me, m' lady?"

"Oh it's you, Alaric," replied Oriana more than a little surprized at finding the village blacksmith where one ordinarily finds squirrels or children. "Well, hello," she said, dabbing off the front of her dress with a fold of her apron.

"I'm a clumsy oaf's, wot I am—all over your bonny festival gown."

"Not to worry. It'll wash out." Given the blacksmith's watery eyes, it appeared he might start blubbing over his carelessness any moment. Alaric was rather sensitive, after all—everybody knew that. So Oriana thought it best to turn the smith's thoughts toward a new course.

"I must ask you, Alaric," she said genuinely bemused, "what in Alfred's name are you doing up there? You're far too big and hairy to pass for a songbird, you know?"

"Oh, Miss Oriana, you make me fer to laugh, yeh do," he chuckled, sniffing back his welling sniffles. "No I'm jus' tryin' ter—em ... get a bet'er view o' course, beggin' yer pardon."

It was then the smith's burly brown arms and hands attracted her notice—in particular, what he was holding. In his left hand the blacksmith was clutching a miniature barrel in goblet form, dripping red wine from its bottom. His other hand was holding fast to a higher branch.

"A better view of what, pray?" she asked, lifting her eyebrows intrigued.

"Now meanin' no harm, yeh understand, Miss Oriana, ter the lord an' lady an' their fine guests," pled the hairy smith. "But I was wantin' a good look-see at the other nobles as they arrived—'fore they took their seats down yonder at the white fathers."

"But you've seen our nobles plenty of times, Alaric," observed Oriana, perplexed by his statement.

"Yeah, well…em, it's—it's Lord Thorgrim, yeah, Lord Thorgrim I'm wantin' to see. I heard tell from, em…ah, Garrick, who'd heard from one of his mates in Warminster, that Lord Thorgrim would be wearin' his new corselet."

"Do tell," added Oriana dubiously but smiling all the while.

"Yeah—special made Garrick says it is, just for tomorrow's tournament."

"Did he?"

"Yes, ma'am. Now seein' how I probably won't get no chance ter see this fine piece of smithin' near close enough for me own likin', I figured a bird's eye view might be the next best thing when he passes by."

"That was very clever thinking," said Oriana a little more brightly this time. "I should think that height would provide a most excellent perspective indeed. You know," added Oriana, pretending that a new idea had just come to her, "those boys I just passed—I'll just bet that's what they were talking over, too. Initially I thought it a most curious dialogue, but now that I've heard your tale, I feel rather silly to have so perfectly misconstrued their topic."

"Ahum," coughed the blacksmith in the middle of a large swig, his face staring down stunned. Wine was drizzling in large droplets from the ends of his moustaches. "Wot's this now, ma'am? Who was sayin' wot exactly?"

"Some of the village lads—they were discussing your same curiosity. I overheard a group of them as they were playing a match of buzzard bounce."

"Talkin' 'bout Thorgrim's armour, were they?" asked Alaric, sounding a bit taken aback, apparently baffled at Oriana's report.

"Yes, not far—just there, over the hill," remarked Oriana, pointing. "They certainly shared your enthusiasm all right—kept going on and on about how they'd happily give up a full day's serving of bread and milk just to have a tiny peek."

"Did they now? I mean ... well, I shouldn' be surprised in that. Not one bit I shouldn' be. After all, who wouldn't fancy a gander at—at a fine piece o' craftsmanship like that?" he muttered still sounding a little off kilter. He took another nervous gulp from his wooden reservoir.

"Craftsmanship is it?" Oriana said half smirking. "Yes, I suppose I can appreciate your interest in Lord Thorgrim's mail, my studious smith. Your curiosity is purely professional. That's highly admirable of you, Alaric. I commend you. One can hardly reproach a man for availing himself of so rare an opportunity—a chance to expand his knowledge and further his craft."

"Why, Miss Orie, that's—that's that gift of yers shinin' through again," he muttered some more, "always able to see right ter the truth o' things, yeh can. Bless my anvil, that's just wot I was aimin' to do." He took another time-consuming draught from his bucket-sized goblet.

"Doubtless that's the answer, my honest smith," she returned archly and nodded. "Yet in truth, if I were addressing anyone but you, Master Alaric, I might have construed things differently. For I myself have just received word that the incomparable Lady Branwen, daughter of said Lord Thorgrim of Warminster, is just arrived and drest out in a sumptuous kirtle of purest godweb silk, and perfumed with the most redolent of lavender oils, *and* is also due under this *very* elm at any moment. Yes, master smith, if you were anyone other than yourself, I might think it *she* who motivated such an ascent to those lofty boughs."

"Now, Miss Orie!" cried Alaric nearly slipping from his perch.

"But I believe you when you say your curiosity lies only in some forged bits of shiny iron circles."

"See here, Miss Orie," he stammered again, looking most sheepish indeed.

"And where is your faithful wife, Freydis, hmm? Still down yonder by the fish pond, minding your children, I'll wager?" yelled Oriana whose voice teetered on the brink between disgust and laughter. "I see what you're about! A man your age! Why you should be ashamed of yourself, leering down at a poor unsuspecting noble lady who's but recently sixteen. I have a good mind to—"

"Now just a moment—that's—that's not fair that. I don't want yeh gettin' no wrong impressions 'bout me, Miss Orie. You've got this whole thing all wrong, yeh do. After all, I—wot I mean to say is—wot I told yeh was the truth. Well, a fair chunk of it at any rate."

"My dear, Master Alaric," laughed Oriana so frightfully she doubled over, clasping her hands to her knees. "I am only having a good Brunanburh Day laugh at your expense. I do not *really* think ill of you whatever your true motives for such a climb."

"Cruel—that's wot that is. Nearly made me 'eart give out on me," whimpered the strong smith still struggling to catch his breath. "That's all that wee joke nearly done!"

"I'm sorry, Alaric. I simply could not resist the pleasure," she responded, unable to stop laughing. "I'm sure you'll recover just splendidly."

Alaric took a deep gulp and sighed. After a pause he said:

"Well m' lady seenin' as you're here and that—been meanin' ter 'ave a word with yeh anywise, I have. I wonna thank yeh for all this fine drink and vittles. I know the whole village wants to thank yeh loads for it too. I've got a feelin' it was you as planted the idea of these extravagances in Lord Elgar's head, awright. This 'ere ruby wine is the best I've 'ad since, well … probably before yeh was even foun …"

He coughed suddenly in a most obvious sort of way.

"What did he just say?" Oriana wondered to herself as his coughing drew her notice.

Hurriedly, the smith carried on just as if he had never muttered or coughed. "Before yeh was born. A right honest wine; fit more fer the king's table than fer the likes of me, I shouldn' wonder. You do know that people down in the village've been sayin' you've won Lord Elgar's ear faster than anyone 'xpected. You're Lord Phillip's daughter through and through, yeh are. An' don't go thinkin' folk aren't rememberin' his gentle ways today neither—'cause they are, you can take me word for it."

"Alaric," began Oriana brightly, her eyes going slightly misty, "that means more to me than a thousand words of gratitude."

Alaric smiled and took another sip. "If yeh don't mind me sayin' so," he went on, "it's also my belief half the folk here from Frome and Warminster wouldn't be here neither if it weren't for you."

"I just wish I could have similarly persuaded Lord Cadwallon to bring some of his cottagers from Shaftsbury. He's an impossible, disobliging man. They scarce celebrate even the great church holidays. He's brought none but his own household and a handful of serving slaves—the poor wretches," said Oriana with a sympathetic scowl. "Thank heavens Lord Elgar has never shamed Oakleigh Manor with that vile practice."

"I'll not argue with yeh o'er that, Miss Orie. You and me are o' like mind there, that we are. Put me and me family out o' house and home, that dirty business would."

"Well, I really must be getting on, Alaric. You caught me on my way down to the henge. Lord Elgar's about to introduce the men of Malmesbury and commence the feast. And look," she said, holding up her wooden buckets, "wouldn't you know it— someone forgot to fetch these candles from Finwine's workshop as I had asked. You will come up for the speech and entertainments after the feast, I hope. I should be very sorry not to see your family in attendance."

Oriana now thought the blacksmith was definitely shewing an interest in returning to the terrestrial world.

"I dunno if I fancy fightin' the crowds, but I ain't dead set against it. Yeah, there's a beard-on-a-gnome chance[1] you might find us lurkin' in the back," he said, looking as if he were counting the number of suitable stepping branches below.

"Wonderful. I'll be looking for you," returned Oriana earnestly. "Incidentally, you must tell me before I go, how were you able to climb this elm with that enormous wine goblet in your hands? I can't for the life of me see how it was done short of flying."

"Yeh know, now that yeh put me mind ter it—strange thing is, I can't rightly recall that meself," said the hairy smith with a puzzled air.

"Best ruby wine you've had in ages, huh?"

"Yeah, a bit too good, maybe. How d'yeh reckon I ought to get down?" he asked with an anxious voice.

"I really couldn't say," said Oriana with a wide grin. "But you might ask your understanding wife who—ah yes—is arriving just now."

Alaric turned and stared in the direction Oriana was pointing, his eyes nearly starting from his head in a frightful way.

"She bade me inform you that she's been looking everywhere, *everywhere*, for you—very cross she was. But after she learns your tale of, uh, Lord Thorgrim's armour, was it?" she laughed, looking over her shoulder as she strolled away grinning, "I feel sure you'll find her a *big* help."

---

[1] Popular myth in Selwoodshire held that beardless gnomes were greedy and cruel and the bitterest of foes of the stout-hearted mountain dwarves. According to legend, a small number of gnomes could, and would, grow beards equal in length to some of the shorter dwarvish beards. They could never grow the magnificent, full, knee-length beards, however. Some gnomes would do so that they might infiltrate the fortified dwarvish cities and steal from them the enchanted mountain heart-stones. Because it was believed this ability was so rare among gnomes, the expression beard-on-a-gnome chance was often used in Selwoodshire the way you might say a slim chance.

CHAPTER 3

... to Portents

The sun sailed just beyond noontide when Oriana reached the eaves of Sycamore Henge. There, just outside the ring of mighty trees, past a brake of nut bushes and robin's pincushions, stood the roasting pits and brick ovens constructed some years back for servicing noble company during high festivals.

Oriana walked toward one of the newer scrubbing tents pitched beside a row of young hollyhocks. Aidith, one of Oakleigh's best dairymaids, was just coming out, burthened with a basket of dirty dishtowels.

"Oh, Aidith," Oriana said hurriedly, "would you be an angel and run another errand for me?"

"Willingly, ma'am. Name it?"

"Would you count the remaining cheeses for me? I haven't had a chance."

"Certainly. Where shall I find you?"

"Let's see," she paused to consider. "How about in the newest larder tent? Say, half an hour?"

"You may depend upon me for it," said Aidith and was off at once after a quick curtsey.

Unfastening her apron, Oriana dashed into the scrubbing tent and, dropping the candle buckets near the washbasins, made a quick inspection. She took one look inside a tub half filled with old soapsuds and threw her hands to her head.

"That will never do," she said irksomely. "I wish I had seen this before I sent Aidith off."

Continuing her inspection, Oriana noticed a stack of very comfortable-looking, yellow seat cushions piled high in the corner. At first she was annoyed that the servants had neglected to place them on the banqueting benches, but the irritation passed almost as soon as it emerged. And in no time at all, unable to resist, she plumped herself right on top of them.

"Just for a few minutes," Oriana said to herself, as though needing to assuage a guilty conscience for resting. "I have to get off my feet, even if it's only for a few minutes."

It wasn't too awfully long before Oriana caught herself nodding off. She knew the very real danger of that and thought she had better get up before it became a daylong slumber.

And then, as she sat up yawning, it came once again! She began to have that same curious sensation she had in her room. Someone was watching her; she just knew it! She did not like this feeling at all, not one bit! In fact, she was beginning to wonder if she was going positively mad because there was, of course, no one in the tent with her.

Oriana got to her feet and raced toward the door-flap when, suddenly, she froze. Someone was whispering just outside! She could hear the muffled tones through the back wall. She probably would not have stopt had it been one of the scullion lads or serving girls. But it wasn't. She recognized that voice all right. The sound of it made her stomach turn in protest. It was Lord Cadwallon. He was speaking barely above a whisper to Lord Elgar, but she caught every word.

"Now why should they have come to the serving station so far from the other guests?" she wondered. This was very odd indeed. It was certainly the last place Oriana ever expected to find the proud lord of Shaftesbury.

Oriana's first impulse was to make some exaggerated clamour

or, at the very least, clear her throat to make clear that the gentlemen were not speaking in private. But she hesitated. Why had she?

She knew it was impolite to eavesdrop, and yet there she was, doing just that. Perhaps it was Lord Elgar's anxious tenor wresting her attention. Or maybe it was the secrecy of their liaison making it impossible for her to declare her presence.

Whatever the explanation, premonition or mere curiosity, Oriana remained silent, glued to her spot listening.

"Is this really necessary, Elgar?" whispered the lord of Shaftesbury. "Honestly, what can be of such import that was not addressed at court last Thor's day?"

"It may prove of even greater import, Lord Cadwallon, than either of us can conceive," returned the lord of Oakleigh. "Indeed, until very recently it was only the dawning of suspicion. Things are now otherwise, I deem."

"Suspicions, Elgar? ... Great machinations!" cried Cadwallon irritably. "Please do not say you have brought me to this paltry peasant station to relay some news of the king's ailing health? I realize we did not take this matter under counsel, but this is hardly news."

"Shh. Please, Cadwallon," whispered Lord Elgar. "No, this has nothing to do with His Majesty Athelstan."

"Come, what is this then?" he snapped, sounding both bored and annoyed. "I can tell you it's quite beyond my faculty to guess."

"The phenomenon."

"The what?" asked Cadwallon languidly.

"The heavenly phenomenon," replied Lord Elgar. "You do follow me, do you not? The recent celestial occurrence?"

"And I just said it was beyond my faculty—I should have known. Prophecies and portents—yes? Is this *truly* the lord of Oakleigh who now speaks to me? You are sounding dreadfully similar to that deserter of yours—that Greek, Phillip."

Oriana gasped out loud! She covered her mouth to prevent

another. "How dare Cadwallon speak so contemptuously of my father," she thought scornfully.

Instinctively, she picked up one of the filthy dishrags and wound her arm back as though she might somehow throw it through the tent wall and right into Cadwallon's smug face.

"What was that?" asked Cadwallon.

"I heard nothing."

"Are you sure?"

"Quite…and he was Cypriot, not Greek," Elgar explained in a sharp whisper sounding rather affronted by Cadwallon's remarks. "He lived just beyond the abandoned city of Amathus before coming to Wessex. And he was no deserter. Besides, you can hardly speak to that, Cadwallon, when, as I recall, you were on the eastern flank and nowhere near our vanward."

"Are we quite finished?" His tone sounded as though he had every intention of leaving. "Do you not suppose my Egwina, not to mention your Mildreth, will soon be seeking our hiding place?"

"Stay, Cadwallon, you must hear me out," whispered the lord of Oakleigh pleadingly. "I spoke nothing of this last week for fear of rousing anxieties. You know as well as I that many in our counsel are given to overreaction. And I certainly am not of a mind to enter on the subject with anyone else and imperil the mirth of our festival. What is more, I have just this morning heard tidings of which I believe you should know."

"And thus here we stand, is that it? Concealing ourselves in these shadows like two fugitives evading the reeve's hounds? All right, Elgar, now out with it."

"The new stars," he answered in a bluff manner. "This is what troubles my mind. Have you noticed how all five have grown brighter?"

"You'll be astonished in this, I'm sure, but it has quite escaped me," said Cadwallon coolly. "What new stars?"

"*You must be jesting?*" whispered Lord Elgar in a shocked way. "I know they are as yet dim, but I refuse to believe you can be so little acquainted with … that is to say, in matters such as—"

"Lord Elgar," interrupted Cadwallon, "not everyone is a stargazer … or philosopher."

"Then I take it I needn't ask if you have observed their colour or motion."

"Do continue, lord," said the Lord of Shaftesbury phlegmatically. "I can scarce tolerate the suspense."

"We weren't entirely certain at first. That is, Phillip and I were not sure, but Oriana on the other hand—now that was positively astounding. She made a disturbing prediction late one night three years ago after falling into a curious fit—no, a trance. Yes, it was definitely more of a trance—something about the treachery of Tad Svarti, whoever he is, and the master being freed from Malgorod and … and the slaying of lands."

Oriana nearly gasped a second time. This time she had checked her astonishment. Her curiosity was suddenly made all the greater knowing she played some mysterious role in Lord Elgar's tale. What on earth was he talking about?

"Even to this day I do not believe she can recall that evening."

"Spare me the anecdote, Elgar. Now what is this? Come to the point, old man," said Cadwallon, sounding increasingly bored.

"Where ought I to begin?" Elgar paused for some time. "Well, for start, Cadwallon, their colour is extraordinary. Each star is of a different hue: red, yellow, blue, gold, and silver."

"Blue and red stars, Elgar? Preposterous! Are you sure it is not you who jests with me?" he asked sardonically.

"This is no Brunanburh jest, Cadwallon. I assure you."

"Really? Then how do you explain why this is not on the tongue of everyone at court or, for that matter, throughout the whole of Christendom?"

"Perhaps for the very reason you have failed to notice them," replied Lord Elgar, sharply. "They are still dim and obscured if viewed within the context of the greater constellations. You must first know where to look and then have imagination enough to isolate these five from their companions. It is not as easily done as you might suppose."

"Apparently not," Cadwallon agreed. "Now, Lord Elgar, if you would be good enough to hurry your inevitable apocalyptic appraisal of this, I should very much like to return to my mead and company less grim."

"In a moment, I shall oblige this request to your complete satisfaction, I'm sure. For you have not heard all, my lord. There is more to tell," continued Elgar. "The position of these stars is just as extraordinary as their colour. They have formed a ring in the northern firmament. Four years ago it was not so apparent they made any pattern at all. Of course at that point they were dimmer and farther apart."

"Farther apart? Are they not stationary as all others of the stellatum[1]?"

---

[1]   According to the Ptolemaic construct of the universe devised around 150 AD, the fixed stars reside in the eighth sphere beyond Saturn. The stars were regarded as stationary given their fixed positions relative to one another, which distinguished them from the motion of the planets.

"No, to the contrary. Not only are they mobile, but they are traveling in two disparate ways. Each one appears to be gliding inward to a fixed central point—to a convergence perhaps. That convergence, Cadwallon, is the North Star! They are racing to join with it."

"What!"

"It is so, lord. For years, their distance from one another had been so great and their speed so slow that Phillip and I hadn't noticed their motion. But as their light grew and their pace quickened, it became evident that they were, in fact, forming a ring in the northern sky."

"Lord Elgar," said Cadwallon irritably. "You would have me now believe these stars not only travel about, but that their pace *quickens* as well?" Cadwallon sounded incredulous.

"You seemed disinterested at first. Do I detect a change of heart, or better yet, of mind?"

"Just continue, lord, or you'll soon find these sycamores your only audience."

"Yes, their momentum grows," replied Lord Elgar shortly. "Not only is each star moving toward one another, but the rate at which they move is accelerating. As it is, my lord, the haste of their junction is now so rapid one can nearly detect the movement with the passing of a single night."

"Let me be certain I understand you fully," said Cadwallon haltingly.

"Go on."

There was a brief pause.

"You say each star is moving, and they are moving in the direction of a collision with each other, and the speed of this imminent junction steadily increases?"

"I should say you do, indeed, understand my meaning fully. Yes, that is it precisely," added Elgar.

"Have you made any calculations on the year of this convergence?" he asked quickly.

"On the year? Yes, that is beyond question. If things continue as they have, it will definitely occur next year—"

"Next year!" roared Cadwallon who evidently forgot they were still meant to be whispering. "When exactly?"

"Shh, my lord—we shall call attention to ourselves. You have to realize, Cadwallon, I have been working off Lord Phillip's notations, and they of course ceased two years ago. But if his measurements are accurate and my skills to be trusted, I should guess sometime in early spring at furthest."

There was another pause, a longer pause.

"You did say they move in two different ways, did you not?" asked Cadwallon at length.

"Yes, I was just coming to that," answered Elgar, stopping, perhaps in thought.

"Well?" asked Cadwallon impatiently. "What of it? How is it manifested?"

"This is the most extraordinary part. The stars revolve in unison around a fixed point. The point of the impending conjunction—the North Star, as I said." He cleared his throat. Oriana could only guess the expression Cadwallon was making.

"Imagine it in this way," continued Lord Elgar. "The stars spin together just as the great wheel of our water mill turns on its axle-tree. In one evening, the stars make nearly a quarter revolution—so it is plainly seen if one knows where, and makes the effort, to look."

"This is almost too much to accept."

"Could I fabricate such a fiction?" replied Elgar earnestly.

"Yes, I daresay, you probably could—just to get the better of me. But I am willing to believe, on the present occasion, you have not. Yet I am puzzled why you have said nothing to me in all these—how many years did you say you've known of this—four? Not a word in four years till now?"

"I have already given you this answer," whispered Elgar whose turn it was to be irritable. "Until today, I had as yet only guessed at the importance of this wonder. Now it is no longer suspicion but a growing certainty."

"Why? Have you received some secret counsel from the king on this?" asked Cadwallon swiftly.

"Well … no—not directly from the king exactly. No, I haven't."

"*Not directly?*" echoed Cadwallon. "How do you mean—ah! His court astrologers at Winchester! Is this your meaning?"

"No, I have had no word from them."

"Lord Elgar, proceeding on the assumption that what you tell me is as things truly are—"

"They are," interjected Elgar.

"Than I am utterly disinclined to believe His Majesty is in complete ignorance of this matter. Surely he must know! It is inconceivable to my mind that he has elected to say nothing of this to anyone," insisted Cadwallon. "Do you truly tell me all? You are certain you have had no communication from His Majesty?"

"You make me repeat myself, Cadwallon. No, no word from the king has reached me. But I have yet to tell you of today's tidings. You may find this to ease your mind. It would seem the king has not been idle. I have it on good authority that an emissary of high repute, a prelate in strange vestments, as I have been told, has arrived from the Eastern Empire to take up this very issue with His Majesty at Cheddar. I have also heard he was in possession of some strange device, a star chart I believe he said it was."

"Who said?" asked Cadwallon hurriedly. "Who is this authority?"

"Well, if you must know—it was Brond."

"Brond? Who is he?" he asked curtly. "He must be a lord of little consequence, I'm sure. I have never heard mention of him before."

"I should be surprized if you had. He is no lord great or small. Presently he is my … well, my stable master. But, I have been giving serious consideration to conferring on him the duty of high marshal."

"An ostler! A ceorl!" cried Cadwallon sounding aghast. "Now, look here, Elgar, look here. You are a lordly thegn of high renown and have the distinction of one of His Majesty's closest aldermen. You have duly earned the admiration from the great earls and bishops throughout Wessex and Mercia, and not least of all, you are my friend. Yet you perplex me to great consternation. Why do you insist on maintaining such social intercourse with your peasant rabble and lending credibility to their gossip?"

Oriana made another angry gesture with her dishtowel in Cadwallon's direction.

"Brond has been a trusted servant to my household these many years," said Elgar firmly. "He has my every confidence. If he says he met just such a man as I described, then that is indeed what transpired. I know him to be a man of his word."

"Have it your way, Elgar," retorted Cadwallon. "For the moment, we will suspend the question of his credibility. Tell me, where did he meet this pilgrim?"

"Near Southampton. I dispatched Brond there three weeks ago on an important errand. He and this stranger met on the high road, heading in opposite directions. Brond said this stranger claimed to be on official business to see King Athelstan and needed directions to Feldway Lane and on to the old Roman road running west from Winchester. Brond, in his usual shrewdness, struck a bargain with the priest. He promised to give the directions only if the priest would in turn allow him to see the map he was holding. Brond explained he had a great fondness for books and maps even though he could not read them."

"And did the priest oblige his request?"

"Partly," said Lord Elgar, continuing his story. "Apparently the cleric was sympathetic to Brond's intellectual curiosity. He did oblige, yes, but with some reluctance, it would seem. According to Brond, he made clear what he was holding was no map of the local roads but a rare astrological chart. In the end, he permitted a quick glance only at the parchment but wouldn't allow Brond to handle it. As they parted, Brond thanked him, and then the priest made a most unusual remark."

"Yes?"

"He told Brond to pray for a favourable prophecy."

Again, there was a brief silence. Oriana wondered what the two of them were up to. Were they planning to end their private conference?

At last Elgar broke the silence, saying, "I trust you find my news of stars and foreign interest real enough articles to mitigate even your mistrust of portents and peasants?"

"When did you say this occurred?" asked Cadwallon clearly skirting Elgar's last remark.

"You mean when did Brond meet the priest?"

"Yes."

"It must have been sometime last week while I was attending your court," said Lord Elgar reflectively. "He did not name the exact day. He only just this morning told me of this encounter as he was taking my horse to stable."

"That means he would have already passed through Shaftesbury if he were riding north on Feldway," cried Cadwallon excitedly. "He must have traveled through my lands the very moment we were in counsel. This is outrageous! Why did I not receive notice of his trespass from my own peasants?"

"It is not impossible, Lord Cadwallon, that a great deal happens under your very nose that is never brought to your attention. Perhaps if you were to treat your ceorls more like the free Saxons they are and less like swine, you might find them more obedient to your will."

"On that score, Elgar, I am convinced we shall never hold common ground."

"More's the pity, Cadwallon. More pitiable for you, I think, than for your villagers."

"Spare me your sentiments," spat Cadwallon indignantly. "So how are we to interpret these developments, your stars and this easterner? Do you suppose the king regards it as a prophecy like the priest?"

"I should say you have rightly guessed my mind from the beginning," Lord Elgar went on. "For myself, I do take this to be a portent, or prophecy if you prefer. Yet for good or ill, I cannot guess—even my learned steward did not attempt meanings. Bear in mind, I have only become convinced of their importance this morning with Brond's news, but I have yet to suppose the *manner* in which they are important, though I fear it is not impossible some evil may come of it. As to the king's thoughts, my hunch is we shall know his mind ere the autumn leaves begin to fall."

Yet again, the lords fell silent. Oriana, meanwhile, seated herself quietly back onto the cushions. She could feel her head beginning to spin. This was entirely too much! Five moving stars! A trance!

Then, at last, Oriana heard from afar, "Father?...Father, where are you?"

"That's Edgira's voice," said Cadwallon.

"Yes, I think it is. I'm really quite touched, Cadwallon," laughed Lord Elgar. "Your attentive daughter longs for your company."

"Hardly! She is merely bored, no doubt—or hungry, or both. Come, Elgar, our talk is at an end."

Oriana heard the lords head back quietly in the direction of Edgira's calls. Oriana's mind was racing. Just then it seemed that Penda's fib to Bathilda earlier that morning was forcing itself into painful reality—a sort of petty curse coming full circle to trouble her here. Now Oriana really did have a headache!

What was she to make of all this? Her head throbbed, saturated with a legion of unanswered questions. It pained her to admit it, but the truth was staring her in the face—she was just as culpable as Cadwallon. She too had failed to notice this celestial awakening. Why had she?

She was not unaccustomed to studying the stars; she did so often. She couldn't understand this. And what was this trance? Lord Elgar was right. She had no memory of it whatsoever. What was this prediction? Malgorod? The slaying of lands? Was there more? What else had she said?

The throbbing in her ears increased. And what of her father? Why had he never mentioned this trance to her? Had there been others like it? In all their lessons, in all their intimate discussions, not once did her father address this trance or these strange new stars, not once! Maybe their relationship hadn't been as close as she had always supposed?

Despite the swirling mists in her head, Oriana was determined to carry on with her duties. She scurried out of the tent unnoticed.

CHAPTER 4

Wonder in White Grove

Oriana reached the interior of Sycamore Henge minutes behind Elgar and Cadwallon. Her thoughts were reeling.

"How shall I ever be able to concentrate on my duties now?" she said privately as the nobles were settling down to their respective tables. "If only this headache might pass. Would that I had a pinch of willow bitters just now!"

Quickly, Oriana strode over to the lord and lady of Oakleigh.

If the faldstools and tables, tents, awnings, and pavilions had all the appearance of being randomly scattered throughout the south meadow in the peasant quarter, the same could not be said of the nobles' accommodations at Sycamore Henge. Everything was in order—truly elegant. From the greatest to the least of details, everything had its appointed place.

Five long tables draped with costly, cream-coloured linens were carefully arranged at the centre of the grassy nook. They were situated end to end in an arc with plenty of room to pass in between. Each was well laid in the best taste. Silver candelabras newly polished, dinner knives, brass goblets, terra-cotta plates, and wooden mazers were set according to the number of seats. All the nobles were seated next to one another on the same side that the serving maids and scullion lads might better serve them from across the opposite end.

Each noble family from Selwoodshire's four villages was honoured with its own table. A fifth was reserved for this year's distinguished guests—seven warriors of the Warden and Freemen of Malmesbury.[1]

To have seven such esteemed knights at their festival was treat indeed for the people of Oakleigh. Rarely did visitors from Malmesbury attend Lord Elgar's estate during high feasts as they generally held their own celebrations in their home county of Wiltshire. That these captains had accepted Lord Elgar's invitation did the lord of Oakleigh a great honour. And so, theirs was the centre table, the table of renown, and it was well merited. But for the valiant men of Malmesbury, as so many had observed that day, there would be no victory celebration—for, indeed, there would be no high king of a united Britannia.

Each table had an unobstructed view of the centre stage. From there the lords and ladies would be regaled with an assortment of evening amusements. Even the ceorl peasants could enjoy the festivities as they would eventually gather in the back along the edge of sycamores.

Oriana had the itinerary all worked out. Lord Elgar would first mount the stage to welcome the day's guests. Next, Father Oswald, the itinerant priest of Selwoodshire, would give the benediction, as he always did at high feasts. After the banquet Lord Elgar would present his victory speech and recite from the Great Chronicle. Thereafter, Oriana would herself introduce the individual entertainers—musicians and minstrels, jugglers and tumblers, buffoons and bards.

Oriana guessed his lordship probably wouldn't object to giving the victory speech. Indeed, it was likely he was already plan-

---

[1] Two years ago to the day, thirty-four villagers from Malmesbury led a fierce charge at Brunanburh that helped turn the tide of battle in the Saxons' favour. As reward, King Athelstan granted them noble status along with six hundred hides of land to the south of their village.

ning to do so. Lord Elgar was rather fond of giving speeches, especially on such occasions where the excess of pomp and pageantry made his dull speeches seem better and his mediocre ones nearly grandiloquent.

"Still, I wish I had run over some of the details with Lord Elgar before now," Oriana said to herself as she neared Oakleigh's banquet table.

By now, more than half of the nobles were seated at their tables laughing and drinking, waiting for Lord Elgar to commence the feast. Lord Cadwallon and his daughter, Edgira, were standing some way off, whispering amongst themselves and glancing about with what might pass for furtive looks. Edgira looked stunning as ever, her well-formed and perfectly positioned curves shewn to advantage by her close-fitting gown of yellow samite and her long raven tresses spilling down her back, straight and lustrous. She drew many eyes. Edgira of course loved to have herself admired whenever the opportunity arose; this was a widely acknowledged fact in Selwoodshire, and it was also widely acknowledged that this, above all things, Oriana detested most in her former friend.

At Oakleigh's own table, Lady Mildreth had already entered into what looked to be a most important conversation with Governess Bathilda and Chamberlain Cerdic. Lady Mildreth seemed much annoyed, which, thought Oriana, was nothing out of the common. Lord Elgar, meanwhile, sat gazing upward with languorous eyes at the blue above, plainly indifferent to his share in their discussion.

"…and there I was," cried Bathilda in a mighty fluster, "walking up and down Feldway, calling out her name and fearin' the worst—even braved a search deep inside old Selwood himself—against my better judgment too, I might add—faërie folk've been seen in there, you understand. 'Wimple-chokes and midge-hives!' I shouts when the truth of it finally come to me. And wouldn't you know, as soon as I set to—"

"Oriana!" interrupted Lord Elgar, rising from his seat and throwing back his russet cloak. He slipt round the table to receive his acting stewardess. It appeared Governess Bathilda was also eager to have a word with her, attempting several times to catch Oriana's eye.

"So you have got here at last," he said merrily, clearly pleased at her entrance. "You are very nearly late, child. What's kept you?"

The lord of Oakleigh was of middling height and build, clean shaven, with cropped ash-blond hair and grey, candid eyes, and, on the whole, quite good-humoured looking. He stood before Oriana with arms crossed in front of his indigo tunic. He winked at Oriana, suggesting he really wasn't angry.

"Forgive me, your lordship, my lady," she said with a curtsey, nodding first to Lord Elgar and then Lady Mildreth. Lady Mildreth didn't trouble herself to look up. To be sure, the lady of Oakleigh gave every appearance she was convinced in the happy belief that the patch of turf Oriana presently graced was very much unoccupied indeed. "I had intended to greet you upon your arrival this morning, but my attentions have been most attenuated. Much has occurred this day, my lord, which has not been answerable to the course I had in view."

"So I see," he said, noticing the red stains on Oriana's fine new kirtle. He then looked down at the dirt splattered at the bottom and shook his head. He was still smiling. "Ever my attentive busy-body you are," he added with approbation. "But I must say, we were beginning to wonder if you would ever stoop to join our humble—"

"*Oriana!*" roared Lady Mildreth just then in her usual cheerfulness and likely within many of the nobles' hearing. She was staring down at a cloth napkin that she was busily folding, unfolding, and refolding as if suddenly afflicted with a neuro-sis for uncreased linens. "I trust you have resolved to end this abominable running about. Have you given no thought to how eagerly some may have expected you? Ladies Branwen and Ele-noora have already twice inquired to your whereabouts."

"Have they indeed?" remarked Oriana shortly.

"Quite! And I must say I scarce knew how to reply."

"The truth should have served well enough, I imagine," replied Oriana directly with just a tinge of flippancy—doubtless the result of her lingering headache.

"Do not answer me in so insolent a tone, young woman," snapped Lady Mildreth angrily. Now was she looking up at Ori-ana with hateful eyes. "You forget yourself! Such base, imperti-nent manners. Ah! Here is something." She hissed with a scru-tinizing stare and pointed her stubby finger with great satisfac-tion. "Look, all of you—look at the hem of her new dress. Just as I expected. My, what an egregious want of rectitude you do exhibit. Well? What do you have to say for yourself?"

Oriana looked down, considered a little then answered, "'Tis' just the mark of the earth's sweet caress, my lady," was her answer. This she said as if reciting a favourite line from a half-forgotten poem. There was song in her voice. She smiled over her sudden cleverness.

"What?" shouted Lady Mildreth with answering contempt, pounding her pudgy fist into the table and bristling the black hairs on the mulberry-size mole adorning her left nostril. "Upon my word, I simply do not—cannot understand this creature!"

At once, several noble ladies glared rudely at Oriana from their tables. Lord Cadwallon and Edgira did the same.

"Mildreth, I say!" interjected Lord Elgar.

"It will wash off, my lady—no worries," explained Oriana confidently, fancying that she would soon gain the upper hand in their latest row.

"And look—I am affronted! Look at those red stains down her front," sneered Mildreth, now flailing her beefy arm as she glowered at Oriana. "Appalling! Wine no doubt. You see, my lord, this is how she repays your generosity. Ingratitude! What a pity, girl, you are not in possession of the refinements that recommend our Lady Edgira, such lofty breeding!" Mildreth screwed her shoulders round and pointed at Edgira still in private counsel with her father behind them. "She is all gentility—propriety itself. I daresay *she* would not ill-spend her energies consorting with those of a lesser pedigree and spoiling her clothes thus."

"Indeed, I am quite of your opinion, ma'am," said Oriana with utmost candour. "I do not suppose our gracious Lady Edgira has ever maneuvered in circles that could not afford her some advantage at court or, at the very least, effect a better change of opinion in those above her in station."

"Obstinate, wilful creature!" snarled Mildreth with a withering glance, her face reddening. Now was she fully within her magisterial element. Finding fault with Oriana on any occasion or impulse was easily Mildreth's favourite amusement; always far quicker to censure than to applaud was the lady of Oakleigh, but Oriana had got use to such strictures by now.

"You would do much better to emulate gracious Lady Edgira's respectability than to invent faults she patently does not possess," she carried on sourly. "My, how you refuse to accept that it is the proper observance of decorum which is the essence of our nobility. You make it plain enough you disdain this widely held truth."

"Lady Mildreth, if it's all the same to you," added Bathilda quite reasonably as she straightened from her usual slouched position so often brought on, poor woman, by her alleged rheumatics or some other imaginary disorder. Like an old mother hen, ever with a watchful eye in matters concerning Oriana, Bathilda now looked keen to get a word in before Lady Mildreth could further upbraid her pretty darling. "I think it might be best if we just let drop—"

"Your actions," continued Lady Mildreth with another spiteful outburst and rudely interrupting the governess, "give very decided expression to your selfish disregard for the dignity and repose of Lord Elgar's house. Playing the part of a serving girl indeed! The very idea! You have much to learn about the proper role of steward. Now, I will have no more of this—I insist you sit down this very instant."

It would not be ungenerous to suggest Lady Mildreth was of a much less agreeable sort than her husband. But fortunately for Oriana, she had few dealings with the proud lady of Oakleigh, having seldom to report directly to her eminence, and that suited Oriana just fine. The less she saw of her, the better. For as long as she could remember, it was her governess, Bathilda, who superintended her upbringing while her father was away at King Athelstan's court. It was she, and not Lady Mildreth, who filled the void in her heart—the emptiness of never knowing her own mother. Next to her father, Bathilda had always been first in her affections.

Oriana knew much of Lady Mildreth's spite arose from the sudden death of her two-week-old son, a loss made all the more painful as he had been their only child. Oriana always tried to bear this in mind whenever Mildreth roared. Such a loss, of course, had its weight in explaining her bitterness, but Oriana knew there was more to it than that. Indeed, it was the uncommon favouritism Lord Elgar lately showered on Oriana, attentions which undermined Mildreth's authority at every turn, that also contributed to her resentment; for Oriana had the advantage of being able to persuade Lord Elgar in matters where Mildreth simply could not. And while Oriana was also blessed with that prepossessing quality of being able to find the good in most people, she confessed at having a mighty struggle when it came to Lady Mildreth. In Oriana's estimation, Lady Mildreth was quite beyond any hope of amendment. She thought her fat, fussy, and fastidious: the perfection of conceit itself. She avoided her at all cost.

And then, just as she stood defending herself against Lady Mildreth's charges, it happened yet again! For the third time that day Oriana had that same curious feeling that someone was looking for her—or at her! Was she going completely mad?

She looked all around, first this way then that, over her shoulder and behind. How unnerving it was!

"This simply cannot be my imagination!" she muttered softly. "What is going on?"

She could form no guess.

"Are your paying attention to me, girl?" growled Mildreth testily as she crossed her arms in front of her overly-abundant bosom. "Display some dignity and sit with the rest of the house."

"Please, Lady Mildreth, in a moment. I—" stammered Oriana, who now felt an urgency to confront whoever or whatever was haunting her. Yet as she looked about, there was no one *to* confront.

"I was about to ask Lord Elgar something. What was it?" Oriana puzzled, still flummoxed over this returning anxiety and momentary loss of concentration.

"Oriana, dear? You awright?" asked Bathilda, rising from her seat with a worried countenance.

"Yes, that was it," she said to herself, still staring off into space.

Oriana turned and faced Lord Elgar. "My lord, by your leave, I should like to meet with the servants one last time." She thought it best to appeal directly to the authority of the lord of the manor. "I have to sort out a couple of things in the new scrubbing stations. When I last looked, there wasn't nearly enough water in the tubs. The candles, I also fear, may be in short supply, and I need to count the—"

"You don't *need* to do anything of the sort," growled Mildreth once again, visibly vexed that Oriana was yet again circumventing her authority. "You simply *chuse*, or perhaps *prefer*. Yes, I think prefer is apter to the situation at hand—preferring to busy yourself with things managed capably enough by others better suited for such purposes—those bred for it! No, no, you will do no such thing!"

"Mildreth!" demanded Lord Elgar on the brink of unbridling his temper. "Enough! Enough! Great fens of Athelney![2] Compose yourself, wife. I say, this is hardly the place for such a scene. What's more, I heartily disapprove of your tone. It quite overreaches the occasion. Such severity upon our junior-stewardess is misplaced."

Seething, Mildreth crumpled her napkin, her lips curling down with a choleric quiver. "My lord, have you not seen—"

"Once again, Mildreth," continued Lord Elgar, cutting off his wife, "you shew yourself disposed to rallying and rash judgments before all accounts have been heard."

"But her indiscretions! Such insufferable...it does not beseem our," she said spitting and sputtering, and by this point positively apoplectic. "Well, I was merely—as you say, my lord."

Well now, how could Oriana possibly forbear cracking a tiny smile at this? Nonchalantly, she covered her mouth.

"Humph!" Mildreth breathed in a surly way. Snubbed, she straightened her back and squared her shoulders with an ill grace. She was scowling furiously at Oriana, her blubbery jowls and portly chins suddenly crimsoned in dozens of sweaty blotches.

---

[2] Sixty-one years earlier, King Alfred the Great fled west of Selwood Forest to the marshes of Athelney where he re-mustered his battered forces. On Easter Sunday he began the fortification of a small island in the marshes from which his army would harry the Danish raiding parties. After seven weeks of successful guerilla attacks, Alfred stole quietly from his fort to rally his army at Egbert's Stone, believed to be in Penselwood. At length, Alfred's army advanced to Ethandun where the Saxons won the most decisive victory against the Vikings. Since that day "Great fens of Athelney" became a common invocation in Selwoodshire for patience or fortitude.

That ended the matter flat.

"Oriana, let me be clear in this," said the lord of Oakleigh in a sincere aspect. "I have entrusted you with a prodigious responsibility this week and, I must say, you have far exceeded my expectations, both in the planning and execution of errands large and small."

"Then you *are* pleased. I was so hoping you would be. I was beginning to have my doubts." At Lord Elgar's commendation she at once felt the weight of a ponderous load lifting from her shoulders.

"Indeed, I am pleased," he said, nodding pleasantly and placing his hand softly upon her shoulder. Mildreth gave a low objectionable hiss. "As far as I am concerned, you are shewing yourself amply ready for the responsibilities of stewardess."

"Thank you, my lord," she replied, making another bob-curtsey.

"Of course, you may go if it will comfort your mind. But make haste."

"I shall hurry my return, lord," and so saying Oriana darted off at once.

"You'd better be quick about it, child." yelled her governess after her. "The final gentlemen from Malmesbury should be arrivin' any minute now."

<hr />

Despite Bathilda's behest, Oriana was gone a good deal longer than she meant. But it wasn't her fault. Whilst inspecting the remaining stores, she had stumbled upon an exceptionally rapacious and most ill-tempered sow that had snuck into one of the larder tents. The bloated porker was racketing all about and devouring as many plums and apples as her sagging belly could hold—a truly alarming quantity, to be sure! This led to some discussion and then dispute between Oriana, Aidith the serving girl, and one of the scullion lads over how best to get the sow out—all of them proving ill-adapted to the task. And after the pig tipped up a third barrel, spilling a peck of chestnuts at least, cracked two more fine crocks, then positively pulverized a pumpkin-coloured pipkin, Aidith was sent off after the village swineherd. It was a ticklish thing to manage, but eventually the four of them were able to coax her out of the tent with a handful of rotting turnip marrows and moldy cabbage leaves.

Soon afterwards, Oriana hastened back. It was time she did, for there was scarcely enough time to explain the schedule to Lord Elgar. She had, of course, fully intended to do this before hurrying off, but Lady Mildreth's latest tirade had pushed the thought clear out of her mind. But given Lord Elgar's placid smile, he seemed to have known what he was expected to do all along. Yes, it was entirely possible she had been worrying far too much over every little detail of the festival. But she couldn't help it—she *was* a perfectionist after all.

Quickly and unobtrusively, Oriana made her way straight to Oakleigh's table, taking her seat in between Bathilda and Cerdic who had conveniently arranged for there to be no other available seat—how benevolent! She guessed they probably wished to chat about something—something undoubtedly involving her friend Penda. But whatever it was, it was going to have to wait. Lord Elgar was now ambling toward the centre pavilion.

His guests now all in attendance, Lord Elgar took the stage and turned to speak. "Gentle ladies and lordly thegns," he shouted with outstretched arms. "Proud neighbours of Selwood-shire, faithful countrymen of Shaftsbury and Frome and Warm-inster. I bid you welcome to Oakleigh Manor.

"Do not be alarmed," he laughed, pointing to his right. "Already I see our brave Lord Éthelhelm of Frome despairing over the unhappy prospect of giving audience to tiresome words on an empty stomach."

Everyone turned to his table and laughed—everyone with the exclusion of Lady Mildreth. She never laughed. Lord Éthelhelm smiled and gave a stiff, rather awkward wave in reply, as his children, the twins Elenoora and Thurnstan, chuckled lightly in their sleeves.

"I shall not long keep you." Lord Elgar went on, "I agree that victory speeches are more palatable at feasts' end, for this is not that speech—not yet. In one thing though, my dear friends, we cannot delay. This year we are given a rare privilege. Our great festival is today made greater with the company of our guests of honour—the valiant men of Wiltshire."

Cheers began to rise.

"I and Lady Mildreth, along with the rest of my house, my chamberlain, Cerdic, and junior-stewardess, Oriana, make welcome our northern neighbours. People of Selwoodshire, let us give thanks to those sturdy knights, without whose courage we should be harkening on this day to the cries of lamentations rather than the mirth of celebration. My lords and ladies behold! I give to you the Warden and Freemen of Malmesbury."

Lord Elgar gestured for the honourees to rise. Without delay, the men of Malmesbury obliged Elgar, nodding and waving to a thunderous applause from the other four tables. As the cheers abated, the tallest of their company, standing behind the centre of the table, raised his longs arms and spoke:

"I, Théodoric, high thegn of Malmesbury, on behalf of all my men, thank you, Lord Elgar and all the good people of Selwoodshire, for this grand reception."

The lord of Malmesbury had a trumpet voice that resonated in rich, baritone notes. Théodoric was not only the tallest of his comrades, but in Oriana's view, the handsomest and most lordly, a fine figure of a man as was ever seen! Even more handsome, she had to confess, than Leofa, her first love. She could not guess his age; he seemed neither old nor untested. He had wavy, auburn hair that fell to his shoulders and a long, braided beard of a slightly redder colour. To be sure, the lord of Malmesbury did not fail in finding an avid admirer in Oriana.

His beard! Oh how she loved it! Oriana always had been fond of beards, long, white beards especially, even more than red beards like Lord Théodoric's, though she could never say why long, white beards exactly. She really did not think beards generally, or for that matter long, white beards particularly, made one look especially handsome. In fact, she had never known any one with a long, white beard. Even King Athelstan's beard, though it was white, was not very long. She could never guess where this affinity came from.

For Oriana, the beauty of Lord Théodoric did not end with his beard.

"My, what wonderful eyes he's got too," she reflected privately. They flashed like peridot under bright sun yet warmed with the hue of new grasses in spring. "And his raiment! How princely it is!"

The lord of Malmesbury was drest in a brown leather jerkin studded with many a bright steel ring pulled over a yellow shirt with billowing sleeves. Girded at his side in a long scabbard richly set with precious stones was a ring-hilted sword nearly half his height in length. Grey like his trousers was his deep-hooded cloak. It was clasped at one shoulder with a bronze-gilt brooch bedecked with gold filigree, garnets, and three ivory rounds.

So great a lord was he, none was his rival that day—not in voice, stature, or address. And as he stood and spoke thus, the tall lord of Malmesbury filled the dingle with his commanding self-assurance—that unique quality that can arise only from the sore trial of battle.

"We humbly accept your gratitude," continued Théodoric graciously, turning to fix his eyes on each of the nobles in turn. "But it would be ill of us to take into possession that which does not wholly belong to me or my comrades alone. Verily, was many a fierce blade wielded by the captains of your shire on that bloody field of Brunanburh. Ever is our king indebted to your deeds withal. Valour was in your hearts that day, and in your step was courage. Long shall your prowess, your dauntless defiance, your unwavering hearts, be remembered in song."

At this panegyric there rose again wide applause, but this time it also sounded from the edge of Sycamore Henge. A sudden crush of daring peasants stood listening and cheering their assent, drawn clearly by the reverberations of Théodoric's oration.

Stirred by their zeal or perhaps following some planned course, the tall warrior unsheathed his sword and held it aloft. Spontaneous or no, he could have chosen no better moment. Just then, the sun shone fiercely through a tiny fissure in a passing cloud, stretching downward to gild Théodoric's blade in shimmering flashes gold and purple.

"Lo! I lay naked before you, Gramling, friend of Adder, rod of the battle-storm, as binding pledge of our fellowship—most ancient of heirlooms from my sires of old it is, forged with the splinters of Sigurd's hallowed blade. Oft has its hardened edge stood me in good stead in times of greatest peril. May it ever protect the free people of Wessex. Behold!" and he cast the great sword bare upon the table.

Emboldened, his men followed suit, brandishing their swords in kind, holding them erect and calling: "For Malmesbury! For Wessex! And for King Athelstan the Victorious! Feeder of ravens!" Then they too tendered their blades to the table so that Gramling might not be in want of company.

For the third time the nobles from their seats and the peasants by their sycamores clapt, whistled, quaffed their goblets, and cheered with a fervour that made the earth rumble approvingly.

"Wonderful! Glorious!" exclaimed Elgar enthusiastically.

"For whose heart could ever falter with such stirring sentiments? Now, my noble thegns and gracious ladies, now for the feast. Let us call upon Father Oswald to deliver the benediction. Father, if you would honour us."

The aged parish priest rose from his seat after a quick nudging-elbow from Lord Thorgrim. He had been sitting at Warminster's table only half-awake. He straightened the purple tippet round his shoulders, reached for his matching embroidered maniple from his belt pouch, draped it over his right hand, and hobbled slowly up to the dais. He leant on his crosier next to Lord Elgar.

"Thank you, Alderman Elgar," he muttered softly with one hand raised. The feeble voice of Father Oswald stood in meek contrast to the thundering blasts that had issued from Théodoric. Oriana thought the juxtaposition almost comical. Perhaps she should have arranged for the good priest to speak first!

"And thank you, Lord Théodoric," he continued sleepily, "that was truly rousing."

Oriana wondered if he meant this to be a joke given his own soporific state just moments ago.

"I will echo the words of Lord Elgar," he said, straightening his back, "and say the free shires of Wessex and Mercia owe you and your men a great debt. But let us not forget, dear friends, to whom we must ultimately pay our gratitude. We would do well to remember that in the end it is to divine providence we owe our liberation from the heathen northmen and those in league with them. I might also remind you, though I hope it needless, that today is also the feast day of St. Tychon, bishop of Amathus, the ancestral home of our beloved steward, Lord Phillip—saints be with him this day."

Oriana gasped! How naïve she had been. Her father hadn't been forgotten after all. It was childish and selfish to have thought so. She should have known Father Oswald, of all people, would not have forgotten him.

"We should remember and honour both men this day as we celebrate our victory. I might also point out, St. Tychon is the patron saint of wine makers in Lord Phillip's island home. Given your obvious love of drink, my fellow Saxons," he said smiling, "it is fitting we begin with the orison of St. Tychon.

"Let us pray: *In nomen patris et filii et spiritus sancti, amen.*"

Oriana was able to follow most of Father Oswald's benediction. From an early age her father had placed her on a steady regiment of Latin—translating the works of Virgil, Cicero, and Boëthius—Boëthius in particular![3] Her father used to say, "If our great Alfred thought Boëthius worth studying then so, too, should you, daughter."

All the same, she was glad her father had never asked her to recite the first half of Father Oswald's benediction. She had never heard the prayer of this obscure Cypriot-saint. She wondered if her father had even known the prayer. He probably did.

As for the ending of his benediction, she knew this well enough. It was from the Gospel of St. John:

This world is fading away, along with everything it craves, Amen.

"Well now that was certainly a demoralizing way to conclude a blessing," she thought. She wondered if anyone else had worked out the translation and thought as much.

"Now are we bidden to table," exclaimed Lord Elgar. "Bring flesh to the board! Wine to the cup! Let the feast begin!" And with these words, the smiling lord of Oakleigh thrice chimed the ceremonial bell.

---

[3] Around the year 890, King Alfred translated those works into English which, as he himself said, "are most necessary for all men to know." Six works in all were translated: St. Gregory's Dialogues, Pastoral Care, and Soliloquies; Bede's Ecclesiastical History of the English People; Orosius' Seven Books of Histories against the Pagans; the compilation of the Anglo-Saxon Chronicle; and Boëthius' The Consolations of Philosophy. For six hundreds years Boëthius was the only source through which the West had any contact with the writings of Aristotle, albeit in a very fragmentary form.

◇◇◇◇◇◇◇◇◇◇◇◇◇◇◇◇◇◇◇◇◇◇◇◇◇◇◇◇◇◇◇◇◇◇◇◇◇◇

Lord Elgar's guests dined until dusk amid a cacophony of conversation, laughter, clanking dishes, a constant coming and going of scullions and waiters, and even more frequent and fervent replenishing calls to the cupbearers. Shadows were stretching slender fingers from the enclosure of white trees as the sun westered to the green shoulders of Selwoodshire. Their repast finished, the time for evening drolleries was fast approaching.

Now you might be surprized to learn that, despite Oriana's exceedingly busy day, she really hadn't much appetite for food or drink. She, at any rate, was much astounded by this. While Oriana was certainly never given to gluttony, she wasn't exactly what one might regard as a dainty eater. Ordinarily, she had a perfectly fine appetite.

Oriana rationalized. Nothing she sampled that day had disagreed with her, so that wasn't it. It was her nerves, it must be— no that didn't seem to be the answer either. She had been anxious that day of course, praying she would not disappoint the lord of Oakleigh—but those sorts of stresses generally made her hungrier, not the reverse.

"Ah! It's Lord Elgar and Cadwallon's private conclave still gnawing me! That certainly must be it. No, this won't do." She couldn't convince herself of this either. For the moment, she had dismissed all those unanswered questions to the remote hindquarters of her mind to puzzle over later. In truth, she was no longer dwelling on their bizarre meeting. Even her earlier headache was now gone and so that could not be to blame. So what was this?

Oriana sat massaging her temples with her fingers. This often helped her clear her mind, but it did not seem to be helping now.

As she sat searching for the root of her restlessness, she was but dimly conscious of the voice to her right.

"I hold you blameless in the whole affair, child," said Governess Bathilda with a most sober bearing. "Why I didn't first check your quarters before that confounding little varlet sent me off on that wild goose hunt, I'll never know," she went on roundly. "Why that no-account, puny, prevaricating imp! Thistle burns and beestings! If I get me hands on his twiggy neck...He gave me such a turn you see, that's all. I didn't have my wits about me, or heaven is my witness, I should have..."

It was beginning! It was coming! The source of her disquiet was revealing itself at last. It was the same queer feeling she'd been having all day, only now, much, much stronger!

Something was approaching! It was not an evil feeling; there was no menace, no feeling of dread. But something, or someone, was definitely nearing, and it was coming with knowledge and disruption. No longer did she feel as if she were merely being watched, for the watcher had come! This was no headache, no disquiet of the nerves, no subjective emotional pang. Its approach was absolute! The truth of it consumed her.

"My, my; couldn't eat another bite," said Chamberlain Cerdic in an after-supper tone of improving humour. He was scratching thoughtfully at the stubble on his pale, protuberant chin. "But come now, did your father really confirm his answer? One grey cat in a cleric's smart pouch? I've been running over that all day, and while it does seem to resolve the first couple stanzas; what about the looming sheets of ice? I think that if you apply..."

It happened suddenly! In the blink of an eye, Oriana was there.

Oriana and her tapestry had become one. The great white stag, the hawthorn tree and green hillock, the silver lane—they were all before her. Gone were Sycamore Henge and all its revellers. The whole of her consciousness was now bent on that single world. And that world was growing—changing. It was astounding—breathtaking! No passive observer was she, indeed no. She was not experiencing a flat, lifeless picture dangling before her as if she were merely standing in her room admiring her favourite tapestry. She was now part of that tapestry, of that world!

"I was right," she said, in that moment of transcendental passage. "My tapestry! I knew I wasn't mad."

Oriana moved her head to and fro, viewing the objects and landscape from changing perspectives. She marveled. Where was she exactly? This could not be her world—all was fuller. She could hear the wind whickering with sweet voices through the budding boughs of trees near and far. And ever the aroma of new life flowed. Green fragrance of the grassclad knoll filled her nostrils as if spring had burst suddenly from an impatient slumber of countless winters. Her mind was overcome with the presence and purpose of life. Every leaf and twig, every blade of grass, each cloud, crow, and shadow was purposeful. Nothing in this new world felt a product of chance—design was ever present.

Oriana eyes were brimming with tears. By some great wonder, she had been thrust into a world in possession of beauty unmarred and purpose fully knowable. She was overjoyed. All was richer, deeper, more alive—the very fabric of being was itself more real than anything she had experienced until then. She basked in the meaning of this new world!

And there, beyond the gnarled trunk and hoary limbs of the hawthorn came the stag. Solemnly he gaited down the glittering arch, the causeway borne upon naught but wind alone. Proud and venerable he seemed, his white antlers piercing the blue above with its many points and his fur shimmering with the soft radiance of an early-morning snowfall. Oriana quailed in his presence, not from fear of some impending dread but from the overwhelming understanding he was aware of her, considering her.

Long did the great stag descend the ethereal lane, his black eyes boring deeper and deeper into her soul. Oriana could not free herself from his gaze. Deep were his sable eyes, deep and dark as the night of a new moon, profound and unyielding—tiny windows opening onto a chamber of forgotten lore and ancient secrets. Yet there was love also in his eyes, love tempered with sadness. Oriana trembled. His stare gave every promise he meant to have speech with her.

Forward she too came, compelled by a will not her own. Ever closer, ever trembling, she advanced to the entrance of the sterling bridge where the enormous creature now awaited her approach. And yet, it was strange, so very strange—though she was most definitely drawing near the great stag, she realized she was not moving at all; for in fact, she was standing perfectly still as if rooted to the very soil!

They were before one another. Neither spoke. Oriana was powerless to resist. Deeper and deeper she fell under the spell of his gaze.

It had begun! A journey she had been awaiting all her life—something ordained for her, though presently she could offer no explanation how she knew this to be so.

Oriana continued her descent through the stag's eyes, only now had they become long, dark corridors with small lights glimmering far ahead. What was Oriana's wonder as she went! Now if you, for one, have ever peered through the wrong end of a play telescope for fun or curiosity when you were younger, you would have a rough idea of the tunnel-like experience Oriana felt as she fell through his gaze. And as she glided ever onward she realized the tiny lights at the far end were no lights at all, but dazzling miniature-white flowers of five petals.

As she continued her journey into the hollows of the stag's mind—or perhaps it was the reverse; perhaps he was penetrating her soul—Oriana could hear from afar a familiar voice, faint but undeniable. It sounded through an unseen barrier, dimmed in the manner a porch light struggles through a damp fog to aid the master returning home. It was the voice of Lord Elgar.

"He must have already given the victory speech," said Oriana to herself. "How long have I been away?"

Stranger still, Oriana was not only aware she could hear Lord Elgar, but she could *see* him as well, standing once again upon the stage. She was wrong. Her consciousness was not wholly with the stag. She was, in fact, still seated behind the table between Bathilda and Cerdic. But this could not be, for she was yet staring at the stag, falling steadily deeper into the wells of his being.

Oriana was dismayed! She was somehow in two places simultaneously. But she felt perfectly intact. It was not at all the sensation of having two halves of one self—two distinct but connected persons; no, that was not it. She was convinced she was one, indivisible whole yet in two separate places at the same moment. Somehow she had become bound up in the paradox of schism without separation.

Nothing in her life had ever prepared her for such a transcendental experience—no banter of metaphysical speculation with her father, no carefree discoveries with Penda in the woods, no sacred pilgrimages to Winchester or Canterbury. No idea or past event served her now.

Traveling ever onward toward the white petals awaiting her at journey's end, she sat listening to Elgar's closing remarks. He was reciting from the Wessex Chronicle. Hushed nobles and peasants were hanging on to his every word with eager faces.

Here, Athelstan King, of earls the lord
and ring-giver to men, and Prince Edmund the Atheling his brother
elders of ancient race, earned this year fame everlasting,
slew in the fight, with the edge of their swords the foe at Brunanburh.
The sons of Edward cleaved the linden shields and hewed their banners,
as was only fitting for men of their lineage.
Oft they carried arms against some foe in defence of their land,
their treasure, their homes.
Pursuing fell the Scottish clans, the mariners in numbers fell;
amidst the din of the field the warrior swate.
From the hour when the sun was up in morning-tide,

gigantic light! Glad over grounds, God's candle bright, eternal Lord!
Until at last that lordly creation set into its westerly bower;
There lay many of the Northern foes under a shower of arrows, shot
over shields,
The battlefield flowed with dark blood.
With chosen troops throughout the day,
the West Saxons fierce pressed on the loathed bands;
hewed down the fugitives and scattered the rear,
with strong, mill-sharpened blades.

The stag blinked. Exactly as Lord Elgar was reading from the
Great Chronicle, the stag ceased his searching. She could feel
that he had finally found what he had been seeking. He was contented. Gently, he eased his clutch from her mind. Oriana's will
was hers once more. Then, calmly and gracefully, the great white
beast bowed. That is, he made a sort of genuflection, stretching
out his right leg and curling the left one under his breast as he
lowered his mighty antlers to the earth.

Oriana knew she must return his polite gesture, but what was
the proper display of respect, or more rightly, deference, to such
a being? Her usual curtsey seemed ill suited, yet so too did full
prostration. By her own impulse, or through some other design,

she crossed her hands over her heart and bent her torso in a deep bow with her face upward, never removing her eyes from his. The stag smiled.

The great stag made ready to announce the purpose of his coming. Oriana could feel her mind had been prepared as tilth, waiting to be sown with the seed of his word.

"No, I…I am not ready," she said to herself, letting her eyes drop. Hitherto Oriana had merely been daunted, awed by his overwhelming presence, but she was never really frightened. Yet now, now she *was* afraid. What message; what truths would he impart? What words would be spoken that could be meant for her alone, someone small and insignificant as she? How could she merit such an embassy, a simple Saxon girl not in the least degree worthy of his counsel?

In a jolt of defence or desperation or denial, Oriana focused solely on Lord Elgar's conclusion of his recitation.

Five kings lay on the field of battle, in bloom of youth, pierced with swords.
Thus the Norse king was forced to flee, the dread of northern foes
To ship's slender prow did he fly; the little ship scurried out to sea.
No slaughter ever was made greater in this island of people slain,
Never before were men so slain in this land by the edge of sword,
since hither came from eastern shores, the Angles and the Saxons,
over the broad sea, and Britain sought,
Behold! fierce battle-smiths o'ercame the Welsh, most valiant earls,
eager for glory, and gained a land so fair.

"Have no fear, precious yearling, daughter of worlds twain," the white stag called to Oriana, his gaze ever penetrating. For a third time her mind was his possession, her will subject to his. She felt sudden shame course through her body; she could not look upon him.

"How dare I ignore? How dare I disobey? I am faithless and weak," muttered Oriana to herself reproachfully.

"Dear one, you are no coward, no miscreant," said the stag

reassuringly. "Do not reprove a faltering will when it comes of humility. I see no evil in you, and though you know it not, I have peered long into your heart—an age at least in some worlds. Be comforted. Hope you may find in my voice, though it is not for all to hear. Verily the strength I have beheld in you may bear fruit of that hope. I say unto you, though my voice is hope, from you hope shall spring. And so, be at peace, yearling of lands twain, while you may."

His voice! His voice! What speech the stag possessed; words formed of ordinary deer clickings and whistlings blended with the soothing tone of a kindly elder. Yet her ears played but a minor part. She listened with her soul, understood with her mind, and believed with her heart. She trembled no longer in his presence.

Oriana thought she should make some effort at speech but found she was completely dumb with amazement. She could find no words suitable for reply.

"Have you aught to say to me then?" asked the stag trenchantly, yet smiling as he spoke.

Again Oriana did not reply.

"As I expected," the stag went on. "Your silence speaks to your humility and to your wisdom. You fear a hasty word lest it seem ignorant or that which is worse—haughty. Not for naught have we waited since the Great Reconciliation was wrought. You elect to listen, not to spoil words. You are wise. Then harken to me, yearling girl of goodly sense!

"For I am come with tidings grave and grim but to them is hope akin. Though I say you need fear me not, my tidings are perilous, indeed. Alas! I come a herald of dread.

"Lo! I say unto you, child of woe. Very near is your world to the final sunderance, the last rending sorrow, should the faceless foe and his fell apostates prevail, a great withering of your world shall come to pass. But I do not say the beginning of the end draws nigh. Nay! For an age and more has that ending already neared. Too long has your race, the folk of Miðgard, heeded craven whisperings of the faceless foe. Alas, it is he who man obeys in his lust for dominion over all else that lives. Behold! Daughter of worlds twain, I have been sent hither to lead a way, to lead you to a final hope. For the end of ending and the world's return should you hope. But come you must first and face the heavy hour."

His words scored into Oriana's thought as strokes cautiously etched onto a sacred tablet. This message she would carry until the end, but this moment she could not preserve. Her mind, indeed this very part or her being, slowly and without resistance, was closing to his realm. Someone next to her was speaking.

"Oh, that's splendid! Congratulations, child, wonderful news. Though I dare say I suspected it would come to this sooner or later." It was the voice of her governess. "You were, of course, listening to Lord Elgar? What on earth's the matter with you? You look so lost. Stitch a smile on your face, child—for goodness sake! Did you not hear his pronouncement? He has just…"

Oriana saw, as though through a deep mist, the white stag turn and walk back toward the silvern arc. Briskly he crossed the threshold, working his way ever up and over. Clouds of gossamer strands sailed underneath as he sped.

With a final spurt of will, she called to him.

"Lord, might I know your name?"

He did not respond, or else she did not hear. Silence was falling all around. And then, as that world was but fully veiled before her eyes, she heard as though across a great chasm: "You must follow me."

In a dim flicker, that world was gone. Oriana saw nothing of the stag, or the knoll, or the hawthorn tree. The silver lane had disappeared along with every leaf, fragrance, and blade of grass.

"How can I follow? What am I to do?" Oriana wondered

WONDER IN WHITE GROVE

despondently, now bereft of that glorious peace. She sat staring at a small wine stain, spreading over the cream-coloured table-cloth. Her hand was twitching beside an upset goblet.

"… made you his heir apparent—that's what 'e done. He's just announced the adoption. You're now stewardess, and before you've come of age no less! Well? What d'you have to say 'bout that, child? Lord Elgar is now your father!"

CHAPTER 5

Of Lines...

Three days had come and gone since the guests departed for home—most of the guests that is. The usual manor activities had resumed. All the tents and awnings had been dismantled, bundled, and stowed, farmers had returned to their sowing, artisans, their crafts, and the children to their chores. Lord Elgar was once again obliged to depart for King Athelstan's court at Cheddar, distant but one day's journey west of Oakleigh, where his duties as the king's alderman were expected to keep him for the next three months. Lady Mildreth staid behind skulking and bossing.

And so the following days were to bring every appearance that all was settling back down at Oakleigh Manor.

But you would be mistaken to assume life had completely returned to normal. It hadn't; at least for Oriana it hadn't. It was now nearly a week since Lord Elgar had surprized his guests with Oriana's unexpected adoption. None had been more astonished by this than Oriana herself—none save one other perhaps.

"Say, that was pretty good. Did yeh see that one? Got three that time."

"That's nice, Penda," Oriana returned stolidly.

"Pay close watch. You're about to be impressed!" he gloated. "Goin' for a fiver this time." Back, back he wound his arm then threw. A flat stone skipped poorly down a wide length of Willowrun Creek.

It was late morning of what was shaping up to be a hot,

muggy day. The air was close and bore a heaviness that acted against an easy breath, an occurrence not too terribly uncommon for Selwoodshire in late Plough Month.

"Uhh! That was bloomin' awful," grumbled Penda, kicking clumsily at some tall rushes and nearly stumbling into the water in the bargain. "Only a one-hopper on that one. Couldn't've been my throw, though—rutty diabolical stone that last one was!"

"Have you heard a single word I've said?" asked Oriana as she sat motionless on a knobby, wooden tree-swing. She was staring out fixedly at the radiating ripples in the water from Penda's last throw.

"Not a one," he said bluntly, but then, putting up his hands defensively, laughed. "Kidding, Orie—kidding. As it happens, I can skip chips and listen to you at the same time. That's one of my other unappreciated talents you know—being able to do two—"

"All right, Penda," Oriana cut in, "fine, but you do sometimes give the impression you're not paying attention."

"Yeah, well that's just it, isn't it—an impression," he said wryly, winding up for a third go. "That's just how subtle I can be. It's guile and good looks that get me by. Some are just born to it, so Mum tells me. Despite external indications to the contrary, m' lady, I've heard every blessed word you've said. What's more, I even—wow! Four! Ha! Top drawer that was!" he vaunted at his throw, which, truth be told, was really not so very remarkable. "Let's see yeh beat that."

But Oriana didn't see Penda's last throw. She really wasn't all that interested in skipping chips at the moment. Instead, Oriana granted herself licence to do the very thing she had just accused Penda of doing—she wasn't paying attention. Privately, she was revisiting the evening Lord Elgar had announced her adoption and investiture as stewardess.

What a very great shock it had been to all present that evening. Mildreth's eyes had flashed at Elgar's pronouncement, then the whole of her complexion blanched as shock turned to disdain. She went chalky pale, looking as one does when just about to hurl half-digested bits of more than half-fetid morsels of mutton pie. Mildreth's view on the matter was plain; Oriana was to be their daughter, and worse, their legal heir! To her would pass all the holdings and income of Oakleigh's twenty-six hides—and that prospect was unbearable.

Mildreth's astonishment was understandable. It had been widely voiced that Lord Elgar intended bequeathing all of Oakleigh's properties and income to Lord Bertolf of Langport. Lord Bertolf was Lady Mildreth's favourite nephew and the wealthiest, most influential man in Somerset, which of course explains why he was Mildreth's favourite nephew! It was also no secret Bertolf was maneuvering to acquire estates in Bath and Frome to secure his political advantage in Somerset. Should he inherit Oakleigh Manor and most of Selwood Forest thereby, he would be in the rather enviable position of holding the wealthiest estates in both Somerset and Selwood.

Surely, as Elgar had no son or other suitable, that is, male progeny, Bertolf did seem the logical choice. This was all normal enough, as far as it went. Yet Oriana still had her doubts about Mildreth's true motives. It was obvious that should something unexpected, something untimely happen to the lord of Oakleigh, Mildreth would stand to profit very handsomely under such an arrangement. Oh yes, should tragedy strike, were Mildreth to become a widow, she would ascend to senior matriarch of her extended family and, hence, could exert considerable influence over Lord Bertolf and the other noble families of Selwood and Somerset.

Oriana did not, of course, suspect Mildreth of palace intrigue, but neither did she underestimate Mildreth's calculating nature—her unsavoury propensity for personal aggrandizement at others' expense. For one thing, Oriana thought Mildreth often offered just a trifle too much encouragement when her husband was called to arms. Dreadful things do happen in battle after all. She guessed this was never too far from Mildreth's thoughts. For another, it was not at all uncommon for her ladyship to embroil Lord Elgar in private disputes between the lesser thegns, disputes almost invariably resulting in bloodshed—Lord Elgar's blood on more than one occasion.

And so, the suddenness of Elgar's adoption of his junior-stewardess was a mighty blow to Mildreth's pride and plotting. For Oriana, it was surprize itself! Never for one moment had Oriana the presumption that Lord Elgar might extend such generosity. Nor, for that matter, did she once suppose he, like so many others in the village, had abandoned all hope of her father's return. And so now, as stewardess, she was expected to oversee the entire management of the manor's farm in Lord Elgar's absence. The responsibility was great. Oriana could only guess what this elevated position might hold in store for her in the coming days.

"I've had it. I'll never top four," said Penda duly, offering Oriana one of his stones. "Why don't you have a go, Orie? Bet yeh can't one-up me this time."

Oriana was only half listening. She sat staring down softly from her swing at a long twig she had just snapped under her heel.

"So what do you make of it?" she asked phlegmatically.

"Make of what?" he said with a half smile.

Oriana put her hand to her forehead, frowning. "Honestly, Penda! Do be serious, won't you?"

"Okay, okay." Tossing his stone, he seated himself on a dry clump of grasses by the tree. He pulled a wide blade and, placing it between his thumbs, blew several notes. "I know! Lord Elgar's stars, yeah? What about 'em?"

"Why can't I see them?" she said dispiritedly. "The past four nights have been clear and yet, nothing, nothing at all. Why do you suppose this is?"

"Blest if I know," he murmured, shrugging his shoulders. He blew several more obnoxious-sounding duck calls through his grass reed.

"A shrewd observation," she said facetiously.

"Maybe you're not looking in the right spot."

"The North Star, Penda? You of all people should know I can find that easily enough. How many times have we snuck out to watch shooting stars, huh? Lord Elgar said they rotate around it. So why can't I?"

"Dunno." *Squeak… Squak.* "Look, if it's any consolation, Orie, I haven't seen them either."

"Oh no you don't, my little tousled-headed friend. You are playing at words," she said, looking up from the stick beneath her swing. "You mean you haven't seen them because you haven't bothered to look. But *could* you see them if you had, I wonder? Well, I *have* looked and cannot. I just don't understand it."

Try as she might, Oriana just could not free her thoughts from the events of the past week. Lord Elgar's report of the five new stars was only a fraction of that which presently racked her mind.

How embarrassed she had been. To be sure, her hasty exit from the festival must have seemed most indecorous of one just appointed steward. And as Oriana had threaded her way through the crowd, Lady Mildreth had been perfectly unable to resist whispering snide remarks to her young admirer, Lady Edgira, who had been very much at her disposal all that day.

"So much the better for all concerned, I'm sure," she had said in a most sanctimonious tone as Oriana swept passed. "The agony of separation! Yet I expect we shall just barely be able to endure the deprivation, however desolate it may render us."

Edgira then gave Mildreth a return look expressive of her sharing in the opinion.

But no such criticisms were made by her governess. Bathilda was nothing if not a compassionate, thoughtful woman, happy to do a kindness to anyone. And she was ever so insightful too—her unerring instincts proving correct again, predicting Oriana's adoption when she herself had not.

"But what will become of Bathilda now?" Oriana had wondered aloud in bed the following morning. "Now that Mildreth is to be my—no, I … I can't bring myself to say it."

And whilst Oriana had kept to herself during the second day of the feast, Bathilda had once again assumed her former role of nursemaid, looking in on her pretty darling from time to time and always within calling distance. "Lady Oriana is quite indisposed today, but she thanks you for calling just the same," said the governess a thousand times that day if she said it once. Oriana had instructed her to relay this message should anyone come to pay calls or inquire about her condition. Naturally, many had.

"Our lady's fallen ill and needs her restin.' God willin,' she'll be able to see yeh off in the morning before yeh leave. Now all you youngins clear out before I sets a switch ter the lot of yeh," she said firmly and turned Oriana's admirers out of the inner ward directly.

Indeed, Oriana had seen no one the second day of the feast (apart from her governess of course), chusing instead to remain cloistered within her private quarters. She hated disappointing Lord Elgar, especially in light of his recent generosity, but a sudden overwhelming anxiety, a sudden need to be alone, much exceeded her sense of duty. She found she could no longer manage—neither feasts nor her nerves.

All that day was spent in thinking. Hardly stirring from her bed, she desired neither food nor drink, counsel nor comfort. Her morose frame of mind the previous morning was as nothing compared to the state in which she had dissolved on that second day of the feast. At the start of the celebration, she had merely been downcast. Her heart aching so in want of her father, Oriana often found her loneliness difficult to bear; his disappearance weighed heavily on her soul and probably would the rest of her life. But now she had this and much, much more to trouble her.

Never had a day been so fantastic, that day of growing stars and rumoured trances, transcendental journeys and dire prophecies. Never had a day delivered such change to Oriana's life.

In the first place, Oriana had no choice but to reassess her rather rigid worldview. Such conventional, empirical reasoning simply did not permit the possibility of what she had experienced. In a moment, the world had become a larger, grander, more complicated and wonderful place. Her former assumptions of life—of being itself—now offered no grounding for explaining her mysterious journey.

She pondered much that day alone in her room. Why had the mysterious stag come to her—her of all people? Why did he call her a child of woe and daughter of worlds twain? What did it all mean? And why did he not call her by her name? What was the meaning of his message—the faceless foe and the end of ending? Could there be some connection between the stag's warnings and what she allegedly told her father about the new stars? Malgorod? The slaying of lands? Lord Elgar had said it was a disturbing prediction.

Her questions were unceasing as she had lain alone and confused, staring up at what used to be her favourite tapestry. Was it still? Oriana wasn't now so sure. Her whole world was standing on its head.

By late afternoon of the third day, the wagons and packhorses had set out for home. Oriana had much rather gone with them, with someone, anyone. It wasn't that she really fancied a trip to Frome or to Warminster or to Shaftesbury specifically, she just longed to be anywhere but home—some secret, quiet spot to reflect on the meaning of such extraordinary things.

"But really, where is there for me to go?" she had said to herself then. "Well, maybe a trip to Frome wouldn't be such a bad idea after all."

Oriana had spent virtually no time with her friend Elenoora on that first day of the feast, just a passing salutation here and there as she volleyed between the peasant quarter and Sycamore Henge.

"A visit to Frome would at least put things to rights with Elenoora."

As it was, most of the guests had departed for home on the third day. There was a handful, however, who had decided to lengthen their visit by an additional day or two—on permission of their lords of course. Most wished for little more than an extended visit with distant relations. Others, apparently, were just plain unenthused about returning to their daily routines back home.

On balance, Oriana's duties had been unaffected by their prolonged mirth. But the situation with Miss Edgira of Shaftsbury—now that, that was another matter entirely. At first Oriana found the situation to be only a slight nuisance, yet it took little time before it became a truly insufferable affair.

Quite out of the blue, Edgira had stated she would not be returning to Shaftsbury with her parents. She too would be extending her stay at Oakleigh Manor. But she would not be staying in the village. Oh no, not she—not the lady of Shaftsbury. Without the bother of asking Oriana's leave, she set herself up very comfortably in her private chamber. What audacity!

Then, not two days into this intrusion, she had appropriated most of Oriana's room for the arrangement of her own personal effects. Worse than all, she even had the effrontery to take possession of Oriana's bed, her best owlet-down pillow, and fine eiderdown quilts for her very own. The situation was insupport-able! There simply could be no enduring her. And this impo-sition was to last—well, Oriana wasn't exactly sure how long Edgira intended to stay.

Oriana could not recall having ever felt so prevailed upon. On top of everything else, she now had Edgira to complete her troubles.

"Why Edgira?" Oriana had asked herself. Why she of all peo-ple desired to stay on at Oakleigh Manor was most perplexing indeed. "We aren't exactly what one might call the best of friends anymore. Is she hoping we might be again? Well if she is, this hostile occupation of my room certainly is not going to advance things in that direction—Exactly whose idea was this anyhow? Was this her decision or at her father's command?" This last question was the one casting about most wildly in her mind. If it was the latter, what could he possibly hope to gain from Edgira's prying? What was Oriana or her room to him anyway? So, in those three days of having to relinquish nearly all her private space to Edgira and her dignity to Lady Mildreth, Oriana found herself making ever-increasing forays into the village, seeking out such society of a less pretentious nature and far more to her liking. Selwood Forest too beckoned on more than one occasion, promising some well-needed private contemplation.

And on that third day, once again robbed of her peace of mind, she had found the lulling current of Willowrun Creek calling. Her morning duties seen to, Oriana had made her way to the north pasture and the large shade tree along the water's southern bank. Penda was already there, lazing about.

"Forget about those stupid stars, Orie. Listen, we'll have a look tonight if it means that much to you, awright?"

"Do I have your word on that?" said Oriana, glaring at him dubiously.

"Need you even ask?" he returned, smiling impishly with his

hand over his breast. "I do believe I detect my lady in doubt of my honour."

"I think you're confusing me with Bathilda," she laughed. "I still say you have loads of integrity."

"Well, since you put it that way, you can count on me. I'll be there tonight. I'm sure we'll see them. Now come on!" He threw away his grass reed in exchange for some more river pebbles. "'fraid you can't top four?"

Oriana began swaying gently in the tree swing, lost in thought again.

Penda cleared his throat in an obvious way. "Why, thank you; I don't mind if I do—that's what comes next, Orie."

"Right; sorry. Uh, I think we'll let your record stand." She paused. "And the rest? What about everything else? Now be honest, Penda. Don't spare my feelings—you won't be doing me any favours. Do you *really* believe me, the stag and the rest of it?"

"Hmm, worried I've changed my mind since yesterday?" returned Penda as he limply plopped a stone into the water. He walked behind Oriana and began pushing her. "Reckon after a good night's sleep I've reassessed everything? Is that it? Well, stop. You haven't a thing to worry about. I still believe you."

"Thank you, Penda," she said as the world began swaying back and forth. "You always come through for me."

"Hey, like I said, don't mention it," he returned nonchalantly. "But if you ever doubted I was your best friend, doubt no longer. Anyone else would say you're a total nutlet if you'd confessed half what you've told me, a right raving nutlet for sure—cracked!"

"You'll find no quarrel with me on that point," she chuckled. "I would grudge no one saying or thinking as much. This is why I confide in you and only you."

Penda coloured. He always did so when Oriana flattered him. In her father's absence, Penda was her one true confidante, and he knew it.

"But I must tell you," she went on hesitantly, "I do have a small confession to make. Yesterday when I said I had had a very strange vision—well, I wasn't entirely straight with you. That's not exactly what happened. The truth is much stranger, much more complicated."

"Orie, I said I believe you, and I meant it, whatever you say it was," he replied with a sincere intonation. "That's what friends do, right? Believing in one another when everyone else thinks you're off your nut."

"Why, Penda, how beautiful!" she said brightly. "I don't think I've ever heard you say anything quite so sentimental. That was precious."

"Yeah, it was at that, wasn't it? Just don't expect it too often," he added. "But I must say, as your father so often did—Mjollnir[1] protect him wherever he is—just remember there can be many truths to a situation and a shed-load of ways to arrive at those truths."

"For instance?" began Oriana and then, "*Hey!* Take it easy! You're going to launch me into the creek!"

"Sorry," he said, easing his push. "I sometimes forget my manly excesses."

The swing slowed. "Much better."

"It's just that, as I see it, there might be more than one explanation for what you experienced."

"No, Penda, I think not—not this time," she objected most emphatically. "In this instance, there can be only one explanation. I was invited—no, summoned is more accurate—yes I was definitely summoned, to another place that is. And I do mean *another* place. Very different everything was. Though strange as it sounds, I can't recall exactly in what way it *was* different. But I do remember I did not wish to leave. I would have stayed if it

---

[1] Thor's hammer

were permitted. That feeling is still with me, even now … Here, help me stop."

Penda took hold of the ropes stopping the swing, his face twisting into a puzzled expression. Oriana jumped down and picked up the slender twig she had been eyeing beneath her.

"Since you mentioned Father, I'll continue the idea." Using the stick, Oriana started etching lines in the scuffed dirt below the swing. "I've been giving this an awful lot of thought lately. Remember how everyone thought I was sick on the second day of the festival?"

"So, I was right all along, huh?" he barked testily. "I knew you weren't sick. What a sneak!"

"Oh, Penda, don't be such an infant," she shot at him. "*Believe me.* I wasn't malingering. I just … well, I just needed some time to be alone—to sort things out. I did nothing the whole day but lie on my bed and stare up at my tapestry, thinking. I forced my mind to probe deeper than I ever thought possible. I had to find some explanation. And then I finally hit on something Father had once said. Now you tell me, Penda, who was Father always so keen on?" she asked eagerly.

Penda looked down at Oriana's scrawling in the loose earth and shook his head, "Who was I kidding? She has gone batty! Now we're playing in the dirt, Orie? *I retract my earlier obfuscation, your honour,*" he said in a tone meant to mirror one pleading before the king's witan.[2] "She is a nutlet!—no hope for this one."

"Plato, right?" said Oriana, answering herself as Penda seemed at a loss for more sensible words. "And what did Plato fancy? Geometry, right? Pythagoras, yeah? Right, that's brilliant, Penda. Thanks," continued Oriana a little frustrated with Penda's diffidence.

"An honest to goodness nutlet. N-U-T-L..." he muttered jovially.

"No more cracks, Penda. Now, look," she said, marking her lines even deeper and clearer. "I think this will help illustrate my point. See these two lines? They don't touch; they're—"

"Parallel. Yes, Orie, I know. Are we now back in the golden years of The Academy[3]?" he asked, staring down at Oriana's tiny furrows in the soil, "and I, your pupil, Sir Penda Aristotle, about to hear a lecture on the forms?"

"And here we have a line that intersects," said Oriana, cotinu-

---

[2] The witan was the king's council amongst whose members the drafting of laws, alienation of estates, levying of taxes, and the proclamation of herebote (the king's edict summoning his subjects to muster the fyrd) were deliberated. King Athelstan's witan comprised nearly seventy lords and high clergymen. In attendance were notable scholars from throughout his realm and abroad. Once included amongst the king's witan were his court tutor, Phillip, of the ancient Roman-Cypriot city of Amathus, and Dunstan, son of Heorstan, of the house of Baltonsborough, who, only six years prior, was expelled on rumour of his practicing black magick.

[3] The Academy was Plato's school for philosophy founded in 387 BC. It was located northwest of Athens within a lush public garden replete with spouting marble fountains, cobbled lanes, and bronze statues of such faërie folk as satyrs, fauns, and nymphs. The Academy was nestled atop a small knoll surrounded by a labyrinth of fragrant hedges and groves of olive trees from which the tragedian Sophocles asserted the nightingale would often sing its Worldsong.

ing to scratch at the dirt, ignoring Penda's taunts. "These two parallel lines could go on forever and would never meet but for the joining of this line. It disrupts both."

Penda shrugged. "So?"

"Just listen! Now let's say this line represents us, or let us say our world," she continued, tracing her lines once more. "We move forward along this line as if it were a river—our own Willowrun if you wish—and time acts as the current, pushing us along—dawn to dusk, new moon to full moon, the seasons. Follow me?"

"Yeah, I'm still with you. But again, so what?"

"Well," she went on excitedly, "let's suppose this line next to it is another world, similar to ours, moving, perhaps along with ours or maybe not exactly synchronized with ours yet still advancing through time in some relation to our own. And so, the two worlds never join. One has no awareness of the other."

"Except where your perpendicular line touches the parallel ones," remarked Penda with a serious expression. "Is that the idea?"

"Exactly!" grinned Oriana, swishing her stick through the tall water grasses as though it were a sickle.

"I still don't get it." he said, shaking his head. "I thought we were discussing your vision. You've lost me somewhere, professor?"

"We have been, you dolt," she scolded. And so saying, she whacked him fair on top his mangy head with her improvised stylus.

"Hey, that smarts! Easy with that club, Goliath!"

"The *lines*, Penda?" she droned. "Don't you ever pay attention to me?"

Penda paused for several seconds, scratching his head.

"Well?" asked Oriana, standing up to her full height and placing her hands on her hips impatiently.

"You mean to say you think this experience was some sort of *real* place you journeyed to—some other realm? A parallel realm, to use your analogy?" he asked, pointing down at her simple diagram, his high voice cracking with astonishment.

"Penda, I could kiss you," she said with a wide grin. "And I would if I could only bend that low."

"Hold that thought till I find a stool."

"I wouldn't want to spoil you," she chuckled. "You know I think you're super." She blew him a kiss.

"I suppose that'll have to do," he said with a wry smirk. At this, he stretched himself along the ground on his side and began tracing Oriana's lines with his finger.

"This may help a bit. Do you recall Father's favourite passage from Plato's Timaeus?"

"By gum, Orie! There you go again!" cried Penda incredulously. "Are you kidding me? Your father had hundreds of *favourite* passages. I don't have the least idea."

"The principal of the triad, silly! Remember? '*It is impossible that two things only should be joined together without a third.*' There has to be some sort of bond in between both to bring them together, yes?"

Penda's face contorted into a look indicating he hadn't quite got on that far in his studies.

"Hang on, Orie," he implored at once, "before you go making this more complicated than need be—"

"You mean before something else goes over your head?" she laughed in retaliation.

"Real cute. I suppose that's meant to be funny! Another short joke, yeah?" he said, sitting up with a jolt and grasping for Oriana's stick as if now intending to give her a sound thrashing with it himself. She was too quick for him.

"Right then," he went on seriously. "Assuming I'm going along with this line business, how do you explain how you got to be in that world in the first place? I imagine your perpendicular line fits somewhere into your theory?"

"I'm glad you said that. I was just about to give you another bludgeoning with my wee cudgel again. It's all there in Plato's triad! The silver road—remember how I said it seemed to be floating in midair? I think that's the connection."

Penda looked dumbfounded. "I'm embarrassed to say this, Orie, but you've just shewn me to be a liar again," he said worriedly. "I suppose I haven't been paying attention to you after all. I don't recall you saying you crossed that ghastly thing."

"Don't worry. Your integrity's still intact. I never said I had."

Penda shot her another perplexed expression, looking as if he had just sucked a lemon—not that he had ever tasted a lemon.

"You'll have to bear with me, Penda. This is the queerest part of all. But I think I now understand it aright. It seemed as though I was already on the opposite side of the road and that if I were to follow the stag across it, I would have simply ended up back at the feast with everyone else."

"What?" cried Penda, his voice cracking worse than usual. "May I make an observation?"

"You may."

"Forget a nutlet, you're plain balmy. What do yeh say we start this whole theory all over again, huh?"

Penda grabbed for Oriana's stick—this time snatching it—and began etching the ground next to her lines with marks of his own. "Here! How about some *nice little circles* instead?" he blathered on. "They'll do loads better. Or maybe a couple of profound ovals? Ah yes! There we are! Squares might even do nicely at a pinch."

"I told you this would be the hardest part to accept."

"No, it's all right, Orie. I've got it, really I have," he said sarcastically, leaning his back against the tree. "This silver road of yours is the only way to arrive at that world, but in order to enter it, you don't have to use the bloody thing. Somewhere we've departed from the dictates of logic."

"Not necessarily, Penda. What if I've always been in that world, waiting, as it were, for him to arrive?" She seated herself next to him with her knees drawn in.

"Always been there?" he echoed in undertones, looking now even more restive than ever. He stretched himself flat again, crossed his hands behind his head, and began watching two finches play a game of "Hide and Seek" in the branches above. "You've always been there, huh?" he repeated rather snidely. "Well that makes sense!"

"That was certainly the feeling, or I should say, *is still* the feeling I have."

"But didn't you just say you were commanded to go? That means you went, right? You left one point for another. Is this another contradiction, master?" he asked with another sardonic stab. "How could you have always been there if you first had to travel, so to speak, in order to get there?"

"Of course, I did arrive, after a fashion. But it didn't seem as though I was returning to rejoin some other half of myself. I was one whole person in two separate places simultaneously. It felt as though my essence in that world had only been roused in order, I believe, to greet him when he arrived."

"So how long were you kept waiting—either one of you? Auh! Now you've got me sounding mental."

"An age, perhaps a flicker in time only. Who knows?"

"Well, I hope you at least had a spindle whorl to help pass the time," he said in a failed attempt at humour.

Oriana threw him a dark look.

"I'm sorry, Orie, but do come along, won't you?" he begged with an air of frustration. "I mean … well, I must say, you're making it awfully hard for me to take you seriously."

---

4   Dangeld was a tribute first paid by Anglo-Saxon kings in 856 to buy off Danish invaders who had settled in the northeast of England. By the eleventh century this region became known as the Danelaw. This extortion had been intermittent before the reign of Alfred the Great and had temporarily ceased after his treaty with the Danish King Guthrum at Chippenham. Athelstan's later victory at Brunanburh and subsequent hegemony over the Saxon, Celtic, and Danish kingdoms in Britain further interrupted this payment.

"Serious? I'm perfectly serious—as serious as a dangeld.[4] And you know who you sound like?"

"Myself, unfortunately? No wait—you wouldn't dare," he cautioned, raising himself on his elbow and glaring with hard eyes.

"Wouldn't I?—Cadwallon! That's just what he said to Lord Elgar during their secret little meeting."

"That hurts," he snapped, sitting up, "cuts straight to the core that does." He pretended to be pulling a sharp stake from his chest. "I *am* trying to help you with this, Orie. Honestly, that seems to be my appointed task of late. But I don't understand any of this business—one person in two places, a giant albino deer that talks in half-riddles, and this silver bridge of yours. Let's just take that bridge for start. You say it's some kinda link between worlds, yet in the end it played no role in your being there."

"I'll try to be clearer," said Oriana as she got to her feet. She had been fidgeting with a flat stone that Penda had dropt and now wanted to see if she could go one better than his last throw.

"It does play a role—an enormous role," she continued. "Its necessity, I believe, is absolute, but not in my journeying to that world—at least not yet, but only in my return from it. It *is* a tie, a causeway if you will. I think the stag wishes me to cross so that I may be even fuller, more complete, somehow, on this side, in this world, than I am at present. He did call me daughter of worlds twain, did he not? Three times, in fact."

"Oh, I forgot about that nugget of clarity," returned Penda, hopping to his feet. "That certainly clears things up. What the devil does that…Ahh five! Must you always one-up me? Why always by just one?" he exclaimed, stomping his foot into the dirt after Oriana's stone skipped effortlessly down Willowrun Creek.

"I hope, Penda, the devil has nothing to do with it," she resumed, turning back from the water's edge. "Initially I took his calling me daughter of worlds twain to be a reference to Father being Cypriot and Mother a Saxon. But now I think it means something altogether more complicated—just don't ask me what exactly."

Penda sighed and skeptically shook his head as he left Oriana's side to have a turn on the swing.

"Really, Penda; stop being hardheaded," said Oriana, a bit frustrated by this point. Then, meaning to be more objective and reestablish her intellectual humility in Penda's view, she added, "Look! I'm not trying to sound like a know it all. I'm not firmly convinced of all this myself. I don't really *know* you might say; what I've been telling you just *feels* to be correct—to be the truth. I'm only trying to offer a rational explanation for what I experienced, that's all, Penda, nothing more."

"Now that sounds like my old Orie, ever rational, ever humble," he said, smiling once again. "So we now come to the point, your point it would seem. But will you not at least hear my ideas?"

"Yes, Penda," answered Oriana, gazing out pensively at the sun reflecting in countless shimmers across the swift creek. "You've been patient with me. Go ahead. But I think I can guess where you're heading."

"Now this may not go down well," he cautioned, "but hear me through. Isn't it probable your experience was just another one of your trances like ..."

"No ... no—" She was shaking her head.

"Like the one you overheard Elgar describing to Cadwallon last week."

"No, Penda, no! Bees and botheration! After everything I've just said," she protested, throwing her hands to her head in a deprecating sort-of-way. She plumped herself back down on the grass. "You exhaust me. No, Penda. Decidedly not. Think, how could it be? I can't remember any of those episodes. You wouldn't even be considering this if I hadn't first overheard their discussion and then told you about it, now would you?"

Penda shrugged, swinging now mildly back and forth.

"It couldn't have been a trance," she carried on fervently. "This event is as clear as a silver bell ringing in my mind. Honestly, it's almost as if it were still happening, right now, all over again. It doesn't even seem like memory at all—shadowy and incomplete. Though at the same time, as I said, I know there are aspects of that world I can't here recall. It was the strangest thing that's ever happened to me."

"Then maybe it was some sort of hallucination like the one I had," he ventured, plainly unconvinced. He dragged his boots to stop his swing, partly erasing Oriana's marks. "Remember last spring when I ate those purplish morels and was coughing up grey chunks for three days? Couldn't it have been something like that? Maybe it was something you ate that made that wacko tapestry of yours come to life in your head."

"*In my head!* Fine! Sure! Okay, Penda!" she answered irritably, finding herself suddenly raising her voice and quite out of temper. "Right, then how would you account for the concreteness of the stag? Hmm? Answer me that! I can assure you he was no phantasm: I could have touched him, I'm sure of it—but I durst not touch him—I wouldn't dare, not ever. Or his message, Penda, the stag's message for heaven's sake! His warnings and instructions! Can you dismiss those as easily?" she demanded. "You weren't there, Penda—such complexity and urgency! Have you ever heard tell of anyone hallucinating a command so important, so fateful, and yet so enigmatic, full of doom and yet not without hope?"

"Well I have to admit, Orie, you have me there—I haven't," observed Penda yet donning still an unconvinced expression. "All the same though, they do say there's a first time for everthing, you know. But perhaps you're right, maybe not for something like this."

"Hang it, Penda," said Oriana, recovering herself. She was still irritable but no longer raising her voice. "There isn't *something like this*, not anything. There's no basis for … that is to say, nothing exists for comparison—nothing. This was unique. Something designed, intended for me. Only, don't ask me why—I can't for a moment pretend to know why."

Penda sat motionless and kept his peace. He seemed stumped, his brow knitted. Oriana could tell he was mulling over the merit of what she had just presented.

"Orie," he said by-and-by in a conciliatory air, "you might've had a promising future awaiting you as one of the king's aldermen. Too bad you weren't born a bloke! *Your convictions and clarity of thought have won me to your view of things,*" he said, emulative of the king's counsellors once again. "*I confess, my pertinacious pretty, I cannot contrive a better explanation than your … your postulate of propinquity … your paradigm of—of,* oh, heck, than your ridiculous lines."

"Thank you. Finally!" Oriana laughed. Yet in spite of Penda's reassurances, Oriana thought his face conveyed quite a different opinion. She couldn't help concluding he still wasn't completely convinced by her explanation, but exasperated by their discourse she was in no humour to offer additional analogies or diagrams. "I know how it grieves you to acknowledge the rightness of my ideas to say nothing of the *superiority* of my insights."

"Let's not carry things too far, Orie," he retorted with a tight grin. "Anyway, on a brighter note, I now have a superior idea of my own. One I am certain you will not counter."

"And what is that, pray?" she asked, happy to change the topic.

"How about that ride you promised me last week?" He jumped from the swing, picked up one last stone and made a pathetic attempt to skip it across the surface. "Abysmal stone!" he bleated when it failed to make a single hop. "Well, how 'bout it?"

"The ride *I* promised?" she repeated, raising an eyebrow.

"That is what I told Cerdic after all, remember?" he replied with a mischievous glint in his eye. "You did say you wanted to keep me an honest man, right? In any case, I figure an invigourating ride might be just the thing you need to clear your mind—I mean, *we* need ... uh, to clear *our* minds. There's still the rest of this mystery to be worked out and what we're to do next."

"We, Penda?" she asked, sounding a bit more motherly than she meant.

"Of course, we! I'm with you come Hel or high weeds."

She laughed. "I thought it was water? Hel or high water."

"Well I'm not willing to come with you quite that far. I'm scared to death of the water—can't swim, you know."

"Right."

"To the stables then? Brond should be there about now."

"I can think of no more pleasant amusement, my little Doubting Thomas," she said mirthfully.

"And on our ride you can tell me how you like bunking with Edgira—"

"Please, Penda. Please! One crisis in my life at a time, if you don't mind."

"Priorities, yeah?"

"Exactly!"

"Well, just the same, I don't think I'd mind the arrangement nearly so much," he opined with an impish grin.

"Cheeky, Penda! Very cheeky!" she said reprovingly. "On the other hand, you know," she paused and stroked her chin, "maybe that isn't such a bad idea at that. Tell you what, tomorrow we shall exchange places, you and I. Come morning I'll just move right in with your mum and little sister, yes?"

"Kidding, Oric. Only kidding," retorted Penda, throwing

up his hands warningly. "Rack and ruddy ruin, don't take me so seriously! I'll admit Edgira's one fine-looking bird—easy on the eyes or Idun[5] has no apples, as they say. But that's the limit of her charms for my part—not exactly Mrs. Personality, that one. Anyhow, I should think you've had enough of switching places ... with yourself or anyone else for that matter."

"Good point," she laughed.

"Let's go. Have you seen Brond's new acquisitions? Well, Lord Elgar's really. They're ace! Come on, I'll show yeh. Last one there has to scrape out the frogs."

---

[5] Idun is a Teutonic goddess in whose keeping were the golden apples of eternal youth, kept safe in an enchanted casket. For each apple she drew forth another emerged in its stead. These were the fruits of immortality, the fruit of the gods. When Idun was taken from Asgard the gods feared the golden apples might fall into the hands of trolls and giants who ever desired to rob the gods of their immortality and cast them from the heights of Asgard. Legend holds that Idun's casket had a twin made of whale bone. There is wide speculation and disagreement amongst faërie loreologists over what became of the second ivory casket.

CHAPTER 6

... and Mad Dashes

Penda was off and running—the trickster! He bounded so abruptly Oriana hadn't been given much time to realize he had just challenged her to a race. He probably figured he needed a head start—and so he did!

Without losing a moment, Oriana had her shoes removed, her kirtle tucked up, and like wind before a summer tempest, shot after her friend in the best of spirits. It took few strides before she caught him up as his legs were rather short.

But needless was Penda's race to coax Oriana into running— she loved it! She simply adored the feel of the tall meadow grasses and moist wildflowers brushing her legs. Often when Oriana ran she imagined herself a swan gliding inches above still waters of some vast sea without shoals or shore. More than once did she wonder why running formed this impression in her mind. So light was Oriana's footfall that it almost seemed she *did* possess wings, spurning neither grass nor flower as she sailed through Willowrun pasture. Rarely did the earth leave more than the slightest rumour of her passing.

Sheep, some shaggy goats, seven milch cows, a family of toast-coloured rabbits, many a ceorl farmer, and one wood mouse suspended their present employment to stare up admiringly as Oriana flew by. Some of the younger lambs bleated avidly at her passing as if wishing to join in the run, but the motherly ewes standing watch would hear none of it.

Presently, Oriana was cresting the brow of a low hill dotted with scores of haystacks and tall ricks drying golden brown—there was the village down below. She slackened her pace and looked back over her shoulder. Penda was nowhere in sight, having yet to emerge over the previous hill. And so, Oriana thought she had better slow down even more. She always did this. In all the years of their friendship, not once had Penda lost to her in a footrace, never noticing, not even once, that Oriana deliberately slowed toward the end of their races. Boys are, after all, supposed to be faster than girls even if they are shorter and younger—Oriana just couldn't deprive her friend of a truth so universally broadcasted! Slowly she trotted on.

At length, the scent of the stables drew near. She could hear Penda closing in, huffing and panting. Oriana went to look behind her, but all of a sudden, a terrific motion caught her attention! She stopt at once. Charging straight toward her with breakneck speed was a fiery chestnut stallion with white legs. He had exploded out of the corral gates just to her left. Rapid panic-stricken neighs rent the air. The ground trembled as the galloping thunderclaps drew close. In a moment, the frenzied steed would be on top her!

And atop the great charger, just barely holding fast in his saddle, was an equally frightened-looking rider. It was Brond!

"Wo-ho Éohmane! Easy, lad!" he yelled, nearly bouncing over the front of the saddlebow. The stallion heeded not his master's commands but continued his charge in Oriana's direction, bucking his rider like an unschooled colt with prickly burs under his saddle. In one of his hands, Brond was holding the severed end of the bridle strap. His other was attempting to catch the snaffle-bit flailing against the charger's neck.

"Gang way, Miss Orie!" shouted the stable-master, now but feet away. *"He's mad! Look out!"*

The horse's eyes flashed with terror; pressed flat were his ears, and his nostrils red, flaring wide. Oriana knew she would soon be crushed under heavy hoof if she did not move in time. Yet she did not move. And it was not fear rendering her unable to chuse between a left or right lunge to safety. Something was compelling her to hold her ground. Something was stirring within her—something swirling—something pulsating—something she had never experienced before.

"Orie, get out of the way!" screamed Penda distantly from behind.

Just then a strange and most unexpected thing occurred. Without the least thought, Oriana thrust out her left arm, palm open and out in a gesture of defiance. She raised her other fingers to her lips and whistled a quick fluttering of high sustaining notes. The tones were enchanting, as though it were the music of a thrush nightingale singing from some unseen thicket.

At once, the steed was snatched from his madness, his shrieks silenced. He came to an immediate stop, hurling his rider overhead like a stone from a sling in a triple summersault.

Splat! Brond fell flat on his back. But by happy circumstance it was of no consequence. He landed safely onto a mud puddle thick with pansies and spongy blades of newly cut turves.

At once, a concourse of rousting blackbirds and throstles began cawing in fabulous fits of laughter from a nearby rhododendron over Brond's ungraceful tumble.

"Brond! My God! Brond!" sighed Oriana, running to where the stable-master lay unmoving on the ground. "Brond, can you hear me? Say something? Oh no! This is all my fault! I never meant—"

"I'm all right, Miss Orie. I'm all right—I think?" returned Brond in a laboured wheeze. He was struggling to regain the wind knocked out of him. He sat up, stretched his arms back and forth then looked down at the mud spattered over his dingy orange and brown tunic. "Nothing broken, not even my pride."

"I thought you were dead," returned Oriana with tears welling in her eyes. "I thought I had—"

"Brond!" panted Penda as he crossed to the mud puddle, sweating heavily and clutching at the stitch in his side. He was puffing for a breath of air, hot and windless with running the long sprint.

Oriana bent over the stable master, trembling with the horror of nearly causing someone's death.

"I'm okay, son," he said gruffly, looking up at Penda with unsteady eyes. "The ground broke my fall, as the absurd saying goes. But I could use a hand up, if you don't mind. My head's still swimmin' an' swirlin'."

"Here! Up you get," said Penda, pulling the stable master to his muddy feet. "I can't believe you're not more done over than this."

"I'm fine … just a little winded."

"Wow!" said Penda with a heavy sigh, turning to Oriana with wide eyes. She was wiping away tears with her sleeve. "That … that was excellent!"

"Oh Brond, forgive me. I had no idea ... I—I don't know what came over me." Still sobbing, she began wiping bits of grass and dirt from Brond's back.

"Don't fret yourself over me, my lady. I'm none the worse, good as new," he said blithely, dusting himself off and pounding on his chest like a lowland gorilla. He coughed and spat twice on the ground.

Brond was a lean, well-built man, though not as muscular as Alaric, the village blacksmith. And he was youthful, no more than ten years Oriana's senior. His tawny brown hair was gathered at the back of his neck with a bit of old shoelace into a short pony tail, now dripping with yellowish clay muck. He had a pointed Vandyke beard, lighter than his hair and a thick, rope-like scar running diagonally across his cheek from under his left ear to his chin—a souvenir from the battle of Brunanburh.

"I haven't quite been feeling myself of late," Oriana said, her voice still quivering. "You're right to marvel, Penda. I don't know what got into me. I say, I *am* sorry, Brond."

"No need for that, Miss Orie," returned Brond reassuringly, stretching his back. "No harm done as I said, and that's what I meant. The way things were shaping up I'd've ended up on my back sooner or later. Would've picked a drier spot though, if given the choice."

"Orie, I can't believe it! That was—that was brilliant!" Penda said repeating himself, his heavy breathing beginning to abate. "I've never seen you do anything like that before. Though I have to say, what goes on inside that thick head of yours, frankly, is a mystery to me. What were you thinking? You might've been killed, you know. Still, it was brilliant. Where in the world did you pull that move from anyway?"

"This time, Penda, I can honestly say your guess is as good as mine." She was staring in amazement at the contented stallion. "I've never *done* anything like that before." So saying, Oriana turned back round and gazed at her friends full in the face, thinking there was about them both a sudden fear and wonder.

"Well it's a miracle's all I can figure, or magick I'd almost hazard to say. In all your fussing over me we've forgotten Éohmane. Look at him, biting the grass as gentle as an old mare at twilight." Brond went slowly to him.

"What startled him?" asked Penda who was also puzzling at the chestnut horse, now tearing lightly at some wild buttercups and swishing his tail as if he hadn't a care in the world.

"Startled son? No, he wasn't startled," replied Brond, shaking his head. "Take it from me: I've ridden my fair share of spooked mounts. He wasn't what I'd call startled. That was sheer terror I felt beneath me."

Oriana grew curious. "Then what terrified him? What happened?"

"That's what's so bloomin' odd. Nothing as far as I could tell," he returned, shrugging. "No sooner had I mounted him when he lit out of the stable like the devil himself was hard on his heels."

"Do horses have heels?" asked Penda comically, tilting his head in a profound way and furrowing his brow.

They ignored him.

"But that's so strange," said Oriana, she too now walking over to the stallion. "Certainly something must account for his behaviour."

"Miss Orie, I tell you there was nothing; nothing at all. It was just the two of us in the stall with no one else nearer the stables than the two of you—not another living soul, not unless you count that ugly grey moth that flew in when he went all yellow-barmy," he chuckled, clearly at the expense of a little pain to his side.

But Oriana did not laugh. Something touched her memory.

"A grey moth?" she asked quizzically, pinching between her lip and chin in thought.

"That's right," answered Brond. "Great, big, ugly, speckled thing. Why?"

Yes, there was something strangely familiar about Brond's moth—something she did not like. But she could not place her finger on it.

"Oh … uh, it's nothing, never mind," she replied and yet went on pondering the matter just the same.

"Sounds like you made a real smart purchase there, Brond. You just bought Lord Elgar one right plonker of a horse—doesn't even need a reason to rare up."

"He's anything but stupid, lad," returned Brond firmly, "an uncertain temper, to be sure—but far from stupid."

"Hey, it just came to me! It's perfect," said Penda with a mischievous grin. "Don't let this little episode get around—keep it under your hood, huh? This one's just got to be destined for our esteemed Lady Mildreth, a prime match of temperaments—neither one needs a reason to go totally mental."

Brond gave a guttural guffaw that looked even a little more painful than his last one. Oriana could not help a smile herself, but did manage to beat back the impulse to out-volume Brond's laughter many times over.

"Here, Miss Orie," said Brond still laughing, "since Éohmane is plainly at your command, why don't you take what's left of the reins. You can lead him back to the paddock for me."

Éohmane did not flinch at Oriana's gentle touch. He went just as easy as a lamb behind her, and within a few minutes, Oriana had got the mighty destrier safely inside the corral. With Brond's help, Oriana unfastened his saddle and severed bridle and slung both over the fence.

Éohmane immediately took to the company of the other four horses that had been monitoring his steady approach. Two were mares, unbroken and restless, each of Arabian bloodstock, one roan, the other a deep raspberry brown. At once, they cantered over to Éohmane as he made his arrival through the gate. Both began vying for his undivided attention. Éohmane seemed most interested in the affections of the roan mare to the other's disappointment. The third was another mare, a bit shorter than the two Arabians with a shiny iron-grey coat and long-feathered fetlocks. A frail-looking foal with a matching grey coat kept to her side. They too seemed emboldened by Éohmane's arrival, if not with the same excitability of the two Arabian mares!

Fine specimens though all of them were, none of the horses were to be compared with the nobility of Éohmane.

"What breed is he?" asked Oriana, pulling the gate shut on their way out. "Éohmane, I mean. I've never seen his like before."

"You have a sharp eye, my lady. I don't suppose anyone in these parts has ever beheld his make. He's an Andalusian, straight from Cordoba—"

"That's in Spain, Orie," said Penda helpfully.

"Yes, I know, Penda, thank you," she drawled. "How beautiful he is, Brond. He's very tall, isn't he? What a long back he has, too."

"Yes, Andalusians are very beautiful animals," agreed Brond, resting his elbows on the fence. "And you're right about his back—loads of space between the cantles."

"I could see that when we unsaddled him."

"Yeah, and he's more than just a handsome mount, isn't that right, Brond?" observed Penda jauntily, now straddling the corral fence. He was swaying back and forth as he was wont to do when excited or nervous.

"Penda's been a very studious assistant to me these past few days on his days off from house-duty—we'll make a proper groom of him yet," he told Oriana. "You're quite right, Penda," he said, nodding. "As I explained only last week to our vertically-challenged friend here—"

"Hey!"

"Andalusians are bred for their speed and stamina. I'm sure you've heard King Athelstan himself has given Lord Elgar instructions to begin a stud farm, right here at Oakleigh Manor. Éohmane is to be the stud! Busy work ahead for him," he laughed.

"Oh that's right. Lord Elgar had mentioned that to me some weeks back. But I thought acquisitions weren't to be made until late autumn?"

"I thought so too," agreed Brond. "But he sent me earlier than the original plans. I traveled to Southampton about three weeks ago on purpose of purchasing the finest stallion in the lot. The ships drew into harbour two days before I arrived—about a week sooner than everyone expected. Apparently—one of the captains' mates told me this—the caliph of Cordoba—can't remember what he said his name is—"

"Um...uh...oh, yeah: Abd-ar-Rahman the Third, you mean?"

"That's it. Apparently he's been mustering his Moorish fighters. Some think he's planning to attack King Ramiro's city of Simancas."

"Really?" said Oriana in a worried way. "How dreadful."

"Yeah. So they put out with their cargo early to avoid the mess. Moors have been rounding up the finest horses. Eight beautiful stallions in all, but Éohmane stood out above the rest."

"Tell her about the Arabians, Brond," interrupted Penda hastily.

"I was just about to ask—I didn't recognize those either," she said to Brond.

"Did Lord Elgar ever tell you about Hugh the Great's donation to King Athelstan some years back?"

"The count of Paris, right?"

"Yes! You've heard the tale, I dare say?"

"I have, but not from Lord Elgar—it was a most generous gift indeed," replied Oriana as she too clomb the fence, seating herself next to Penda. "Father mentioned this to me years ago when I was very young. He went on and on for ages about those seven proud Arabians—'There were never such horses to these.' What a fuss he made. Father always bore a soft spot for horses. He used to say to me, 'Now don't you forget, Orie, in my native tongue Phillip means lover of horses. My parents chose my name with uncanny vision.' Bucephalus, his own steed, was a direct descendant from one of those Arabian mares."

At this, Oriana jumped down from the fence and stole cautiously toward Éohmane.

"Of that I'm well aware! Who could forget him?" said Brond morosely, staring down at his muddy shoes. Lord Phillip's steed had been slain at Brunanburh—Brond had been right there to see it. "What a sturdy bay gelding Bucephalus was. These Arabians are of the same lineage." He looked up.

"Brond's planning to crossbreed Éohmane with—"

"Are you sure that's a wise idea, Miss—"

"Orie, what in blazes do you—"

But she ignored them both. Without thinking twice Oriana leapt onto Éohmane's back and nudged him into a hearty trot, her hair flying behind her in golden waves. The two mares followed close behind. Within no time, Oriana had made three quick circles inside the paddock. She slowed his pace to a walk, made two caracoles—first this way and then that just for the fun of it—and steered him back to the gate. Penda and Brond looked in a great worry, their tight faces relaxing only when she made her safe return.

"Oh Brond!" called Oriana exuberantly. "He's amazing! So smooth and quick witted!"

"I'll take your word for it, Miss Orie," he said, opening the gate. He walked over to the stallion and patted his broad chest. "Today was my first attempt and ... well, that didn't exactly go according to plan."

"Brilliant! Look who's coming!" shouted Oriana, staring out across the south pasture from atop Éohmane's height.

It was Edgira. She was walking in a violent hurry toward them, her long black hair rumpled into a blowsy mess.

"Isn't that your new roommate coming over the hill?" laughed Brond, putting a shading hand to his eyes.

"Not you too! Honestly—first Penda, now you—"

"She looks in an awful hurry," said Penda, jumping down from the fence. "Bit dishevelled too. Hmm. Fancy seeing her out-of-doors; wonder what the excitement is."

"Some very great matter, by the looks of it," sniggered Brond.

"Is there no sanctuary for me?" cried Oriana despondently. "What have I ever done to deserve it all?"

"Maybe she's lonely." Penda laughed.

"Typical!" moaned Oriana, shaking her head quite put out. "She can't have finished her embroidery already."

Éohmane began at once to grow restless beneath her.

"Fine time for her to show up," Penda told Oriana with a thick sigh. "Something tells me we're not going to have that ride after all—first prize killjoy that one is."

She nodded in agreement, her gaze wandering downward in resignation.

"Penda here tells me she's made you all but indigent—taken over your whole room."

"That's one way of putting it. I think from now on, Brond," she said pointing, "with your leave, I'll be sleeping in the hay loft. I expect I'd find Éohmane's company more to my liking."

"I think I might be able to arrange that," he returned with a convincing grin. "Yeah, here on out it's Brond's Bed and Board— has a nice ring to it, does it not?"

"Oriana! Oriana!" called Edgira as she eventually drew near. "I checked the pond first and then the creek, but you weren't there. This was my next guess," she added, not in the least apologetic for the intrusion.

"Hello, Edgira. Yes, that was very sensible of you," said Oriana in the best politeness and forbearance she could manage. "Edgira, I do not believe you have been introduced to our stablemaster. May I present Brond—our soon to be marshal."

Brond bowed politely. "It is a pleasure to meet you, my lady."

Edgira made no curtsey in answer. Rather, she said only, "Charmed, I'm sure," very pompously and with a nasty smile as she eyed his soiled tunic. Little surprize! It was widely understood that Edgira, like her father, held all ceorls in decidedly low estimation. Proud and particular Edgira was, even prim, but it must be said, if she were hoping to appear prim at that moment her tousled hair made it a lost cause. Indeed, she wasn't looking her best.

"Oriana, you'll never guess what's happened."

"Oh, Edgira, I haven't the slightest idea, but whatever it may be, I'm sure it is not my affair," said Oriana, rubbing her forehead to stave off the makings of another headache. "This is precisely why I take my leave from the house—to escape such catastrophes. Now whatever's the matter?"

"It's Bathilda!"

"She knows where I am," said Oriana testily. She was petting Éohmane on his side to steady him. Something was increasingly agitating him, his nostrils blowing hard several times. "She has no cause to be cross this time."

"That's not it at all—"

"I can explain everything," Penda suddenly launched in, sputtering nervously. "How was I supposed to know her stupid cat would be sleeping right in front of the door?"

"What?" shouted Edgira, looking confused and sounding irritated at the same time.

"This morning,"—he turned and looked up at Oriana clearly

trying to palliate something—"when I was carrying in the crushed dogwhelk shells—you know for Cerdic's special purple dyes. Spilt right on top 'im—the menace, lumpy purple blotches all over his stinkin' fur. Serves 'em right though, the manky fur ball. But it wasn't my fault—"

"What's this puny imbecile talking about?" spat Edgira, turning to Penda, glowering. "Who are you?"

"Oh, I'm fine, thanks. Who're you?" retorted Penda irreverently.

"Huh?"

"She sure walked into that one," he muttered softly to Oriana, glancing up with a triumphant smirk.

"This is Penda," Oriana told her and turned to Penda, flashing a scathing look as much as to convey, "Not now, Penda!" Éohmane was stomping and snorting again—goodness! He was growing more agitated by the minute. "You've already met him. The day you decided to move into—"

"I don't know what this fool's talking about. Be quiet!" she demanded with a superior tone. "It's Bathilda! She's in absolute hysterics."

"Whatever for?" asked Oriana.

"Lady Mildreth, that's what! She's expelled Bathilda from the house, from the whole manor—she says she's no longer needed—no longer wanted, in fact!"

"*What?*" shouted Oriana incredulously. "She can't have! What's behind this?" she demanded.

"I don't know—she said Bathilda's days of cockering and... and doting on you are through. I heard every word through the wall as I was waking. She was screaming at her in fact—she even called her an old crone. I was aghast—told her to gather up her things."

Oriana was fuming, her ear lobes going hot. With a jolt, she kicked her heels into Éohmane's flanks, and like a loosed-arrow from its string, shot through the gate and across the south pasture.

"Orie! Wait up!" shouted Penda frantically as he set off after her.

In a flash, Oriana was over the nearest hill. Éohmane was galloping at a speed far beyond that which she had first observed when Brond had been holding on for dear life. Just as fast as she dared, Oriana jumped over Willowrun Creek and by gallops and leaps headed straight for the bailey gate of the outer ward.

But before they were anywhere close to Oakleigh Ridge, Éohmane began to slow unexpectedly. Oriana had not given this command—speed is what she desired most. "What is he doing?"

Oriana was about to dig her heels deeper into Éohmane's sides when suddenly she stayed. Now she understood why Éohmane hesitated! Now she understood what was troubling him at the stables!

Oriana could scarce believe her eyes! She gasped! It was he! He had come for her!

Standing directly in her path was the great white stag! He had appeared from out of nowhere. There he stood. Her way was blocked.

Éohmane slowed to a stop less than a dozen yards from the enormous creature. Oriana's stomach gave a turn then plummeted as if she had been pushed from a tall precipice. Her heart was racing. There was the stag—here, right now, in this world!

Yet something was different about him. It was the stag; of that there was no question, his fur glistening white and his antlers surpassing those of the greatest elk. But he did not seem as he once had upon their first meeting. He was strangely diminished—not in his physical aspect, but lessened in his very essence. Somehow there just seemed to be less of him—a dimmed soul perhaps. Oriana had no answer for this.

But the stag's sway over her had not diminished. Again she

could feel the strands of her mind being pulled, manipulated as strings of a marionette. He wished to speak. He wished for her to listen—to know. His deerish words poured through her ears, a mountain spring rushing to quench a thirsting mind. He opened his narrow mouth and sang these words in a plaintive melody:

Eve chanced fate; that fruit she took,
Such knowledge was forbidden.
Shame and fear fell over all,
Then hallowed disk was riven.
Pride and greed marred deep green earth:
A second, sundering blow.
Atonement make! Thicket seek!
Adjoining waits! Fens of woe!
Fear no blackthorn! Come hawthorn!
For secret path, sing you must,
Ere faceless foe devours,
All sweet life and leaves but dust,
Upon last mournful hour.

The stag went silent, standing still as a bronze statue. Oriana said nothing; she did nothing. Finally, he smiled then bowed before her as he had once done. He turned and sped off in the direction of Sycamore Henge. She knew he wished her to follow.

"What am I to do?" Oriana was faced now with a hard choice. Bathilda needed her help. She could not fail her—not now. For once, it was she who needed Oriana's help. She knew she could sort things out somehow and have her reinstated as governess. But the stag—he had come again! And there was another message, another instruction. "Seek a thicket? Sing for a secret path?" So far she had done precious little but think about their first encounter. Now was the time to act.

"But what do I do? What's the right thing to do? What of Bathilda?"

Oriana closed her eyes. She prayed to the saints for guidance.

"Saint Audrey! Saint Cuthbert! Intercede for me. Help me make the right choice."

After a time, she opened her eyes. Oriana had found her resolve. Her mind was made up.

Oriana spurred the great stallion with a kick. Like lightening, Éohmane bolted forward in the direction Oriana knew she must follow.

CHAPTER 7

Laughter at Anwash

Oriana followed the stag. The mystical creature sped before her, lordly in his going, a stark, snow-white dart through the wind-tossed grasses, yellow-gold flax, and purple irises. How astounding was his speed, and the *way* he ran was the most peculiar thing Oriana had ever seen.

The stag sprang forward with several long strides and then, like the fleetest of impalas, vaulted high through the air in a series of erratic jumps before returning once again to his lightening-fast sprint. It was not at all in the manner ordinary fallow deer run, at least not as far as Oriana or more meddlesome people like you or I have ever seen when we go blundering through our own shrinking forests. Who knows how deer may scamper under happy skies when we are not looking?

Strong and fierce as Éohmane was, he was not disheartened by the stag's mightier speed. At his rider's bidding he hurried his chase undaunted. Oriana was determined to finally have her answers, to learn the purpose of the stag's coming.

"Faster boy!" Oriana shouted, braiding her fingers through the stallion's long auburn mane. "He's making for Sycamore Henge!"

Éohmane urged forward. Now was the stag fewer than a hundred yards ahead as they drew near the white grove. And then, just a couple of strides before the stag would have burst through the ring of trees, he halted abruptly and faced round to Oriana.

She slowed Éohmane to a canter.

That's when the stag once more did something Oriana did not expect. Staidly, he walked up to the grandest and oldest of the sycamores and, jumping upright on his long haunches, began scratching his enormous antlers back and forth against the lowest branch.

"Stay, my friend," she commanded and brought Éohmane to a dead stop. She sat puzzling at this strange sight, the stag's behaviour passing peculiar every moment.

"Gracious! What in Alfred's name is he doing?" she wondered, her wide-set eyes staring unblinking. Every nuance of this fantastic being eluded her. Even Éohmane too seemed to think queer the stag's bearing, shying backwards and neighing a blubbery whinny as he looked on.

The stag continued to scrape at the bark until it began flaking off in long white slivers. A tiny sheaf of bark was collecting at the bottom. Finished, he lowered to all fours, picked up two of the largest slivers of bark in his teeth and turned to Oriana. He sang once more with the same melancholy refrain:

> *White begets white; hard thorn chafes thin,*
> *From faërie ring; thy long-lost kin,*
> *For fast asleep is Gwendolyn.*
> *O withered-haw, unhappy grin.*
> *Two tears and blood to redress sin.*

The stag turned and, with a jolt, bounded forward, the white flakes of bark dangling from his clenched teeth. First running, then leaping high, then running again, the stag hastened southwest, straight for Selwood Forest.

"The faërie ring? Does he mean Sycamore Henge? Could there actually be truth in the old peasant tales?" Yet again her former worldview was being called into question. "Gwendolyn is fast asleep? Who is she?"

What Oriana wanted more than anything all this week was

answers, not another riddle, not another mystery. But the mysteries kept right on coming.

Oriana spurred Éohmane forward. She hoped this chase might finally lead to some understanding, some resolution.

Within moments, they arrived at the eaves of Selwood Forest. The stag approached the wood and darted through a slender gap of an otherwise impassable barrier of tangled briars, misshapen saplings, tendrils, and tentacle-like vines coiling downward from the strangled canopy above. But just before he entered, Oriana heard him sing:

> *Ill-fated rose, new star for each,*
> *Slain and buried for death to reach;*
> *A sacrifice so worlds might teach.*
> *And then thy choice; pixie pear or all as beech?*

Oriana reached the entrance seconds behind him. "New star for each? Does he mean Lord Elgar's new stars? He does, I'll bet. But what of the rest?"

Suddenly, Oriana felt Éohmane begin to lose his confidence. Something was troubling him once again.

"Don't worry, boy," she said, patting the stallion on his side as they bolted toward the entrance. "I know this trail."

Indeed, Oriana knew this to be the entrance to one of several hunting trails Lord Elgar and the other nobles enjoyed when taking sport with bow, horn, and hound. The paths through Selwood were many. Yet no matter which trail one followed there was never really much danger of getting lost as each eventually meandered its way to join Feldway Lane at some point.

Presently, the sun was peering brightly through a temporary break in the low clouds. It made the dark of Selwood considerably darker in an instant.

"Just inside is the old ash tree struck by lightning last summer," she said to herself as she passed into the wood.

Two stately fir trees stood at the entrance. "That's odd," she thought. These Oriana did not recognize. The slender firs seemed almost as gateposts or sentinels perhaps. As she and Éohmane passed into the gallery of branches, Oriana thought their higher boughs bent suddenly together, forming a pointed arch above the entrance.

"My eyes must be cheated by the forest shadows," she said to herself, only half convinced by her own explanation.

When Oriana's eyes became accustomed to the dark and dim, green light of the forest, she noticed the white stag was ahead by several paces, speeding down a winding path. He had not stopt to await her arrival.

What a marvel! The stag seemed to have changed. Here, despite the dark, she could see him more plainly than in the meadow under the noontide sun. He looked closer to the full mettle and magnificence of their first meeting, though perhaps still less radiant. What a beautiful sight he was.

And there were other things too that perplexed her.

"The ash—where is it?" The old tree with its split limbs she did not see, nor did she recognize a single elm, beech, or oak!

"What's happened? Where am I?" cried Oriana in dismay.

Something was not right. She was in a dense wood, and the stag was there—this was as things ought to be. But this was not her Selwood Forest. And perhaps stranger yet...

"Where's Éohmane?" Not only was Oriana in an utterly alien forest, she was standing. She was standing when she ought to have been moving, and not just moving but riding—riding with the great strength of the stallion beneath her.

Oriana spun round wildly, frightened and confused. "Éohmane! Éohmane!"

There was no response—there was no Éohmane. Where had he gone? Why was she no longer riding? She hadn't fallen off; of that she was absolutely certain—for she was standing securely on her feet, calm and unshaken. It was inexplicable. The fiery charger was simply not there—he had vanished altogether.

As Oriana looked about, she noticed the entrance through the forest brambles had also gone missing. She was not at all where she expected to be. She stood disoriented, deep within an ancient wood, a discernible reckoning of place or direction impossible. She felt quite lost indeed!

"Your proud destrier is not here, precious yearling," called the stag, breaking the silence, his voice filling the dark wood. He was not facing Oriana as he spoke but continued his descent down the winding lane. "It is not permitted. None now dwell here but they who reach deep with thirsty roots. This gift is proffered to you alone."

As he spoke, Oriana noticed his speech—it was as it had been upon their first meeting, clear and direct, not in song or half-riddles.

"Fear not for his safety," he continued reassuringly, his voice growing ever fainter as he hurried on apace. "All is well with him. It is your well-being that is of the highest importance now."

"Forgive me, Sire, but I do not understand," Oriana frantically called after him. "Why my well-being? Why I, lord?" Oriana wished to give expression to all her questions in a single breath. "Where are we?"

"Patience, small one!" came the stag's diminutive call. "I know your heart desires answers. The time for knowledge is near at hand."

In her wonderment, Oriana had not moved from her spot. Only did it now occur to her she was no longer following the stag—and he was not waiting.

"Follow me now afoot, and you will have your understanding."

Now was the stag far distant, and though his speed had lessened since entering the wood, it was still very unusual, if not erratic as it had been just seconds ago in the meadow. He was capering and gamboling along the path rather than bounding to terrific heights. He looked cheerful, his step light and gay, even playful.

Oriana shook herself from her stupor and hastened after the stag as he disappeared around an embankment of dangling moss and great-knobby roots. "Where is he taking me?"

As she ran on, she was met by a conflicting sensation. On the one hand, she did not think the forest evil in essentials; yet, at the same moment, she still felt she did not wish to be left alone within it. Oriana sped after her guide with unflagging haste.

While Oriana attempted to catch him up, her thoughts fell to wondering about this unusual place.

"Am I back?" Oriana asked herself as she sped. "Is this the world of our first meeting?" It took very little time before she arrived at a resounding—"No; I do not think it is," she answered herself. "It cannot be. It does not taste the same."

Ahead was a small, grassy hill running up to a level summit thick with towering oaks and straight poplars and carpeted with bracts of mauve-coloured clematis. The stag was already nearing the top.

"Taste? What a strange notion," she said to herself, pursuing her guide. "But that was definitely it. I had tasted that world. My mouth had been filled with its purpose."

Onward Oriana went, now clambering after the stag round a hairpin bend dotted with orange blossoms and tiny plants that you would have thought looked like small red umbrellas, and then further on and up, up another craggy slope.

"For some reason, I can remember my experience of our first meeting more fully here," she thought cheerfully. "I remember now! It was not merely my taste. All my senses had grown in that world—his world. Yes that was it! I can recall all of it. Oh how I basked in the joy of his realm—the joy of purpose revealed."

The very next turn of the path soon brought Oriana to a

low-rising knoll crowned with many a silver-limbed birch. The stag was already prancing upward. As he neared the summit, he stopt to smell a mound of shiny-yellow wood spurge rising along the trail. The stag sneezed, laughed, and then began to dance in its rising fragrance with spry, snappy twirls and kicks. Oriana guessed the petals had tickled his nose. Sight of the stag's glee made Oriana feel like laughing too.

For the second time, the stag faced round to see if she was still following. Satisfied with her progress, he crested over the hill. He had hardly disappeared when Oriana felt a sudden loneliness. The anxiety of being alone gript her every time he slipt from sight.

"Yes, this wood is definitely similar to his world, but it is not identical," she thought as she too now sped by the same yellow wildflowers. Indeed, they did smell very nice.

"Though I imagine it must be related to it in some way; why else would this forest awaken my memory of his realm? My, how I wish Penda could be here with me so he might finally believe, to finally know!"

The thought of Penda brought back recollections of their amusements in Selwood Forest. And now this forest began to remind Oriana of her beloved Selwood—the Selwood she expected to be in at this very moment! The variety of trees and gentle fold of the land bore a striking resemblance to the ancient wood surrounding Oakleigh Manor. Yet this forest felt older and considerably wilder. The trees were heavily hung with thick lichen, and the canopy was dense and similarly clad in formidable tangles of ivy. Rays of light struggled to find a patch of earth to warm. What little light that did manage to peep through never visited long.

Even the smell of the forest, heavy and thick with wet-green, suggested the stuffiness of Selwood on a muggy summer afternoon.

"The smell is not all that unlike that of Selwood and yet—"
Now she thought about it, there wasn't the least breath of wind
as she ran. Oddly enough, there was no resistance to it; the air
merely opened, making way as she went.

So while this forest seemed a dim reflection of Selwood in
certain particulars, it clearly was not the wood of her home.
Apart from the vacant air, something else was peculiar about this
place. This forest had something Selwood did not possess—an
awareness! It breathed with a knowing spirit. In Selwood, Oriana had never sensed a watchful presence. In Selwood, she never
felt like she was being observed!

On and on ran Oriana, pressing ever deeper into the mysterious wood. Now, at every winding turn, Oriana thought the
watchfulness was growing ever greater. And as she followed her
guide's lead the tiny hairs on the back of her neck began to tin-
gle. The forest was alert, attentive, even intrigued. Oriana was
being considered, regarded, and examined by every tree, bracken,
and whin she passed.

It wasn't long before the tingling on her neck grew to a tickle.

"Dear me; what is this I now hear?" she said presently.

The winding path now dropt down a gentle hillside dense
with straight ash trees and scarcely any brushwood to be seen.
On her descent, Oriana marveled as the forest's quiet observation changed with every step. There was a sound, a curious
whispering through the trees, or perhaps *of* the trees. Yes! There
was no mistaking it—it was most decidedly the forest itself. The
great wood was actually speaking to itself in hundreds of tiny
snaps and crackles. From leaf to gorse and flower to frond, a
woody murmuring exchange bantered all around her as she went.
Though unintelligible as the forest speech was, she nevertheless
could not help thinking it to be discussing, even heralding, her
coming. Not for the first or last time did Oriana wonder how she
knew such things to be so.

At this, Oriana began to feel differently about the forest. The fear of loneliness she had sensed upon her arrival was steadily giving way to a reassuring serenity. She felt welcomed. Something was embracing her. She knew. In some way, Oriana knew: it was the very spirit of the wood calling to her. Life sounded glad of her arrival as if a prayer from far-off days had at last been answered.

The trail led on. Over hill and down woody dale, ever the stag ran and ever Oriana pursued—now both in high, good humour. And as their journey lengthened, the forest-speech flowered yet anew. For hours what had been a low wooded-crackling was growing steadily into a soft hymn, exalting and joyful. Now more than ever did Oriana long to discover the meaning of this realm and why the stag had twice led her to worlds beyond her own.

"Has anyone ever had such a week?" she said to herself, recounting all the extraordinary vicissitudes that had occurred in the space of so few days. There were the new stars she had not once seen and her alleged trance too, her sudden taming of Éohmane, and then of course, the great stag himself. And now there was this—the mystery of this new realm and forest hymn in her honour. Uncertainty was unavoidable. Oriana began to question if perhaps she were more than the simple Saxon girl she had always taken herself to be. She wondered if she might ever uncover this truth.

Oriana ran on a wearisome long way till she reached the foot of another rise. She stopt. She listened. The chattering of a swift water was lifting from the other side. What a sound! The plashing cascades were melodious.

Eagerly she clambered up. She was not mistaken. It was even more than melodious—

"Can it be?"

Her ears were not deceived. The air was suddenly filled with a chorus of complementary tones. The water was actually joining in the forest hymn, harmonizing beautifully with the woody notes.

Thither Oriana bent her steps with a glad heart!

Hastily she clomb up ... up. And as she went, the music lifted ever higher as if greeting her with its light, ethereal tones.

What music! Eagerly she fed her ears with its beauty. What delight! To be sure, if you've ever rubbed a wet finger round the brim of your gran's best crystal wineglass when you were younger and more mischievous, you would have a fair impression of the lilting notes Oriana heard just then.

But the music retained still the sound of water rushing. And the churning of the clear melody had the effect also of making Oriana begin to feel overcome with thirst after this dash of—

"Strange, but I don't know." Oriana couldn't begin to guess how long she had been running. Judging by the slanting shadows she guessed twilight to be drawing on. "Have I been running all day?"

When Oriana gained the hilltop and looked below, she at last came into sight of the music's source. Oh, it was a splendid view! There, at the bottom of a narrow vale coursed a swift brook in sharp bends like a blue, spangled ribbon, dazzling and inviting to the eye. It was easily twice the width of her own Willowrun Creek and just as clear as the best glass. The far bank was high with many sharp-looking rocks and dozens of thick, protruding roots embedded like the gnarled and knotted rings of giants.

The nearer bank was much shallower and grown dense with heather and bluebells, and the finest of grasses scattered within. There she saw the stag. He had deposited his cache of white bark along the water's edge and was now drinking merrily.

"We are come to a finger of the River Anwash," called the stag brightly, lifting his head from the water to fix Oriana with his jet eyes. "Refresh yourself, young one, while you may. The water is cool and clear, a gift from He on high above. It is yet without sickness. Come! Imbibe and be quenched."

She scrambled down the hill.

Arriving at the narrow vale, Oriana sidled to the water's edge with a fair measure of trepidation—for she was nearing him. She was walking to him. She now stood close enough to touch him, though of course she wouldn't dare. Oh! She was so close that she noticed his scent for the first time. What a gorgeous smell—a crisp, autumnal bouquet, the fragrance of one born not *in the woods* but one born *of the woods*. It reminded Oriana of every pleasing forest aroma she had ever enjoyed—of crushed autumn leaves and black peppermint, damp earth and young daffodils after a light mist. Truly, he perfumed the entire riverbank. It was ever so lovely to be near him!

Oriana turned from the stag and stooped to drink. The water coursed in glad excitement, dappling yellow and silver and green along its quartz-rich bank with bright flashes. At first Oriana thought the water to be reflecting the sun that had forced her way through the dense roof of leaves. Yet as Oriana looked above, she descried the sun barely to be shining through at all.

"How wonderful," she said gaily. The water actually seemed to be casting its own iridescent hues. Her hands cupped, Oriana ladled the water where it fell swift and foaming over a large rock and drank. It was reinvigourating, exactly as the stag said: cool and clear, savouring of new life and of hope unforsaken.

To Oriana's amazement, it took fewer mouthfuls to satisfy her thirst than she expected. And very surprizingly, Oriana found it gave new strength to her limbs, serving more than an adequate substitute for the noon and evening meals she now realized she had missed. She rose with a glad heart, her vigour restored.

"Here we shall have rest awhile," said the stag, lifting his tremendous antlers, sniffing the air and smiling. "The water bracken sing. They invite us to visit."

"The bracken? Do you also hear the voices of the forest, my lord?" Oriana inquired at once. "Can you understand the meaning of their song?"

"Yes, young one," he returned briskly. "I too hear their song and have faith in their hymn. They bid us to lie with them as their guests. Together we shall be lulled by the gentle water music. Nowhere will you find softer bedding, less the golden goose herself should share her down. Come, let us take our ease here among the bluebells and purple heather and think pleasant thoughts—of acorns and berries ripe, and of green hills with honeysuckle grins."

Oriana happily accepted the forest's offer and comfortably reclined herself on one elbow next to the stag by the water's edge. She relaxed both mind and body, and after a time, the forest's singing began to recede as though it too would take its rest.

Her arms now behind her head, Oriana stared up at the thick canopy of woven leaves, her mind filling with the loveliest thoughts. It was impossible for her to do otherwise; dark thoughts were inconceivable in the quiet of this wood. She wondered if this peace were some enchantment of the forest itself or some efficacy of the stag's presence.

So Oriana and the stag rested for a duration she could not guess. Time seemed to operate differently in this enchanted wood.

◇◇

Morning was just breaking when Oriana awoke from a most agreeable slumber. The air was moist and cooler. A low gilded light percolated between the eastern boughs, and grey dew mantled the forest floor in soft sparkles as far as she could see. The trees too were wet in places and darker looking. It felt a perfect morning despite the fact that not a single songbird was to be heard singing the dawn's return. The stag apparently had been awake for some time. He was just returning from the Anwash.

"Good morning, young one," he said mirthfully.

"Good morning, Sire," she yawned, sitting up slowly from the plush bolster of heather. She rubbed the sleep from her eyes. "I had no idea I fell asleep."

He stretched alongside her. "It is a natural response. Did I not say a softer bed you will never know? Go now. Drink once more and make your ablutions."

After Oriana had splashed handfuls of cool luminescence over her face and hair and drank till content, she took her place by the stag. How wonderful it was to be in this glorious wood on so fine a morning and to be taking her ease with him.

"Now is the time for speech," he said in a serious air. "The forest has made your heart ready, but I fear it will soon be tested," he cautioned. "You have drunk a philtre of the Anwash and have heard the serenade of the wood's awakening. Now is the time right for questions."

Up Oriana sat straight, her emerald eyes wide with anticipation.

"Some knowledge you must necessarily have ere we set out," he said enigmatically. "Though heed when I say that not all you desire shall be made known to you. I will speak only of that which I know. Understand, innocent one, none is granted knowledge of all life's mysteries. As are you, so too am I bound to this truth. None knows all save He alone. But I will answer as I may."

Oriana took a deep breath. "Thank you, Sire," she said, not entirely sure where to begin. "If I may, lord, can you first tell me where we are? I thought you to be leading me into Selwood Forest, and well, I must say, I am fairly certain this is not it."

"You are correct," he chuckled lightly. "We are not exactly in what you name Selwood Forest—Coit Maur as the druids of your country once called it—but we are near."

"Druids," she thought. "So there really were druids once upon a time in Britain?"

Just then, she noticed the stag was no longer smiling. Something had suddenly captured his attention. Quick as thought, he got to his feet, stretched his mighty neck, pricked his ears, and began looking about beadily to and fro. Something had startled him. What's more, he wasn't just startled; he seemed affrighted. Oriana wondered why. "What could possibly give fear to so great a wonder as he?"

Oriana looked round. She saw nothing; she felt nothing. Strange as it was, in spite of the stag's concern, she was not the least afraid; so contented was she in the quietude of this glorious forest.

In due course, the stag lay back down, though his eyes relinquished none of their watchfulness. "Yes, we are near the wood of your home," he resumed, still looking about. "You thought me to be leading you to Selwood, you say. And so I hoped you would believe, but know this subterfuge was not done in evil. It was necessary—necessary for you to be led where you expected familiarity so that you might fully value the unfamiliar by its contraries. Have faith when I say all I have done or shall do is for your welfare—your actualization."

Oriana's furrowed brow and pinched eyebrows must have suggested that she did not understand him.

"Your expectation of the known enabled you to more fully see the true nature of the unknown," he went on, his eyes now glinting with less worry. "Only in facing the unfamiliar can one discern truth in the familiar. And so shall you soon have to decide; for all is not truth—not all ways and thoughts are equally good."

Again Oriana said nothing. Was this meant to be a warning of some sort? What would she have to decide?

"Your impression of this wood is as it is. It is like and yet unlike the wood of your home as it is also like and unlike my world. Here are you both at home and away."

"And where is here?" Oriana repeated, still bewildered.

"We now stand at the heart of the Wood of Adjoining—an unmarred wood between worlds, a secret path to the navel of worlds uncounted—the Omphalos Wood as some call it," replied the stag contemplatively.

Oriana stared back, unblinking, her mouth going slightly open.

"It is difficult to understand in a moment, young one," he went on, pensively fanning the bluebells with his tail. "Presently, I shall say the Omphalos Wood is a transilient realm and though its being reaches out to all realms, some fairer than others, there is but one path leading in. Its secret is known but to a few of the wise; even fewer yet have ventured through. And it is at the very seed of the Omphalos Tree where it must begin."

"Then I *was* right after all," said Oriana more for her own satisfaction than for the stag's consideration. "There *are* parallel worlds."

"You are referring to your discourse with your young friend?" he asked.

"Forgive me, Sire. I was merely talking to my—You know of my friend Penda?" cried Oriana.

The stag smiled. "Certainly I do. And because he touches your life, I am particularly interested in him. Many difficult paths await him—he too shall be tested in time," he drawled darkly. Oriana did not like the sound of this. "Know that all which concerns you is my greatest concern."

While that was certainly a lovely thing to say, it didn't really bring Oriana the comfort he may have intended. After all, why was she his concern? What was their apparent connection to one another? It was a powerful mystery! Why had a tapestry bearing his likeness been hanging in her room for as long as she could remember? What was their special bond to each other?

"What you told your young friend was true, in a certain manner of truth," added the stag. "'Time is a current,' you said. 'Worlds flow next to one another,' you said. You have discovered a truth, my wise friend."

Oriana began to glow with rising self-confidence over the stag's praise, though, at the same time, uneasy at this wondrous being knowing so much about her when she knew positively nothing of him.

"Even your friend's small acts of creation were tokens of another truth."

"Acts of creation, Sire?"

"The creek and his pebbles," he answered pointedly. "Do you not recall how they greeted one another?"

"How they greeted one another?" she repeated, probably sounding more dumbfounded than she had intended.

"Yes."

"You mean what happened when he skipped the stones across the water?" she asked with yet more diffidence.

He nodded. "What did you observe?"

"I'm afraid I saw nothing unusual, my lord, nothing that stands out for comment." She hoped she was not about to disappoint.

"That was not my question, dear one," he said, pricking his ears once again, his eyes beginning to roam. "What did you observe? What did you see that *was* usual?"

"Let's see...em...well, for start, the stones made a series of ripples—" Oriana paused, searching for more. But she could think of nothing more to add.

"That radiated outward," continued the stag for her, "growing larger until they met the boundary of the water only to return once again to their source. Was it so?"

"Yes, that is what happened, Sire." Oriana worried she was

about to fail a very important lesson. She tried to push her mind where she believed the stag wished it to go.

"And so are we headed, yearling daughter. We quest to this same singularity—where the stone met the water. What occurs there radiates outward to touch every other world for as long as time and being themselves endure."

"So, my friend Penda?" she asked, gazing inquisitively into his gleaming eyes. "Am I to understand, lord, he was skipping those stones at your behest, to aid in my understanding of this realm, of … of what awaits me?"

"Not solely at my bidding, dear one, but I did play a part, yes."

Oriana stared down at the green-folded fronds encircling her. After a pause, Oriana looked at the stag. A new thought had just come to her which she wished had not, an idea that now made her doubt she was truly worthy of the stag's commendation. She felt her sudden rise of confidence in jeopardy.

She asked, a little crestfallen, "And my lines? The ones I drew in the dirt, I mean."

"Yes! They too were a gift."

Her face fell. She was silent again. She started ruffling the bottom of her blue kirtle in thought.

"Be not cast down," the stag said eventually. "Do not abash your spirit; for so it is with many of our thoughts."

It was as she guessed. The implications were obvious. The illustration she had drawn for Penda was not solely a product of her own intellect. And then with this thought, she wondered if any idea was ever wholly a creation of one's own mind. Did she not will her own ideas?

"All thought," he went on solemnly, "all wisdom must come from somewhere. You do not suppose that something can come from nothing, do you?" asked the stag seriously.

"No, Sire," returned Oriana, looking up from her dress. "My father once taught such a notion is not logical."

He looked pleased by her response. "Well said. It would seem many of the answers you seek already lie within you. As you say, it is not possible. That something could come from nothing annihilates the very possibility of being itself. Our thoughts have origins, and such beginnings do not always come from mere experience."

"This is because..." she thought for several moments, "because certain thoughts are given to us freely—a gift, as you have said?" she posited.

"Precisely! And of the source of such gifts I sense you have already been taught finely from others. So think no less of your own wisdom. Doubt not the gift of your splendid mind."

This made Oriana feel better about herself. What a whirlwind of introspection she had just gone through.

"As this is true for you, so is it true for me as well," he said, nodding. "But understand, young one, though many of our ideas may be transcendent, that does not mean we do not contribute something to them. By our wills, free to contemplate, can ideas be reshaped for good or ill. Though I say to you, daughter of worlds twain, I count you among the wise, more must your wisdom grow ere your final task is through."

Slowly, Oriana got to her feet and crossed over to the water, mulling over this idea. Again she marveled at the water's singular beauty. Never had she seen a river sparkle so! And studying it, she thought the mysterious current of light somehow gave her courage, courage enough to turn round and ask:

"What *is* my task, Sire?"

He smiled. "Thither are we headed. It shall be revealed when the moment is best."

Oriana returned her gaze to the running current, visualizing how beautiful the sea that awaited the end of this water's journey must be. And then, as she stared at the flecks of light swimming by, Oriana felt something awake inside. She suddenly longed to drift along this current, on a raft maybe—perhaps a raft of singing timbers gathered from this magickal wood, till the water bore her far, far away. Excited within was a yearning to sail ever on, on to that glorious sea at water's end, and then beyond to lands unknown. And so did a faërie wanderlust kindle in her breast—her heart had grown full of it.

But would she ever do such things? How many countless marvels had come into being that she had never beheld?

As these thoughts flashed through her mind, she wished the brook might resume its earlier water music. She yearned for the wild imagery its song evoked in her mind. And then a new thought came to her at once—a darker thought. Why was the water no longer singing? Was it simply silent or had it been silenced?

She turned, whisked through the knee-high bracken, and reclined once again next to the stag.

After another space of silence and glorious peace, Oriana eventually asked, "Can you tell me, lord, why you did not sooner make your return?"

"I returned as soon as I was able, when my quest was completed. My duty obliges me to take many paths, small one. Much evil is now astir, and not all is well in Danuvia, the realm the Miðgård folk call Faërie."

And exactly as the stag said *Faërie*, he jumped quickly to his hooves. He was looking about anxiously once again.

"The Faërie realm? I should like to hear more about that," she said to herself just then. But there was no time for further questions. The stag's urgency pressed in around her.

"We must away anon!" He was staring at the path beyond the river. "Henceforward I fear our way shall grow ever perilous."

Oriana was also looking ahead at the opposite bank. A steep, craggy path rose sheer in front of them.

"I am at home in the forest, Sire, and do not easily stumble."

Yet Oriana did agree, nonetheless, that this part of the path looked considerably more difficult. "So long as I have you as my guide, I shall not falter. I will follow your lead come what may."

"You are brave," returned the stag, gazing now in the distance behind Oriana. "I doubt neither your will nor your step. But I think you do not understand me aright. I said our way will grow ever perilous. I do not refer to the difficulties of yonder path only. Unforeseen evil is afoot. Darkness approaches."

Oriana gasped! She spun round wildly, peering into the stretching shadows with nervous eyes. Again she saw and felt nothing.

"Something stalks in the shadows, precious one. Some black hatred rankles just beyond the edge of my sight and knowledge. I am afraid we travel in secrecy no longer. Something comes, some evil drawn perhaps to your purity. It seeks to devour that purity, as darkness seeks to extinguish light."

Oriana was speechless. She felt seized with a sudden dread. Perhaps the fear of loneliness she had felt upon her arrival to this wood was not unwarranted after all.

"We have tarried here too long."

Oriana stood silent. What could this mean? Darkness is attracted to the light? Just as a ... as a moth is drawn to—

"Before night begins to fall, I fear this evil may beset us." The stag moved closer to Oriana. "We must hie as fast as we may. Now shall I fly as you have yet to see me advance."

At these words, Oriana felt something draw suddenly near in dark proof of the stag's suspicion. But for some reason, she felt she could not express this foreboding to her guide.

It was terrifying! Something *was* definitely approaching, something enormous! Darkness was closing in! As a speeding avalanche of tumbling night this unseen horror menaced, and it was nearly upon her!

"Four surpasses two according to the Maker's design. I advise you take to my back, young one. Quickly!"

But there was no time! Oriana was seized! The black wall had come! Darkness fell upon her!

Like a mountain stone, Oriana instantly fell lifeless to the forest floor, her eyes glazing over. No sooner had the stag urged them to flee than the gift of the forest's joy was torn from her spirit. Someone or something was dragging Oriana's soul down a darkling path.

Oriana's mind was laid bare. She struggled to resist. Love, joy, laughter—these could be her only defence. In desperation, she tried to recall happy memories of her father as a talisman against the hold of this black oppression.

In vain did she resist!

Now was she being forced to recall something that had been gnawing at her spirit for the past week: the private discussion between Lord Elgar and Cadwallon. Her thoughts began to narrow, blocking out all other images save how her father had intentionally kept something from her. He had concealed her bizarre trance and its connection to the new stars from her. Her father had deliberately withheld something from her, something very important. And there were other things too he had kept from her, no doubt—she just knew it! He was keeping things from her! This was tantamount to a lie! He had lied to her! If he could lie, he did not love. He had never loved her!

Oriana's tranquility was dissolving into bleakest despair. She hated; she resented.

And then amidst the height of her agony Oriana heard— shrill and icy cold from afar—a cruel, piercing sound of laughter. It was horrifying. The terror nauseated her. Something was delighting in her torment.

"*No!*" Oriana shouted in defiance. "*I will not listen! I do not believe! I will not believe!*"

The stag had not been idle. As soon as Oriana fell upon the ground, the stag was leaning over her, staring with burning intent into her glossy eyes. In a flash, his spirit was within her, probing her soul as he had done upon their first meeting. But this time the stag was not alone. Oriana was overwhelmed by the concussion of two titanic wills colliding in cosmic opposition. Her mind had become a battlefield—her soul the prize. This dread, this malignancy came to devour, to assert total mastery over her being.

"*Please no!*" she screamed even louder than before. "*I wish to bear life!*"

In quick, tormenting slashes of despair, evil hewed at Oriana's soul: terrible blows meant to destroy her faith in all that she cherished to be true. But the stag defended with equal might. For every fell stroke of laughing mockery came a deflecting white blast of purest hope—blasts in the imagery of tiny white flowers.

Long and bitter was the struggle. Oriana was powerless against their fierce contest. As a drowning child she felt, pinned and battered under a violent weight of crashing waves.

And just when Oriana thought she could endure not a moment more, the dark power weakened. With a final surge, the stag cast the fell laughter from her spirit. Oriana could feel the dark power fleeing before the stag's white luminescence. Her torment of doubt and resentment and fear abated then fled utterly.

The confrontation was over. Oriana was freed. Slowly she hoisted herself up, shivering with fright as she sat gazing wide-eyed at the stag. She was yet nauseous.

Ahead the stag dragged himself wearily to the riverbank. He bent, almost collapsing at the water's edge. The great stag took small sips only. But with every new sip, his strength returned. Slowly he stood. Then, wading out into the water, the stag completely submerged himself under the shimmering surface.

After a few seconds only, the stag burst from the Anwash

like a giant salmon leaping upstream in search of his spawning waters. He landed next to Oriana in the soft heather and rolled amidst its deep purple till he was dry.

Oriana thought he looked his former self once again, if even more determined in his demeanour.

He drew closer to her side, reseating himself.

"Are you well, dear one?"

"Yes … I … I think so," answered Oriana lethargically, "that is … well … it will soon pass."

"I wonder?" The stag had a strained look. "I said your heart would be tested, but I have misjudged the hour of its coming," he said lamentably. "I am afeared the enemy may attempt a return, perhaps in deathly form as well as spirit."

Oriana got to her feet. She was no longer shivering, yet the pain of the black ordeal hung as a cloud over her heart.

"Tell me, lord, who was he? Never in all my life have I known such terror."

"The laughter came not from he of whom I have already spoken: not from the faceless foe himself. He is yet imprisoned in depths beyond fathom. Deep beneath his most ancient fastness in Malgorod does he lie unclad and in torment, consumed with his own black thoughts as he deserves. Such is at least the belief and hope of many."

"Malgorod?" she whispered. It was an evil word. "My trance!" she then wondered privately. "Lord Elgar said I … how could I have—"

"Alas, yes! Malgorod, the fallen lands of Faërie, that black and ruinous realm beyond Danuvia's mournful sea, the shoreless Sea of Tyynimôr.

"But nay! It is not the faceless foe who yet laughs but he who serves him. One of his deadliest servants, a Lych-priest it was, one of the four dread apostates—cheaters of death they are, once loyal brethren of the Magi Order of Miðgard. Alas, does one of their kindred now seek our bearing, though I cannot explain how it is so. Somehow the enemy has espied the Wood of Adjoining. He is searching—searching for you, precious one. But he must not find you!"

At this news, Oriana felt a sliver of death's chill freeze up and down the marrow of her spine.

"Searching for me?" she whispered with renewed fright.

It was a horrible fortune, worse than anything the stag could have told her. The faceless foe, Malgorod, Lych-priests—how could she be connected in any way to things so dreadful?

And then, Oriana felt something welling inside her. She was consumed in a sudden blaze of self-pity. Why was she being hunted? Why did something so evil wish to find her, to harm her? She had not asked for any of this. She, in fact, deserved none of this!

Oriana grew angry. Her self-pity was collapsing into renewed resentment.

She turned and faced the stag. "Why me?" she demanded angrily. She must now, at this moment, have her answer. She would brook no further delays to these mysteries.

But the stag simply smiled back at her, not smugly or triumphantly, but warmly and lovingly. No scorn was in his countenance. He spoke nothing.

Twice had Oriana now directly asked the stag this question, and still did he not respond. For a second time she was denied.

Oriana stared fearfully into his dark eyes. But what exactly did she fear? He of the dread laughter, or the quiet strength of the stag himself? She couldn't now say which.

Why would he not simply, directly, plainly explain what she had to do with all of this? Her resentment was deepening.

Just then Oriana realized, as if jolted by her greater conscience: "Ah! But that is exactly what this evil desires!" she said to herself resolutely. "He wants me to resent! He wants me to hate, to fear!"

Oriana threw her hands to her face, feeling she might sob at any moment.

The stag sighed. He was not now looking at her but down at his crossed hooves as if troubled. "Still does the lychcraft enervate your heart. They have become mighty indeed! I have done all I can for you, small one. Only through the force of your own will can the black cantrip that yet lingers be expelled from your soul. I can do no more."

Oriana took a deep, cleansing breath. She struggled to clear her mind. And then, at that moment, Oriana heard—very soft at first but rising, rising until it swelled in stupendous crescendos—the carol of the wood, returning in her moment of need. The trees and every other rooted being were singing to her from all corners of the wood. And then the Anwash too! It too was now joining with its own ethereal harmonies.

The water music was speaking to her. And now did she understand. As her guide had done only moments ago, Oriana walked to the bosom of the Anwash, drank of its essence, and then, like the stag, immersed herself fully in its vigour.

Light! Colour! Indeed every hue of the rainbow Oriana had ever seen and many more that she hadn't—lovely colours abiding beyond ordinary sight, one moment distinct, the next, combining—were suddenly swirling about her, swilling her, healing her. In a moment, Oriana found herself floating, standing upon nothing, yet at the same time feeling not at all submerged in water. In fact she wasn't even certain if she was holding her breath.

What wonders the Anwash worked! Like the final vestiges of a fever draining from its host, all the resentment Oriana had first harboured for her father and then for the stag started to melt away in bright crystalline gusts.

Cleansed of her dark thoughts, Oriana swam to the bank and

lifted herself onto the bracken, flinging water of sparkling light from her long hair as she threw back her head. She got to her feet feeling hale and invigourated. She went to the stag who stood watching—who stood waiting.

"Well done," he said, nodding his great antlers. "The Lych and his dark dwimmer spell have you resisted—even defeated, defeated for the present. But you have not destroyed. They shall return in time, I fear."

"I beg your forgiveness, Sire, for my insolence," said Oriana sincerely as she stood streaming wet in countless crystal droplets.

"There is nothing to forgive, young one," he returned patiently. "You have nothing to unsay. Today you have born yourself bravely and gained honour."

"Oh, Sire, I daresay you do me more credit than I merit."

"Nay; it is well deserved. You have shewn strength in your resistance and freed yourself of the Lych's curse."

"Thank heavens we were so near the water. I see it serves as a powerful defence against evil."

"Think not it was the philtre of the Anwash alone that vanquished the black enchantment, for it was your will and no other at work. The Anwash gives only encouragement and concealment. Now come and dry yourself among the bluebells. Listen to their final song and be warmed ere we depart."

In surprizingly little time, Oriana was dry as a bone. The forest hymn had indeed brought warmth as the stag had promised.

"I feel much better, Sire," said Oriana, getting to her feet spryly. "What immense power our enemy wields. I hope I never meet this devil again."

The stag drew a deep breath. "Would that that could be. I predict many perils await us still. Things go evilly in Faërie. The Lychgate grows weak—sooner, far sooner, than ever I thought it may. Even now as we speak, I expect the deathless ones begin to breach its mighty spell. The enemy is amassing, gathering new strength from across the sea. Now is the time for haste! I think it best for me to carry you for the rest of our journey. Come!"

Though Oriana dreaded the thought of having to face such evil again, she thought his request almost equally terrifying. As yet, Oriana hadn't grazed a single hair of his immaculate coat. And now, she was being asked to regard so perfect a creature as a common sumpter, a mere beast of burden. She quailed at the thought of something so pure being subordinate to one as imperfect as she. How could she bring herself to throw the whole of her unworthy being upon him?

"Come," he called again. "We must away!"

Her hesitation occupied but an instant. At the stag's adjuration, Oriana leapt to his back, the force of her jump proving barely enough. Somehow, he was even taller than she had supposed, several hands higher, in fact, than Éohmane's tall withers.

She was bestride him! They had made contact. Flesh met fur. She was at once overcome by his presence, their physical touch completing their metaphysical bond. His essence was hope, and she was to be carried by hope. "But hope in what?" she questioned.

The white stag walked to the water's edge, picked up the two large slivers of sycamore bark which he had earlier deposited, sniffed the air, and sighed. Grim was his visage.

They set off at once!

CHAPTER 8

Of Whitethorn and Wine

With a terrific spurt, the stag bounded over the wide brook, landing solidly atop the far bank. But for her mastery at riding, Oriana surely would have reeled backward, head over heels, for a thorough wetting in the Anwash below. Nimbly did she hold fast, clapping her hands round the base of his enormous neck and securely lodging her knees into the folds of his fur just above his bulging shoulders. For now, she held fast, but Oriana was uncertain how long she could remain thus upon his back.

No longer capering, the stag shot up the path with ever gathering speed. Soon the crystalline plashing of the Anwash was no longer within hearing.

The forest had become a speeding, green blur. Whipping twigs and noose-like vines whistled by Oriana's face with alarming nearness. And on more than one occasion did she barely avoid certain decapitation, ducking and dodging oncoming branches just in the nick of time. With the stag's high vaults and lightening sprints, wide leaps, and sideways dashes, Oriana seriously doubted that she would come out of this race unscathed. But in spite of these hazards, she found the whole thing, slaps, scratches, and all, to be the most exhilarating thing she had ever experienced.

Without once stopping the stag hurtled through the labyrinth of ancient trees over a distance Oriana was finding difficult to fathom. The forest was proving vast beyond her imagination.

Her own Selwood, running fifteen miles in length and nearly six across, was dwarfed by comparison. Already, she guessed the stag to have run at least twice the length of Selwood Forest and perhaps farther. The great stag was astounding. Not once did he tire or founder with a poorly landed hoof.

Sometimes Oriana felt as they jumped over fallen trees and ducked beneath hanging branches that she was no longer balanced upon the stag's back at all, but instead flying alongside him. Again she fancied herself a white swan in full flight, gliding over calm waters. As lonely white pilgrims she imagined the two of them, hastening toward some sacred reliquary hidden deep and quiet amidst the sorrow of a newly troubled world. By hoof and wing did they fly. But whither exactly were they speeding, she still could not guess.

They had been winding their way through the bottom of a mossy vale that contracted steeper and steeper and were now passing into a much flatter section of forest. What excitement! What joy! All her senses were excited. With the stag's Herculean speed and herself in imagined flight, Oriana was finding it difficult to dwell on anything but the thrill of journeying.

"Oh! But I mustn't forget our peril," she told herself presently.

She was discovering there was something about the stag's presence that made her forget unpleasant things. And now that she actually sat atop him, touching him, this calm only deepened.

"Danger of a different sort also lays ahead, innocent one—the peril of choice awaits you, indeed two choices, I expect," warned the stag as if in response to her own private admonition. "None knows what the future holds, nor what consequences our decisions may bring. For you, daughter of worlds twain, the perils of the Primrose Path await, the path to certain deception. And when the heavy hour comes, you must have a care. A small test only of the enemy's malice have you endured. Their shadows are many." He paused as with a troubled thought. "Should your heart misgive, should you falter in the end, a slave to the ene-my's ruinous will shall you become. So I say, beware! Beware the Primrose Path. Beware the enemy's crooked words! Few are able to separate their counterfeits, their sophistry from that which truly is. Deceit and truth together the enemy wields to realize his ends. For such is the Lych's strength."

At these words Oriana could feel darkness creeping over her heart once again in spite of his healing touch.

"But do not despair," he added reassuringly, "you will have wisdom enough for the trial, I ween."

So the stag and Oriana continued through the Wood of Adjoining with the fleetest of speed, a flight matched only by those borne aloft by wind and wing. After what seemed like hours of such haste, Oriana found herself nodding off till a sud-den sideways jolt revived her.

The narrow trail now brought them to a gradual thinning of the forest. Ahead Oriana could see sunlight growing ever brighter. Oriana guessed they would be exiting the wide wood before long.

"Shall we be traveling much farther tonight, Sire?" asked Ori-ana. She was becoming a little fatigued and more than a little hungry. She wished she had brought a flask filled with a nour-ishing draught of the Anwash. But she had no flask. Nor did she have provender of any sort. She had not at all expected to be setting out on a journey the previous day.

"Yes, young one, I am afraid we must, through early eventide and beyond."

Not once during their flight had the stag slackened his pace. Oriana thought his stamina easily thrice that of the greatest warhorse.

"I marvel at your endurance, lord," she said, leaning forward to relieve a little of the pressure from her bruising bottom. "Do you not tire from distance or burden? I know my weight to be nigh on nine stone at least."

"Yes, I do tire in time," laughed the stag once again in his hearty deerish clickings. "Weariness takes me as it does all others. Do you not suppose the same life force coursing through you also brings life to me? You and I are not as different as you may imagine."

Oriana felt she should have known this all along. He was, after all, as real in body as in spirit, even if both gave every appearance of being grander than any living thing she had ever met.

"Though I think," the stag went on, "my strength is simply more stubborn than most. It is slower and less willing to pass than the strength of aught that goes on four."

"Or two, to say the least," she returned lightly.

He nodded. "It is so."

"But I have felt, Sire, from the moment of our first meeting, and do even now feel, that I am able to draw strength from your strength," she said feeling a little embarrassed that her present questions had the ring of complaint. "I will trust in this. I will not give thought to food or rest until you desire as much."

The stag turned his great white head and smiled up at Oriana. "Your trust is another gift and does you credit. But I would not ask such a thing of you, my strong friend. Before the sun retires fully to her bedchamber we shall have our rest."

◇◇

Presently, as Oriana was beginning to think there could be no end to it, the forest began suddenly to grow ever brighter and thinner. And just then, at the very next turning, the wooded trail they had been following for what felt like the better part of a full day let suddenly upon a wide open heath fringed on their left by distant hills gazing out, grey and jagged. All about them lay saxifrages, soft purple ling, and a few straggling elms and fir

trees. Thick cornel and crowberry shrubs and aromatic wood-
bines there were too, stretched before them.

They had finally emerged from the Wood of Adjoining!

Oriana gazed abroad and above, blinking in the path of the
slanting sunlight shining in her face. It was her first full glimpse
of sky in this world. Early dusk was upon them, the sun now
westering into a saffron-streaked horizon, casting warm tints
upon the land. It was a beautiful, pastel sunset but not unusual
in any respect. It could well have been a typical twilight vista at
Oakleigh Manor.

Now was she also able to reckon their direction for the first
time, if indeed she could trust this sun to be traveling a like path
as the sun of her world. If so, they were heading north.

Oriana turned in her seat to gaze upon the distant trees trailing off southward behind them. Almost as tiny shrubs did they
now seem in the lengthening distance. It took little time before
they were out of sight entirely, so great was the stag's speed.

Then, it happened that Oriana noticed the air. For here upon
the open heath, quite unlike in the forest, the wind did not dis-
solve in front of her as she went. As a sun-drenched sheet, her
hair flew and snapped behind her. What a delight to feel Æolian's
cool breath on her cheeks again. Wind in one's hair whilst riding
an enchanted stag is not a thing to be missed!

"Does the … our foe, that is, know of our destination?" Oriana could not bring herself to utter that despicable word *Lych*.
There seemed some foul potency in the very word itself.

"He seeks it, yes, with hatred and envy, bent on further
spreading his master's decay," said the stag darkly. "Long had we
regarded this realm concealed—protected from any direct evil.
Alas, on this day are we shown to have been in error. My mind
is clouded by their penetration, dear one. There is an ill chance
the enemy may also know of our intentions. It is not impossible

we may find them already waiting, waiting to thwart our design, though still do I hope against this fate."

"And how strong is this hope, Sire, if I may ask?" she said worriedly, bobbing with ever increasing fatigue on the stag's mighty back as they sped. "How may we hope in this?"

"By your own strength of will are we given hope," he answered confidently.

"My strength?"

"Yes, through your defiance of the Lych spell," he returned earnestly. "Discovering our quest was the purpose of the enemy's attack on you, I deem."

Oriana rolled this thought around in her mind. Perhaps that was one reason for the attack. But there was a second purpose. The fell laughter had said so itself. She took care to think no more on it. It was dreadful.

"Your defiance," he went on fondly, "also weakened his hold on you—closing the Lychgate to his mind. As I strove with our enemy, I learnt they are seeking our errand and our destination. He was hoping to rob this information from you."

"So that's the reason!" she exclaimed in a moment of epiphany.

"Quite!" returned the stag. The low-rising hills of the glen were smoothing out before them. The air too seemed to be changing—wetter and less pleasant. "This is why our quest has been kept from you—for your protection and our secrecy. Long has the enemy possessed an evil empowering them to peer into the minds of the unsuspecting. And as such knowledge of our mark has been denied you, there is an even chance our intentions remain hidden from their gaze."

"But is there no danger we might, in our very travel, be lead-ing the enemy to wherever it is we are headed?"

"An astute deduction," said the stag approvingly. "Were it not for the Anwash, that would be a very real danger, indeed. From its cleansing water are we both shielded from unfriendly eyes.

Take heart! Still do I hope the first stage of the Mundi Redien-dum will go unhindered by the forces of darkness."

"Mundi Rediendum?" thought Oriana, wishing to know more but resigning to their need for secrecy.

"Let us hope things shall thus come to pass, for we cannot suffer a second such error of my judgment," he said lamentably. "It is yet a mystery to me why I was unable to feel the enemy's presence here in this sacred realm. His coming should have sent a terrible ripple through the fabric of being. It would seem I have already proven to be an ill guide this day."

"Nay! Say not so, Sire," insisted Oriana, patting the stag's side tenderly. "You will not fail us in our quest. I'm certain of this, even if—" she gave a small laugh, "even if I don't know what our quest is exactly. I believe in you, lord."

"And you say it is you who draws strength from me," the stag remarked warmly. "Now is it I who finds solace in your words, dear one."

◇◇◇

The rocky heath was ever widening and leveling before them. At length they entered a brown champaign of sodden flatlands whose tall, wilting grasses whipped at the bottom of Oriana's feet as they went. The wind continued to grow ever moist and . . . and odd.

Hours slipped by as they passed over the darkling bent. And then, the stag did something he had yet done. For the first time since fleeing the banks of the Anwash, the stag began to slow.

"Sire, by your leave. You spoke earlier as though you believed the—well, he of the evil laughter might return." Oriana was glad the stag was finally slowing. Perhaps this meant they would soon be resting.

"Yes, indeed he may, but that, I believe, will depend entirely upon your choice. Yes, it is very likely he may come again."

"By my choice?" she said more than a little surprised by the stag's comment. "Well, I would certainly *chuse* for that horror not to return if I have any say in the matter."

"That is a choice you may make," he remarked benignly. "But I believe you will do what must be done. The wisdom to make the right choices I see within you."

"And how will I know what the correct choices may be?" she said desperately.

"Trust to the strength of your mind and the purity of your heart," he said, slowing to a walk. "Remember our lesson—the lesson of your gifts and their origins. Trust in that which has been given to you."

Oriana was brought some comfort by the stag's rede, but she still did not like being left in the dark about so many important things. She was afraid, afraid of he who lurked somewhere in the distance or ahead perhaps in the deepening shadows. And she worried of the future of unknown choices awaiting her. What decisions would she have to make? And why did her decisions matter so in the first place?

Finally, the great stag came to a stop. Evening was hurrying its descent, the sun low and red. For some time now Oriana had been watching the landscape change—first from dense forest to open glen, and now the earth was grown damp with naught but spongy turves and coarse shrubs in sight for a league or more, the air ever stale. He had conducted them to a tiny spring flowing westward whereat a thick brake of elderberry bushes grew directly atop the slow, trickling current. Hundreds of dark green, featherlike leaves splayed outward as if to shade and cool the water below. Their white flowers were in bloom, lending their cover and beauty to the deep purple berry clusters hanging below.

"This shall be our final rest before our errand is done."

Oriana leapt from the stag's great height down onto the

boggy soil. She stretched her stiff legs and back. Wearily, she walked over to the shiny purple drupes.

Just beside the thicket, the stag in turn dropt the thin flakes of sycamore bark, which he had been carrying in his mouth all the while.

"Are the berries edible, lord?' asked Oriana eagerly. She was famished from the long ride. "Were we now in the fens of Somerset I would have taken these for elderberries and not bothered to ask before indulging. But all is new and strange to me here. Indeed they are the plumpest berries I have ever seen."

"They are quite edible: more than passable, I can attest. They are one of the reasons I chose to lead us in this direction—but not the sole reason, mark you," he replied, sniffing the white flowers.

"And the water, is it fit to drink?" asked Oriana hopefully.

"It is not the Anwash, but it will slake well enough—for the present, it is so. It is yet to savour of the hand of progress."

"The hand of progress?" whispered Oriana but asked nothing of this mystery.

And so they rested and dined amidst the quiet of dusk's lengthening shadows. Oriana and the stag surveyed the drooping branches for the darkest and juiciest elderberries. But espying the very best fruits was not at all easy, as all were absolutely wonderful!

Oriana folded the middle of her blue kirtle into the mold of a wide apron pocket, stuffing it with as many berries as it could hold. She thought her guide equally adept in his own method of collection, sniffing out and biting free the purple gems with all the care and efficiency of a royal bean counter counting the king's royal feorm.[1]

---

[1] The feorm was an annual food-rent collected from select villages to sustain the king and his household for twenty-four hours. Such taxes were sometimes commuted with an equivalent monetary payment. By the time of King Athelstan's reign, the obligation of paying such dues usually fell to noblemen only and not the ceorl-peasants. This tended to further undermine the economic autonomy of individual ceorls as the obligation to pay taxes was the distinguishing characteristic of all freemen.

Oriana dined on her fruits standing, hoping warmth and feeling might soon return to her thighs and bottom. And return they did. Like the Anwash, the elderberries brought nourishment surpassing that of their kind in her world. Then, with a few sips from the spring, she was contented once more.

Oriana returned to the elderberry thicket, stretched along the ground next to the stag, and snuggled herself against his soft underbelly. She tried to relax her mind along with her body. She could not. As was frequently the case, she found she could not quell her curiosity. Would they soon reach their mark? Would she even know what to do once they arrived? And something she hadn't considered until this very moment now sprang to her thoughts: What was she to do after she'd done whatever it was she was meant to do? What then? Would she ever return home to the woods and fields and good people of Oakleigh Manor?

"I feel the time is now ripe to give what you asked of me at our first meeting," said the stag calmly, lifting his great head to gaze round at Oriana.

"Asked, Sire? I don't recall having asked anything of—
Oh … your name?" she said, remembering just then that she had
asked for the stag's name as he sped over the silver causeway.
"You mean to give me your name?"

"Yes, precious one," he returned with a smile.

Oriana sat up quickly from the pillow of the stag's soft under-
fur, crossed her legs beneath her, and looked into his jet eyes. She
was met with a sudden giddiness, feeling as a child waking early
on Christmas morning. She would finally have what she eagerly
awaited these several days.

"Whitethorn is my name," said the stag without preamble,
"or at least as it is expressed in your Saxon tongue."

"*Whitethorn*," repeated Oriana slowly, savouring the sound.
"What a lovely name, Sire," Oriana said, beaming at her guide.
She repeated the name in her mind over and over, thinking she
had once heard this name long ago. "Whitethorn, it sounds
so … well, right some—" And just as she was about to say *somehow*, it came to her at once. After a pause she said, "Why … why
Whitethorn's another name for a hawthorn tree!"

"Your agile mind serves you well," said the stag approvingly.
"I was rather hoping you would appreciate my name."

"Are you then related?" asked Oriana avidly, "you and the
great hawthorn of your world—of my tapestry?"

"Of it and all hawthorns in a manner of speaking—yes,"
replied the stag, straightening his head as if to survey the way forward. "You are, I trust, aware what the hawthorn tree embodies?"

"Yes, I see now—it's beginning to make sense," piped Oriana,
her face warmed with understanding. "Hope. That's what the
hawthorn symbolizes. Local folklore in our shire suggests the
hawthorn is ever the emblem of hope."

"In your shire and all shires—in all worlds," the stag said
pointedly. "And hope is the bane of our enemy."

"It's such a beautiful name. May I—I mean, by your leave that is…" Oriana did not complete her question, fearing the request might be impertinent.

"Of course you may call me Whitethorn, dear one," replied the stag, nodding his stupendous antlers.

"And you, Sire," asked Oriana respectfully and ever so haltingly, "that is… may I be so bold as to ask… would you care to call me Oriana?"

"I would be privileged to call you by your true name, should you and your rightful name ever meet."

"What… what did he say?" Oriana asked herself suddenly stunned. "My rightful name?"

Oriana was just about to ask for some clarification on that point when the great stag said, "I know your heart desires more, small one. But I can say no more, for I know no more of this mystery myself. I am but a messenger of a higher will. This is a truth that can be discovered by you alone. It falls to us each to discover our own paths to understanding, for there exists certain knowledge that cannot be given from one to another. So it is with your name."

How very disconcerting this was for Oriana. She had always been immensely fond of her name. Oriana was of course no typical Saxon name. Her father had once told her he chose it in remembrance of their eastern island of Cyprus. It was a perfectly apt name, for *Oriana* literally meant "Maid of the East." Her father had given her this name. She loved anything her father had given her. She loved her name.

Now of course Oriana didn't wish to get into a flap over this, but this was going just a little too far. Was she really meant to abandon a name she so fancied, a name so fitting to her person and given by one she so loved? How could she lay aside something given to her by her father? Why should she have to discover a new name for herself? It didn't make sense.

She shrugged and had a good sigh. "Perhaps this answer too

lies ahead," she thought, watching the sun fall to join the grey-ing, distant rim of the grassy levels.

Oriana turned her mind back to their present quest. "Our errand, Sire … Lord Whitethorn," she added cautiously with a smile, "tell me, if—if it is permitted, why have we flown with such urgency all these many leagues? Have we hastened merely to reach our goal ahead of the enemy, if indeed they do pursue, or must we arrive by some appointed hour? Very little of this is clear to my mind, as you well know."

"What does your intuition suggest?" replied the stag, tapping her heel gently with his enormous hoof. "Listen to your heart."

Oriana closed her eyes and searched. "I think, Sire, we run for both reasons: *from* pursuit and *in* pursuit ourselves—we pursue a moment before it passes, the heavy hour as you have warned."

"You reason very properly," he replied, nodding with approba-tion. "You are correct. Again I say, many answers do you already carry within you."

"But my heart does not tell me, Sire, or perhaps I am yet a poor listener, what time we aim for," she said, reaching up for a low-hanging elderberry she simply could not pass up.

"Are you aware what day we departed your realm?"

"Well, let's see," Oriana paused. She was counting on her purple-stained fingers. "You came to me on the first day of the feast, and that was … em—that was the sixteenth—then you returned … hmm, five days later. And we slept through the night at the Anwash. So today is … today is the twenty-second. At least in my world it is. I cannot begin to guess what day it is here, lord."

"It is no day and all days, dear one," said the stag mysteriously. "But it is your world which matters now—that blessed mortal realm. Your calculations remain true. This is a day not without significance—"

"Yes! Of course," she exclaimed after another short pause.

"Tomorrow is the Feast of St. Audrey—the Summer Solstice, when day lives longest. 'When night fears light,' as we say in Selwoodshire. Tonight is the Solstice Eve!"

"Indeed," said the stag, sounding pleased with her answer. "Tomorrow is the day when we live in His fullest illumination. But what will eventually follow?"

"What will follow?" she echoed, thinking she did not fully understand the question. "You mean in the following days themselves, lord?"

"Yes."

"Well," she said, getting to her feet for another good stretch of her back. "In time, night will lengthen, Sire. Dark will grow strong until winter fully sets and day begins to lengthen once again."

"One chance to begin, therefore, ere the celestial portal to your world shuts. By the spring equinox will it be closed forever. And who knows what may come of that? We must snatch this chance before it is too late. Verily is tonight the night for which so many have waited—hallowed midsummer's eve. We must reach our mark ere the witching hour strikes."

The stag got to his hooves and led the way to where the spring widened just beyond the thicket. He lowered his head as if looking for something.

"A parting treat before setting out," he said merrily. "O elder-umbles! May you bring us good fortune."

Oriana stared, wondering what he now had in mind. A hearty treat did sound very pleasant indeed!

"Pick nine of the elderflowers and bring them to me," he instructed, nodding toward the thicket.

Oriana was only a few seconds plucking the tiny aromatic petals and speedily walked over to the spring.

"Drop five in the water in token of the five sacred amulets."

"Five amulets?" she thought. "Oh no! Is there no end to what I must learn?" She cast the petals in the water.

"Now the remaining four," he bade. "May each serve as a bane to the fell Lych-priests, who hate all sweet things."

Oriana released the rest. Nine white flowers now floated in the lazy shallows where the water bubbled over small rocks.

Again, the stag bent his head to the water to drink—or so Oriana expected. But he did not drink. Rather, he dipt the ends of his antlers into the water, removed them, and breathed across the water's surface causing the subtlest of ripples. The flowers vanished.

"Amazing! Where have they gone, Sire—I mean, Lord Whitethorn? Have they sunk down beneath the soil?" she wondered yet again.

"Wait!" The stag told Oriana. "Look now! They have joined the water. Come and taste!"

The water had turned a pale yellow. She bent for a closer look. It smelt wonderful. With ready delight, she joined her hands and sampled it.

"Why, it's heavenly!" she observed in a most approved manner. It was magick! Plain and not at all, simple—it was magick! What other powers must lay hidden within him?

"It's so light, Sire, crisp and dry. Is it—"

Now did the stag bend to drink. "It is, yes, elderflower wine. A sweet cordial many times distilled to gladden two weary travelers—a treat seldom to be had in the world. And as is true in your world, here too a draught of elderflower wine is best sipped at midnight under a clear plenilune, but we shall not have that pleasure, not this evening."

"What a beautiful treat," said Oriana, sipping, almost giddy in her praise "How delicious! Thank you, Sire! This is delight itself!"

"Drink till your heart's content, dear one, for it will not inebriate. Healing and protection, rather, are its virtue. These I deem will be needed sooner than we should care."

They finished. The stag nodded to Oriana. Night was coming on. It was time for them to depart.

"No further nourishment shall we find on this journey," said the stag in a much graver tone.

Oriana vaulted to his back, found her point of balance, and pressed her knees. He in turn gently lifted the slivers of sycamore bark. She wondered why he continued to carry these.

"Ahead there is nothing to sustain life, only despair," he went on darkly. "We are come to the low marches of the Festering Fens. Thither through its desolation we must pass till we stand upon its murky core, but go we must. Though have a care as we tread. By its sickness will your thoughts grow ever dark. And it is then that you must summon the hope of the Anwash and healing of elderflower wine."

"I had no idea, lord," whispered Oriana tremulously. "I was rather under the impression this was a world of loveliness only. That is why the intrusion of the—" Oriana durst not name the fiend, "the laughter and his black sorcery felt such an affront to this world. How could so unhappy a place exist here, here of all places?"

"It is a long tale," he began soberly. "In time, perhaps you will come to know it fully; perhaps ... perhaps you may even come to witness it fully, such would be a queenly gift."

"Whatever could he mean by that?" she wondered.

The stag started to the east. Oriana pressed her hands in around his shoulders, staring ahead uneasily. Whether owing to the stag's warning or her own premonition, she was definitely beginning to like the look of the boggy way forward less and less. Dismal the brown levels ahead suddenly seemed.

"Once, not too long ago, indeed not too long ago for some, was a single act of evil committed." Oriana listened intently to his darkening words. "And it was committed, I am sad to say, in your world, in young Miðgard, dear one; though I suspect that sad day would seem many an age passed to you. Somehow that evil punctured the membrane of this world, bringing with it a spreading ruin as it came."

"What, Sire?" she asked impatiently, her curiosity getting the better of her. "What was this act?"

"A fleeting moment of desire and reckless passion it was, desire which begot betrayal, betrayal ending in a will for power and dominion. It soon came to pass that these acts spawned greater destruction than any among the wise could ever have foreseen. But such is the precarious nature of a will that is free."

The stag sighed and fell silent for several seconds as though he needed time to collect himself. He looked very troubled indeed.

"As is the nature of this transilient realm, this realm which lies between Faërie and Miðgard and all lands ever to be sung into being," he resumed eventually, "the black wake of that evil now threatens to reach out and poison all other worlds. As a lonely drop of ink set to clear water, this evil was. In little time, it returned home to its dark progenitor many times fouler and mightier in its wake."

"The radiating ripples returning to their source," observed Oriana in a hushed tone.

"Verily! And such now is our course." Just then, he stopt and turned round to the elderberry thicket. "Look your last upon flower and leaf, innocent one. Look your last while you may."

And so Oriana did; with a deep sigh, she gazed at the delicate flowers and fine berries. She felt fear coming for her once more.

Her guide faced back round to the east. "Thitherward we must now tread through choked and dying lands—and thence, who can say? We must reach our mark, that source of transilient sorrow, ere moon and midnight join. Let us go!"

CHAPTER 9

The Festering Fens

They had passed into unhappy lands, to the last stage of their journey, and that stage was darkness. There was little light above. There was even less light in Oriana's heart. They had come to a world forsaken by all that was good—nearly all.

Long before Oriana and the stag crossed into the Festering Fens, the sun had sought refuge beneath the marsh's western brim as if to avoid seeing the ruinous lands for herself. Indeed, Oriana wondered if this vast waste had ever known the joy of day, as though it be a land abiding forever west of the sun's rising. All was dead darkness, a dark beyond that of mere night.

"Why should the sun ever wish to come to this dreadful place?" wondered Oriana gloomily. "Why would she bother? I don't suppose there is anything green here that would welcome her cheering glow anyway."

The stag had been splashing and squashing his way north through foul-smelling mires for hours. Presently, Oriana was sitting uneasily atop her guide, squinting into the black ahead. She could see little save the faint outlines of small hillocks. "Or maybe," she said to herself, "maybe they're heaps of clumped earth or dunghills or perhaps even some sort of strange rubbish middens. They're awfull, whatever they are."

She looked above. Like the sun had very sensibly done, the struggling stars were taking their leave too, one by one. Clouds as heavy, black curtains were unfurling from the west, bringing even greater darkness. Within moments not a single star was to be seen. Rain threatened. And with this threat, Oriana felt a deepening gloom close in about her as if the sagging clouds possessed in themselves a menacing will, waiting to drown them in hard spates of resignation. She felt not at all welcome.

Nothing was pleasant about this part of their journey. The farther they went, the colder and fouler grew the air. Oriana drew herself in closer to her mount for some added measure of warmth and relief from the swirling stench. She buried her face into the thick fur of his neck, which served in some degree to seal out the offensive fumes. Yet, to Oriana's disappointment, even his forest fragrance proved inadequate against the overpowering odour.

Here was a stink more obnoxious than that of ordinary marsh. Something more was fouling the air.

"The Festering Fens indeed!" she bemoaned to herself. "There could hardly be a more fitting name."

Oriana could more or less tolerate the stagnant smell of rotting peat, but this was not that odour at all. This was the offence of fermenting cesspits and gangrenous flesh and of yet another filth she could not identify. All about them, black waters bubbled and hissed as if repudiating their very passage.

Never had Oriana known such an altogether ghastly, such a forsaken place. Her nostrils burnt in the acrid vapours, her stomach turning in on itself. Just as she had felt when violated by the Lych's icy laughter, Oriana thought she might become physically ill.

Even the stag himself appeared changed in the gloom. No longer was his coat glistening white but more unto grey-ash, pallid and cheerless had it become. Oriana wondered if this were night's deception or the more pernicious despair of these wastes seeping into his soul, dulling his inner radiance.

And he had slowed considerably, but not this time, she

gathered, for another rest as they had enjoyed at the elderberry thicket. Perhaps it was the difficulty of landing a solid footing in the shifting mires or maybe it was his spirit that flagged, menaced by the despondency of this wiery realm. She could not say which. The only certainty in this torment, it would seem, was the way ahead would offer no improvement.

Yet in that gloom, Oriana was able to acknowledge one fortunate happenstance: there had been no further sign of the enemy, which of course had been a constant source of worry. This was the only part of their journey she hoped might go unaltered.

"Lord Whitethorn, had you not suggested earlier that I take to your back I should have soon requested it myself," she said, coughing into her sleeve. "I can see nothing in this dark. It's almost as if we were crawling through some deep crevice in the forbidden caves of Cheddar Gorge back home. And this stench!" she went on. "Phew! It is overpowering. Does it not oppress you, lord?"

"Indeed, it does. An unfavourable wind blows this night," he said ominously. "Yes, I am most oppressed by it, to the very soul I am, and not merely in its stench. Yet both dark and reek will pass as we come to the end of our journey," he added a bit more encouragingly.

Just then, Oriana noticed the stag's breathing was beginning to sound pained for the first time on their journey. "So he can fatigue," she thought, feeling increasingly anxious at the sight of his struggling.

"Light will return, and the fouled air will clear," he went on. "Yet the sadness will endure until our task is through."

"How, Sire, how will there be light?" she asked, fixing her eyes on the impenetrable pitch above. "Shall the moon somehow punch a hole through these storm clouds? If he can, I hope he will soon do so. I expect it would be a considerable improvement to things."

"He will come when summoned. Wait and see," he said, now plashing even more vigorously. The fouled waters were now deepening with every step.

"But when he brings his silver light," he continued with a cautious air, "you may not think things much improved. Do not look to his light for comfort. You will find nothing pleasing in his glow. Be it known, dear one, that it is sometimes best to let some truths lie hidden from our notice. Not all truth edifies as the Anwash. Not all that is true brings encouragement. For when you behold the progress of craven deeds that now beleaguers this realm you may find yourself in need of such strength and healing that wash and wine provide."

"Progress?" she wondered again. "Whatever does he mean— surely not the state of this terrible place? He can't. Progress means advancing to something superior, something beneficial— an improvement of some sort, as in progressing with my studies. How can this be said of these wastes?"

Soon, Oriana and the stag came to the deepest sloughs they had yet traversed. Now were the poisoned waters lapping against the stag's tall shoulders, increasingly splattering Oriana's legs and dress with foul-smelling grime as they went. She would have looked in a shocking state, a very sorry sight indeed were there any light to tell the tale. How Lord Whitethorn was managing to find his way through a dark so abject, Oriana could only wonder.

"Truly, it is better that some truths should lie hidden," she thought miserably, trying her best to wipe off the clinging filth. "I shudder to think what produces this scum."

With this thought, it struck Oriana that the stag's coat remained unblemished. True, it was still pallid in this lair of dark, yet it was perfectly unstained. This was certainly not for want of spewing stench, made plain enough by the black drippings from Oriana's heels. To the contrary, streams of filth sprayed every time the stag lunged forward, but none of it hit, or at least did not, or could not, or durst not, cling to his fur. He appeared to have some immunity against this filth. Oriana only wished she had as much!

Oriana glared above, feeling just about as wretched as she ever had. Still was there no sign of the moon, only low sagging clouds foreboding imminent downpour. Yet even in the moon's absence, if she had to guess at the hour, she would expect midnight to be drawing nigh—the witching hour as the stag had so named it. She wished that hour might hurry its arrival so their task might finally be completed—whatever that task may be. But would this mean bath and rest would follow? It seemed unlikely.

"Lord Whitethorn, what do you suppose has become of the enemy?" asked Oriana after a time. "Do they pursue?"

"Nowhere can I feel their hatred, precious yearling. But that does not mean I take all to be well. Not until the Mundi Rediendum is set in motion shall I be at ease."

"Sire, if I may ask, what is this Mundi Rediendum? I've been hoping we might return to our earlier discussion and to that subject especially, if it is safe for us to discuss."

"It is safe enough. Long has the enemy already known of the Order's hope for the Mundi Rediendum, but how and where it is to begin has thus been kept from their thoughts. Yes, you are right," agreed the stag, nodding after a pause. "It may even help to pass the time in this filth—the way ahead promises to be long and difficult."

Oriana coughed again, asking, "So what is this—this Mundi Rediendum." But before the stag could respond, she let out a miserable "*Aauhh!*" in consequence of a thick batter of flying ooze spraying suddenly down the back of her long hair. Utterly revolted, she reached up, flinging off the sticky muck as best she could. Oriana had always possessed a strong stomach, but it was being sorely tested on this final leg of their journey.

"I am sorry, dear one," said the stag apologetically, "but I'm afraid it can't be helped. We shall be rid of these fens ere long. Go on."

"Well," coughed Oriana, composing herself, "I was about to say, I've been searching for some answer to what this Mundi Rediendum may be, and I must say, I am a little uneasy at my reflections. Of course, it could be this vile place clouding my judgment—I'm not sure. My thoughts are ever dark here."

"It is as I warned—the black spell of despair it is you feel," he returned ominously. "But this time it comes not at the fleshless hands of the Lych, not directly I should say. It is the sadness of this world that darkens your heart."

Just then, the stag, to Oriana's great surprize, slowed and came to a halt. She had not expected them to stop even for a moment until they had reached their mark. As a grey island in a sea of black he now looked.

"Before we discourse on the Mundi Rediendum," he carried on, "you must invoke the living spirit of the Anwash philtre and elderflower cordial. In these shall you recall your strength. Their charm courses through you still. Only now is it subdued by the despair of these fens." He lifted his head. "Here, young one, close your eyes. Now take hold my antlers."

"Your antlers?" gasped Oriana. She was stunned, reacting as one might if asked to lay hands on something sacred, indeed in a manner as if his antlers were some gilded reliquary housing the bone of a beloved saint.

"As you say, lord," she said apprehensively.

Hesitantly, Oriana reached up to the lowest fork in his antlers, closed her hands ever so cautiously at first, and then, with a fair measure of uneasiness, gript tightly. Immediately, the smooth texture reminded Oriana of another silky surface she had once felt. It was curiously familiar to ... to—

"My tapestry!" she thought excitedly. "His antlers feel just like its pearly surface."

"Can you again taste the water music?" asked the stag avidly. "Do you now hear the sweet savour of the wine?"

"No, I'm … I'm afraid I—" she stammered, still fixated on the texture of his antlers. "Wait—yes, I feel them both now. Oh, I had forgotten how lovely the music is. Already I feel better. I say, whose heart could ever be grey with such beautiful accompaniment? Even amidst the bowels of these bleak lands do I feel the vigour of rekindled joy. And the elderflower wine! I can feel its healing power surface yet again. My heart feels now less dark."

"Good! Very good!" he said cheerfully.

With that, the stag lumbered forward, resuming his laboured push through the black waters.

Feeling much restored, Oriana returned her touch to the warmth of the stag's neck. The healing of wash and wine came none too soon. For at that exact moment, the wind began to moan with greater ferocity, wafting rottenness of the deep meres with renewed anger. Rain was certain.

At this point, it seemed to Oriana that the stag was veering their course in a slightly new direction—a little east, maybe, if they had still been traveling north, but of course, it was impossible for her to know with certainty in the dark.

"Now to your question," said the stag as the sour wind chafed Oriana's ears. "Tell me first of your own thoughts on the Mundi Rediendum. Is your mind still plagued with doubt, even now after recalling the hope of wash and wine?"

"A bit, Sire, yes, I'm afraid it is," she said disappointedly. "I cannot turn away from my first impression of what this may be."

"And what is this impression?"

"Well, for start, I am prepared to say, just from the words themselves, it must be a returning of the world in some way or another."

"That it is," he said, nodding. "What else does your heart reveal?"

The wind increased its angry howls. It seemed to detest their very discussion.

"I'm thinking back to your counsel at our first meeting," she said, coughing twice in response to the gathering wind. "You said I should hope for the end of endings, for the world's return-ing—and so, Mundi Rediendum—the world's returning. Is that it?"

"Yet again, I say your heart sees clearly. What more does it perceive?"

Splash! Plablump! Oriana's lap was pelted with more projectile stink. She paused, wiping herself clean for a second time though with little efficacy. "This is insufferable, Sire."

"I am sorry you must endure this ruin," said the stag, shaking his head ruefully. "Please continue."

"Well, I must confess, it's at this point where I falter. I am still at a loss for exact implications," sighed Oriana heavily. "I think this is where I most require your guidance. Ought I to view this returning of the world as a renewal for man himself?"

Oriana felt the first cold rain drops at this question.

"Indirectly, yes. As a corollary it may be so, should it come to pass. But not directly."

"That's what I suspected, Sire," she answered in a worried way, "and it is that point precisely which confuses me. This notion of man's renewal that is, I must say—well, I should say I am a little bewildered, even a bit troubled at this, if I may be wholly frank."

"Why is that?" he asked with a consoling air. "Why should you be troubled by that which may bring hope to the folk of Miðgard?"

There was no time for Oriana to respond. Suddenly all was alight! Exactly as the stag spoke these words, there came from the west three terrific lightening bolts, flashing across the sky, illuminating all that was below for many leagues. For several horrible moments, Oriana beheld the ruin that had for so long been concealed from her sight.

She saw much in those fleeting seconds. Everything was alien and unnatural in every respect. Nothing looked a possibility of her world or any world she could ever envisage.

Oriana now realized they had been wading through a terrible desert, a desert whose sands were black ooze and innumerable lumps of hideous floating debris—broken crockery bits, perhaps, and misshapen canisters of all sizes. Littered all about them in all directions were heaps and heaps of the most unsightly rubbish, indeed the vilest offal that ever was seen.

A great many of the awful items looked to be a sort of narrow-type costrel or glass beaker maybe, but not of ceramic, or glass, or any material she had ever seen. They were shiny but not at all pleasing to the eye. Some of the containers were clear. Others were coloured. Some possessed strange symbols, which Oriana thought might be writing. Others were plain. All were covered in thick scum and stench.

Amongst these, and no less abundant, was a quantity of large knobby rings—centreless wheels perhaps—floating like rotting corpses in the deep meres. Again, she could not identify their foul make, but they looked almost of blackened leather. Yet leather it could not be; it was far too grotesque—too fiendish.

And perhaps ghastliest of all these horrors was this: a legion of tall wooden crosses, leaning and broken, marching off, rank upon rank, into night's endless dark. Some were strung together at their tops with rusting metal cords. Others bore similar cords, only severed, dangling from out-stretched arms like the strands of snapped-spider webs. Oriana was mortified at the mockery, for mockery it did seem—evil and taunting. Oriana thought the endless procession of derelict crosses surely stood in effigy of the most hallowed of all events in her world. Crosses they were, but utterly unholy, evil, and twisted.

"Oh, Sire! How horrible! How can this be? What a vile, evil world you have brought me to."

The stag sighed. "I had hoped you would be sheltered from this vision until the end. Would that the lightening had not revealed these horrors. It may now make the beginning all the more difficult. There's some evil at work here, some malignant intent behind those flashes, hoping to discourage. Let us pray we are not too late."

Oriana closed her eyes tightly. She had never seen such ugliness. Seeking solace in the stag's fur, Oriana tried to recall the beauty of her own shire. The image of this waste made it nearly impossible for her to picture the fair fields and orchards, cottages and crops of Oakleigh. She feared she might now be perpetually traumatized. How could any world fall to such filth, such unnatural estrangement? What devilry was at work here? Was this what Lord Whitethorn meant by a world of progress?

Onward they trudged. There was no conversation for some time; Oriana hadn't the heart for it.

Ever the stag pressed forward, yet Oriana now made no effort to wipe the spattering filth from her body. An ever-swelling despondency was consuming her.

Eventually the stag broke the silence. "I think we should resume our speech. It may help to comfort you."

"Yes, Sire, I will try if you desire it," said Oriana languorously.

"Then let us return to the Mundi Rediendum: now most of all is this talk needful." He paused as though thinking then continued: "I ask you once again, dear one, why do you fear that which brings hope?"

Oriana gave the question serious thought, saying at length: "I believe this has been my reservation all along, lord. All my life I have been taught to believe that One has already come for man, One whose act of sacrifice has brought us hope. And so I am forced to question the necessity, or even the truth, of this returning, this other renewal."

"Really? In what respect?"

"Well, lord, on the surface it sounds, at best, superfluous and, dare I say, at worst, even blasphemous, if you'll pardon my boldness."

"There is nothing to pardon," he said reassuringly. "Your mind is following a proper route. But in what way do you suspect blasphemy?"

"In this way, Sire: How can anything be added to that which is already complete in itself? If I am correct in my belief, His great sacrifice needs no amendment. His act of universal redemption lacks nothing."

"So far, young one, we have yet to part company. All that you say is consistent with the Mundi Rediendum."

There was a pause. Perhaps the stag was waiting for her to respond. She gave no response.

By-and-by the stag resumed: "On this point you must think. What if something should transpire in your world, something at the hands of man to cause the Miðgard race to utterly abandon faith in the promise of His sacrifice? What then?"

"I do not know, lord," remarked Oriana, pausing to think. "The end of all things, I would imagine. But how could such a thing come to pass? How could man, himself, bring about such a thing?"

"Easily could it be so!" replied the stag quickly. "Ruin brings despair, and despair destroys hope: From that, one belief shall come to replace another. Man's faith in his own knowledge, his lust for dominion—these may come to replace man's trust in Him. And that dominion can only deliver ruin upon his world, hence despair and the annihilation of hope itself, you see."

At these words, Oriana began to smell a different odour, far off but approaching steadily straight ahead. It was merging with the sickening stench that already oppressed them.

Something was burning! It was neither wood, nor peat, nor any sort of dried bramble she could imagine. Briefly, Oriana thought it the stench of smoldering privy ditches as fouled the air back home during the annual winter purge. But that was not it either. The only impression she could form in the dark was smoke from some ghastly combination of dirty lamp oil and soured-mutton grease. She then tried to picture what could possibly bellow such a plume. Oriana wondered if the smoke came from a type of tall shaft-furnace similar to the one Alaric, the village smith, used to smelt his iron. If it were, it must be many times its size to produce this reek.

Oriana lifted the top of her kirtle over her nose. It made little difference, so she returned to pressing her face to the stag's neck for relief. That was better—but not nearly good enough.

"Take heart, small one. We are nearing our mark; soon will the worst be over," he said reassuringly. "Alas! We must make for yon poisoned smoke. It is our firebare, our beacon, a reprehensible guide, but our guide nevertheless. There lies our way and our hope and perhaps ... perhaps the enemy in waiting. We must be vigilant."

On and on the wind and rain continued, refusing to relent in the slightest. And with every splashing stride the stag took, thicker and ever noxious the smoke grew.

Eventually Oriana resumed her questioning. "Tell me more, Sire. I still feel the need to 'get to the bottom of things,' as my friend Penda so often says. Still does doubt gnaw at my heart."

"Then let us assuage that doubt once and for all," replied the stag comfortingly. "You said His great sacrifice needs no amendment. To you I say, you need not doubt your former learning. Yet I counsel you not to place all trust in your store of knowledge alone, thinking it whole. Many more truths await you."

"Oh, Sire, believe me, I do not. On the contrary, I often wonder how deficient my learning has been." It now required a prodigious deal of concentration for Oriana to continue with their conversation in the mounting smoke, cold, and damp. "On the one hand, I am determined to remain open to all you might reveal to me, yet I am still reluctant to place faith in anything that might contradict His blessed teachings. I do not mean to frustrate you, Sire, but I still know not what to think or believe."

"Be at peace!" he commanded warmly. "Do not fear my tidings. I have not been sent to undo the truths you have learnt. Nay, rather! I come with reaffirmation of your beliefs. Behold! What you believe is so! To your world has been sent He among high. Through the great event has man been given hope beyond his world and is thus blessed."

"I am glad to hear you say so, lord. It is a comfort to me."

"Wait, young one! I must ask you, what of the world created for man's stewardship, His first mighty and hallowed act of creation? Does it have similar cause for hope?"

By now Oriana had grown accustomed to the stag's method of answering her questions with a counter question of his own.

Yet this question caught Oriana a little off her guard. He had pressed her with some pretty difficult ideas these two days, but this one, she thought, may have been the most perplexing of all.

"The world, Sire?" she said in a timbre betraying her confusion. "When you say the world … the world's hope—I take it you mean—that is, I should think you refer to … I'm sorry, Lord Whitethorn. Once more does my wisdom fall short. I have no answer for you. In fact—and I am most embarrassed to admit as much—I do not understand the very question itself. How can a world hope?"

The smoke was now beginning to overpower all other offensive odours. But this was no improvement.

"You trust that it is man alone who has faith in the goodness of what may come to pass? It is only man who desires all to turn out well? Man alone who trusts in a happier tomorrow? For such is the essence of hope. Is this what you believe?"

"I—well, that is to say, Sire—" stammered Oriana, attempting some semblance of a reasonable response, "yes, I guess I do suppose that. It is only man who is given hope; only man *can* hope."

"Such a notion would not bode well for the quiet ones of your world," drawled the stag. "What would you say of the wood and the rivers and the seas of your home? What say you of the hills and vales, meads, levels, and downs of your dear country? Think you they have no spirit, no voice of their own with which to sing their own hymns of hope? Have they no song similar to that which you have harkened to in the Wood of Adjoining? Do you suppose there to be no crystalline water music in your world, no serenade by bluebell or heather, spurge or whin?"

"For my part, I must confess, lord, I never … well, I never had occasion to consider such sentience a property of my world," said Oriana still struggling to find even the smallest amount of comfort in his fur from the driving rain and billowing filth. "Not once, ever, have I heard such wonders of my home. Thereby, I never imagined a state so purposive could there exist. I thought it only a quality of those realms you have shewn me—that of our first meeting and of the Wood of Adjoining."

"That is what you assumed, yes," he remarked firmly, "that such things could not be in your world. Always are assumptions humbled by the unknown. Remember my words, 'Here in this realm are you at home and away.' And so you are."

Oriana mulled these ideas around in her mind for several minutes. Could her world have such a voice? Could her world have such song? Was it similarly sentient? Could her world actually be aware as the Wood of Adjoining? Despite her love for all things green and growing in her world, indeed the things she loved best, maybe she had never taken the trouble to open her heart and listen?

"Sire, I believe I never considered such wonders as I had no indication of such reality. Unhappily, I have never heard the fields and woods of my home in song."

"'For everything, absolutely everything, above and below, visible and invisible got started in Him and finds its purpose in Him,' quoth the prophets of your world, did they not?"

"Er…yes. Yes, I know the verse you mean," she returned, after taking a few moments to think about what these lines meant. "Yes, such is written and accepted as true."

"And did they not also saith, 'We fix our eyes not on what is seen, but on what is unseen. For what is seen is temporary, but what is unseen is eternal'?"

"Quite, Sire," agreed Oriana.

"Hence we might well add to these verses the *heard* and *unheard* as well! The *unheard* has purpose in Him; the *unheard* is eternal. And so I ask you now, because such wonders, as you say, were not *heard* in your world, they therefore cannot exist? Is this a just appraisal of your view of things?"

"No, Sire—indeed, no!" said Oriana emphatically.

After a brief pause the stag continued. "This may help you better understand the full nature of your world beyond its mere physical properties. Let us return to our discussion of ideas, but not to their origins this time. Think on this for a moment: Have you ever seen an idea?"

What an unusual question. She closed her eyes, searching for a new image that did not involve her parallel lines or Penda's stones.

"Well, Sire, I think I may have an example for you," she replied, not wholly confident in what she was about to say but continuing with her thought just the same. "Just yesterday afternoon—I think it was yesterday—at any rate, Penda suggested we go riding. And so we ran to the stables with that purpose in mind."

"Yes? What of this?" asked the stag keenly, continuing his slow wade.

"Well, that was his idea. I saw and heard him make the suggestion. We ran together. I experienced his idea."

"Nay! Not his idea, small one!" he rebuked swiftly. "He alone experienced the idea. You must realize ideas are very private matters. They like to keep to themselves, in a manner of your speech. You experienced the *expression* of his idea, the *manifestation* of his idea. But you did not see the idea itself. How could you? Ideas are not comprised of what the Ancients[1] in your world once called *matter*. Ideas are not material."

"Oh! I think I understand you, Sire!" she responded with sudden epiphany. "I merely experienced him acting upon his idea. Yes?"

"Precisely!" said the stag approvingly. "And so as is true for

---

[1] This is a reference to such ancient Greek philosophers as Leucippus, Democritus, and later, Aristotle, all of whom theorized the atom as a basis for matter as a separate realm of being from mind and spirit, which are non-material.

our example of ideas so does this truth hold for all that weaves through the fabric of your world. Being exists and phenomena occur that you will never come to know if you trust to your senses only."

"I am beginning to understand your lesson, Sire," said Oriana, a little more emboldened, despite the discouraging wind and rain. "Just because I do not hear my world in song, I oughtn't to assume such singing is not possible, just as man believes in the existence of his soul, for instance, without ever having seen it, or—or believing, he has ideas when an idea has never been seen. These unseen things are just as real."

"Splendid!" he said with affirmation. "But if you accept all this to be true, why doubt the possibility that your world may indeed be expressing hope *in that singing*? Why doubt the world's desire for its own betterment, the restoration of its original purpose—the purpose to live *with* man, *for* man as his provider, not *in spite* of man, the purpose to give freely, lovingly to man. Bethink you the world brought into being to be ravaged by the hands of avarice and might?"

"No, never, indeed, I do not."

"Then, I ask you again, why doubt the world longs for this restoration?"

"I should not doubt, Sire," she owned at once. "You are right. It is wrong of me to make such assumptions, though I suspect it might be difficult for me to convince others in my world of this truth."

She was referring to Penda, of course!

"Why should it be difficult?" he asked with an incredulous tone. "Did not the Great One say unto your kind, 'Blessed are they who have not seen and yet believe'?"

"Indeed, Sire! He certainly did!"

"Perhaps this will bring some greater measure of clarity," he said with a contemplative air. "Allow me to put my question to you in a different way. What if I were to ask you if you believed there was hope *for* your world, hope for the restoration of that perfect state He ordained for it?"

Oriana was silent in thought for several moments. "Ah, yes!" she exclaimed with sudden understanding. "Of course! How could I be so blind? This dark is no excuse for a blind mind. You mean the hope that the world might be protected from falling into the state of these wastes? I understand you, Sire. Indeed what an unhappy … forlorn … Godless place this is," added Oriana, staring with disgust through the dark and stench.

"You are nearing understanding, young one, but you are not fully there. Do you recall my earlier words? I sang of man's sins before we entered the Wood of Adjoining. Part of the answer to the Mundi Rediendum lies in that verse—a verse entrusted to me many ages ago."

Suddenly, at these words, the storm broke fully upon them. Freezing rain began to lash at them in driving sheets. In a moment, Oriana was submerged in the icy rills bearing down upon them. Along with the rain, the fouled wind too grew all the angrier. It was now a mighty gale of rotting breath, shoving at them with brutish force. Even with the protection of the enchanted wash and wine, Oriana began to shiver from cold and wet.

Hence their progress began to slacken considerably the stag himself, nearly stumbling several times.

Oriana closed her eyes again, which little changed her sight, buried her face as deeply into the stag's neck as possible, and tried to dwell only on his wisdom. Sighing for even the least of shelter and a short rest, she did all she could under the circumstances to fortify her mind and body from the besieging wet and reek of this world.

"The verse?" she asked herself.

O the misery! Oriana was completely drenched. Yet Lord

Whitethorn seemed indifferent to his being soaked. But was he soaked? Oriana couldn't tell.

After a long pause she said, shouting through the wind, "Yes, I have it now, I think. You sang, 'Tew tears and blood tew redress sin.' By that I take it you mean man's sins against one another. The world falls ever ill when we harm one another, yes? The world suffers by our pride or avarice for instance, or through such wickedness as murder or betrayal. Is that the answer?"

"You stand upon the threshold of all we now seek, but you have yet crossed over to that truth. We must recall these lines as well:

> Eve chanced fate; that fruit she took,
> Such knowledge was forbidden.
> Shame and fear fell over all,
> Then hallowed disk was riven.
> Pride and greed marred deep green earth:
> A second, sundering blow.

"Verily," the stag went on, "is it through sin that your world withers alongside many other worlds in sad company. But not through man's evil against one another is your world in peril."

The storm was howling and swirling so furiously it seemed to be contriving against both their advance and their words. But the stag would not be intimidated.

"There is a final point I think worth consideration," he called through the rain. "Tell me, what is the nature of sin?"

"Well," sighed Oriana, struggling to give voice to her thoughts, "Father Oswald has always instructed that ... that sin is when we act deliberately in a way contrary to His ... His great will—acts of wilful disobedience."

"Very succinctly put." The stag was changing their direction once again. Within a few strides, Oriana noticed they were emerging from the spattering depths of the stagnant meres. So did they now at last tread upon more solid ground.

Ahead, Oriana could dimly see a flattened hummock opening before them. Dead grasses there were, sealed beneath the same mounds of hideous refuse.

"The priest," he went on, "has given you truth, and you have accepted his gift. This is good. So ask yourself, has not Miðgard also been given to you and your kind, freely, as another gift? Would you not agree that your world is His creation, an act of His holy will?"

"Yes, lord, wholeheartedly. Completely!" she shouted to be heard. "Who would not acknowledge such blessings in this ruin?"

Oriana coughed several deep coughs, to purge her lungs of the obnoxious smoke. She was beginning to think herself nearly done in from the misery of this realm. The smoke and pungency of rot and molding dung hung yet around her as an unseen reminder of its ruin.

"So now I ask you, would it therefore not follow that if man set to ruin Miðgard, the very world of His creation, the world of His will, whether through his own design or in heeding some false promptings of the enemy, that too would be tantamount to what you and I regard as sin?"

"Yes, absolutely, Sire. All that you say is beyond question. There can be no other view of things!" she conceded, shivering and sniffling. What was her misery! "I...I can only say in my defence that, until this very instant, I have never had such..." It was storming too furiously to allow of her continuing in speech much longer. "I've never had such thoughts or visions revealed to me. Yes, Sire, I believe it would be a sin to wantonly ruin that which He has created. But again, lord," she drawled heavily, "is it possible that the world could be ruined at the hands of man? I freely admit we destroy one another at a will. Our appetite for war and conquest seems sometimes insatiable—our own campaigns against Danes and Britons, for example, attest to this, but the world itself? How could such devastation be wrought?"

The stag came at last to a halt. "Can you not conceive of such possibilities even here among this dying land?"

"Perhaps here, and only here, can I think of such a realm, yes," replied Oriana despondently. "The dark and filth of these moors suggest the work of daemons, but surely not of man. And so, Sire, I say but one place comes to mind—Hel, if I must put a name to it."

"Not Hel itself," returned the stag stanchly, "but one of its spreading dominions. Say, rather, this ruin is unto the likeness of Malgorod, for such has it become. We shall see if man is capable of such atrocities. But now, now has the heavy hour come for you! It is time for you to dismount and chuse as you may."

CHAPTER 10

"... Or all as Beech"

Oriana stood shivering in the dark, filthy, cold, and exhausted. And as she was no longer seated upon the stag, she hadn't the advantage of his healing touch. A draggled, wretch of a creature she felt, blind in the black of this world, drenched, and still largely uninformed. He said the time had come at last, but time for what exactly? Despite their discourse on the Mundi Rediendum, she still had no clear understanding of what this was. Presently, all she knew for certain was it had something to do with the world's returning to its natural state and that it needed reviving as a result of man's sins against it.

But what of it? What was she to do about such things? And what was she meant to do now? She still had received no instruction. Her ignorance made her feel empty and alone, even naked in spite of evening's dark cover. And in this nakedness, she sensed her own vulnerability, an unwary fly winging perilously toward a web unseen.

"You are now in danger, small one," called the stag darkly through the slashing rain. "As our touch is now severed, so too is the protective enchantment also broken. Now will our enemy's search be made easier if they know but where to look. Yet we must take that chance. The time for stealth is passed. We must act."

Oriana watched as the stag hurried over to what looked like a large circular mound reaching up from the dead grasses. It was nearly as tall as she. She squinted at the odd hump as the stag dropt something from his mouth on top its jagged surface.

"Ah!" she said to herself. "The sycamore bark—in this dark, I'd nearly forgotten he was still carrying them."

The stag turned to Oriana. Fey and grim he suddenly looked. "You may want to cover you ears," he warned, "I expect this is going to be loud."

"Oh, my stars, what now?" she said, just as she threw cupped hands over her ears. The wind and rain were already howling with such anger she could scarce imagine what noise could rival it short of thunder.

Just as she had seen him do at Sycamore Henge, the great stag jumped to his hind hoofs and threw back his enormous head. And then, with terrifying force, he hurled his antlers downward, smiting the top of the mound like the sledge of a smith striking his anvil.

"*Enough!*" The whole world was filled with the loudest, lowest, and longest rumble imaginable.

What a noise it was! And it had come from his antlers! It boomed many times greater than the greatest thunder clasp she had ever heard. If you have a good enough imagination to picture a tuning fork the size of the tallest skyscrapper in your world striking an equally large block of wood, you would have a near notion of the sound his antlers produced just then; that is to say, if your imaginary tuning fork could also produce words!

Oriana guessed there would have been lasting damage to her hearing had she not heeded the stag's suggestion and promptly covered her ears. But she wished he would have also advised her to sit, for the concussion of the impact knocked her hard onto her already-bruising bottom.

Long the word *enough* echoed over and over as if the wide waste was roused slowly from its slumber in angry agreement of the stag's condemnation. At length the booming echoes drew faint then trailed off utterly into the dark and howling storm. And exactly as his voice began to fade, another curious thing occurred. The white slivers of sycamore bark began to glow ever brighter and fierce atop the small hill.

"Oh! I can see now," she said with disgust. "Why it's … it's no mound at all. It's a—How brutal! Who could have done such a thing! It's despicable!"

Oriana could even make out the type in the spreading light of the sycamore slivers. It was the stump of a colossal beech. The signs could be plainly read. It had been intentionally felled with many cruel axe strokes while yet strong with green life.

"What a tree it must have been!" Indeed it was so large, Oriana could well have lain across its surface with her arms stretched overhead like a diver and still not have met its diameter.

Gently, he bent the tips of his antlers to the glowing bark. "Enough of their ruin! Enough of this despair," he called in a deep, melancholy tone, as though in answer to the fen's reverberating cry of woe.

No sooner had he spoken these words than the glow from the strands of bark began to flow outward to fill the whole of the trunk's surface, its top now a translucent pool of molten silver—a repository of collected moon-glow it looked.

The stag bent down yet again and, as he had done at the elderflower thicket, breathed over the shimmering surface.

"*Solestitia*! Vanquish the dark!" commanded the stag in a voice terrifying in its resolve. He breathed again upon the trunk.

What a wonder! Just then a dazzling shaft of silver radiance shot up from the chipped surface of the stump. Light spiraled upward like a spinning corkscrew with all the ferocity of a twisting cyclone, stretching not from sky to earth, but in the reverse rather, as if lifting up to ravage the dark above.

Slowly, Oriana picked herself up and watched, to her amazement, as the winding light pierced the heavy, sagging clouds. Instantly the driving wind and rain ceased. And then quick as thinking, the clouds rolled back in on themselves till the evening sky was released from its dark oppressor. The rotting odour of the rubbish heaps too gave way as if swept clean by the rising light.

With the clouds and stench went also the winding beacon of light. In an instant, the luminous vortex detached from its base, flew upward with a terrific force of suction, then flattened in the sky in wide whirling spirals like a floating maelstrom. Spinning with ever gathering speed, it condensed smaller and smaller, collapsing in on itself until it spiraled down to a single point and vanished altogether.

So the light from the slain beech was gone. But it was not the end of light itself. For by this time, the moon had come and was at his full, shining down like a great silver dish.

What had been glimpsed only for a moment in the earlier lightening flashes lay now fully revealed before her. Of course,

Oriana was relieved the raging tempest was no longer battering her, but she could not say she felt now much better.

What a sight, what an awful sight! A nightmare in full wakefulness!

Oriana threw her hands to her mouth. She was mortified. The slaying of the giant beech was one thing, but this! This! It eclipsed the loss of the beech many times over.

Oriana plumped herself back down on the blackened sedge, sinking her face into her hands.

"I am sorry for you, dear one," drawled the stag sadly, seating himself betwixt Oriana and the enormous stump. He looked tired. "Deeper is their ruin than ever I had supposed. Could we have proceeded in blindness, I would not have summoned the moon. But the need for his shine is absolute."

Oriana lifted her head. She peered through the gaps in her fingers. She made the spaces a little wider. Oh! she could not bring herself to look fully upon it.

It lay ahead of them by less than a hundred feet. It was the hawthorn tree of her tapestry—the hawthorn of the stag's world! Or was it? All wrong it was. It did not look as it should. It was even larger than she would have expected, nearly as large as the felled beech must have once been, and it was completely beset on all sides by an impenetrable hedge of hideous blackthorn. As a bulwark set to deny passage the blackthorn seemed. But it was not the sight of the choking hedge upsetting her most—

"Come. We haven't much time." The stag retrieved the sycamore bark from the stump and headed toward the hawthorn. Oriana started to her feet as in a dream state, and followed him across the blackened hummock of shriveled rushes.

The moon had traveled high enough to peer directly down upon the wide ruin. Under his cold radiance, Oriana and the stag came now and stood before the great hawthorn and its black barrier.

"It's dead!" thought Oriana horrified, feeling suddenly as if death might soon be reaching out to her as well.

Yes, it was dead. And to Oriana, it looked as if it had happened fairly recently. It had been burnt, badly burnt, almost beyond recognition. What little remained of its lower branches were bending mournfully into the grotesque brambles of blackthorn below.

She then surveyed the top of the tree. This may have been the grizzliest sight yet. Its upper branches had been mutilated. Down the centre of its crown a wide path had been cleaved to allow passage of three of the countless rusting cords webbing the night sky from their broken crosses.

All at once Oriana saw something she was surprized hadn't sooner captured her notice. In her anguish over the slain hawthorn, she had ignored the pungent smoke still hanging thick in the air. The smoke had not left with the other obnoxious fumes—and now did she understand why. She beheld its source!

Behind the hawthorn, by little more than a mile at most, rose four devilish-looking towers. Each was many times the height of the oldest tree of Oakleigh Manor. And they were wide. She imagined their gaping jaws at the top could easily swallow the space of Oakleigh's large fishpond several times over. It appeared that her earlier guess of tall shaft furnaces hadn't been too far removed from the truth. They were belching foul purple dross high in the air hurrying to take the place of the departed storm clouds.

Oriana turned from the towers and blackened hawthorn and gazed about in anguish. Now did she begin to understand at last: for under the fullness of the moon's light Oriana saw that the fate of the beech and hawthorn were no isolated acts of brutality. Amidst the countless articles of strange floating refuse and leaning crosses were untold numbers of mangled stumps, their thick rinds cracked and rotting. Twisted limbs and severed crowns by the thousands lay also hurled upon the earth like old bones stript of meat. It then occurred to Oriana that these clumps of broken tree limbs and rubbish were the strange hillocks she had dimly noticed earlier in the storm's dark.

Oriana turned to the stag. Grief was in his eyes. She was speechless.

"Yes, dear one," he said gravely. "Now do you gain understanding. The Festering Fens had once been a realm of life, a joyous forest blessed with its own song, but it is no longer singing; now only echoes remain. Verily was the whole of this world once a great wooded realm. What now remains only as the Wood of Adjoining had once filled the far greater Omphalos Wood—the wood at the centre of worlds uncounted. It is here, and here alone, at the very navel of this ruin, where the Mundi Rediendum must begin."

And in all that ruin, Oriana could not help but feel the hawthorn was the most grievous loss of all. Why did she have such an affinity for this tree? Why was her life bound to it and Lord Whitethorn, thereby?

"Is it *the* tree, lord? *The* hawthorn?" asked Oriana eventually, returning her eyes to the sad sight of it, "the one of my tapestry and your realm?"

"That remains to be seen. What shall become of it depends on your choice. Come."

They crossed to the tangles of blackthorn. When Oriana came to the edge, she saw that it was more than twice her height, its dead branches bent with many shriveled and poisonous-looking sloes hanging beneath. As far as one could tell in the soft glow of moonlight, the dense barrier looked doubly thick as tall, giving every indication that naught could penetrate it, let him be as small as the smallest vole!

"Through the blackthorn does the first of your choices lie," said the stag with a grim expression.

"But how, Sire?" asked Oriana much bewildered. "This hedge is a most formidable obstacle. There isn't the slightest gap."

The stag did not reply. She thought for a moment.

"Perhaps if we walk around it, we'll find some way through," she suggested in a falsely optimistic tenor.

"Perhaps," he answered with a slight nod.

"Maybe there's a narrow breach in it, somewhere I might be able to squeeze through." So saying, Oriana skirted round the barrier for a careful search then, finding no way through, doubled back in the other direction. She soon realized there was going to be no weak point at all in this defence.

"What I wouldn't give to have Durendal[1] right now," she muttered, staring at the impossible task ahead. "Very well then, I suppose there's nothing for it but to try and force my way through these tangles."

Carefully, Oriana attempted to bend one of the branches downward to squeeze through. But, as she soon found out, it would scarcely budge. Oriana then pulled with a will, harder and harder, but do what she could, it did not the least good in the end, and, in spite of her caution, she managed to hook her elbow on one of the terrible thorns. It started to bleed.

"Oh, pooh!' she cried, her elbow now stinging. "This is no good at all! I'll never get through this beastly hedge."

She turned to her guide. He looked back blankly, saying nothing.

"Right then, let me think," she said, staring up at the moon. The poisonous green and purple clouds were reaching out ever farther from the towers to blot his gentle glow.

"There must be a way," she went on, now on the verge of owning herself finally beaten. "Why else would I have been brought

---

[1]   Durendal was her father's ring-hilted, pattern-welded sword. It was given to him by King Athelstan himself during the ceremony of Lord Phillip's investiture as alderman and royal tutor. Nothing was ever seen of Lord Phillip's blade after his disappearance at Brunanburh.

here if not to find a way through? But how?" Oriana was beginning to fear they had come all this way just to be disappointed
by her failure in the end.

And then, "Wait—fear!" she said excitedly. "Fear is the clue—
it's in your verse!" she said to him.

It *was* fear Oriana felt! But it wasn't just the fear of failure;
she feared the very look of these groping thorns.

It was with this thought that Oriana recited a portion of the
stag's verse:

> *Fear no blackthorn! Come hawthorn!*
> *To secret path, sing you must,*
> *Ere faceless foe devours,*
> *All sweet life and leaves but dust,*
> *Upon last mournful hour.*

"That's it!" she cried. "There must be a concealed path through
this hedge. The instruction! I must sing!"

The stag was smiling with great enthusiasm.

"But what am I to sing?" she puzzled. "What song could work
enchantment over a hedge?" Oriana pressed her fingers to her
temples, as she was wont to do when quick decisions were in
order.

"What ought I to sing to a thicket?" she continued "What to
sing? What to sing?"

She considered and considered, until, "Maybe … maybe, what
would sing to a thicket?" she wondered. And then, "Not to a
thicket, on a thicket!" She was closing in on her answer. "A song
bird!"

She had almost forgotten the happy singing of bird laughter
in this strange realm utterly devoid of beast or bird.

"And of their sweet company, whose music is fairest? The
thrush nightingale, of course! That's it! My strange whistling to
Éohmane, that's what it had sounded like—a nightingale."

And at this, just as she had done to snap the fiery stallion from his mad fit, Oriana raised her fingers to her lips and warbled the same series of soothing notes.

Whish! Crack! Snap! The melody of high chirpings shot through the hedge, cutting a wide path like a giant billhook as it went. Branches, flinders, and thorns flew into the air, exposing an open path leading straight to the charred trunk of the hawthorn.

Oriana stood gaping at the power she just commanded, her heart pounding with triumph. It was much more shocking and impressive than her influence over Éohmane had been.

"Excellent!" extolled the stag, nodding briskly. "Well done, daughter of worlds twain. Again I see our faith in you has not been misplaced. Your strength begins to bud. Soon will it be in full blossom. Can you not now begin to understand your importance to this quest? For I, myself, knew not how we were to proceed. It is ordained that we all must shoulder our burdens and face our appointed tasks. The way through the blackthorn was for you to discover, not I. You have done very well indeed."

"Thank you, Sire," answered Oriana still flummoxed by what she had just done. "Only, please do not ask me *how* I did it."

"You needn't worry," laughed the stag, "I will not ask this of you. Nor is there such need. You will discover the depth of your inner song in your own time. Come now! We must enter. And you must lead."

Oriana walked warily between the looming walls of groping thorns. Even in death, the blackthorn barrier seemed aware of their passing—and that awareness was contempt.

There stood the hawthorn, its hollow trunk cleft wide. It was a sad scene. The bottom had been burnt even worse than the upper half rising above the blackthorn hedge. She wondered how long it had lingered in such torment before finally passing. Her heart was heavy with grief.

Oriana stared perplexed at the deep crack. She knew it well, and not merely from the image of her tapestry or even from her brief time spent in the stag's world. She had been near it before—very near it.

Her next impulse was to ask her guide what she was to do next, but realized at once how little would be gained of any asking—for this was her moment; the answer was for her to uncover. And so she asked nothing of him at all.

Oriana reached the trunk and peered inside its dark chamber. There was just enough moon-glow filtering through the fissures and holes of the charred wood to discern the space within. She thought the interior large enough to serve as a rabbit's warren or possibly a den for martrons or brocks or—

"Or even a cradle for a baby," she thought to herself. At once, Oriana was struck by yet another of her own odd notions.

She continued surveying the tiny chamber for some sign, something that might lend itself to instruction. As she leant in for a better look, Oriana reached up, placing her hand on the charred bark along the edge of the opening. Instantly, she felt a curious sensation similar to when she had first laid hands upon Lord Whitethorn. She was given a tiny jolt of sorely needed hope. It was not the overwhelming surge she had felt upon his back, yet hope it was still.

"I say! They are related," sighed Oriana, considering again the significance of his name. She withdrew her touch and turned to Lord Whitethorn to see if she could find the tree's resemblance in him—

But as she turned, Oriana was met with sudden dread. Lord Whitethorn wasn't there! He should have been right there behind her in the blackthorn pass. But he wasn't; he wasn't anywhere!

"Master!" cried Oriana at the top of her voice, her stomach dropping into emptiness. "Lord Whitethorn! Where are you?" she shouted again doing her level best not to panic.

There was no answer. Fast as she could, Oriana tore back through the pass and looked all around till her vision was strained. The great white stag was nowhere to be seen, nowhere at all. Her great white guide and protector was gone!

Part Two

The Dragaica Bride

CHAPTER II

Skulls from Above

"No, Oriana, positively not," she scolded herself. "You are not to cry. It won't help matters in the least."

But she was so very afraid. She could have easily cried, and nearly did.

Oriana was all alone, stranded and unfriended at the very centre of the most dismal land she had ever known—the dead wastes of the Festering Fens. And to crown all, she still had her errand before her, something very important—but what? Lord Whitethorn hadn't said. All she knew for certain was she had to make a choice—two choices, in fact. But between what alternatives and to what ends?

"Saints preserve me! Where's he gone?" she said, feeling even more wretched than she had in the wind and heavy downpour. Her knees went weak. She felt faint with fear and exhaustion. Had you been there yourself, you would have had the good sense and manners to help Oriana to your comfortable reading chair and offer a cup of tea to steady her nerves. But of course, you are not there, nor are there such pleasant things as reading chairs or Tetley in the Festering Fens, as I daresay you probably know.

Oriana, to own the truth, still hadn't quite got over her fright from the ordeal at the Anwash, and now with Lord Whitethorn's vanishing, she was completely terrified. She felt more vulnerable than ever, knowing it was only a matter of time before he of the sinister laughter would return. Deep down there was a small voice, a grim foreboding, telling her she should have known things might come to this in the end. Lately, it seemed she could never rely on those she loved to be there for her in times of need. It was her father going missing all over again! More likely than not, it was this recurring fear of loss that had made her so anxious every time she lost sight of Lord Whitethorn in the forest.

Presently, as Oriana wondered what was to be done next, three curious things happened almost at once. Loud cracklings and snaps sounding suddenly from the blackthorn enclosure put an end to her musings. She spun round sharply. The terrible walls of thorns were closing in on the path! Whatever she had done to prise apart the fiendish hedge was now waning.

What was she to do, all alone and without aid or advice? Where was she to go? What was she to think?

But there was no time for thought. She had to act!

Her heart spoke. Like summer lightening, Oriana darted back through the shrinking corridor toward the hawthorn. And it was well that she happened to be looking down as she sped or she would have missed them in the dark. She stopt abruptly! There on the ground between her feet, right in the middle of the path, lay the two slivers of sycamore bark. For the third time, she had forgotten all about them.

"Then he had followed me in," she said in that moment of consternation. "But I wonder, did he mislay them by some accident or leave them intentionally?"

Quickly, but gently, even reverently, she lifted the white sheaves of bark.

"What's this?" she said curiously.

Something shiny was on top of both—something small and twinkling, reflecting the full moon above. They looked as liquid droplets of purest pearl, each about the size of a wee barleycorn.

Oriana could speculate no further. For the very next thing she knew a large grey moth, speckled white, was flying straight toward her much faster than a moth ought to be flying. In fact, it was a great deal more like a mighty peregrine diving for his prey. It flew entirely too fast for Oriana to ward off. But fortunately, she hadn't needed to. Seconds before colliding into her, it alighted atop a particularly long thorn, its wings splayed wide apart. It sat eerily still.

A deathly chill clutched Oriana. The same icy fear she had felt along the banks of the Anwash was upon her.

"I've seen this dreadful thing before. I'm sure of it! But where?"

To Oriana's left and right, the towering walls of black needles were closing in ever apace. She would soon be consumed in a torment beyond any description you would care to read.

"That's it! The morning of the feast, at my window...and...and—Great Guthrum's guile! Of course! Éohmane! The grey moth at the stables! Brond said it entered just as he went mad."

Try as she did, Oriana found she could not avert her gaze from the white spots on the moth's wings. She was transfixed, incapable of drawing back.

Suddenly, Oriana gasped in horror. "They're no spots at all. Why, they're—they're skulls!"

In an instant, there was a second identical moth just next to it on a thorn of its own and then a third and a fourth, their number increasing every moment. From the corner of both eyes, she saw a great swarm pelting down from the sky like ashen-grey hale.

Then, to Oriana's complete bewilderment, there came a high-pitched, crackled voice from inside the hawthorn's trunk, sounding as if crossing a great distance:

"Orie! Are you mental? Run for it!"

That voice! Oriana thought she should be able to recognize it but could not.

And then, as though in answer to the warning call, "Stay! You disgusting crossbreed," commanded a deadly voice she knew all too well. It was a voice she knew she must honour. "Attend to me or your filthy white guide shall not be spared!" It was the voice of the fell laughter, taunting her from somewhere within the closing blackthorn! He had come again, and he was no longer laughing!

"*Oriana!* Don't listen to his rot! Make for the tree! Hurry!"

The cruel hedge was now but feet from shutting tight.

"I must submit," whispered Oriana as the moonlit world dissolved grey before her eyes. A gathering fog was beginning to rise from the surrounding fens.

"Of course you will obey," he hissed malignantly. "You have no choice, have you? You who bring ignominy and ruin, you are an abomination to being itself—"

Oriana's mind seared with the burn of his icy voice.

"The witching hour draws nigh. Reach out to my servants, and I shall take you in. I am now your only hope. Do it not and you shall repent it, for both you and your guide shall come to no good end."

Oriana did as she was commanded. She stretched out her hand to touch the moth nearest her. For there was nothing else that could be done.

"*Orie!* For Frig's sake, don't touch that thing! Get inside, hurry!"

"But I must—"

"Do it now! Touch my flesh!" he hissed vehemently.

"Come on, Orie! It's perfect! Think! One cracked trunk for a half-cracked nutlet."

"Nutlet?" she thought. That did it! Oriana was brought back to her senses. In that single, perfectly absurd word, Oriana's heart grew light, recalling in a flash all the love she bore for her friend. Oriana had regained her wits and her will.

Quick as thought itself, Oriana withdrew her hand just before touching the vile wing and scuttered back down the closing hedge. In she went, squeezing herself sideways through the hawthorn's trunk.

Snap! Exactly as she pulled her foot to safety, the blackthorn hedge clamped shut like the jaws of a giant Venus flytrap, completely sealing Oriana inside.

Oriana knew not what to expect. She bore the faintest hope she might see her friend, Penda, waiting for her inside. But, sadly, and to be honest, expectedly, he was not there.

Oriana, of course, had never been sealed up inside a tree before, nor had she ever given thought to what such an experience might be like. But then if she had, she never would have dreamt of this, never in four or forty fortnights of Fridays!

At once, Oriana put aside thoughts of the brutal hedge and the enemy mustering just beyond its enclosure. She was even too much astonished to ponder the whereabouts of Lord Whitethorn or how Penda was able to call her to safety. She could think now of none of these things, for now—now! There were ever so many marvels before her!

CHAPTER 12

"Tew" Tears and Blood

Oriana found herself crouched at the edge of a cavernous hall filled with a silvery light several times brighter than ordinary moonshine. Slowly, tremulously, she got to her feet. She was staring up at an immense dome of charred and dangling timbers, utterly lost in amazement, the moon plainly to be seen through the splintery cracks. In fact, were the walls and crumbling roof not of wood, Oriana would have guessed this a giant's cave, just as those described in her favourite childhood tales. It was certainly wide enough and tall enough to be a deep underground cavern. As an ant Oriana felt, staring up at the inside of a scorched drinking bowl flipped upside down.

"Greetings, Oriana of Oakleigh," said the most beautiful being Oriana had ever met with or would ever again behold, a being as lovely as the day itself. "I bid you welcome. Come, step into the light."

Oriana was at once struck motionless, unable to budge for fear. She did not step forward as asked. She stood perfectly still in the soft soil, dumb with astonishment.

Ahead, a glorious wonder beckoned to Oriana from the centre of the hall. It was a lady—perhaps?—seated upon a most curious throne and bathed in a glow of silvern brilliance. Oriana was utterly bereft of words and very nearly all her breath in addition.

What a marvel she was—of such surpassing, such seraphic beauty, and yet somehow incomplete in form. On the one hand she did not appear to be fully corporeal, not wholly in the world of physical space. Yet neither did she have the look of a phantom. Her very being appeared to teeter on the narrowest edge between the material and spiritual worlds, not amorphous but not completely solid either. Numinous was her aspect, even terrifying in the awe she effected in Oriana.

"Don't just stand there gawking on the stoop, my child. In you come!" she commanded to Oriana, gently but inexorably. It was the loveliest voice Oriana ever heard or ever would hear again. This time Oriana obeyed, edging her way cautiously nearer.

"Surely a goddess she must be!" thought Oriana. For the lady exuded, in her one person, every attribute of such beings Oriana had ever read about in her father's ancient texts. In that first moment, Oriana thought the lady shone with all the beauty of Aphrodite, whilst yet possessing all the fierceness of Artemis. She calmed with the wholesomeness of Hestia but daunted with the deep wisdom of Athena and severity of Hera.

Her raiment further spoke to her divinity, arrayed as she was in a vibrant hanseline, looking of woven flower petals and threaded gossamer—no dress could be lovelier. Upon her head— no, floating just inches above, rather, was a slow spinning halo-like coronet inclosing her brow with five spectacular jewels. Each gem was the size of a walnut and scintillated its own hue of gold, silver, yellow, blue, and red. And the lady was tall, close to Oriana's height and probably a little taller. Yet what was positively uncanny indeed was the lady's hair. It was the express image of Oriana's hair in every particular—the same colour down to the last strand, with even the same wavy texture to match.

And there was her throne too! Oriana's wonder increased. Such a throne! Such a wonder! Oriana couldn't help but goggle at it, for it was just as wondrous as the great lady herself. Exquisite it was, tall and ornate; Oriana doubted any emperor ever possessed a finer one. Yet it was clear at a glance that no carpenter could have crafted it. Though it was in shape similar to all wooden thrones, comprised of individual timbers, cunningly joined and shaped, what made it unique lay in how the individual pieces gave no appearance they had been cut from any tree. For the timbers were themselves yet living—reaching, coiling, and visibly breathing! Each delicate piece of wooden tracery seemed to be borrowed somehow from its mother tree, not hewn or hacked, but simply loaned while still alive so that it might be joined with other like members to form a new living whole in their union. Indeed the lady's throne was a living work of craftsmanship, roots, bark, leaves, and all! "If ever a thing belongs to the realm Lord Whitethorn called Faërie," she said to herself, "this surely must."

And there, flanking either side of her throne, were two identical, deeply engraved wooden columns, imbued with the same curious life essence as the throne. They towered thrice the height of the high-back throne in the likeness of great gnarled peepul roots reaching up out of the soil. Though the columns' entwined tracery was similar in many respects to the living throne, it reminded Oriana of the illuminated artistry she had once seen on the venerated Lindisfarne Gospels[1] some years back. Strange though it was, she couldn't help wondering if the crowded spirals and fantastically complex interlace on these pillars were somehow the inspiration that had once guided the hand and mind of the manuscript's artist.

It would not be well at all to avoid describing what rested atop each column—an immense crystalline orb filled with the

---

[1] Having been occupied for two hundred forty years, the monastery at Lindisfarne was abandoned by its community in 875 just before its total destruction at the hands of Danish invaders. In their flight the monks brought with them the body of their most revered saint, St. Cuthbert, along with other treasures including the priceless Lindisfarne Gospels and the legendary sword of St. Cuthbert. After wandering for eight years, the monastic community settled finally at Chester-le-Street in the shire of Northumberland.

compressed shimmering of moonlight. For indeed, they looked as miniature moons themselves held firmly aloft by a multitude of thin, woody fingers stretching up from the rootish columns. It was obvious at a glance that it was the light of these orbs flooding the doomed hall and immersing the lady in its tremulous shine.

"You cannot begin to imagine how long I have awaited this moment," said the great lady, fixing Oriana with her tender and yet terrible eyes. Oriana stood now in the silvern light of the large orbs, only feet away from where the wondrous demigod sat surveying her.

"Ah! how lovely you have thriven; such remarkable beauty. And your eyes! What a strong likeness, exactly as I had wished! So very like the king's eyes are they!"

"The king's eyes?" wondered Oriana quite taken aback. "What king? King Athelstan? Why should my eyes resemble his?"

"Now tell me, my child, for I must know, why come you alone?" she asked in a concerned way. "Where is your conductor, the great heorot?

But Oriana still could not answer straightaway. Her mind was reeling. She remained speechless, her eyes bent on the jewels dancing above the lady's fair head.

"I must warn her, the moths—the enemy," thought Oriana, but instead could only splutter, "I...I..." totally tongue-tied, her mouth having gone all dry for wonder and fear.

"Come, come. None of that now, my sweet," said the lady gently. "You need not fear me or my hall. You have entered the Seed of Life, where worlds shall be renewed. No harm can come to you while you are in my keeping."

"I...I thank you, Your Majesty," whispered Oriana most timidly at last, her heart in her throat all this time. She knelt and lowered her head as she had been taught to do upon her first introduction to King Athelstan.

"Arise, my dear," the lady said, her severe eyes boring steadily into Oriana. "You must not prostrate yourself before me. The innocence of your heart perceives majesty where none exists. Nay, child, kneel not before me. Indeed, were it possible for me to rise and duly welcome you as you well merit, it would be I who bowed before you."

"Bow to me?" wondered Oriana at these words. And just as soon as she set herself to pondering this odd comment, she then considered, "What does she mean if she could rise? Is she lame?"

Upon closer observation of the throne and its occupant, the answer at once impressed itself upon her mind. Things were not as she first supposed. Apart from the lady's lips and eyes no other part of her body was moving—not an inch.

Now she understood. It was horrible! The throne was not a refinement, not a thing meant for the pleasuring of royalty at all. No! In fact, the lady seemed to have actually melded with it. Its stretching branches were growing into and passing out through her not-quite-translucent, not-quite-solid form. O! What a perfect reversal of perception it was. What Oriana had just regarded as a marvel of ethereal and likely faërie workmanship, now seemed altogether diabolical.

This could mean but one thing—this was no hall at all. It was a dungeon! "I seek then your pardon, my lady," begged Oriana, rising to her feet. She was beginning to subdue her fear though in awe still of the lady and her hall. She would now warn her of the gathering enemy and Lord Whitethorn's disappearance.

But suddenly she didn't feel so well. Maybe she stood up too quickly or maybe it was the sum fatigue of journeying and marveling catching her up. Whatever the cause, Oriana nearly swooned as she rose. She tottered and staggered backwards but soon regained her posture. She was nearly at rope's end from fatigue, filth, and fright. Remembering Lord Whitethorn's advice, she searched within for the last vestiges of wash and wine but soon discovered they too were now fully exhausted just as she.

"My dear child!" cried the lady lamentably. "You are in need of rest and victuals after such exertions, to say nothing of a bath." Closing her eyes, she paused for some time. She seemed to be sunk in deep thought, drawing perhaps on some long, half-forgotten memory.

Minute after weary minute passed by and then:

"Ah! To bathe," continued the lady with mournful intonation. "Seeing you, my sweet, puts me in mind of feelings I had thought died out of me! 'Tis such a distant memory! What I would not give to revisit the far-off delights of bathing with elven maids in spring's morning dew! How the snows did melt soft upon the hills! Indulgence! Sweet indulgence!"

The lady took a deep breath, saying at length, "But alack, I have no such comforts to offer you. O heartache! O anguish!" she cried suddenly. "Now I am met with the last and greatest of my torments: to be unable to aid the one I love."

Oriana looked on in pity and confusion as tears began to well in the lady's eyes and thought, "The one she loves?" Oriana was dumbstruck.

"Yes! I must! I shall!" shouted the lady at once, still as if she were talking to herself. "I have long wondered what I might say when finally in your presence. Now I see your purity, there is no other course for me to follow."

Her words were growing ever swift.

"I shall not keep this truth from you," she continued with an air of self-reproach. "Nay! Nay! Before I avail myself of your confidence, you must know the truth. Yes, I will tell you. My shame shall not be concealed from you, not from you, my sweet.

"From my sins do worlds uncounted face ruin so imminent and despair so certain," she continued on the brink of tears. "Yet only now in the sight of your sufferings do I understand the final reach of his cruel deception. O misery! O torment! That you should bear my punishment! Curse the day that made me captive to his designs! Curse it, I say!"

Oriana weighed the lady's comments silently. "Her sins? His deception? Whatever does she mean by all this?"

"For I knew in my heart," maundered the great lady rapidly, "that He on high would refuse to sanction our union. But I cared not. I did not listen. Selfishly did I obey my desires and open all my heart to him. You can have no idea how afflicted I was by his betrayal. Oh! How wretchedly I have suffered!"

Oriana thought the lady's ramblings sounded of one who has gone a very long time indeed without speaking to any other living soul, so muddled they were. "Yet it is I who bears the blame. I should have perceived he was not to be trusted, but ever is passion a corruptor of judgment. Such was my failing."

Oriana was so exhausted she felt beyond the point of working out the meaning of any more mysteries. She wished to simply lie down for a long, well-deserved slumber and wake with all the unusual occurrences of the past week, fair and foul alike, well behind her.

"But come," resumed the lady after a pause, "our time is too short to recount all my sins—we must turn to matters at hand. The hour is come, Oriana of Oakleigh. The Mundi Rediendum must now be set in motion! So tell me, how came you to enter my hall without the white heorot? Great is his need here. Come, tell me, where is your guide?"

Oriana took a deep swallow to pluck up what little courage she possessed. She cleared her throat. "I was just about to tell you, my lady. He has not come, he—" But she cut herself short. Something distracted her.

Just then, Oriana noticed a yellow-green light beginning to rise from the earth, encircling her and the great lady in a wide glowing ring.

"Wait a minute," thought Oriana. "That's not right. Why did I say that? He had come with me. He was captured. I must warn her—"

"This is very shocking, most distressing news, I am sure," said the lady, her eyes alit with worry. "I expected to see you enter the Seed of Life together. The need for the heorot's presence is absolute. He knows this himself! For the Lay of Ethélfleda clearly states:

> O hoary head, tall points so keen,
> Grim tidings you must give
> To purest heart, then make haste,
> By wood and wash and fens of waste.
> Dragaica Bride! O Litha maid!
> Solestitia Eve!
> Guide and thee in Seed of Life,
> Atone for others' ruin rife.

Steadily, the yellow-green glow forming a circle around Oriana and the lady grew stronger. And it was changing. Oriana could see shapes, tall figures perhaps they were, emerging from the wreath of light. All the while, Oriana heard a low humming issuing from the moon globes crowning the woody columns.

Oddly enough, the lady, to Oriana's great surprize, seemed disinterested in these things.

"It is a great mystery how you have come to enter my domain when he has not," said the lady, her narrowing eyes betraying her shock at the stag's missing. "Pray continue. Am I to believe you have traveled all this distance from our precious Miðgard to the hidden omphalos of renewal without his guidance?"

Oriana shook her head. "Nay, my lady!" She continued gazing side to side in wonder at the new light enveloping them. "That is not my meaning at all. Forgive me, my lady. It must be my weariness. I have been unclear."

Oriana was certainly astonied at the morphing green nimbus

and rising hum of moonlight, but still more was she perplexed why the great lady had yet to take even the slightest interest in this curiosity. Was she perhaps unaware of it?

"Your verse speaks truly," said Oriana earnestly. "Twice has Lord Whitethorn come to me bearing frightful tidings, which, I confess, I still do not fully understand. He has guided me through the Wood of Adjoining, to the Anwash and elderberry thicket, and through storm and stench of these fens. But for his defence, my lady, I should have fallen permanently under the black incantations of the ... the Lych-priest; such was Lord Whitethorn's name for the evil that assailed me. I fear this same foe may now hold him captive."

"*What?*" cried the lady, her eyes lit with alarm. "You were assailed by one of the dreaded four? The fleshless apostates are come? Here to the World of Adjoining? It is not possible!"

"That was what Lord Whitethorn seemed to believe at first," returned Oriana hurriedly. "The attack came as a very great shock to him too."

"This is unimaginable. Where did this attack occur, my child?" she asked quickly.

"Along the banks of the Anwash ... well, a tributary of it, so Lord Whitethorn said it was."

"*The Anwash!*" she bellowed in astonishment even louder than before, her voice echoing deep in the hall. And for a split-second, Oriana thought the lady's arms had twitched despite the penetrating interlace of groping switches holding her fast.

"Your tale grows ever more difficult to accept. The Anwash is the very source of the Adjoining's secrecy. Its waters are the most sacrosanct of beings in this realm. If you could be assailed there—" She did not complete her sentence. She seemed flush with sudden dread.

To be sure, the lady's fear, in combination with her own certainty of the enemy's mustering, made Oriana feel very far from safe here, despite the lady's earlier assurance of protection.

"Continue, child," resumed the great lady. "In what manner did the enemy attack? Did he present himself in form or spirit only?"

"He attacked in spirit alone, but that proved more than enough, my lady. It was horrible. He defiled my soul with the vilest bewitchments of despair and resentment and hatred. He even threatened me with … with—"

But just as the lady had done, Oriana too could not bring herself to complete her thought. She fell suddenly mute. In this, the lady's eyes shewed interest at once, her searing gaze attempting to tease the answer from Oriana's silence.

"Say on," pled the lady urgently.

After a pause Oriana breathed deeply. "In the end, Lord Whitethorn succeeded in casting out the enemy. It was a bitter contest of wills. I felt nearly crushed under the weight of their struggle."

"This is evil hearing, my child," she cried nervously. "How in the nearly infinite number of counterfeits has the enemy located the true Omphalos Wood? How? How? Where our counsels have erred I cannot begin to suppose."

Both fell silent. Brighter, ever brighter and more distinct the yellow-green light was growing around them.

"When, my child?" asked the lady eventually. "When did our foe return?"

"Haven't I already said? Just heavens! I haven't!" cried Oriana. "Here! Here! Just moments ago—just as we approached the hawthorn! A thousand pardons, my lady; forgive me my dalliance. I don't know what has come over me. It must be their bewitchment again, clouding my mind. I meant to warn you as soon as I arrived but—"

"*The enemy? Here at the Seed of Life?*" she shouted in a tone betwixt fear and anger and contempt. The twigs and vines of the lady's throne began to writhe as though in response to her shock. "Go on, dear. Tell me all."

"They're here, my lady. Just beyond your hall!" exclaimed Oriana again. "As soon as we were about to enter, I turned to ask Lord Whitethorn a question and discovered him missing. He just vanished into thin air. It was then that the enemy came. A host of devilish-looking moths descended from the sky and held me in their spell."

"Moths, you say? Did they bear skulls?"

"Yes, my lady," she answered fretfully. "They were grotesque."

"Flesh-seekers!"

"That was when his terrible voice came to me again," continued Oriana. "He exhorted me to obey his commands or Lord Whitethorn would perish. That's when I heard my friend, Penda. It was the sound of his voice that delivered me from their evil. It sounded like he was calling from inside the tree."

"Oh, my lady! Please tell me, whatever must we do? Without Lord Whitethorn's protection I feel utterly defenceless. I am very much afraid."

"I cannot imagine what has gone wrong, my child," said the lady mildly, not meeting Oriana's eyes. "Nor can I find reason for why I do not sense the enemy's presence. If they have beleaguered the gates of my realm, here, as we speak—I just cannot understand this."

The lady closed her eyes again and said nothing. Oriana stood puzzling—puzzling at everything. In the first place, the great lady! Who was she? Why would a being so seemingly divine as she be condemned to such torment? What could she have done to warrant it? In the second place, it appeared the lady bore just as great a part in this strange business as Lord Whitethorn himself, and yet, she too seemed caught completely at unawares by the enemy's presence. And on top of all these things, Oriana was still very much bewildered over the curious ring of chartreuse light surrounding them and why the great lady with all her strength and wisdom continued to give no notice of it whatsoever.

"I think I may have it," said the lady in due course, opening her eyes and staring intently at Oriana. "Tell me what this devil said to you at the Anwash. Tell me all. You said he threatened you. What was this threat?"

Oriana did not like this question at all. She hoped it had been avoided altogether. The memory of the enemy's threat made her very uncomfortable. It made her feel unclean—as unclean on the inside as she presently was on the outside.

She withdrew her eyes from the lady and, as she was not in the least disposed to say more, looked down at her tattered kirtle, muttering, "I have got myself very grimy indeed. It will never come clean."

For the next few seconds Oriana stared and stalled...stalled and stared, until, "Look into my eyes, my sweet," insisted the lady, bending her eyes sternly on Oriana. "It may be indelicate to insist, but you must tell me, however painful it may be. Be not afraid, not here under my ward. As long as I sit in the Seed of Life, no harm shall come to you. Now tell me, what did the enemy say to you?"

It was a memory she hoped to forever suppress, but feeling obliged to do as the lady asked, Oriana recalled his black words despite its pain.

"He taunted me with dreadful images—most of which concerned my father. And then,"—Oriana breathed deeply— "he threatened me with—"

There was a pause.

"Go on. What were these threats?"

"I cannot repeat them," she said, her voice quivering. "Please do not make me say. I dared not even mention it to Lord Whitethorn himself."

The lady stared at Oriana severely. "*You must tell me,*" she then demanded with an intonation one wouldn't dare contemplate disobeying. "I do not wish to importune, my child, but his threats may help explain the heorot's disappearance."

"Very well, if it must be known. He was hissing and laughing at me... he threatened that—that I would be taken bodily. He laughed and promised I would be ravished with such violence that I should never be able to bear fruit. He warned that a flame would be set to my womb, reducing my Seed of Life to ashes and—" Oriana stopt herself mid sentence. She felt as one who's just had a bucket of ice water dumped over her head.

"The devil! Take no heed of his threats, my child. Such is the like of the dread apostates. Much of their power is spawned from the fear they instill in their victims. Now come; think no more of it—"

"My lady!" cried Oriana in reply, her breathing intensifying. "Your hall! The Seed of Life! That was his meaning! It must be. I mistook it to be a threat against my person, but it wasn't. Our enemy seeks to thwart the Mundi Rediendum. Lord Whitethorn said so himself. This is how they intend to go about it. He's the one responsible for burning your hall, he must be."

"The burning of—whatever do you mean, child?" remonstrated the lady in tones of dismay. "Recalling the enemy's assault on you darkens your thoughts, I see."

"That's got to be the answer, my lady," continued Oriana with a heaving bosom. "Don't you see? He set a flame to this hall before we arrived. Even Lord Whitethorn did not expect to see it so ruined. He said the enemy might be waiting for us. On the other hand, the enemy did say *my* womb, *my* seed of life? Still it must—"

"My darling, I fear you are yet belyched!" said the lady quite sharply. "The Seed of Life is impervious to ruin. It cannot be touched."

"I beg your pardon again, my lady," returned Oriana startled by the lady's sudden annoyance, "but I must take exception to this. What of the scorching all about us? Even from the outside the hawthorn is barely recognizable."

"Hawthorn? Whatever do you mean?"

"Why your tree, of course, my lady—even from within it looks on the verge of imminent collapse—"

"Desist, my child! Desist! Why do you seek to distress me?" cried the lady, though making some effort to resume her earlier calm. "You mustn't say such impudent—such, such falsities. Open your eyes fully and see, my child! The Seed of Life is a realm of green and life. It is immaculate. Just as lush as upon my arrival; it is unchanged. The last remnant of the garden of Granusion it is."

"Then you do not see this hall as I, my lady?" inquired Oriana meekly. "What of the blackened timbers and wide fissures? Can you not see the moon peering in through the cracks above?"

"I should say I certainly do not!" insisted the lady implacably, clearly still vexed at Oriana's persistence though managing to restrain her voice. "You are indeed mistaken, I'm sure!"

"I crave your pardon then once again, my lady; I mean no impiety, but it seems one of us is under some dark enchantment. I would happily submit it is I who has fallen victim to our enemy's conjuring were it not for Lord Whitethorn's own observations. He himself beheld the ruin of the hawthorn just as I."

It appeared the lady was now in her deepest anguish yet. Gradually she opened her eyes wide and, forcing back her tears, drawled in a shaky voice:

"Oh, sweet Oriana! I am at a loss for answers. Nothing is transpiring as it has been foretold. The white heorot ought to be present and yet is not. The Seed of Life cannot be maimed, and yet you say it lies in ruin. Far and wide have the servants of the faceless foe sought the hiding of the white heorot and the omphalos of worldly return. Yet even their darkest sorcery could not give such advantage. Something has gone dreadfully wrong. We have been plotted against. That is the only answer! Someone has betrayed the Order of the Magi. But which guild I wonder?"

"The Order of the Magi!" wondered Oriana curiously. "Lord Whitethorn had himself mentioned this once. Who are they?"

At the sight of the lady's despair, Oriana grew increasingly troubled. She could feel what little resolve she still possessed beginning to vanish.

"What now, my lady? What's to be done now?" she asked again, feeling panic setting in. "What do you advise?"

Slow, very slow, was the lady to answer. "Nothing, my sweet—nothing is to be done. All is lost," was her pitiable reply. The lady was inconsolable as she fell now to weeping and wailing. "This means the very end to all our hopes and plans, you understand? Your errand is failed. For naught have you tholed through peril and pain. Now shall your world hurtle toward an age of darkness, of steely-waste, and ash, and hopelessness—a state contrary to my essence, a world of unnatural extension. As for me, I shall ever linger in this morrowless torment—for my duty was beneath the moon as His vice-regent, but I have proven faithless. Such is my just desert, but not yours, my sweet, not yours. You have a stout heart and have done your best, but all is up. Without the sacrifice of faërie flesh and the gift of the heorot's lamentations, the enemy is victorious."

As though in response to the lady's resignation, the dazzling chartreuse light swirling and steadily changing shape round them flashed suddenly and became complete. What had been but mere light was now linked hand in hand!

Scores of effervescent young women in yellow-dagged kirtles and emerald scarves thin and festive encircled Oriana and the lady in a wide ring. Adorned they were with golden chaplets on their heads and long necklaces of crystal dewdrops that jangled below their scarves as they danced. Their long sandy hair was lank and shot with green and argent silver strands. Each maid looked close to Oriana's age, though seeming to have passed those years in a world quite apart from her own, for Oriana had never seen girls as thoroughly halcyon as these. Indeed, the very sight of them lightened Oriana's heart, making her long for her younger, carefree days before her father was much away from home. And in their presence, she was reminded of the times she once danced in happy rings on the vigil of the Summer Solstice.

"Hang on," she thought presently. "Isn't that this evening? Dance in rings? A faërie ring! It must be. They must be! Surely they must be faërie maidens. Perhaps they are the daughters of this great lady, come to honour their mother."

Their dance ended. The young maids stood now perfectly silent and smiled at Oriana, appearing not in the least troubled by the great lady's present woe.

"What a marvel," Oriana whispered to herself. "Lord Whitethorn, the great lady, and now these wondrously fair maids—how narrow minded I have been my whole life. I suppose the old peasants' tales are true after all! Oh, Father, how I wish I could tell you my mind is indeed now open to much wider possibilities. I never should have doubted the beliefs of our good villagers."

The maids continued to smile at Oriana, but the great lady was herself not smiling. She sat with eyes closed. Hers was the sad visage of defeat.

"All the unmarked years, all the ages I have passed, lost in my grief," she told Oriana in the lugubrious manner of one whose mind was elsewhere, "all the secret counsels of magi and faërie folk, all your toil and my hope for absolution have been for naught..."

"We beg thy leave, O lady, of the blessed mortal realm," sang the girls together in perfect unison. Their voice was pure melody—a sublime fugue surpassing the finest of Gregorian chants. "But Lady Natura cannot see them. Needless is her despair. She knows not that you bear them still."

"Please! Who are you?" burst Oriana, her eyes darting from one young maid to the next, not knowing whom she should address. "I don't understand what is happening. The great lady, you mean? She is Lady Natura, *the* Lady Natura—the lady of worldly myth? The lady of Claudian and Statius?"[2]

"We know not of those named Claudian or Statius, but the lady who sits before thee truly was once Lady Natura," continued the maids in song. "That was before her choice, before she fell. She is the lady no longer. Now she is but a lonely dryad, cursed and bound to the fate of her tree—the Omphalos Tree."

"And, please; who are you?"

"We are your kin from beyond the wide chasm. We have come to aid in the return. We come to sing the Dragaica and proclaim the Dragaica Bride."

"The what?" asked Oriana. Her head was swirling with dizzying unfamiliarity. "Did they say my kin?" she thought at the same time. "How can we be related?"

"The Dragaica—the song of summer's solstice," they answered in rising crescendos of harmony. "Now is the long-awaited vigil. We come to sing and dance and to serve—to serve thee, our lady. For thou art the chosen one; thou hast survived your abandonment. Now art thou to become the Dragaica Bride; for it is written: only the betrothed of the Mundi Rediendum may release Lady Natura from the Seed of Life. Behold! for it

---

[2] Publius Papinius Statius was a lyric and epic poet born in Naples in 45 AD. He later moved to Rome where he became a highly acclaimed court poet. In his major life work, the Thebaid, Lady Natura is personified as leading a crusade against that which is unnatural. Claudius Claudianus of Alexandria likewise moved to Rome in 395 and is regarded as the last of the great Latin poets. In his De Raptu Proserpina and De Consulatu Stilichonis, Lady Natura is similarly personified as a supernatural but subordinate being of aged beauty.

is also written that the Dragaica Bride must set free Ethélfleda, queen of fairest Danuvia."

"Look," retorted Oriana, perhaps a bit too sulky, but it couldn't be helped. "You must excuse my directness, but I have been told nothing of my part in any of this. I have been kept in complete ignorance, and I am at my wits' end," she went on desperately, hot tears welling in her eyes. "So please, do not suppose I know anything which may be of any service here to anyone, for I haven't. I no longer even know who I am, nor have I the least idea what I am meant to do about any of this!"

And at that, Oriana's spirit gave way. Poor Oriana! Utterly spent, unable to stand on her feet any longer, she plumped herself down in the soft earth with pardonable resignation. But just as she was about to give herself up to an agony of despair and bury her face in her hands for a private cry, she noticed she was yet holding the two strands of long sycamore bark.

"And without the breath of the white heorot," resumed the great lady whose continued despair seemed to know no bounds, "it is impossible for you to return to your world, my child. Yes, yes, impossible I say; for it was through his breath that you were brought to me—Ah, what's this? I do not reproach you, my dear. That's it, my love. Sit and have a good cry. I would join you if I were able. And then … then I would suggest a prayer. It is not for me to do, for my realm was beneath the moon and sphere of fire, but I linger in shame—I forsook my rightful place. Now am I condemned and have no voice. Pray to Him who resides beyond the Stellatum, beyond the Primum Mobile, He who dwells in the eternal light."

"If you please, our lady, we know what ails the great dryad. If you would but reveal them to her," continued the maids in song, "she sees them not. She sees only that which belongs to her world. So long as you bear the faërie flesh, she sees naught but you. You must separate: thou from the flesh."

Oriana had not exaggerated when she declared she felt in utter ignorance of these matters. And when she let go the sycamore bark, she did so in the expectation of absolutely nothing. But nothing is not what occurred!

At the very moment the bark fell to the soil, two spectacular beams of light shot with a resounding hum from the orbs of moon-glow.

"How extraordinary!" exclaimed the great lady as a joyous light came into her face. "It's a miracle!" She was no longer in the throws of despair. She began to rejoice! "The faërie flesh and the white heorot—he has grieved my Gwendolyn. You have them, my child! You have been truly blessed. What a gift you have received! It is a miracle, I say!"

For when Oriana relaxed her hold on the white bark, each of the giant moonstones cast a tiny arc of silver light down upon the sycamore bark, laving the ground in drenching waves of rippling moonlight.

"The Silver Causeway!" exclaimed Oriana jubilantly. "They look precisely the same, only smaller. Of course! That's it. They must be bridging another world!"

Presently, so many things were happening that Oriana could scarce keep track of them all.

Next to the slivers of bark, a young shoot broke the earth and began reaching up from the soil as if an entire growing season were squeezed into a few seconds. With the blink of any eye the shoot had sprouted into a small hawthorn sapling with a single white primrose in full blossom.

"Now! Oriana of Oakleigh, we haven't a moment to lose," implored the great lady in booming tones.

But despite the echoing volume of her command, Oriana nearly missed what she had said. For at the same time, the ring of young maidens began to sing anew, swaying back and forth hand in hand. And their song was not now as it had been. No longer were their voices sweetened with their blissful fugue.

"*Solestitia Litha Ukon Juhla Lunae Lux. Solestitia Litha Ukon Juhla Lunae Lux.*" Over and over, the faërie maids sang such a mournful dirge as made Oriana feel at once sorrowful, the sort of deep and numbing sorrow one suffers at the unexpected passing of a loved one.

Oriana's mind was in tumult. The great lady was joyful, ecstatic over the sudden good fortune. Yet the young maids were in obvious mourning. Why were they?

"Hurry, my child," commanded the lady again. "The time is now. Lay aside your doubt and fear. Truly are you the chosen Dragaica. The witching hour is upon us. Complete your errand before it is passed."

Oriana was about to entreat to the lady that she hadn't a clue what she was to do next, but at that very moment, she noticed, to her very great astonishment, that she was no longer wearing her filthy blue peasant kirtle. Oriana was now arrayed in snow-white petals in the form of a wedding gown. It was similar to the hanseline of the great lady, but of pure white. And she was perfectly clean!

"It must be the faërie maids' singing," she said to herself just then. "I feel ablution in every note—their voice cleanses as the Anwash."

And then, Oriana felt something resting upon her head. She reached up. It was a wreath of interwoven wheat. She replaced it immediately.

"*Solestitia Litha Ukon Juhla Lunae Lux. Solestitia Litha Ukon Juhla Lunae Lux,*" sang the choir of faërie maidens.

Precisely when Oriana replaced her wheaten anademe, she noticed two curious articles lying next to the hawthorn sapling. One was a dagger of purest jacinth crystal—blade, handle, pommel, and all. The other was an ordinary wooden spade.

Oriana knew not what Lady Natura nor the faërie maids meant by chosen Dragaica, or why she was now attired as a bride, or what these objects were meant for—but she was not disheartened. There was dire urgency in both the lady's command and the maids' mournful plea. And in these Oriana found her readiness to complete the task. With roused application, she straightened herself to her full height and stared intently into the lady's eyes, awaiting her instruction.

She waited. She waited some more. What was her agonizing state of suspense! For there was yet no instruction! The maidens were continuing their requiem while the lady, in turn, simply bore down on Oriana with eyes awful in their anxiety.

"This is completely maddening—madness out of mind!" thought Oriana with overwhelming frustration. "How can I possibly know what's to be done, when I've been kept in the dark about these matters? Why didn't Lord White—wait! Maybe he did!"

Oriana began to draw on her memory again. But suddenly she felt something wasn't quite right. She struggled. It was happening again! Evil was reaching out to her mind. It felt a cold, clasping hand, rotting and deceitful, smothering her mind, stifling the memories she needed most. It had come! It was here; the very dread which had been over her ever since her attack near the Anwash.

"Fight it, Oriana; fight it," she thought determinedly. "You know whose vile touch this is. Don't let him block your thoughts. Think! What had Lord Whitethorn said?"

Oriana stared at the young hawthorn with its single, lovely flower. The flower had five petals. It was so beautiful, so fragile—the only green and growing thing she had seen in this realm of waste. It was the only sign of hope, indeed, the only thing worth preserving. It should be—no—it *must* be, tended and nurtured, loved and nourished so that one day its progenitors, in all their multitude, might one day cover this world of ruin with ever spreading leaf and flower and hope.

"I have it!" yelled Oriana out loud. "I remember!

> *Ill-fated rose, new star for each,*
> *Slain and buried for death to reach;*
> *A sacrifice so worlds might teach.*
> *And then thy choice; pixie pear or all as beech?*

Yes, she had it. And what she had, what now confronted Oriana was a moral dilemma. This delicate, delightfully musk-scented rose was the one in the verse. It was the ill-fated rose, and it had to be sacrificed. An awful choice lay before her.

"What a perverse choice," she grumbled to herself. "Would they have me destroy the one thing worth preserving in this world of ruin? Surely this can't be right! Why destroy this single ray of hope? Why destroy this? Why not the belching towers of filth? Why not the fiendish crosses? Why can't they be sacrificed—why can't they be the things destroyed?"

Oriana of course knew the answer to these questions, just as surely as do you. Destroying these things would be no sacrifice at all. Oriana knew perfectly well that a true sacrifice is when we will to lose the very things most precious to us. And of all things valuable in any world, the wonders of creation are the most precious above all else. To rid the world of filth and dominion would be a pleasure, not a sacrifice.

"Make the first of choices, my child," said the great lady serenely but emphatically. "The trysted hour hastens to elapse."

Oriana was always loath to destroy any form of life. At home, she never cared for what some regarded as the thrill of the hunt, despite her skill with a bow. She often wondered if Lord Elgar and his retainers derived pleasure from the satisfaction of procuring needed meat for the village or from the mere act of slaying their prey. She always hoped it was not the latter.

Oriana picked up the crystal dagger. In gripping its handle, Oriana was in turn gript with an incontestable truth—all life necessarily comes of pain, then struggles, and then, in the end, must perish from the living world.

"But why? Why is the natural state of being so cruel? So iniquitous?" she wondered with sudden existential doubt. "One must die so another may live? Is life naught but pain and struggle and then ending? Why? Why must the very order of things, the balance of life be so savage, so ruthless—so unjust?"

Oriana brought the edge of the crystal blade to the base of the sapling, her eyes watering. She moved her hand to strike. She wavered for a moment.

"Precious yearling! Daughter of worlds twain! I implore you—stay!" It was the voice of Lord Whitethorn reverberating through the domed hall. Oriana quickly glared around, yet the great white stag was nowhere to be seen. "Do not this evil deed! You have been deceived."

"Young one," his voice continued. "You sense that the sacrifice is regrettable. You stay your hand from disdain of killing without need. You are wise and merciful, but the need is great and you must chuse."

Yes, this was also Lord Whitethorn's voice, yet his words seemed now to contradict what he had just commanded.

"You must not do this deed. Do you not recall my words? *'For you, daughter of worlds twain, the perils of the Primrose Path await: the path to certain deception. And when the heavy hour comes you must have a care.'* This is that heavy hour! Now is it come! If you destroy this life, all that you love in your world will share its fate."

As Oriana stood hesitating, she knew she had to chuse and chuse quickly.

"The portal is closing, my child," urged the lady, her eyes flashing beseechingly. "Opportunity passes."

Oriana gazed up from the flower to the lady. She noticed that the five glowing gems floating about her head were growing ever dimmer.

"Innocent one! You do not delight in killing. Decide for yourself, but needful is the right choice. Should you chuse poorly, should the Mundi Rediendum never dawn, a day will come when man will utterly devour his world, the mountains and seas and meads of sublime wonder. And it shall come to pass without remorse, for it shall come at the hand of progress."

"Lies, young one!" the stag insisted. "Heed not this calumny. Do not allow your mind to be deceived by the enemy's sophistry. You must do as I command! Protect the life before you."

"If there should come a day of such ruin," he continued ruthfully, "man shall be well prepared to pass through the gates of Hel, for by their deeds will they have already rendered their world fit for the denizens of Hel's domain. For Malgorod shall his world have become!"

"Lies! Deceit! With guile the enemy speaks! The perils of the Primrose Path are before you. Do you not recall? I said by your choice may he of the fell laughter return. Lay down the blade! Destroy this life, and he will come for you. You will be in greatest peril. You must by no means commit this evil or forever shall you rue your choice."

Oriana clutched her forehead in angst. What was the right choice? Both seemed the right thing to do. How was she to know? Oh, how bewildering and maddening it all was! What was she to do?

She thought—quickly she thought. And then by great good luck, just as she was nearing the breaking point of her nerves and sanity, she hit upon something else Lord Whitethorn had once said:

"Such is the precarious nature of a will that is free."

It was true! Free will was precarious. Though one is free to chuse, those choices are often bound to, or in reaction against the erstwhile decisions of others. How often are one's present choices guided in response to the wise or foolish decisions made by those who come before us?

Precarious or no, independent or circumstantial, her will was her own. Lord Whitethorn understood this. He had never insisted she obey his commands—to merely do as she was told. Not once had he given direct injunctions; he only advised, suggested. He never demanded she do anything! Her will was free—free to chuse.

No longer could Oriana respite—no further thoughts had she to spare for her choice. Without delay, Oriana observed the dictates of her mind rather than her fancy, chusing the course most difficult, the course so opposed to her deepest scruples.

Her hands were trembling. Again she raised the crystal blade and with a single slash the young hawthorn lay dead by her side.

It was a ghoulish sight. To see the only fair thing in all this waste now also in ruin, slain at her hands, was agonizing. She hoped she had not chosen evilly.

Silence fell. The opposing voices of Lord Whitethorn were no more. And as if in response to her choice, the lady's hall began to quake with a frightful violence, crumbling and cracking worse than ever. It would give way any moment.

"*Solestitia Litha Ukon Juhla Lunae Lux. Solestitia Litha Ukon Juhla Lunae Lux,*" resumed the maidens just then. For reasons of their own, they had not concluded their dolourous chant. It was plain by their urgency—there was more still to be done.

"Right! Now what was the rest of it?" she thought quickly. The answer came to her none too soon.

"That's it! 'O withered-haw, unhappy grin. Tew tears and blood tew redress sin.' But to whose tears do I turn? The lady's tears? She had shed tears when I arrived. And to whose blood?

No blood has been shed—well, just my elbow by the blackthorn hedge."

Now when Oriana had first listened to the stag recite the verse, "tew tears and blood," that was precisely what she heard, "tew." She did not, of course, have the benefit of seeing the word spelt as "two," as you had first seen it and have no doubt already worked out the answer.

The hall was beginning to rain even larger chunks of charred timber. The arcing light of the twin causeways was also ebbing. But the light was just enough for Oriana to notice, once again, the two crystalline drops yet clinging to the sycamore bark.

Oriana picked up the bark, scrutinizing the tiny droplets of liquid pearl. She puzzled for a short space and then peered back at the great lady. Her eyes were closed. She was no longer speaking. And beneath each closed eye was a single teardrop.

"Think, Oriana! Drat it! What was it? What did she just say?" On and on she wracked her memory, staring still very intently at the lady's tears.

"Of course!" she said at once. "That's it! 'Without the sacrifice of faërie flesh and the gift of the heorot's lamentations the enemy is victorious.' The gift of Lord Whitethorn's lamentations—she said he grieved her Gwendolyn. Lamentations—grieving— she means his tears! By Alfred, that's it! The two droplets on the bark, they're his tears. Ugh! Oriana! You numbskull! *Two* drops—it isn't 'to' tears and blood it's *two*, the number— 'Two tears and blood.'"

"*Solestitia Litha Ukon Juhla Lunae Lux. Solestitia Litha Ukon Juhla Lunae Lux*"

Oriana lost no time. Grabbing the wooden spade, she dug up the remaining roots of the sacrificed hawthorn and dibbled down deeper yet. Gently, she placed the dead sapling and its wilting white rose into the earth.

"I hope I get this right," said Oriana anxiously to herself, all over shaking with worry of wrong choices.

Atop the white primrose, Oriana interred the white slivers of sycamore bark in the loose soil.

"*Two tears and blood.*' Well, I just thought as much, myself— all life comes of pain."

Suddenly, Oriana twisted round with a jump! There, just to her left was a table-sized plank of charred wood that had just flaked off from the ceiling nearly crushing her beneath. How would she ever survive this destruction?

Now in a terrific twitter, Oriana turned her gaze to the young maidens yet singing hand in hand. "I certainly can't ask it of them. Besides, they did call me the Chosen One, the Dragaica Bride, whatever that means." Oriana took a deep breath. "Right then! There's nothing else to be done."

Oriana picked up the dagger and, clenching her teeth, pricked her thumb and ring finger. Pressing the two together, she dript two drops of blood over the tiny earthen mound. In a sudden flash of yellow-green light, the faërie maids were gone, and with them went also the tormented spirit of Lady Natura, vanishing in a silvery puff of smoke from her throne.

"Victory! My child, it is done!" called the lady's voice through the noise of crashing timbers; it was a departing voice, a dissipating tone as of one calling ever lower from behind a wooded hill. "You have procured my deliverance. I am eternally grateful to you. No longer am I confined to Llynarian's seed. As I now speak to you, my spirit draws closer to its rightful abode beneath the moon. My penance is at an end. I go now to my rightful place whence I never should have left. Once had I provided man with abundance; once when my spirit alone was wed to Danuvia, O sweet Faërie, how gentle was your silver touch! Of all matrimony under the Maker's eye, Miðgard and Danuvia was the fairest!"

It was getting worse. More and ever larger timbers were now crashing all about Oriana. She would be crushed any moment.

"I return, my child; I go to edify those who yet listen for my song and believe. For Miðgard the Mundi Rediendum comes! Now shall the wielders of Worldsong be emboldened with renewed strength and deeper understanding, for now are these needed more than ever. Fire! Water! Rock! Wind! You are directionless no more.

"Now behold, my child, behold! Prepare your nuptials. Go and see!"

Crack! Oriana glared above. A slab of burnt timbers the size of a cottage roof was hurtling down directly on top of her. There was no escape!

But then, just moments after the second drop of her blood met the earth, there came a second blaze of consuming light. At once Oriana felt herself whisked away from death's door in a blanket of soft white.

CHAPTER 13

Of Petals and Beards

"Have I died?" wondered Oriana in a hazy twilight state deprived of nearly all her senses. "Gracious! What has become of me?"

She was dismayed. Her body was touching absolutely nothing at all; in fact she wasn't even certain she still possessed a body. Not a sound to speak of could be heard; there was naught to experience, which is to say there was naught but a consuming white light that soothed and warmed.

Perhaps she was only dreaming? No, this didn't feel like any dream she'd ever had. Maybe she was waking from a dream? Ah! That seemed far more likely; she did feel well rested. And at some point she must have eaten a most excellent and fulsome supper too for she was no longer hungry.

"How all so very odd this is!"

By-and-by the white light began to diffuse. Now could she see movement at last, distinct forms and colours materializing all about her, especially beneath her. Then there came a sudden whiffling and whirling of wind, too. In fact, it looked like … and it sounded like … like the world was flying up at her. She was falling!

From what mere sight and sound suggested, that was certainly a reasonable impression. And Oriana would have screamed a truly frightful scream had she not felt at once that no air was rushing about her. Actually she was standing quite motionless and not falling at all.

Just then, the memory of the trial at the lady's hall, the Seed of Life, washed over her.

"Have I done it? Is my task over?"

Oriana was in great hopes that in this spell-like state she might be returning to her home. After all she had completed all that needed doing, hadn't she? Had she not faced the heavy hour and made her choice? Had she not reasoned her way through the enemy's deception—the Primrose Path as Lord Whitethorn had warned? Was that not what he had meant: her decision to sacrifice the only fair thing in that world of waste for some higher, albeit elusive, good? Did her choice not release Lady Natura and set into motion the Mundi Rediendum that was to save her own world from some impending doom? Her task, her quest was completed, right?

"Then again," Oriana told herself uncertainly, "didn't Lady Natura say that was merely the first of choices? And hadn't Lord Whitethorn himself also mentioned two choices awaited me? Well, at least the heavy hour is passed. Of that there can be no doubt."

At these reflections Oriana noticed her clothes. She was once again donning her blue gown—well, what had once been her blue gown. It was now very nearly all black, still begrimed with the disgusting filth of progress.

Perhaps this was the sign. She was no longer wearing the ceremonial wedding gown. Perhaps when the spell of swirling light lifted, as she so desperately dared to hope, she might find herself sitting comfortably by the hearth in her room.

◇◇

At last the dazzling aura was gone. Finally could Oriana see clearly. But what she saw disappointed greatly, for she was not seated on her high-back bench where she and Penda once sat warming their feet. She knew this was too much to hope for.

"What can this be? Where am I?"

Oriana found herself in a lush garden under a bright sun shining younger and many times gladder than the sun of her world. But Oriana could not say she was *standing* in the garden as she initially supposed. Rather, she appeared to be hovering just inches above the ground in spite of the fact her feet were telling her she was standing quite firm upon some solid, if unseen, surface.

Oriana stared unblinking, marveling yet again at this new wonder!

What was slowly being revealed to Oriana was a realm completely without blemish. What she *felt* was a world that had never known shame.

The garden was filled with the plumpest of fruits, crisp-looking vegetables, honeycombs dripping sweet-smelling ambrosia, and blackberries the size of cabbages. Though Oriana had of course never been to this precise spot, she had experienced the essence of this garden before, for it was replete with the same fullness and meaning of the stag's world. It bore a like wind that chattered through bough and happy leaf and was perfumed with a green fragrance heralding a purpose long ago ordained.

That was when she beheld the black serpent. He too had a purpose! He was dangling limply from the branch of an unusual looking tree at the centre of the garden. Oriana had never seen the like of this tree before. It seemed a mingling of every variety of tree she had ever seen and many more, she guessed, she hadn't. And then she noticed the tree had given life to a single, moist fruit glistening enticingly beneath the young sun.

"Wonder of wonders! It can't be." Oriana pondered as she pieced the images together. "It can't be *the* garden, can it? *The* event?"

But when Oriana saw the woman approach in all her innocence and nakedness, all doubt left her. "How beautiful and ageless she is. Yet I had always supposed her to be fair-skinned like myself. But this must be it. It must be her."

The woman stretched out her hand to the fruit. It was not an easy thing for Oriana to watch. For one thing, Oriana felt a strong connection with the woman's naivety and curiosity. To own the truth, it was empathy Oriana felt for her just then. From what she had read of this moment and what she now beheld in the lady's countenance, Oriana believed she understood this woman fully. What the unassuming maid desired was not power or riches, but simply to know, to gain wisdom. And what was wrong with that? Was not wisdom the highest pursuit? All men by nature desire knowledge; Aristotle had said so himself. Apart from her first desire to love and to be loved by a family of her own, were knowledge and wisdom not also what she herself sought beyond all other things? The introspection was disconcerting. Oriana did not like imagining herself in the woman's position. Would she have made a different choice in her stead?

The maid picked the fruit. Oriana wished she could have interceded, warning her of the serpent's deceits. But it was impossible. She learnt at once she was but a passive observer, unable to interact with any facet of this realm.

That's when something very strange indeed occurred. At the precise moment the maid bit the fruit, Oriana saw something she could not explain. The whole of her mind was filled with the single image of a white flower cracking along the edges of its five petals as though it were a thing of glass struck suddenly with violent intent.

◇◇◇◇◇◇◇◇◇◇◇◇◇◇◇◇◇◇◇◇◇◇◇◇◇◇◇◇◇◇◇◇

Whoosh! Oriana was whisked away from the garden and again enveloped in the warming white aura. For a second time, she saw shapes and colours and sounds swirling in all directions. This time, however, Oriana abandoned even the faintest hope that she might be returning to her home and loved ones. Oh! How very cruelly she missed her beloved Oakleigh Manor.

When at last the shroud of light cleared and her vision restored, Oriana found she had alighted softly amidst a gathering of rather wild-looking people drest in simple fur garments. They were seated round a large bonfire. Cool and brisk was the noon air, and the yellow-gold leaves of what sparse trees there were to be seen suggested midautumn.

The men were adorned with long necklaces of feathers and animal teeth as the women, in like manner, were festooned with brightly florid garlands. On the outskirts of the clearing was a cluster of matted-hide structures held upright with rough-hewn timbers and curiously large bones.

Stretched in all directions, as far as Oriana's eyes could reach, was a flat grassland strewn with yellow anemones, pink asphodels, and other untold wildflowers. The fields were teeming with butterflies, honeybees, and small gregarious birds that chattered and played.

Oriana floated just at the edge of the group, studying the odd gathering. None save the eldest of the band, whose eyes darted in Oriana's direction just as she appeared, took any notice of her arrival.

Oriana was stunned by the elder's glare. "Does he see me?" she wondered.

For a brief moment, she feared the elder might raise a cry at her presence, but after a couple seconds of hard staring and a concentrating expression, he too gradually returned to his business. He was principally occupied with flaking off tiny bits from the edge of a flint point with a small antler tool in a most methodical and meticulous manner. It was very fine craftsmanship, to be sure. Oriana assumed the worked stone to be the final touches of a spearhead, noticing a long wooden shaft leaning on a hunk of limestone beside him.

Everyone else just as busily devoted themselves to their tasks as to their laughter. Some of the men were minding a spit with, what was beyond any doubt, the largest roast Oriana had ever seen. She thought it smelt wonderful, despite the fact she really was no longer hungry. The other men were either fashioning similar stone implements as the elder or on their knees scraping hides that appeared to have been recently procured.

Not too far away at the corner of the group sat a small gathering of women nursing their young whilst discussing something evidently important given their attentiveness. And next to them were yet more women, some stitching hides together with short bone needles and long strands of sinew as others peeled and twisted fawn-coloured fibers into tight cords.

No one in the band seemed disinterested.

"True, primitive and untidy they certainly do look, but what does their appearance matter."

All were contented, even more than content: just as joyous as any people one would wish to see. For them there was nothing menial in providing the essentials for life and happiness. For them there was no abstraction to their work, their labours not a thing apart from their lives or their desires or from the very nature of life itself. Though it is likely some in your world might regard such physical labours as nothing short of toil and moil, it was plain these communal necessaries lent satisfaction, meaning, and purpose to their lives.

It was then that a rushing sound and barking of dogs was heard. Oriana spun round, thinking for sure she would be toppled over by a group of children running wildly. Had she been wholly in that world, she certainly would have been trampled underfoot. With sticks waving overhead, a dozen or more children were chasing after a pack of dogs yelping in close pursuit of three geese that had just landed in their camp.

The children ran right past three women sitting a little distance away from the rest of the camp who, presently, were bent over an infirm boy lying bloodied on a large bear skin, his side apparently gored by some tusked animal. They were applying a thick brown salve to his wound.

"What an unusual village this is," remarked Oriana, eyeing each person in turn. "Where are their crops and livestock? I wonder how they keep themselves."

Oriana then began wondering—and it was really much more to the point: "What is all of this anyway? Why am I being led to these places, the garden of gardens, and now this odd village too? What purpose can it have for me?"

It was at this last question that Oriana saw the lightening bolt strike sudden and quite near.

"And now lightening on a clear day? My, what wonders are being revealed to me!"

Even odder than lightening under a bright sun was the absence of a trailing thunder clasp. But even that was not the queerest thing, not by far. Exactly where the lightening smote the ground, an arc of silvery light vaulted from the earth, lifting ever skyward till eventually melting away into thin wisps of cloud.

Instantly all stopt what they were doing and gazed fixedly at the arc of silvery light now shaping into a colossal bridge. Clambering to their feet, men, women, young and old, began wailing and running wildly about.

At first Oriana guessed these simple people to be terrified by the supernatural marvel. But the longer she watched, the more it became clear their cries were not of panic but of celebration. And they weren't running at all; they were dancing, dancing and embracing one another as though recognizing this sight, welcoming its return.

Oriana's eyes traveled up to the arc of sterling radiance with a good measure of recognition. The glimmering lane was exactly as she had seen before—it was the Silver Causeway of her tapestry!

Then came a second swift flash high above! But no bolt of lightening was this. The flash came from atop the causeway precisely where it melted into the clouds—a wash of light as though someone had abruptly opened a door in a darkened hallway onto a dazzling, sun-drenched room. Though the wide lane looked but a single strand of silk where it touched the clouds, Oriana could nevertheless discern slow movement crossing its surface. Something was speeding downward from the sky.

In little time, it had become quite plain. It was glorious. Myth had sprung to life! A company of tall, radiant beings was hastening down the wide arc in bright two-wheeled wagons drawn by the most heavenly steeds. There could be but one explanation. They had come from Faërie; she just knew it! For so the flash atop the causeway *was* a door—a portal opened unto lands beyond.

Though the company numbered men only, Oriana knew them in an instant to be the kin of the fair young maids of Lady Natura's hall. For in their noble faces was the same light of unfading stars, and in their eyes, shone wisdom ancient and unyielding. Upon them was the visage of knowing—the knowing of mysteries to worlds young and old and secrets sought since time itself was conceived.

Oriana would have called their white steeds horses but for their graceful swan-like wings and single spiraled horns reaching out through their black forelocks. Each steed was bridled with gold fastenings hitched to a war-wagon[1] of crystal topaz and wheels of milky-white opal. Three tall riders shod in turquoise

---

[1] The Saxon tongue had no equivalent word for chariot; "war-wagon" was a fairly good synonym. Even the Great King Alfred himself used the compound "war-wagons" when translating Orosius' Seven Books of Histories against the Pagans to describe the chariots of Egypt's pharaohs. In a like manner, Alfred translated the city of Troy as a Saxon "burh," the Roman vestal virgins as "nuns," and the maritime exploits of Philip of Macedon as the seafaring adventures of a "Viking."

scale armour richly gemmed stood in each: one commanding the golden reigns from the centre as archers bearing emerald quivers and body-length, *S*-shaped bows stood vigilant on either side.

The whole camp was at once on its feet. Everywhere went the disquiet of expectancy. All in the band cheered or sobbed with joy over the approaching lords.

One by one the shimmering carts encircled the camp in a wide ring as though intentionally giving a wide berth to the jaunty gathering. From their wagons, they waved in gratitude of the clan's hearty welcome yet spoke nothing to them in return. Nor did any dismount—none save one only.

His was the last wagon to cross the threshold between silver and earth. He rode by himself though he was himself not alone. Beside him sat a large wooden box, simple and unadorned.

In he drove through the cordon of wagons, coming to a halt next to the roaring blaze. It was obvious to Oriana that he was their king, for as tall as the fair men were, he was taller and fairer still.

Oriana then noticed his eyes. She gasped. What shock! Oriana was stunned; for as similar as Lady Natura's hair was to her own so too were his eyes identical to hers—green, large, and widely spaced.

"The king's eyes!" she exclaimed completely thunderstruck. "Lady Natura—she said I had the king's eyes. This must be the king she meant. But how? Why? I don't understand. Why should our eyes resemble? We cannot be related, it's … it's just not possible."

The tall king was adorned in a simple white tunic and a belt not at all simple—a girdle of pure goldleaf it looked. At his side hung a long sword protected within a dazzling scabbard of purple crystallized foxgloves.[2] Yet the most conspicuous article in

---

[2]   Foxglove is sometimes called faërie thimbles or faërie fingers. It may well be called this as lore of the king's scabbard, so perfectly fashioned at the skilled hands of faërie artisans, came in due course to the notice of faërie loreologists.

his dress by far was his crown. Wooden and tall it was—very tall, nearly half as tall as he in fact, with eleven slender points.[3] Atop each wooden spire was a thing one would never expect. Oriana at least thought them unusual, for they looked like ordinary black rocks about the size of a child's fist; indeed, they were not the least bit extraordinary. And then there was his ivory horn too, slung over his shoulder—this, on the other hand, was most extraordinary. Rimmed in gold were its bell and mouthpiece while bright carbuncles ran up and down its curved length.

Relaxing the golden reins, the king lifted his horn and winded a mighty blast, clear and commanding.

As though in answer, a tremendous commotion suddenly could be heard clamouring down the Silver Causeway. A host many times longer than the company of faërie warriors was racing now over the silver cobbles. Closer, ever closer they sped—a legion of every manner of mythical wights, entering the world of mortals. There were horses with the torsos of men and women; people with the shanks of deer; short stalwart men with thick, knee-length beards and deep, colourful hoods; and very-wee people only inches high with delicate monarch-butterfly wings and bright satin shoon curving at their tips. And there were many more such wonders besides! Now, Oriana wasn't quite the student of Faërie that you are or she would have recognized in an instant these lovelies as centaurs, fauns, dwarves, and sprites.

All Oriana could do was smile and shake her head as wave upon wave of such glorious folk spread into the wider world of Miðgard.

---

[3] It is widely held amongst Faërie loreologists that the modern German word for eleven—*elf*—derives from the eleven points of the fabled crown of the high king of Danuvia. According to paleolinguists, this word first entered old German when the northernmost tribes were visited by the king of Faërie prior to the great age of wanderings of the fifth century AD. It is believed the Faërie king went in secret to a remote tribe of Frisians in order to conceal Idun's twin casket from the gaze of Malgorod. The casket was lost mysteriously during their migration to Roman Britannia with the other Angle, Jute, and Saxon tribes.

"I wonder why they've come?" she said to herself at length. "Well, maybe it isn't for them at all. Perhaps this is another gift, and what a gift! Maybe they come simply to make the world of man a little less bleak. What a blessing they are."

As the final faërie persons were lost to sight, spreading out in all directions from horizon to horizon, the tall king at last stept down from his wagon. A hush descended over the band of primitive onlookers as the king removed the lid from the wooden crate and held aloft the crystal disk.

Oriana's mouth fell open! so awed was she. It was as if one of the passing centaurs had kicked the wind right out of her. She was breathless. The crystal disk was in all probability the most perfect thing she had ever beheld—as perfect, she thought, as Lady Natura was ineffably beautiful.

The disk was a bit larger than a typical Saxon round shield, yet no circle was this. Rather, the disk was in the shape of a flower with five petals, perfectly white apart from the tips, which glowed in a different hue. In fact, were it not for the thin rims of colour the large crystal would look an enlarged replica of the white flower in Lady Natura's hall—

"The one I destroyed," said Oriana with remorse. And then, "Great Alfred!" she exclaimed with sudden realization. "The colours at the tips—yellow, blue, red, gold, and silver—why, they're the same colours as the gems of Lady Natura's diadem and . . . yes, that is what Lord Elgar had said—the same colours as the new stars. It all adds up. They're connected in some way. This just can't be coincidence! But how exactly? What's the relationship? What does it all mean?"

That's when Oriana noticed it—something on the disk she would have thought impossible of something exuding such perfection. Indeed it was not flawless after all. It was cracked, and not with one hairline imperfection but deep fissures round each of the petals. In fact, the longer she stared, the more Oriana puzzled over what bound the frangible pieces together. She imagined it would take little to fully tear it asunder.

And then it occurred to her. "I wonder!" she began to surmise. "I wonder if this is the field of white I saw crack when—when the lady of the garden committed her deed."

Just as the king held the disk high for all to see, the three women caring for the injured boy covered their mouths for shock when their patient rose suddenly from his mat.

Slowly, and clearly pained, the boy hobbled over to the king's side. The king said nothing to him, but bent on one knee, gently resting the disk upon the ground. With long slender fingers, he set to scratching at the earth rather cat-like, hollowing out a shallow bed, then placing the disk inside, and covering it completely with the dark soil. When finished, the king took compassion on the boy, nodding in sign of his permission. The boy stretched out his hand haltingly to the disk, touching it ever so gingerly at its centre. Then, removing a handful of dirt from the disk, the boy rubbed it into his wound with immediate effect. At once he let out a small shriek, grabbed at his side with his fist clenched, and fell weeping to his knees.

At that point, one of the three women (his mother most likely) got hurriedly to her feet and ran sobbing to the boy's side. She embraced him, mopping away her tears with her braided hair. Oriana realized why both wept, for she saw that the boy's wound was completely healed. Mother and son rose, sobbing, and humbly thanked their benefactor.

The others in the band probably would have reacted with similar sobs of gratitude had their attention not been drawn at once to the wild cereals blooming in masses before them. "Another gift!" thought Oriana. Pushing up in between the tundra grasses were the tallest and healthiest of grains. A terrific profusion, indeed a distending ocean of robust cereals, blue sage, and purple thyme, was suddenly to be seen swaying in gentle waves under the sun's approving rays. Oriana could not help but think how impoverished, how insignificant, the oats and barley and wheat of Oakleigh Manor seemed by comparison, and theirs were regarded as some of the richest in the whole of Wessex.

But what clearly made the band happiest by far was the immediate arrival of hundreds of exceedingly large beasts grazing afar in groves of pink-flowered terebinth. Never had Oriana beheld animals so immense. They were every bit as big as a cottage, with curving tusks many times the size of the wild boar of Selwood Forest. *Another gift!* Oriana guessed these must be the living examples of what they were now roasting over their bonfire.

There was little wonder why so many cheered, laughed, and danced with thrusting spears. They would probably never know hunger.

"I think I now understand how they manage," said Oriana to herself. "They hunt and forage that which has been provided for them. So is this what Lady Natura meant when she said, '*Once had I provided man with abundance; once when my spirit alone was wed to Danuvia*'? But what did she mean her spirit alone was wed to Faërie?" As Oriana marveled at the seemingly inexhaustible bounty, fully prepared to believe all would forever be well for the small commune, a very shocking thing occurred!

At once Oriana was roused from her happy musings when every archer from his war-wagon had suddenly fitted a slender arrow to his bowstring. And just as quick, the tall king had retrieved the crystal disk, brushed it cleaned, placed it safely back in its wooden chest, and mounted his war-wagon, his fearsome sword unsheathed.

Great was Oriana's dismay! The archers were actually pointing their fully drawn bows at the band. One certainly needn't to have understood the band's language to discern that their cries of joy had turned instantly to calls of horror and bewilderment. In response, some of the younger and stronger-looking men brandished their flint-tipped spears in readiness.

"What is this?" Oriana asked herself dumbfounded. "I thought these faërie warriors had come to aid, even to teach, maybe."

The bowmen now but awaited the king's signal to loose their rain of death upon the confused band.

"Why on earth have they turned on these simple people so suddenly and without provocation? Are they to be slaughtered like swine—women and children and the elderly alike?"

Oriana searched for intent in the king's narrowing eyes, those eyes of deep wisdom and ancient lore. Again, she was confused, for she could derive no hint of malice from his gaze.

Just when Oriana was certain the king would at last give death's command, the smoldering bonfire burst forth in a terrific blaze. Terrible tongues of red flame stabbed upward and outward, four times the area of the original campfire. Those closest to the explosion were instantly incinerated.

It was absolute bedlam! Women ran with their babies, the old with the aid of the young, and everywhere was the stench of burning flesh. But no one seemed to know exactly where to run. Some scrambled away from the blaze straight for the encircling wagons despite the formidable bowmen. Others took shelter in their leantos, while still more ran wildly about in circles, pinned between death by flame or arrow.

That was when a second blaze leapt from the earth just next to the first. Cries went out! Oh, what was their dread!

Oriana's eyes darted with yet greater perplexity between the terrified band and the tall warriors. It was difficult to glean any understanding or intention in their stern faces, though Oriana now thought she perceived the tiniest glint of fear in the king's bright eyes.

Still the warriors had not fired. "Why have they even nocked their arrows?" The very next moment the earth began to shake with a great violence. At once, the large, tusked beasts grazing far off began to stampede in all directions—some in the direction of the camp!

Then came a great convulsion. The earth heaved and broke loose all around the blazing turrets into a fine powder. On seeing this, the rest of villagers decided to take their chances with the grim archers, running directly for the ring of war-wagons.

How mistaken Oriana had been—quite mistaken! The archers had not been aiming at the band, for they were not following the frenzied mob with their arrow tips. All their concentration was now bent on the stabbing red pillars.

And Oriana saw why! For what burst out of the ground beneath the twin blazes was the most monstrous spectacle Oriana had ever met with. Up came a hideous black snout from the earth, lifting the shafts of fire higher and higher, the red flames spewing from horned nostrils.

Down rained the arrows upon the monstrous head. Little was their efficacy. Another volley of arrows and then another—all failing to pierce the pustulous black hide.

At last, the entire blackened beast had emerged!

The dragon was even more horrifying than all those described in the old tales Oriana had heard as a child—for this was no tale at all. Her desire to run, to hide, to flee for her life, was all consuming. To actually see the winged serpent in front of her gave Oriana a fright passing endurance.

Just as the dragon took to flight, it unfurled hideous, batlike wings, crushing all to the ground in a mighty gale of fear as they bellowed. Slime dript in thick, mucus-like globules from the wyrm's[4] scaly underbelly, a reek of rottenness going before it like a consuming pestilence. Even the proud white steeds of the faërie warriors shied backwards several paces from the ris-

---

[4] Wyrm, or worm, is the Saxon word for dragon.

ing menace, yet still did they hold their ground, for lo! the noble beasts of white fled not in the face of death.

As the repulsive creature slithered higher and higher, the very air was snatched instantly from the sky, leaving in its place naught but choking gas and red flame.

And there was more to fear than his malignant breath. For his claws were like broad swords, and the spikes splayed along his tail were as boar-spears with dreadful-looking barbs. Oriana shuddered to imagine the carnage these would deliver should the serpent decide to turn and give battle.

So overwrought was Oriana at sight and stench of the dragon she almost failed to notice its rider. Something in human form sat on the wyrm's back, wrapt and hooded in a cloak that looked of raw flesh. The figure appeared quite small against the backdrop of his gigantic mount, but it had to be at least treble the height of the tall warriors themselves. Oriana could not see his face; fully shadowed it was by the grotesque hood of flayed skin.

But the rider's screams Oriana could hear quite plainly— clear and icy. He commanded his winged serpent with piercing shrieks devilishly reminiscent of the foul laughter Oriana had grown to fear. Yet it was not the same cry. In its rending shrieks Oriana heard unmistakably, and knew, somehow implicitly, the wailings of infants abandoned to torment and death in the wild. The cry of sorrow and pain was his fell voice.

The dread wyrm and its death-clad rider soared ever higher to disappear at length behind the cover of an approaching storm cloud. Oriana was finally relieved of the horrid spectacle.

◇◇◇◇◇◇◇◇◇◇◇◇◇◇◇◇◇◇◇◇◇◇◇◇◇◇◇◇◇◇◇◇◇◇◇

Whoosh! And for a third time, Oriana found herself enveloped in the blanket of comforting white.

"Please, oh please! Let this be the end," prayed Oriana. But it was not to be. There was more for her to see—there was more for her to learn.

The next instant, Oriana found herself in a stony, sun-scorched country, the twilight air sultry and close. She was staring at the back of a tall figure, hooded in an exquisitely embroidered magenta cloak. It was walking in long, hurried strides over the burning sands away from Oriana. In its hand was an ordinary wooden hoe, similar, though cruder in design, to the hundreds used daily at Oakleigh Manor. Ahead by several furlongs was yet another primitive band not too unlike the one Oriana had just quitted.

The cloaked figure was racing toward the tiny band with great urgency.

But suddenly the shimmering figure stopt in its tracks, turned in Oriana's direction, and threw back its silken hood. Once again was Oriana short of breath by what she beheld. Just as when she had entered the lady's hall, Oriana was again met by a beauty that utterly astonished her senses.

It was no *it* at all—he was a man! Oriana was stunned. What beauty! What unspeakable perfection! Oriana wholly forgot herself with lust. He was far handsomer than Leofa, her first love, or even Lord Théodoric of Malmesbury for that matter, whom she had only recently regarded as the finest looking of men. With his long, silky black hair and porcelain white skin he was even more captivating than the tall, fair king she had just admired. He had to be an angel; there were no two ways about it. He must be divine!

For the merest of moments, Oriana thought she had been spotted when the angelic figure spun round, but soon understood him to be gazing in the distance over her shoulder. All at once Oriana heard a rustling in the shrubbery behind her. Difficult though it was for her to withdraw her gaze from his beauty—so lost in passion, so gript with obsession was she—Oriana turned to see what had seized his attention.

Not too far behind Oriana, a rather frail-looking cow was dropping a calf in a clearing of dense broom shrubs. Nearby, a gaily plumaged starling, much handsomer than starlings generally are, was roosting in a fig tree, studying the birth and singing a doleful refrain.

But instead of licking clean and nursing her young as is a mother's wont, the cow turned tail and sprang away directly as if jolted with a terrific fright. That was queer enough in its own right, but then the wobbly legged calf, crying desperately after her fleeing mother, was suddenly enfolded in a dazzle of spiraling water, fire, earth, and wind that fizzed and sparked till the calf was no longer to be seen at all.

Like the mother cow, a great terror seized suddenly upon the observant starling. He mewed his finest feathers in a great flapping and took to flight, piping and chattering in the wind.

When the flurrying elemental vanished, so too had the calf. In her stead rose a naked woman from a crouched, fetal position. Oriana recognized her in an instant, for in her shone a loveliness rivaled only by that of the angelic presence who stood watching, smiling with approval. The woman was Lady Natura!

Man and woman beheld one another. Then, walking slowly one to the other, they stopt and stared long into each other's eyes. Neither spoke. There was scarcely a breath drawn between them until they touched. And it was there, atop the shriveled grasses under the sun's glaring eye, that they embraced with the abandon of fullest passion, recking neither shame nor judgment.

◇◇

Oriana was at once whisked away. Yet this time she was not enfolded in the warming white light. This new place, this new time, merely opened before her eyes fast as thought itself.

She was gazing still at Lady Natura, yet now was she no longer naked but clad in simple skin garments. A group of women similarly drest surrounded the great lady in a field of wild cereals and sparse tamarisk shrubs. The angelic being was there too, though his appearance seemed not now so beautiful. He was passing a hoe to Lady Natura, pointing at the soil and then in turn to the wide assortment of tall grains. In his open palm, there rested a handful of germinating seeds. He pointed angrily to the earth again and again, giving her the strictest of instructions. Lady Natura adamantly shook her head in defiance, but the tall being bore down on her, growing ever angrier and more insistent by the minute.

Eventually, the great lady relented in her torment, obeying his command. Down she swung the flint hoe, a most terrible and irrevocable deed, a deed wholly and utterly consequent on her lover's black coercion: for this was not her will at work. She lacerated the earth deep and sad.

◇◇

Again, Oriana was thrust in a new place. Lady Natura was weeping, the sky lead grey and just as sullen as she. Now Oriana stood amongst a gathering of the same crudely adorned women and, presumably, their husbands and children. Before them stood a wide table—or altar perhaps—lit with many torches. Lady Natura's lover, that ineffably beautiful being, he from whom these simple people discovered that first crucial step to dominion—control and manipulation of the land—was nowhere to be seen.

Behind the table stood a man with a long brown beard raggedly kept, a beard Oriana did not like in the least. He wore a tall headdress of antlers and woven twigs and armlets of painted shell and animal teeth. His left eye was blind—its empty socket black and mangled—the other, deep-set and surly looking. Held high in his hands was a rush-woven basket filled with loose chaff and loaves of unleavened bread. With a *whish* and a *whoosh* he flung, flipped, and recaught the loaves and chaff over and over again for the crowd's unbounded amusement.

Oriana listened intently to the hum of their wild voices. And for reasons she could not give, she was able, or perhaps permitted, to understand their speech.

"The medicine has passed to us!" roared the man defiantly from behind the altar, his voice raspy and unpleasant. "Do you see? By our hands can we produce!" He was throwing loaves into the frenzied crowd.

Everyone cheered, pushing and elbowing wildly to be the first to lay hands on the coveted bread. A lame man in the middle of the crowd was very nearly trampled to death in the crushing pell-mell.

Indeed nearly everyone was shouldering and shoving to the front. Not so Lady Natura. As it was, she stood alone weeping, some way off from the others, her tear-streaked face gravely mirroring the tilled furrows marring the earth behind the altar.

"Our days of searching are at an end!" shouted the headman, continuing to cast the small loaves into the jostling crowd and glaring greedily with his useful eye. "We roam no longer! We depend like children no longer!" Louder grew the applause. "Come! Let us make this oath together! No longer shall we rely on the Great One to provide! No longer must we trust to faith! The medicine to produce is ours! Now do we control our fate!"

Wide came the cheers as they held aloft their loaves with outstretched arms.

"Did I understand him correctly?" wondered Oriana aghast. "Is he actually suggesting they no longer should trust in Him? Have they lost all faith? How could these people consent to such an evil oath? Do they place their will above His design?"

<hr />

In an instant, Oriana was removed from Lady Natura and the parched world. She was now peering down upon a snowcapped mountain immeasurably high. A great way up the mountainside a colonnaded temple of polished marble reared itself along its western summit.

She gasped and covered her mouth. What a calamity was unveiled before her!

The depredation was enormous! Thousands of mangled and scorched bodies lay heaped in slushy red snow before the temple gates. Some of the bodies were those of the tall, fair warriors, yet many others did not look at all of their kin, for they were less than half their height with stout, thick limbs and strong shoulders and wavy, long beards red, brown, or blonde—blonde chiefly. Dwarves, Oriana guessed they were, recalling the faërie tales of old. Splintered axe-hafts and cracked linden shields, shattered swords, and ategars lie in ruin next to their fallen owners.

And there was also among the slain a third sort, brutish and foul-looking, as perverse in their grotesque disfigurement as the tall faërie lords were resplendent in their beauty of still pools under winter starlight. Some of the fiends were tall and bow-legged, others short-limbed with wide sunken chests, yet all had the same dark, boil-ridden skin and fanged snouts. By them were strewn the broken and bloodied blades of their curved scimitars and dragon-embossed shields.

Mounted atop the slain, coiled high as a blackened hilltop, was the great plundering dragon, his yellow cat eyes staring cunningly through heavy wrinkled lids. Its flesh-cloaked rider had already dismounted and was scavenging ruthlessly among the carrion. With ghoulish delight, the cloaked horror flew from one body to the next, despoiling the dead of their broken axe handles gript still in their masters' frozen hands.

Oriana looked on in horror as the shade then designed to commit a great atrocity. At once, he began tying together in a bundle the broken birch handles with the spilt entrails of the slain. Seizing several of the smaller axe blades, he then bound them to the bundle in like fashion, their notched edges thrust outward. With fiendish delight, he laughed over his deed, spitting from under his deep hood a trail of acid-green venom upon the melting red snow.

In this way did he ascend the temple stairs, the bound weapons of the conquered raised above as a sceptre for black incantations.

"*Ex sapientia ab imperio cum fasce lictoriae!*" imprecated the cloaked devil in his deathly cry of slaughtered newborns.

With a rending boom, the silver gates were heaved from their crystal hinges and hurled cruelly to the bloodied snow below. Then, as a poisoned vapour, he poured through the cella and into the temple's inner sanctum, bent on defiling the sacred space with his vile intent. There, at the centre adytum on an altar of purest gold, arian-silver, and ivory inlays, sat the unadorned wooden chest.

<hr />

In dizzying confusion, Oriana was back in the sun-scorched world of the primitive band and their sacrilege.

"Together let us break this bread to honour what we have achieved by our hands alone!" vaunted the high priest triumphantly, standing yet behind the tusked altar. "Our eyes are open at long last! Now do we know as the gods! Now do we make as the gods!"

◇◇

A blink of the eye and Oriana was back in the world of ice and death. All about the mountaintop, a fresh snow was blowing with a terrific fury, covering the dead in a cleansing layer of white. The hooded carrion sat hunched upon his black mount. In the palm of his clawed hand shone the crystal disk, its five fissures wider than ever. His other hand was cupped above, as if preparing to contain some mighty release.

Next second, Oriana noticed a large but otherwise unexceptional fallow stag such as one can see any day in the forest. He was ascending the snowy height behind the dread stead. Reaching the summit, he suddenly halted and stared sorrowfully at the noble slain. Neither the winged serpent nor his rider gave any notice of the stag's arrival, nor did the stag look once at them.

◇◇

Another blink and Oriana was amidst the band crowded anxiously round the altar.

With his fist shaking up at the heavens in clear repudiation, the high priest called, "All glory and honour is ours, forever and ever! For our will to power!"

In concert, all in the band broke bread and ate, all save Lady Natura—she walked alone, head lowered among the injured tilth.

◇◇◇

Sound! There was naught but sound upon the icy summit. With the volume of all the world's waves crashing down as one upon a single grain of sand, the crystal corolla burst asunder in a nebula of blinding white light! Then was made a second sound just as measureless and terrible as the first: it was death's rider. He gave a wail that nearly stilled Oriana's heart. Out from his smoldering hands clenched in agony flew the red and yellow, gold and silver petals, each one sinking below the lofty, snow-enameled peaks in opposite directions, north, south, east, and west. But then Oriana saw that he was yet clinging desperately to the remaining petal—the blue petal. Though now the crystal was no longer a pretty thing. What had first appeared to Oriana as the cool blue of winter sky, now suggested the blue of blood-drained flesh. It looked the pallid blue of death newly come.

The crystal would not be molested. Like a spark set to tinder, the grey-blue glow consumed his withered hand, then his arm, and then the whole of his cloaked body till both he and his devil's steed were utterly consumed in its deathly radiance.

Just then, a dazzling blue light flickered high above the uppermost mountain peak. It flashed bright through a break in the snowy clouds as though a new star had come suddenly into being. It shone but a moment only and was lost. And in the dwindling of the starry light went also the terrific blaze enfolding both dragon and his fell rider.

Oriana clutched her face in horror! As the blue fire vanished, there was left the black serpent lying dead upon his bed of corpses. And the flesh-clad horror who once sat astride him was nowhere to be seen. Only his fell cloak of young flesh remained, stretched over the dragon's putrid hide exactly between its jagged shoulder blades. There too, pulsating and steaming in hot vapours atop the bloodied cloak, breathed evilly the blue crystal amulet.

Oriana searched for the stag that had just arrived. There he was! He too was lying just as lifeless as the dragon amongst the rest of the slain, if indeed it was the same stag. In death, he had grown easily twice his size, his antlers, nearly thrice. And he had gone completely white, whiter even than the new-fallen snow now covering the carnage afresh.

Oriana gasped! The lifeless stag she recognized in a moment. "Lord Whitethorn!"

◇◇◇◇◇◇◇◇◇◇◇◇◇◇◇◇◇◇◇◇◇◇◇◇◇◇◇◇◇◇◇◇◇◇◇◇◇◇

In an instant, Oriana was returned to the torrid world of the band. It seemed no time at all had elapsed, for just as the unconsecrated bread was being devoured, a tremendous rumbling began to shake the world. Slowly the sky went dark as the sun hid herself in shame behind the moon's passing. And then all the land was filled with His voice—the radiating source of all voices. His voice was wroth!

Cursed be the ground because of you!
In toil shall you eat its yield all the days of your life.
Thorns and thistles shall it bring forth to you, as you eat of the plants
of the field.
By the sweat of your face shall you now get bread to eat.[5]

His words echoed across the land, filling valleys and sheering cliffs. Terror and shame smote the band. Men groveled and cowered in the dark like frightened beasts, repenting their ill faith with terrible moans. Women too chastened themselves, tearing at their hair and beating their breasts as they fell prostrate to the furrowed ground.

And then something truly heartrending, indeed one of the most lamentable tragedies suddenly befell the world of man—all the enchanted folk who had once crossed the Silver Causeway were now slipping from mortal sight, land by land, country by

---

[5] Genesis 3:17–19

country. Some sought dark mountain crevices; others vanished under deep shadows of ancient forests or returned in sad company back across the Silver Causeway to far-off Faërie. But however they fled, it was plain all willed to distance themselves from the shame that man had once again brought to Miðgard.

◇◇◇

It was now nearly impossible for Oriana to follow the tumbling images. Like the quick thumbing of a living book, Oriana darted from one world to the next.

What Oriana now saw speeding before her eyes were strange lands filled with great stonewalls and battlements, fountains, and aqueducts, paved roads and market squares, palaces, temples, and statues. But what she understood, what was being revealed to her mind on a separate plane of knowing, was very different indeed from what her mere senses revealed.

All was the reverse of the world known by the healthy and happy people she had first encountered by the bonfire. Oriana could give no explanation for how she knew such things, but for every stone building Oriana physically beheld in this whirling vision was a corresponding knowledge of people working harder and living less well than people had ever done till that age. From this new world could Oriana feel the torment of diseases not known to the earlier bands. And she could smell too the reek of crowded cities bulging with a terrific multitude. She could taste also foods bereft of the life-giving vigour once contained in such foods gathered in the wild. Truly, for every impressive marble fountain coming into view came with it a society built upon rigid class distinctions where one's rank depended not on the gift of one's inherent talents but merely on the class of one's parents. For every high temple, ziggurat, or pyramid flashing before Oriana's eyes, flashed also the sins of human sacrifice, endemic warfare, conscription, taxes and slavery, and the first poisoning of clear rivers and laying waste to forests ancient and good—indeed, all the maladies occasioned by the spreading canker of urbanization.

Despite the fact Oriana was somehow able to establish such meaningful links between these shifting images and their dire consequences, she was quite unable to give expression to this further, this forgotten yet culminating fall of man as a concept unto itself. Of course had you been able to accompany our friend Oriana on her transcendental journey, you could have easily pointed out that she had just witnessed what most history books in your world invariably champion as a glorious achievement—the rise of states!

Onward the visions continued, but now they resumed a pace she could more easily follow. Again, Oriana found herself in the presence of Lady Natura. The great lady stood alone and perilously close to the edge of a tall precipice. Her face was lined but not by age it seemed. Rather, hers was the careworn visage of ignominy. In her eyes shone remorse—remorse for unavowed passions and blind obedience to the blasphemous teachings of her lover.

"Why is she all alone? Where is her lover?" wondered Oriana, pity welling inside her over Lady Natura's anguish. "Has he abandoned her at her neediest hour?"

Along the edge of the dizzying bluff, a grove of young hawthorn trees grew thick. One of them possessed an exceptionally long branch reaching out above the deep abyss. Despondently, the lady clomb the tree, inching her way at last to the bowing end of the far branch.

She lowered herself, dangling in abject resignation from the cracking limb. Oriana was mortified. Her intention was obvious. Oriana wanted to reach out—she wanted to help the lady in her darkest moment of despair, but it was no good.

"*No!*" screamed Oriana. The most beautiful woman in all creation plunged inexorably to her death.

Flash came the silvery light; then the dazzling arc; and then the white-winged steed galloping across the causeway, its rider straddled above, gripping tight the golden bridle. It was no other than the tall king of Faërie himself! Like wind borne above the great Sea of Tyynimôr, the white mount charged beneath the lady seconds before death could claim her for its own. The king pressed the limp body of Lady Natura close to his bosom as they vanished behind the unseen door of light in the low clouds.

<hr />

"What is it?" asked the king eagerly. "I must know. Is it a girl as I have foreseen?"

Oriana was now inside a magnificent hall of golden timbers hung with glittering tapestries, the floor so splendidly flagged with tiles of polished morion and jasper that it would be difficult to make you understand just how great was its luster. The room was exceedingly spacious and smelt of cardamom freshly ground. The whole of it was drenched with a dazzle of young starlight dripping steadily from long slender icicles high in the ceiling, drips of starry dew that warmed the air clear and bright. All manner of rare and wonderful items of imaginative shape there were too filling the hall from end to end. Lady Natura and her nurse were in the far bower behind a drawn privacy brocade that looked of woven clouds studded with brilliantly lighted sapphires and purple amethysts.

"This must be somewhere in Faërie," observed Oriana brightly. For the room itself seemed alive, possessing in itself the same life essence as Lady Natura's throne, yet with none of its sinister will.

"Yes Sire, indeed *they* are, I should say," called the nurse from behind the screen. A robin was perched on her left shoulder as she spoke. "You have twin daughters, Your Majesty."

This seemed a far happier sight. There was Lady Natura. She had just given birth to twins. She was lying on a bed shaped from mother-of-pearl with posts of polished alabaster and hung round with silver chimes. A waterfall of sparkling turquoise pouring out of thin air was its headboard, though causing no damp where it met the soft pillow below. The blue sheets were of the finest samite.

The gaiety of the moment, however, was short-lived. At once Oriana saw things take a dreadful turn for the worse. Lady Natura was not moving.

"And the Lady of Miðgard?" the king inquired anxiously, pacing the hall back and forth behind the screen, wringing his hands.

Somewhere from without, a sad bell began to toll as if from a lonely tower.

"I am sorry, your highness," retuned the nurse, "she has perished in bringing forth their lives. Her spirit has been sent to Llynarian—to the Seed of Life. The mortal realm must await her return. I am truly sorry for you, Sire."

◇◇◇◇◇◇◇◇◇◇◇◇◇◇◇◇◇◇◇◇◇◇◇◇◇◇◇◇◇◇◇◇◇◇◇◇◇◇

On perceiving the king's grief, Oriana saw the world change once more with a flash before her eyes. Instantly she found herself in a glade of mighty oaks hung with many lamps from silver chains under a starry sky. In the centre of the small clearing stood a single tree, but not an oak—it was another hawthorn, but not just any hawthorn—this one was it! Oriana was certain! There was no mistaking it! It was identical to the tree in her tapestry!

An old man, a young boy, and the king of Faërie were there too. The king was a sight, clad in the beauty of the stars themselves. And he was holding a baby.

"King Gwyn ap Nudd! We are honoured, Your Majesty," said

the wizened old man in crimson robes as he bowed his head in token of his fealty. He had a long, curly white beard streaked with brown tucked behind his black belt.

Oriana stared at the baby. She recognized her at once. "She's one of Lady Natura's twins." But in a moment her thoughts went dark. "Why is the king holding only one? Where is her sister?"

"Melchior," nodded the king, smiling back at the old man. "Liu Shang also sends his greetings."

"Wait a second," said Oriana astonished. "I know this place. I've seen these people before, once—no several times, in a dream. To be sure, I've dreamt this very meeting many times."

Oriana could remember their names too—so vivid were these dreams. "That's right," she said as she heard their names being mentioned. "And the boy's name is Dunstan—I remember now."

She listened intently to their conversation, able to recall nearly every word spoken. Eventually the two men sent the wide-eyed boy on his way.

"Be comforted, my friend," said the king eventually to the old man. "Here at least I may be able to help. Behold! For the king of Danuvia shall he point the way to his sibling."

Oriana watched as the tall king handed the child to the old man and dashed over to the hawthorn. She knew what was coming. The king removed his colossal wooden crown and placed it reverently inside the gaping trunk.

Then came the wide ring of chartreuse light.

"Why it's—it's the faërie maids!" exclaimed Oriana with eyes wide. "From the lady's hall."

"What a beautiful child, Your Grace. Have you ever looked upon anything prettier?" said the old man eventually with mournful eyes. The baby girl looked up at him, amused with his long whiskers.

"The baby!" said Oriana with a feeling of certainty and yet

denial. "Gwendolyn! Lord Whitethorn ... and Lady Natura too said ... The baby! And she loves the old man's beard too!"

"Then may we now ... may we now know the answer?" asked the old man as he ran behind the much taller king. "Surely we are to prepare the lady's return to her rightful place beneath the moon?"

"And the lady, too!" cried Oriana at once. "Lady Natura! He means Lady Natura."

"I must ask the patience of the Order yet again," said the king to the old man, now in front of the forest lane. "Yet the hour will not be long in coming, I deem. Soon will the five stars be joined, and hence the hour the hidden amulets must be rejoined—"

Oriana gasped for the least air. "*The five stars!* Lord Elgar's stars!"

"It is written that by the queen's hands alone shall the Hawthorn Disk be restored ... *should* she ever be freed in Malgorod! For this is, of course, the great gambit we make, Melchior. Should the child survive to womanhood, she will require the aid of all the Order."

"It is then a grave choice, Your Majesty," observed the old man, loosening the child's grip from his beard as he prepared to hand her back to the king. "What a bitter sacrifice. Abraham of old could himself have known no greater sorrow."

"His beard!" whispered Oriana a second time, her breath nearly failing her completely. "His long white beard! The baby! She loves it! I too love long white—I've never known why—Oh no ... no, no, no! This is all becoming entirely too much. The baby can't be—I mean, I can't be ... My father is Cypriot and Mother was Saxon—that's flat!" Oriana was doing a poor job of reassuring herself of these facts. "But why do I know this event so well? Why the recurring dreams?"

There was no time for further speculation.

Whoosh! All was the warmth of white light; and soon, sooner than she knew, Oriana was taken by a deep, glorious sleep once again.

When at last Oriana awoke, she felt something she had not sensed in what seemed like ages—solid ground! She was lying on her back perfectly becalmed, peering up at thin slivers of sunlight slicing through a cloud of musty air she had just stirred. There above were dangling, hair-like roots and manky clumps of sod and green tousles of weeds all around.

Oriana got to her knees, for there was no room to stand in the tiny hollow of the tree. It was uncomfortably tight. She looked around. Even from inside, Oriana could tell it was a hawthorn tree that now housed her. To her adjusting vision she guessed there to be nothing but bright fog beyond the narrow fissure in the trunk.

And just as soon as Oriana set herself to pondering how and why she had been taken to so many wonderful and terrible and familiar places, she suddenly heard:

"Oriana!" It was a hoarse and laboured voice that called. "Thistle burns and beestings! Is that you in there my dear?"

"Can it be? Could it actually be?" Oriana's heart rose in the sound of her calling.

"Lord above me!" cried the wheezing voice. "Worried me out m' life, yeh have. I jus' dunno what's to be done with yeh!"

It was Bathilda! It was her governess! She was home!

CHAPTER 14

Calls on the Mist

Up jumped Oriana from her knees, banging her head smart on the low opening in the trunk.

"Bathilda! Here I am!" she shouted with a desperate cry from her heart. She clambered out, rubbing her head. Stars and plum-colour spots were dancing before her bleary eyes. Above her right eyebrow a considerable lump was sure to follow the sting.

But the pain mattered little, so glad was she to be home at last. She was giddy! Overjoyed! Bathilda would be there to receive her with open arms.

"*As I live and breathe!*' That's what she's going to say next—I just know it," Oriana said to herself, giddier and giddier.

"Oh, Bathilda," she cried aloud again in a great flutter, trying to collect her senses. "You can have no idea how happy I am to see—"

Oriana stopt. She rubbed her eyes. She rubbed them again. Her mouth fell open. Hope darkened.

It was a horrible, horrible surprize.

"Wait—this can't be!" she cried, clutching at her breast. Oriana was heartbroken—for there *was no* Bathilda!

"Please—no! No! I'm sure I heard her calling for me just now. This just can't be!"

Oriana turned about wildly, glaring in all directions with strained vision. She was deceived. Oriana was standing just outside the hawthorn, stranded still, lost and forgot at the foulest place that ever was seen.

"No! No!" she cried again, her voice trembling.

She stared round at the tree. It was the same hawthorn all right, though not now as it had been when she entered, for it was no longer scorched throughout but restored to new life rather, enormous and wild and altogether magnificent. In the blossom of early spring it looked, beautified with hundreds of musk-scented white roses and scarlet fruits the size of grapes that tantalized with the beaded shine of a pre-dawn mist. Even its mutilated crown was whole once more, the rusted cords defiling its upper boughs now gone.

And there also was the path straight ahead, reopened through the same loathsome wall of blackthorn. It too was returning to new life, as if slowly being reawakened by the many flowered limbs of the hawthorn, now themselves penetrating deep into the black barrier. Beyond hedge and path, and above, and all around was a clammy fog, dense with the white light of day. But what day?

At first sight, Oriana thought there was something curiously familiar about this fog roaming ever closer and thicker and colder—eerily cold.

"It's the white mist I saw between the changing visions."

Indeed, it looked so similar that she very nearly regarded her present surroundings as yet another fleeting image, another memory sprung to life. This thought hardly lingered; the next moment, she realized this light, this fog eddying ever nearer, did not *feel* or … or even *smell* the same, not one bit. It had none of its comfort, none of its warmth. No, it was not the same.

Her eyesight steadying after the nasty clunk to her forehead, Oriana could now distinguish odd lumbering movement off in the distance through the fog.

"Bathilda?" she called out again in desperation. But even

before the name passed her lips she knew quite well the chance of her mistress actually milling about in the Festering Fens was beyond remote—it was absurd.

Oriana gasped. Fright seized suddenly upon her! All her senses were alert! Something dark, indeed, many dark things—bent and misshapen—were prowling in the mist just beyond the blackthorn hedge. Horror! Dread! Her terror was every instant growing! Ahead a snuffling and grunting of wild beasts, deep and threatening, was edging closer, the heavy tread of clawed feet clamouring and scraping.

That was when it came! Her blood grew cold. At once there arose in her an icy chill, creeping over her heart. She had felt this terrible bite before. Shards of steely ice needled her insides. Her heart beat violently.

This could mean only one thing. It came just as sudden and terrible as it had before!

"*Bathilda, indeed!*" scoffed the very same voice Oriana had heard while inside the tree. It was Bathilda's voice all right, seeping through the fog in all directions at once. Yet there was something dreadfully different about it.

"How dare you now call to me?" scolded Bathilda's voice. "Have you forgotten how abominably you forsook me? After all I have done for you! After all the love I have showered on you! What have I got to show for it now?"

Oriana fell to the ground in the force of the woman's scorn, collapsing breathlessly against the hawthorn's trunk. She could not speak, nor scream, nor cry. But for her heart now racing, she would have thought herself turned to coldest stone. Oriana knew by the reproach in the woman's voice that this could not be her Bathilda. No, indeed no, it was … it was surely … Oriana desponded! This could not be happening!

"Why did you abandon me, child? Why? Tell me why!" called Bathilda's voice through the mist, only now was it horribly reshaping into *the* voice—the icy voice of he of the fell laughter. "Have you the least idea what that horrible woman said to me—what she did to me?"

Inch by inch, the misshapen, creeping things drew nearer. And then he laughed in the most maleficent way imaginable. "Ungrateful wretch! How dare you expect to find her waiting to fetch you home. Do not feign you bear any love for anyone but yourself. Comfort? Aid? You deserve neither. You forsook the one who loved you most, and why—for excitement and heroism? To satisfy your idle curiosity? Your childish inquisitiveness? She deserved better of you. What an evil choice have you made. Do not imagine me deceived into the belief that you acted to serve some higher good, for I cannot be deceived. You serve none but yourself—so high-minded you are! By your own wickedness do you bring ruin upon yourself!"

Oriana did not react, not in speech or action. To have heard the calls of her mistress become the savage upbraiding of the enemy, the very ruin of her hopes, was more than she could endure.

What could she do? Was this the end? Was she going to die? She was alone and unfriended. She was afraid—trapped like a butterfly in a treacherous web. The terror was unbearable.

Oriana's breathing was getting away from her. Panic was in every rapid breath. Her ears began to ring. She could feel her head bobbing limply to her chest in consequence, her consciousness ebbing out fast.

Though she knew she would be hard put to it, Oriana understood she must get hold of herself before nodding off, fading perhaps forever, expiring utterly from the living world. She must calm herself. She must gather up her courage, and quick!

Onward the dark shapes crept through the mist. Whatever could they be? She could nearly make them out. It was terrifying. Terrifying!

The enemy's interrogation would not cease, his voice crying in the stale wind, forcibly striking her ears. "Have you given even the least thought to her present suffering? And she is suffering— of that I can assure you. Ah! But you owe her no consideration, do you? This is your mind. Such conceit! But your treacherous ways shall be righted. My master will teach you loyalty—one way or another."

With what little concentration she could summon, Oriana managed by slow degree to stem her panicked gasps. Her mind had become utterly chaotic. How did the enemy know such intimate things about her? How had he come to know so much about her personal relations, or for that matter, her very thoughts themselves?

Agonizing as it was, it could not be avoided. She could not pretend his charges hadn't been made. They had to be confronted head on.

And so, Oriana began contemplating the merit of the enemy's words. "Is it true? Am I really selfish and proud?" Still were Lord Whitethorn's warnings of the enemy's duplicity sounding in her ears, but this could be no deceit.

Oriana took the enemy's assertions much to heart. What he claimed was horribly and shamefully true. *Not once* had she thought of Bathilda since arriving to this strange world, not even for a moment. It was true; he was right—Bathilda's expulsion from Oakleigh was the thing least present in her thoughts. She had forgotten all about her. True, her mind had been preoccupied with the wonders *and* the horrors of this realm to say nothing of her attempts to work out the meaning of so many mysteries. But these excuses would not do. Oakleigh Manor had always been Bathilda's only home. Where was there for her to go? To think it took the enemy to recall her beloved Bathilda to her mind! Her behaviour was despicable. There could be no denial; there was truth in his dreadful shrieks. How could she possibly claim to have any regard for her mistress now—how could she? She had completely forgotten her. Nothing, nothing could be said in her defence.

Oriana was at once filled with shame and self-reproach. She could never forgive herself for this.

Through half-closed lids, she watched as the fog slowly lifted. A choking wind bearing the same burning stench of the monstrous smokestacks began to blow strong from behind, clearing away the fog, little by little, as it went.

At last, she could see clearly. But nothing apart from the hawthorn itself had improved in the least. The ruin of the Festering Fens was even greater than she had seen under the moon's silvery radiance. Only now under the sun's disapproving glare did Oriana behold just how complete was that ruin. The illimitable scope of the fiendish debris, broken crosses, rusted tangles, and stump upon mournful stump was staggering to the imagination.

How could any world fall to such ruin? This cannot be the purpose intended for it, not for it or any world. Is this what Lord Whitethorn meant by the hand of progress? The progress of death and decay only!

There was but one small glimmer of life and hope in so vast a sea of despair, and its strong trunk was now the only thing standing between Oriana and utter resignation, supporting both her back and her spirit.

And in the mist's parting, she beheld them too! Oriana suddenly found herself face to face with the enemy. This was the breaking point. The impulse to simply lie back and embrace death was overpowering. But her tree would not permit it. As strong fingers were the thick ridges of bole and bark, running up and down her back, holding her fast, denying her wish to abandon life for the despair and death of this ruined world.

Oriana could scarce look upon them. Hundreds of hunched creatures, some in grey, threadbare rags, others in rodent-fur jerkins, and still more in rusting-mail hauberks were assembled in front of the black hedge. What she had supposed in the dense fog was so. Several of them were indeed scudding down the path with vile, toothy grimaces, snorting and slavering as they came.

"Ai, we can see 'er now lads," sneered one of the bow legged fiends drawing nearer. He was brandishing a broad scimitar. A round grey-blue shield blazoned with a black dragon in a long cape hung at his back. "Jus' look at 'er! The ogress! Been 'avin' a good roll about in the muck she 'as by the looks o' things."

"Partial to it she is, I'd say—the filthy cur." growled another, pointing a black arrow at her from his arbalest as he shoved his way forward. He also bore such a shield, he and all the rest of his foul company. "Find the smell appealin', do yeh?"

"A right dainty dish she'll make, I'm sure!" snarled one from the back.

Oriana had seen these self-same devils before! Their squashed snouts, chipped fangs, and swarthy skin were identical to those of the disfigured beasts she had seen bestrewn across the battle-field by the mountain temple.

"D'you like 'at sort o' thing missy—gettin' all smeared over with nasty?" spat yet another with a leer. "Makes 'er real fetchin' don' it mates?" With this, the entire company began chortling in beastly jeers. "Does somin' for yeh, huh, troll-hag? Give yeh nice tinglies all over, do it?"

"Yeah, I jus' bet she's itchin' to play," snorted a fourth as they were nearly atop her. "Ain't yeh missy, ain't yeh? Can see it in the waif's eyes, can't we, lads!"

Only at the Anwash had Oriana ever been assaulted with such lurid, such lascivious taunts. The threat of violation, body and soul, loomed certain yet again.

She was alone. She was defenceless. She was going to scream.

Closer they crept down the blackthorn pass; so great was the reek they gave forth! They smelt exactly as one would expect—indeed, smelling precisely as they looked. Oriana thought if any creature belonged in this land of putrid waste, these fiends surely did; for they cast a stink akin to the Festering Fens itself, despite the fact they were not covered in its filth as she. They were the Fens incarnate.

Baying and drooling, they stood just feet from where Oriana sat slumped in resignation against the great trunk, their crooked blades and short boar-spears and black arrows poised threaten-ingly at her slender neck. Dark, roving eyes glared beadily up and down the whole of her tender body, a savage hunger flashing across their wide faces as they considered her every angle with beastly indulgence.

"'ows 'bout we all 'avin' a bit 'a fun with missy 'ere first, 'fore 'is eminence arrives," growled the one in the front lustily. "Looks right juicy under them rags, don' she? Bet she's unsullied too—still a maid, I'll warrant."

Then, with the point of his notched gavelot, he began poking her tattered dress. Oriana struggled to resist. Even in her half-conscious state, she knew full well what these devils had in mind.

And then, as the fiend continued tearing at Oriana's clothes, there was heard, "*Silence!*" thundering from somewhere, perhaps everywhere. "Stay! You Formorii dogs, or you shall go back to hunting flies! I have not arranged for her to be brought hither for your amusement!"

Oriana opened her eyes fully, jolted by his powerful shrieks. Those nearest her also reeled backward as if startled by his presence. A murmur of dread filled the rest of their dark ranks.

"You are to stand guard, nothing more," commanded the shrill voice angrily from somewhere within the hedge of blackthorn. "Your reward will come in due course, when I am finished with her—when I learn where she has hidden it."

Panting and spitting through broken teeth, the hunched devils withdrew several paces.

"What—what did he just say?" wondered Oriana anemically, struggling still with her erratic breathing. The deformed beasts were so foul and her fear so acute that she had come terribly close to missing what the sinister voice had just claimed.

"Did he say he arranged it?" She was completely thunderstruck! "That can't be right."

What was Oriana to think? Was this truth or the artful dissembling of which she'd been warned?

Oriana was losing the battle with herself. Her breathing was becoming uncontrollable once more. She was ashamed of herself. Courage deserted her. In facing her own imminent death, she was not at all as brave as she would have hoped. In the end, it seemed she did not possess the strength Lord Whitethorn or Lady Natura had mistakenly imputed to her. She could not subdue her fear.

"Of course it was I, you fool," he hissed disdainfully, but this time Oriana felt his voice stabbing at her mind just as she had experienced at the Anwash. A hand of rotting flesh was gripping her soul, his mind peering with unobstructed vantage at her most vulnerable thoughts.

"The filthy white beast did precisely as we expected." His shrieks were changing yet again, the voice of Lord Whitethorn coursing now through her mind. "*And so my master bids me give expression to his gratitude for your faithful service to our cause—but there is more to be done, precious yearling. You will complete what you have begun. You will shew me where it abides.*"

These were lies. The enemy was lying to her. She simply could not reconcile herself to the idea that everything she had endured was really just a part of their dark calculation. But how could she judge?

"Lies think you?" he called hatefully to her mind, his voice resuming its usual venom. "Your conceit ever condemns you to ignorance. You dare say I lie—you whose illegitimacy brings destruction to every realm it touches? Foolish girl! And you wonder you are always left abandoned in the end?

"Lies? Lies you say I speak?" he went on disdainfully. "I alone have sought to counsel you in truth, but you have scorned my wisdom. You would not obey, believing it I who deceives. Pitiable creature! I do not suppose you were warned that whoso slays the Omphalos Rose of this world shall be imprisoned to it evermore. Were you even once told you could never return home if you chose such a path? How cruelly you have been mistreated. A scurvy turn indeed have your friends done you! Can you not see you mean nothing to them—nothing beyond the mere expendable means to their wicked ends? Did I not warn you in the witch's dungeon such an evil deed would come at your peril? Yet you insist I tell naught but lies. You shall see for yourself if I lie."

Suddenly, there was a terrific thunder clasp, yet no flash had heralded its boom. At this, Oriana's gaze was drawn immediately from the slavering horde to the poisonous clouds rising from the distant smokestacks. Out from these came a disgusting sight: overhead a river of glutinous pitch and broken rubble was spilling downward. As vomit it came, a hideous grey-black profusion splattering the ground in a dark pool directly atop an enormous stump and swallowing it whole.

How vile! It was the very stump of the felled beech on which Lord Whitethorn had once laid the sycamore bark to work his enchantment. It was gone now, completely sealed in hardening sick and grey chippings. The destruction of the colossal beech was now complete with insult.

But then, something happened that took Oriana completely by surprize. In that moment of torment and overwhelming fear, she felt a refreshing breeze suddenly whiffling through the whole of her being, laving her soul with welcomed joy. It was as though someone were reaching down for her through a drowning current, pulling her to air and safety.

"Close your mind to his, dear child," spoke the loveliest voice imaginable to her mind. "He is coming and must see no more of your thoughts." It was Lady Natura's voice. Oriana was not alone. She was not abandoned after all. It was she, Lady Natura! She had come to her rescue.

Or was it? Doubt was ever present within her. How could she be certain now of anything? How could she ever trust anyone or anything ever again? Was this more of the same? Was this just another of the enemy's tricks?

"This is insufferable! How can one ever discern truth from deception?" Oriana's mind was ablaze with the frustration of ignorance and doubt.

As she thought, as she doubted, Oriana was yet transfixed to the arc of hardened filth suspended in midair, incapable of averting her eyes as one is so often unable to do when met with a ghoulish sight. Something was now rushing down along the dark surface with terrifying haste.

Closer, faster, it drew near. Oriana stared. She trembled. It became clearer. The rushing grey blur was become a hideous sleigh pulled by four terrible beasts she could not identify.

The misshapen devils were also craning their thick-welted necks upward, and removing their dragon shields, they began beating upon them ferociously with the flat of their curved blades, shouting:

"Master is come! Master is come! Lord Koschei the deathless is come! Come, Lord Koschei, come!"

"Have faith my sweet! Suspend your disbelief," continued Lady Natura consolingly. "In His divine mercy has He seen fit to grant me these remaining words. Take counsel with your heart. Listen—listen and believe. Believe of the truth it sings. The enemy cannot now hear my voice."

And precisely as the lady filled her mind with loveliness, the hideous voice spat to her mind.

"Yes! Why indeed should you not believe me? Why should you not accept that you have been manipulated?"

It was exactly conterminous to that of the lady's immaculate call.

"None can assist you now," exhorted the lady with all the serenity of a summer rain at twilight.

What a curiously disconcerting phenomenon this was. Oriana could hear and understand all of the enemy's icy taunts within her mind and yet feel and understand too the lady's calming words without distraction. Unlike what you might be imagining, it was not at all like trying to understand two people speaking to you at the same time, which is of course impossible to do. Side by side—as different as night is from day—hope and doom called to her, but they were not joined in their call.

"You must trust to your gifts," she continued. "The mystery of Worldsong waxes within you. Trust in your own strength. You can defy him!"

"How?" she asked desperately. "How may I resist him?"

Oriana closed her eyes to the nightmare before her and, without proof or reason in this world of deception, trusted blindly yet again to the lady's counsel. She searched deep within for some measure of defence against the enemy's probing mind. At first, she found nothing until her thoughts coursed back to her first moment of need, to the Anwash and its crystalline water music.

Instinctively, Oriana began humming the same haunting tune in her mind, reproducing with precision all the same ethereal notes and symmetrical harmonies.

Something was happening! Something was growing! Like a spinning and growing sphere of blown glass, a gentle shield spread instantly across her mind, encasing her thoughts in an orb of impregnable crystal.

"Impressive!" he laughed malevolently through her ears from somewhere deep within the encircling hedge of thorns. "But oh, how futile it is! Too little, too late, I am afraid. How very sad for you this is. Your feeble powers cannot protect you from what awaits. I have read nearly all that is needed. And as for the location of where you and the rest of your pathetic guild have hidden it, you will happily take what your heart desires and oblige me with that knowledge."

Oriana's ears rang and seared, his voice piercing with the sting of icy hot needles.

"Time presses, my child, and there are things you must know before we are parted," said Lady Natura grimly. "You must prepare yourself. War approaches, and its coming shall not be as in all the countless days of yore. No longer can the free folk of Faërie protect the Miðgard race from the forces of the faceless foe. Dread now lurks in fair Danuvia—alack! Dread Fáfnirson begins to stir. Now shall fair Danuvia require aid of the blessed mortal world. The debt of Faërie's agelong stewardship lies now upon your world. But first, dear child, first must the dissolution of the guilds be undone. All the magi must emerge from their hiding, for the strength of all the Order will be required if Faërie and Miðgard are to endure. Seek the magi guilds. Follow you they must to fair Danuvia. Ever darker, ever mightier does Malgorod grow since the coming of the Lych-priests to those ruinous lands of Faërie. It is natural; only such faithful wizards, sorcerers, warlocks and druids of Miðgard as yet remain may defeat the fell Lych-priests, those fallen and faithless magi of Miðgard. Such is the quest laid before you as I understand it now aright—the fate of worlds uncounted is at stake! Restore the magi guilds before it is too late. From Malgorod, doth war now come!

"And so, my child, the first battle begins with you! The time is come, Oriana of Oakleigh. Take heart, my sweet, take heart! He is come—he of the dread apostates is come. The enemy's Lych is here! Take courage! He comes with death at his side. He is coming for you!"

"Yes—I will have it! You will happily tell me where it is hid!"

Her eyes watering with pain of the enemy's voice, Oriana gradually reopened them to see at last what had been haunting her since she first crossed into the Wood of Adjoining. And what she saw—what had come for her and her alone, here at the very world where consequence radiates outward to every other world—was worse than the worst of imagined nightmares. The terror was excruciating! Death was come for her, and there could be no escape!

CHAPTER 15

Pome in the Thicket

A rush of claws and stench! The misshapen fiends scudded back down the blackthorn pass, trampling over one another in a terrific hurry. With raised faces, the entire company at once began to howl like rabid jackals as the iron-spiked sleigh drew near their opening ranks. Down, ever down and dark it sped, gliding upon runners of ashy smoke and drawn by four fearsome black hounds, if hounds they were: each was easily the size of a bull with great curling ram horns. They were vicious, snapping and snarling; frothy saliva dript hot from bared fangs.

Then, even before the sleigh came to a complete halt, the foremost helhound lunged suddenly headlong like a fur-covered serpent, biting off the arm of the nearest devil just below the shoulder. Blood spewed; gruff shrieks rended the air. At once, the other hounds joined the fray with explosive tumult, clawing and tearing at the bloodied body writhing sinuously on the ground till nothing save his shield and rusted mail remained. From the other fiends, out of reach and not in the least afraid, there came a terrific roar of chortling and applause as if no other spectacle could have better amused them.

What terror! What extremity of horror! Oriana imagined herself plunged suddenly in the lowest level of Hel.

And the sleigh! A carriage fit for no other than Lucifer himself! What a dreadful sound it made! For in its ashy wake came a horrifying wail, a cry sounding of the far-off keening of multitudes. At once, Oriana knew inexplicably—she knew it to be the lamentations of untold mothers. It was the keening of heart-break she heard!

The bitter wailing made Oriana sink into a despair she did not think possible. One needed but a momentary glance at the sleigh to understand the bewitchment. Completely covered in porous, flaking-orange rust it was, with iron spikes crenellating its railings. And adorning each iron spit were tiny cracked skulls gruesomely impaled. This was an evil inconceivable to Oriana's mind, for no adult skulls were these; these were the skulls of infants! And beneath the tiny skulls, thrown over the corroding sides like mats to be dried, were small hides of—

She was going to be sick! In an instant Oriana's hand was over her mouth, gripping and pushing at her face, struggling to arrest the nauseating reflex panging within. For it was obvious at first sight that the draping flesh had come from the same owners as the skulls—it was the flesh of human infants. Hel! Hel! She was in Hel! There, swarming all about the pinkish hides—Hel! Hel! She was in Hel!—tearing and feasting in a frenzied orgy were the very same skull-speckled moths. Like tiny, incensed vultures— Hel! Hel! She was in Hel!—they were shredding the raw flesh then flying off with tiny bits of gore clutched in their pinchers.

And she saw him, too—at long last Oriana beheld him—the most terrible of all the enemies, save the faceless foe himself. Oriana beheld him! She beheld the Lych-priest!

Down the cadaverous form stept from his sleigh of carnage, dropping his silver-handled whip in exchange for his wooden staff. And just as he alighted in triumph upon the poisoned marsh, the tormented keening of his sleigh fell silent from the air.

The Lych-priest was a terror beyond endurance. Swathed was he in filthy leaden-grey robes, tattered and paper-thin. His face was not to be seen, concealed completely beneath the dark obscurity of his hood. Slowly, with laboured strides, he crept straight for Oriana, leaning upon his crosier twisted and thick with many cruel-looking thorns, an enormous pallid-yellow fang arched upward from its tip like a terrible slashing byl. His other hand was concealed fully within the shadowy folds of his robe.

Naught of him could be seen save one hand and his feet. Emaciated they were, with only the sallowest of rotting flesh draped hideously over splintery bones white as death. As he neared, Oriana saw that he too, like the sheets of mangled flesh, was enveloped in swarming grey moths. She hadn't first noticed them, as they blended almost completely into the grey of his robes. As a swarm of enraged hornets, they shot in and out of his frayed sleeves and up under his drawn hood and then, after flying straight to the raw flesh dangling from his sleigh, returned forthwith to his rotting form.

Oriana, on the very verge of denying the possibility of what her senses were revealing, then noticed several of the moths were clinging firm to his exposed hand, regurgitating tiny droplets of pinkish slime onto sections of protruding bone. Straying between horror and disbelief, she watched as the dripping gore stuck like paste to his protruding bones then grew till the scabs and open sores were covered anew with the raw flesh of innocents.

So in this unholy manner did the grey carrion approach Oriana, shambling forward as a starveling leper, relying wholly upon his staff as an invalid's prop. Step by laboured step, he passed between his minions. Some were kneeling and fawning sycophantically at his rotting feet, while others cowered and cringed, prone upon the ground like rats, covering their monstrous faces as he went. All were stone silent.

Closer, ever closer, he crept toward Oriana, a great stink of rottenness going before him, filling the pass with terror. Even his own thralls would not, or could not, look upon him as he passed—for they too feared his coming.

"Now is the time, my child," called the sweet voice of Lady Natura in that moment of damnation, her voice starting to go faint. "Now you must see to your second choice. Trust in your wisdom, and question not that you are the ordained one—the Dragaica Bride. But understand, child, though you have procured my release and set into motion the first stage of the Mundi Rediendum, you have yet to declare your vow and consummate this union."

As doom drew nearer and the lady's voice ever dwindling from her mind, something bizarre began to occur. Time itself seemed to be slowing its pace. Onward came the creeping dread, yet for each menacing step the leper took, there ought to have been two more steps at least in addition.

Step, staff, limp; step, staff, limp. Death was coming for her . . . slow . . . unnaturally slow.

"Greetings and well met," said the grey cadaver in a voice Oriana did not expect at all. It was a voice that soothed, a voice calling with all the gentle sincerity of a princely heart. Every word, every pause, invited her confidence. "A rare pleasure this is indeed. From long afar have I traveled to aid you in your hour of need. I am now come. No! No, do not take fright, child, for I bear you no malice—I wish only for your good. I come with opportunity at my side—a second chance for you to redeem your errant prepossession. And as it shall not pay you a third visit, I trust you will not squander such opportunity with further foolishness. One last chance have you been granted to make amends."

Eerily slow, he lurched onward through the black thicket holding Oriana's gaze, though she in turn found no gaze in him.

"What shall you chuse?" he continued in his chivalrous tone as he limped forward. Oh, his voice! It was ever so sweet. Yet his approach, his dreadfully slow approach, was ever so terrifying. "Shall you condemn your great white guide to endless torment just as you abandoned your mistress? So foolish, so gullible is he, so easy to harness to our will. Give heed when I say his life shall pay the forfeit if you further hinder me. But you will not be of ill faith. You will not permit his death. No, you will do what is needful to spare him."

Oriana spoke nothing in return, wishing only that she could tear her eyes away from his loathsome form. Once again, Oriana began to weigh his claims. Why should she believe anything he said? What proof did he offer that Lord Whitethorn was indeed suffering? But his voice! His voice! She could think of nothing except his alluring voice of truth.

"You are afflicted with undue skepticism; the shadow of doubt is upon you."

"How can a voice be so lovely, so incorruptible?" She just had to accept—to believe. At once she loved him and dreaded him.

Step, staff, limp; step, staff, limp.

"O ye of little faith, why do you doubt? Such did He once ask of his slave—He the greatest of all deceivers."

It was different. It was changing. His glorious voice was now twisting back to the daemonic hissing to which she had become accustomed. Indeed, his speech changed so abruptly it was as if even he himself had no mastery over his own maniacal caprice. Every word burnt cold.

"Foolish whelp!" he laughed frostily. "You regard as virtue to believe without seeing—such is the folly that broods in your mind. You deceive yourself! In the end, even you do not trow such tripe. Still must you see to believe! Proof you need? Here then is your surety! See and believe what I have reft! Know it is not I who deceives!"

In the slowed bewitchment of time, the tall shadow withdrew his fleshless hand from the fold of his robes and held aloft his trophy for her to see and despair.

"*No!*" screamed Oriana. It was a desolate cry, a cry of disbelief. "It can't be," she thought desperately to herself. "It's just some black incantation—some dark spell! It cannot be his!"

The hunched fiends leering just beyond the brake of wilted blackthorn burst with garbled jeers and laughs.

At once, Oriana flinched as it came hurtling through the air toward her. But she was not fast enough. The horror of it all was magnified many times over when his prize struck her forcibly across the face, slicing a deep laceration before tumbling to her lap. Beads of sticky warmth formed at her left cheek. She clasped her hand to her face.

"Made a right pollard of 'im, Master 'as," jeered one of the hunched devils with vile snorts. In response, there came an eruption of taunts and laughter from the rest. The helhounds too began barking ferociously.

"It is his," she thought, completely mortified and yet enraged at the same time, as violent blows to the face are apt to make one.

Her eyes were cast down. There it was upon her lap, a sight so completely destructive of her hope. Yes, there it lay—a jagged and bloodstained length of Lord Whitethorn's antler.

"There can be no antlers anywhere like his," she said to herself as she fingered its pearly surface, putting an end to her doubt. The broken antler now had none of its former glow—gone was its healing power. An inert, lifeless object had it been rendered, mere matter without spirit.

"What have they done to him?" Anger and frustration rose at once to compete with her fear.

"Now is your greatest peril upon you!" continued Lady Natura, ever fainter and sounding completely unaware of the injury Oriana had just sustained. "If you are prepared to undertake this quest and consummate your union, you must first swear to the fullest measure that final oath of fealty and devotion. But know this first, my child. A terribly grave choice it will be, and it can only come of a choice freely made. Know fully the consequence before you determine on it. Mark well what I say. Should you wed yourself to the Mundi Rediendum, you must sacrifice the very thing you desire most in life. Yet know also, in your sacrifice rests all our hope."

Step, staff, limp; step, staff, limp.

It was a nightmare—a nightmare! Death came! Lady Natura counseled! Pain consumed!

"Be not sad. Rejoice, I say," continued the grey horror, resuming his kindly tone as he lumbered forward unnaturally slow. "Rejoice, for you are finally rid of him. The stag is evil and not to be trusted, though perhaps you have already guessed this. Yes, I see that you have! Any fool could see by your face that you think as much. Imagine, your brave and honourable guide fleeing at the first sign of my presence—flying to save his own wretched white hide, only to be snared by his own cowardice in our trap. He must be purified of his evil. And I," he laughed again, his shrill voice resurfacing. "I shall find great pleasure in administering his purification personally, as you, wicked girl, as you stand idly by, watching helplessly with the knowledge that it was you who laid the great beast low in your disobedience. For if you disobey my command, I am afraid this regrettable purification shall moreover come to you. Now, do my bidding and complete what you have begun for my master."

Oriana sat stone still, her hand yet pressed to her face. Blood was trickling warm down her cheek and out through the cracks in her fingers.

"Alack, I must depart, my sweet," sighed Lady Natura, her voice ever dimming.

Step, staff, limp; step, staff, limp.

Hel was nearly upon her, rising to receive her.

"Chuse well, my child, else ruin take us all! Farewell!"

In that surreal state, in that contradiction between death's slow approach and the lady's wholesome voice, indeed between the black macabre and pain of her physical place and the reaffirming love of the lady's spirit swilling her soul, Oriana thought she might go positively mad! How could such opposites exist in life—in being itself? She sighed for something to root her sanity—some mediating context through which she might reconcile such counter realities. Oh, how she longed for—how she desperately needed something tangible, something real to which she might cling for even the smallest thread of understanding or hope or courage.

And in her torment, Oriana searched through mind and space till at last her eyes lighted yet again on the hawthorn's white blossoms and glistening red berries reaching undeterred into the blackthorn tangles ahead. And in these did Oriana at last find her resolve. They were an icon of defiance—a rejection of evil and fear, a small emblem of hope in a world of utter hopelessness. In the approach of death's certainty, flower and fruit had shed none of their beauty. Yet they were more than beautiful, more than inviolate, they were undaunted. They had refused to wilt in the face of death. Indeed, petal and pome shone with a courage and purity unknowable to the misshapen horde groveling at the feet of fear.

Verily in these did Oriana find her strength. Though her end seemed certain—whatever it may mean to come to one's end, to actually die—just as the countless primroses before her, she too would refuse to close the petals of her spirit and wilt in the face of terror. She was resolute. If in fact, what the enemy had said were true, if she had somehow been serving the enemy's will unbeknownst to her or Lord Whitethorn or the lady, she would do so no longer. She would do nothing the enemy demanded of her. She would never do as he commanded, come what may!

"Leave me," he panted just then, his breath pestilence and decay. In answer, a great noisy fluttering bellowed his shadowy robes. At once, the skull-speckled swarm shot out from under his hood, flying back to feast upon his sleigh of flesh.

It so happened, at that very moment, Oriana then did a very brave thing. Regaining her breath, she took courage and rose firmly to her feet, her hand pressing still to her bleeding cheek. She was more terrified than she had ever been in her life. But with all her will, she endeavoured to hide her fear, refusing to give the enemy any further satisfaction. Gone was the spirit of Lady Natura. And time, in all its horror of uncertain becoming, seemed to have suddenly resumed its normal operation.

Oriana stood silent. Alone she was with death pressing in as close as arm's length, his terrible shadow thrown full upon her.

"You dare stand before me," he whispered in a deadly voice, rottenness coiling through her pained nostrils. "That is most inadvisable."

At this, he raised his thorned staff, its horrible fang brought inches from Oriana's ear.

"*Sssit!*" she heard in protracted hissing so deep she felt it rumble the ground underfoot. It sounded of an impossibly large serpent hissing from across a great gulf of nothingness. Yet it was not the cloaked terror who had spoken. The hissing had come from the fang on his staff!

And so, in a moment did Oriana find herself seated without incident, just as she had been, the coarse bark of the hawthorn boring into her neck and shoulders. She hadn't fallen, nor had she been violently forced back downward. She was simply sitting as though she had never stood to begin with—as if time had merely been set back.

"I see you are susceptible to neither prudence nor wisdom," he scoffed at Oriana in a dreadful whisper. "Foolish shrew! I implored you to reach out to my flesh to save your nefarious guide, but you refused me. Pity! If only you had so done, things would be much easier for all. Yet you follow no rede but your own. Did I not advise you to stay your hand from delivering death to the bewitched rose? But you disobeyed to your own folly—to your perpetual imprisonment in these mires. Be that as it may, in spite of these transgressions, I will shew you clemency and renew my invitation, though you deserve it not. I will take you in, despite the greater wisdom of all others who sensibly abandon you. I alone have it in my power to release you from this imprisonment. I am now your only hope—so is your future cast, shame of world's twain."

It would come at any moment, just as soon as he learnt she would not do his bidding. By sword or sorcery, she would soon be slain and then nothing would matter. There would be no choice for her to make, right or wrong. Whatever it all meant, these stars and crystal disk, returning worlds and a world between worlds, the faërie king and Lady Natura, faërie maids and daemons, dragons and twin babies, guilds and magi, and Lord Whitethorn himself—whatever purpose there could be in a world where such things existed, it would have to be discovered by others, for she knew she would not outlive this day—indeed she would not survive this very moment.

"Do not disappoint me a third time," he begged now softly once more, speaking as though he were a kindly grandfather. Ever closer he leant over Oriana. "Do not cause your own destruction. Do not embrace the *nothing* that awaits you at life's end. Has it not been written that death is nature's remedy to all things? Not so for our order. We have conquered nature. We have escaped death. Now do as I command, and so too shall you defeat death, as I and my brethren have done. Take what your heart desires and live! *Live!*"

Oriana held her peace. Whatever these strange new gifts sprouting within her may be, these mysterious—perhaps magickal—properties, she knew she had no power that could rival his black might. But she had power enough to deny him— that at the very least she could do. And so, Oriana would not look upon him, resting her eyes instead on the tiny scarlet fruits, that emblem of hope fixed once more in her mind.

"Ah! Good! Good—look well upon them. At last you are brought to reason," he said approvingly, his drawn hood turning in the direction of Oriana's gaze. "You desire the fruit. I can see this in you. Good—very good. Wherefore should you have given it life if not to partake of its nourishment? You have only to do as your heart desires—stretch out your hand and pluck the nearest fruit. The mark grows ever clearer upon you. Take the fruit, and you shall be as wise as you are now foolish. It is your only hope."

The enemy was wasting his foul breath. She would never do as he commanded. She would deny him and then—then he would strike, and all would be over.

Oriana folded her hands in front of her, and closing her eyes to all before her, she heard, "Prayer? How supremely droll, but completely pointless," he rebuked with a sardonic tongue, his hissing and shrieking resurfacing. "What misapprehension you do wallow in."

But Oriana was not to be turned by her fear of the enemy, her fear of death, from discovering His will. She could feel her thoughts were yet veiled from the Lych's groping mind, encased still in the sphere of impregnable crystal. It might well prove she could do nothing to stop him from destroying her body, but her will, her soul would never be his again.

"Stupid girl!" he laughed. "Unpardonably stupid!"

Oriana strove bitterly to ignore his taunts, so unceasing they were, her mind wild with fear and hard thinking.

"The depth of your ignorance is astounding! Can your tiny mind grasp no truth whatsoever? Prayer?" He spat savagely. "Mere conceit! Do you not suppose the cruel one has already ordained all things in accordance to His foul omnipotence regardless of your trifling desires? Think you His divine workings might be subject to your insignificant supplications? What beliefs you cling to! It is only through your impudence, your vain worship of self that you expect your tiny petitions might effect some favourable response in Him.

"But enough; this ceases to amuse me!" he shrieked impatiently. "It is clear I am unable to make myself intelligible to your common mind. You waste my master's precious time! Now attend to my bidding forthwith, or it will be the worse for you—I assure you. Eat of the fruit before you, and at last what you and your pathetic guild have concealed shall be revealed to me!"

Reluctantly, Oriana opened her eyes to death's impatience. Though the grey horror towered over her still, her vision was not filled with his black rancor. She had willed her gaze away from him and on to the countless small scarlet fruits and white roses smiling in the face of death.

This was the end. She now knew what must be done and what the dire consequences would be. She was going to die!

Her hand clutching still at the pain surging from her cheek, Oriana looked not upon him as she rose unsteadily to her feet again. As a lone sapling, tiny and insubstantial did she tremble before the terrifying might stretching over her, a greying storm come to devour.

"No! Indeed, no!" declared Oriana in that moment of supreme terror. It was the first time she had spoken directly to the enemy, her quivering voice she knew to be fully belying her courage. But she cared no longer. She *was* afraid, and she came by her fear honestly. She would not stoop to deception herself; she would give no affectation of courage where none existed.

Numb and shaking as she stood in the face of death—yet with a will of iron, recking nothing for the fell stroke that was sure to follow—Oriana said at the last need, half mad with terror, "So long as I draw breath, I shall do no such thing that will give you strength. I am the Dragaica Bride. By my troth do I pledge myself to the Mundi Rediendum. As an oath, I renounce all your works and the ruin of your minions."

Silence … silence … a deafening silence, deep and cold, fell between them. What was perhaps mere seconds seemed eternal. Her defiance had sealed her own fate. He moved to strike.

"*Fool!*" he drawled with malignant breath that poisoned the air. "Impudent, wicked tongue! You die by your own words!"

No changing her mind now! After a long struggle with herself, the choice had come. Her choice was made.

At the precise moment the grey horror raised his staff and made to remove his hood, Oriana reached into the black thicket, plucked the nearest fruit, and bit it!

<><><><><><><><><><><><><><><><><><><><><><><><><><><><>

Such was Oriana's fate! Such was her decision, a choice not easily or lightly made!

Just moments before doing the very thing she swore she would never do, Oriana had done some hard thinking and quick too despite her fear and throbbing pain at her cheek. As she had discovered in the lady's hall, Oriana knew the answer to what she was meant to do, the second choice she was to make, had to be contained somewhere in what Lord Whitethorn had already revealed to her. In spite of all the enemy's efforts, he had failed to make Oriana lose faith in her guide.

Prior to her making so crucial a decision, Oriana had again recalled, sitting with folded hands and trying to ignore the enemy's taunts:

> *Ill-fated rose, new star for each,*
> *Slain and buried for death to reach;*
> *A sacrifice so worlds might teach.*
> *And then thy choice; pixie pear or all as beech.*

"Right then," she had said to herself just before eating the pome, "I suppose I've already seen to the first bit back in the lady's hall, but what's this last part: a choice between a pixie pear, whatever that is—and all as beech?"

As soon as Oriana had repeated the final word of the verse, the answer at once impressed itself upon her. She was not going to allow herself to be confused between homonyms again—between *beach* and *beech* as she had been between *to* and *two*.

"Oh! I see," she had gone on, "he meant a tree—a beech tree—this beech. The one here, just beyond the thicket. If I don't chuse the pixie pair, all will suffer the same fate as the beech. By all, I'll bet he really meant all—everything—nothing less than the whole world, maybe all worlds—perhaps even the Faërie realm too. That must be it. If I don't make the right choice, all that grows green shall be felled and covered by the black vomit of the enemy. It's as Lord Whitethorn warned: '*Ruin brings despair, and despair destroys hope: From that, one belief shall come to replace another. Man's faith in his own knowledge, his lust for dominion—these may come to replace man's trust in Him. And that dominion can only deliver ruin upon his world.*' This is my second choice—I have to chuse a pixie pair over utter ruin. This is the next stage of the Mundi Rediendum, it must be!

"Oh, but hang it all," she had thought in frustration. "I haven't the faintest idea what a pixie pair is, or for that matter, what I'm even meant to do with them even if I knew what they were? If only I had—"

She paused. By great good luck—perhaps it was luck—the memory of something she had heard on the morning of the Brunanburh feast leapt suddenly into Oriana's mind. Freydis, the blacksmith's wife, had said something about a pixie pair by the fishpond.

"But what were they?" she had gone on struggling to remember. "There must have been two of something she was referring to—a pair of something. But two what? Jiminy-gems, Oriana, think! Quickly! Two what? It was something she was talking about at that moment. Was it something she was holding? And they would've been small—pixies are said to be small—two small what?"

Despite her caution, Oriana had of course been doing it all over again— thinking *pair* instead of *pear*.

"That's it. It was something she was holding—something she was working on. That's it—I've got it. It was a wicker hanaper— she was just finishing it. But there was only one, and it wasn't as small as all that. Actually, it was rather—wait! By gum, are you thick skulled, Oriana! It's not the basket—it's what she was handing me from the basket. She said she had been gathering them. I remember!

"Oh dash it! I hadn't seen what they were. I was watching her son fish. She must have been handing me two small—no, I think I remember seeing only one ... Ninny-hammer, Oriana! Dunderhead! That's what you are—if anyone ever deserved the mantle of village idiot, you certainly do! I've done it again. It's pear like a fruit—a pixie pear—a small fruit!

"That's what Lord Whitethorn meant by a pixie pear. That must have been what Freydis was offering me, a tiny fruit."

"And look here! Look! Why they're all around me—tiny

crimson fruits. They're everywhere. That's what a pixie pear is! It's got to be! It's the hawthorn pome! That's the answer—I know it.

"But now what? What am I supposed to do with it? That much, I'm certain is nowhere in any of his riddles. Am I to pluck it and bury it like the primrose and sycamore bark? Maybe I'm supposed to eat one. They are fruits after all, and they do look ever so … Don't be a fool, Oriana; that's just what he told you to do. That's what he's counting on. You'd be playing right into his hand.

"Then what? Where shall I find the answer? If it's not in Lord Whitethorn's verse … The visions! The first vision!"

The obvious imagery of a woman being tempted to eat a similar red fruit broke instantly upon her.

"Why else would I have been led to her, to that first act of sin, if not to ensure I do not repeat the same mistake? That much was at least in his verse—

> Eve chanced fate; that fruit she took,
> Such knowledge was forbidden.
> Shame and fear fell over all,
> Then hallowed disk was riven.

"What? Is that it? The vision holds the answer? But it's so simple—the answer—what I'm to do. It's so obvious! Eve had been tempted by the serpent to eat the fruit. I am being tempted to do the same to save my life. She gave in to her desire for knowledge; she succumbed to her curiosity. Shall I succumb too? To my fear? No! I have been warned.

"So that's it. It's got to be it. Both Lord Whitethorn's verse and the vision were meant to caution me against making a similar mistake. It's so clear. Even the enemy too has given similar warning, though I doubt he himself realizes it. Yes, I'm sure of it now—the enemy has been very careless! He commands me to do precisely as she had done. It's simple. I merely need not repeat her mistake. I will make a right choice. The enemy has very foolishly given me the very reason why I should not do as he demands.

"So that's the answer. All I must do is declare my rejection of him and his demands. That's what I must do with the pixie pear: I must proclaim I will never eat of the fruit he offers. I must cast it aside. That settles it.

"Hang on, Oriana. Are you sure you know what you're doing?" she continued, quizzing herself with lightening speed. "What about the lady's last words to me? She said my choice would come at a sacrifice—that I must give up the very thing I desire most in life. Think what that might mean! Both she and the faërie maids had called me the Dragaica Bride, hadn't they? Lady Natura said I was to prepare my nuptials. And she even said to be fully wed to the Mundi Rediendum I would have to consummate the arrangement by a choice of free will. To be wed ... to be *fully* wed, but that would mean ... if it truly were a wedding, a marriage to this quest perhaps, it might mean I really would be married. If that's right, then there could be no marrying another. Oh, no—I think I'm beginning to see. Cuthbert's casket![1] Is that what she meant by sacrificing what I want most? She can't have meant that! But that is what I want most—to fall in love and have a husband, a happy home, and children; to live a full life in the beauty and tranquility of Oakleigh Manor. Is that what's being asked of me? That I should never be permitted to know man; that I should be denied the love of husband

---

[1] Cuthbert's casket was a popular euphemism in Selwoodshire to express a sudden realization of one's doom. It likely arose from the scene depicted in the Anonymous Life of St. Cuthbert in which St. Cuthbert leant upon his staff, looked to the heavens, and predicted the defeat of the mighty Northumbrian army. Since such times, prayers were made to St. Cuthbert to bring water forth from barren ground and to nourish crops when planted out of season. King Athelstan himself donated an exquisitely embroidered stole and matching maniple to be interred in St. Cuthbert's casket in 934.

or child? How can anyone ask such sacrifice from another? It's too much! It's unreasonable to demand…Wait, Oriana, no one is demanding anything—no one except the enemy. He's the only one demanding, just as he had done when I was about to sacrifice the primrose in the lady's hall. The choice is merely offered to me. It has to come of free will. I do not have to accept. Yes, I do see at last—mine is the choice of woman and is the bitterest of sacrifices save the sacrifice of life itself.

"What do I do then? Is defeating the enemy, is halting the spread of these Festering Fens, this progress as Lord Whitethorn so called it—is preventing the ruin of worlds really worth sacrificing all the happiness I had ever hoped for in my own life?"

It so happened that as Oriana had finished sorting and tidying all the conflicting bits in her mind and arrived flatly at her decision to reject the pome, something began nagging at her intuition. But there was no time for it. Not a moment could be spared on second-guessing or indecision. She must do as her reason suggested—she must reject the pome.

Meanwhile, as Oriana had sat with closed eyes and hands folded piously in front of her, the enemy had assumed her to be praying all the while and not just thinking. This is what was troubling her conscience. At the most critical time in her life, indeed at the point of making the most important decision *in* her life, she began to feel she shouldn't trust to mere reason alone. She must do as Father Oswald had always instructed.

And so she did. She prayed. But at the end, instead of comfort and reassurance, she was met only with yet more doubt. It was not the sacrifice that she doubted; that she felt was beyond dispute—she would have to sacrifice having a family of her own. What was now in question was how to *make* that sacrifice. Her will to do what was right was clarion. But how to express that rectitude—this is what now perplexed her. Such is where her prayer led. Was she really meant to reject the pome in the thicket before her?

Things no longer seemed so simple after all.

What a wholly and utterly bizarre notion she was now considering. She was mystified! Could the right thing to do be precisely what the enemy was telling her to do? This stood logic on its head! Or did it?

"But how can that be?" she thought, agonizing in her search for truth. "It's the enemy's influence. Surely that's it. You're being deceived. I must reject the pome he offers!

"Wait, Oriana—both Lord Whitethorn and the lady said to trust your inner strength. Well, it's telling you something. Something's not quite right about this business. Can't you hear it? Listen. Things are not as they seem.

"Now, Oriana—blast it, will you think? Try and see the enemy's mind. Why not? After all, he's been reading yours for— who knows how long. So think! What would you do if you were the enemy?"

The enemy would ever be a weaver of lies—of this she was certain; from this certainty she began to disentangle the enemy's mind. Even above fear, deception was his greatest weapon. As such, even when he was not lying but using passing truths or half-truths, it would only be done to fulfill his deceitful ends. If telling the incidental truth along the way would help ensnare her in some final deception, then that he would assuredly do. So much had Lord Whitethorn warned. Yes, the enemy was very practical; the means would always be justified by the end. If he had to tell the truth in order to foist a greater lie, so he would do.

"Fine, but I'm still no nearer to deciding what's to be done with those dratted pixie pears. Focus, Oriana. Focus on his mind. Know his mind. What's his game? What's he playing at ..."

As no answer immediately befriended her, she began to feel

herself lost in despair, until such time when, at last like lightening, it flashed fully upon her mind.

"I have it!"

It was another gift! Instantly, her mind enkindled with certitude.

"By Alfred, I have it! I have it! It isn't simple at all. Fool that you are, Oriana. He hasn't made a mistake. He knows quite well what he's doing, comparing my faults—my curiosity, my pride—with the first of all ladies. I should have known. He's far to cunning to slip up like that.

"It stands to reason! His only hope of convincing me to do the thing he really desires is to trick me into believing that I would be doing precisely the thing against his will. That must be it! In the end, he must know I would never consent to do his bidding even on threat of death, for he must know that I know I'm as good as dead anyway—marooned here in this world of waste. So why wouldn't I defy him?

"That's what he's counting on," she reasoned with herself. "He fully expects me to disobey him. That's his mind. He needs me to reject the thing he offers—to see it as a thing of evil to be shunned. Perhaps the fruit isn't evil at all? Perhaps they're not really his to offer anyway! That's his plan—it's got to be. I will be deceived no longer! I have to make an end of this! At last I see through his crooked words."

And at this, it occurred to Oriana that she had been mistaken about a good many things all along—even about the Primrose Path itself.

"So this is the moment Lord Whitethorn had warned. This is the heavy hour, not my choice in the Lady's hall," thought Oriana as she came to a new understanding. "This is what he meant—the choice of greatest self-sacrifice, the moment of consummation, the act of greatest peril. This is the Primrose Path. I've even been wrong about that too. He hadn't just meant a primrose path figuratively, as the path of deception, which much of this has certainly proven to be. Ever in his greater wisdom, he meant it as literal fact as well. For see, the blackthorn path is an actual primrose path, the pass is festooned with primroses!"

Now was it clear. The path now blocked by death and his fell minions *was* the Primrose Path, but it was not just the path of deception; it was the path of hope, and life, and courage, and a will to conquer fear.

Oriana understood things plainly. This indeed was the heavy hour come for her at last. This was the moment she must now commit herself wholly and unconditionally. This was the task appointed for her, perhaps long before she was even born. She was the Dragaica Bride: her charge, the Mundi Rediendum. She would not fail those who yet hoped, whoever they may be, that the world—her world, perhaps all worlds—might be restored to their original teleos—the ordained purpose of worlds to have being in harmony with all creation, not as victim, not as casualty of man's dominion.

Now, of course, while it took you quite a goodly stretch of time to read what exactly had been swirling about in Oriana's agile mind, it took her far less time to actually think it all. Ideas are wonderfully swift like that—particularly for one who is no other than the daughter of worlds twain!

And so as we have already seen, with her mind made up for the second time—but this time for good—she declared, knowing she stood on the very brink of death.

"No! Indeed, no! So long as I draw breath, I shall do no such thing that will give you strength. I am the Dragaica Bride. By my troth do I pledge myself to the Mundi Rediendum. As an oath, I renounce all your works and the ruin of your minions."

"Fool! Impudent, wicked tongue—you die by your own words!"

Again, at the exact moment the grey cadaver raised his staff and started to remove his hood, Oriana reached into the dark thicket, plucked the nearest fruit, and bit.

In a moment, Oriana was consumed with a fresh impulse of joy as the bitter juice of the pome surged through her body.

"No!" roared the towering menace in deadly hatred, his wroth bursting forth with overwhelming might. Up went his staff. Down, down it came! With what might did he smite the ground! *"Curses to time!"* he howled again, shaking with rage. Instantly, blue flames burst from the staff's fang. So terrible were his shrieks that his own helhounds and dark servants whimpered in pain or fear.

So, while Oriana may have done precisely as the enemy had commanded, it was plain that it was not at all what he had actually wished her to do. Despite all the enemy's cunning and strategems, in spite of all his wiles, policies, and evil hatchings, in the end, he was discomfited by Oriana's perseverance, wisdom, and self-sacrifice.

Oriana made a good choice!

CHAPTER 16

Time for Silver and Song

Air. *Clamour. Movement. Light.* All was suddenly in flux, unaccountable, and strange. Almost nothing was as it ought to be.

Or such at least was Oriana's impression of things following the Lych's hateful shriek. Time and being had become swept up in a whirlwind of disorienting confusion. This was more than the unnatural slowing of time she had just experienced at the Lych's arrival. This was a bewilderment Oriana had never before encountered—experiencing time behaving as though it might be a child's top spiraling out of control.

Could it be that everything was happening at the same time, or perhaps in reverse, or even over and over again? Why was time behaving so? How could she hope to make sense of anything unless one thing led to another and then another and so on? But nothing was occurring that way. Nothing was right. Her very mind seemed to give way in consequence.

Though perplexed as Oriana was over the total disruption of time it was extraordinary how at peace she felt in spite of it all.

"Maybe this is how it always is when one's about to die—confused but carefree," she thought in placid acceptance of her impending death. "Perhaps time simply ceases or gets all muddled when one reaches her end. With the end of one's being so too ends one's time, I suppose. Well, if this is how it must be, so let it come. I will pass as all others before me."

◇◇◇

Just as soon as Oriana bit the fruit, she found herself prone upon the ground. A mighty tremor, shaking deep to the very foundation of this strange world, toppled Oriana and all the hunched devils beyond the thicket. But not the cloaked horror, not he— he would not be cast down. He remained bending over Oriana ready to deliver death.

Time. Time. There was another hiccup of time! Sights and sounds were now whirling round her and in front of her, coming and going, stopping and repeating.

"Was that…was that a battle?" For a moment, just for the merest of moments, it looked as if thousands had stood arrayed with goodly battle gear and fierce accoutrements just beyond the brake of smoldering blackthorn. Surely a battle it must have been! There had been blinding flashes, shining helms and grinding howls, the clanking of armour and parrying swords, the battle cry of fair voices, and swelling trumpets, and the fluttering of bright gonfalons there were too. And there also was the Silver Causeway; for a spilt second, Oriana thought she had seen the shimmering of wide silver reaching down from the heavens. There was probably a natural sequence to it all, there just had to be, but it was well beyond Oriana's current power of comprehension.

It was then that something else happened to augment Oriana's bewilderment. As if trying to derive meaning from a world without the normal flow of time wasn't difficult enough, she now had this to reason through.

If Oriana had to guess, it was the moment the blue flames burst from the end of the Lych's staff, incinerating nearly everything in its path, when it probably happened.

She had experienced this before. It was the queerness of the Brunanburh feast all over again. Oriana found herself confronting, once again, that same transcendental dualism, that exact, ineffable phenomenon she had encountered upon first meeting Lord Whitethorn. For the second time in her life, Oriana was one indivisible whole in two very separate places—indeed in two separate worlds. Her very being had become bound up with that paradoxical state of schism without separation. She was there— in the world of her tapestry, the world of Lord Whitethorn. Oriana was gazing out along the arching surface of the Silver Causeway and yet seated too by the renewed hawthorn awaiting her end at the hands of the Lych.

Yes! Oriana's other nature *was* reawakened in his realm—that world of omnipresent meaning and verdure, the world of the grassy knoll and wide swarth, the hawthorn and Silver Causeway. She was again one with that perfect place where nothing, however small, seemed a product of chance or devoid of significance.

Yet there was much now that was different. Oriana was rushing across the dazzling cobbles in long, hurried strides, not staring up at it from below as she had once stood in readiness to receive Lord Whitethorn's word. For alas, there was now no word to *be* received, for there was no Lord Whitethorn! The balance of being had been clearly upset by it—his absence—cleaving a palpable void in that sentient and otherwise consummate realm.

Oriana hastened over the Silver Causeway; she hastened toward imminent collision.

"Get you gone, scourge of Malgorod!" demanded Oriana in stentorian waves across the length of the causeway. She was calling to a grey-robed form gliding effortlessly toward her along the same reflective surface. He was not staggering or limping but hurrying just as she.

"Be gone, I say! For I am come! Through the pome, through the Dragaica Bride am I come!"

"Hang on—did I just say that?" thought Oriana with her familiar consciousness. But it had to be she who was calling thus. She had certainly experienced the sensation of speech, feeling her lungs swell with the young air. And she had felt her lips moving too, moistened as she spoke with the purposive nectar of that world. Yet the voice that echoed with such authority was not that of her usual demure register; it spoke with a knowledge and strength she could never expect to attain.

So odd were her raiment and weapons here. She would have given anything for a polished looking glass just then. To her astonishment and her fancy, Oriana saw she was arrayed in the likeness of a great warrior-princess whose rival could be no other than Lady Natura herself!

Strapped tightly to her left arm was a most extraordinary shield. Wide and nearly round it was, cunningly wrought in the image of a single flower petal and burning yellow bright with the captured shine of young suns.

In her other hand, brandished as a war hammer, was a curious stone sceptre slightly longer than the length of her arm. Carved round its stone surface at both ends were four human faces, capped off, first at one end and then the other, with dazzling balas rubies that flickered in their own scarlet light as if lit from within by tiny candles.

Yet it was not these things that made the stone sceptre altogether curious. That came at its very top. In the fashion of a modern trophy in your world, a large, upright golden ring about the size of a noble's armlet rose from a silver bezel imbedded in its ruby base. And standing atop the very extremity of the golden arc, tall and straight as a keen-eyed sentinel, was a crystal-white figurine of a stag—a totem of Lord Whitethorn it looked.[1]

But her transfiguration ended not at her shield and sceptre.

---

[1] For a rough impression of what this unusual talisman looks like one can do no better than to view the imitation whetstone sceptre currently reposed at the British Museum. It's part of the Sutton Hoo exhibit. That it is a counterfeit is easily detected as the terminal knobs are merely painted red and not rubies; the stag and ring are made of simple bronze; and perhaps most telling of all; the stag's antlers are entirely too small.

The body and limbs Oriana saw moving below her gaze were fully clad in the same white crystal of the stag figurine. She was immediately reminded of the faërie armour of the tall lords who gave battle to the black dragon, similar yet not identical. Rather than a mesh of overlapping turquoise scales, Oriana's hauberk was more a gown of flowing white feathers. And though Oriana could feel her body moving effortlessly and independently of the light mail, it certainly appeared that the long feathers had actually sprung from her flesh, leaving bare only her feet and hands and what little she could see of her neckline.

"Be gone with you and return withersoever the black wyrm now hides," Oriana demanded boldly. "Nowhere in this realm is purpose proffered to you. Be gone."

"Hides?" scoffed the cloaked figure as he raced in long strides along the Silver Causeway toward Oriana. Hatred was his voice, but its venom was not the shrill cry she had anticipated, if anticipate anything at all she could in this transcendental realm. There was nothing in the least exceptional about his voice. It was not shrill, not a shriek at all. He spoke just as any other ordinary man. And unless Oriana was very much mistaken, he was not as tall as his other nature towering also at this moment above Oriana amidst the smoldering blackthorn of the Festering Fens.

"Even here do you display a pathetic want of knowledge," he went on scornfully, sweeping ever closer with raised staff. "Ever shall ignorance be your demise. Hides? Filthy were-swan! My master hides no longer. The crystal bulwark is shattered. In Danuvia my master hunts again."

"Unbidden slave of Malgorod—" trumpeted Oriana with all the severity of a goddess who has been defied.

"What is this voice?" she wondered in overwhelming perplexity. "How can I be saying these things?"

A few more strides and they would collide.

"The ruin of your calumny ends with you!" she called. "As

shriveled leaves under tempest's rebuke shall your dark cantrips fall lifeless before me."

"End? No! Half-breed scum—" shouted the Lych-priest maleficently, blood now dripping dark from every crooked thorn of his staff and onto his—

His hands! They were completely ordinary. They looked just as hands should—not a splintery bone or gangrenous sore to be seen. Both his voice and his hands were ordinary in this realm. Why?

"We *have* no end," he laughed. "We have just arisen!"

"Perfidious tongue! Banter no deceit with me!" Her shield was rising, the golden ring on her sceptre filling its empty circle with the soft twinkling of morning dew, whiffling the brisk scent of winter nearing.

"Bane of living worlds," she thundered with overwhelming disdain, "your lychcraft is at an end!"

This was nearly impossible for Oriana to comprehend. Her single mind had to make sense of two worlds at parallel moments. For as Oriana, the swan warrioress, prepared to smite the enemy along the Silver Causeway, Oriana, the humble Saxon girl, continued to stare in horror at the shrieking menace rising above her as she sat, slumped against the hawthorn, awaiting her end.

In a transport of rage, the Lych stretched out the Hel fire from his staff. The terrible walls of blackthorn were incinerated at once. Blue flame was upon her! Oriana crossed her arms in front of her bloodied face to hide her eyes from death's final stroke.

But death had not come! She was not devoured!

Suddenly, Oriana felt a sharp, frosty splinter coursing from her bloodied, out-turned palm—the one that had been nursing her lacerated cheek—and into the warmth of her heart. There was an explosion deep within her. Then out from her heart, a wintry tempest surged in repudiation, flying back to her blood-stained hand with terrifying potency.

In a moment, Oriana had uncrossed her arms and gasped in wide wonder at the blizzard of snow and ice blowing furiously from her scarlet fingertips. Steam lifted thick about her as the enemy's flame was doused with broad flakes and tiny crystals of drowning white.

But Lord Koschei was not foiled. He lurched forward in answer, and with a single wave of his rotting hand, both flame and frost vanished with the rising steam. And before Oriana could hope for or will another defence, her hands and legs were pinioned with terrible iron cords, indeed the same cords dangling with orange rust from the legion of broken crosses overhead. The pain was excruciating.

Loud rose the chortling and vile castigations from the hunched onlookers. They had gotten back to their clawed-feet and were closing in for better sport through the smoldering remnants of blackthorn.

❖❖❖❖❖❖❖❖❖❖❖❖❖❖❖❖❖❖❖❖❖❖❖❖❖❖❖❖❖❖❖

Meanwhile in the parallel world of Lord Whitethorn...

Oriana was astounded. She just never would have believed such a thing possible.

The Silver Causeway was not impervious to ruin. It came as a very great shock when Oriana saw its sterling glow reshaping underfoot into the like of the odious black scar that had served to speed the enemy's sleigh of carnage down from the venomous clouds and into the world of the Festering Fens. The Silver Causeway was reshaping into a causeway of death.

For just when the Lych raised his staff, conjuring spates of dark blood to rain upon Oriana, up swung her sun shield to ward off his attack. Like spent arrows, red gore glanced ineffectually off the crystal surface, bespattering the silvern cobbles below.

The filth was sacrilege. As acid set to pearl it was. At every point gore defiled silver, pungent vapours seethed higher and higher, leaving behind terrible blotches. Like a plague, the black sores spread ever wider and deeper until every spattering blemish was joined together in one great malignancy. A canker it was, stretching ravenously to consume the sterling fabric upon which Oriana stood waiting to lay the enemy low.

Oriana attacked. She raised her sceptre. Forth rushed a mighty deluge of crystalline music out from its golden ring as though it were the great Sea of Tyynimôr itself, roaring through the porthole of a scuttled ship.

For a moment, it appeared Lord Koschei might be swept over the blackening causeway with the rapids and eddies rushing from her sceptre and down into the clouds of gossamer below. But not for long did it seem. Here, too, was he far too quick!

His staff would not be defeated. With a sudden rush of foul air, every drop of cleansing wash pouring from Oriana's sceptre was immediately siphoned through the fang of his staff and cast high into the air with his other hand. At once, the rising water reshaped into the like of a poisonous green furnace cloud.

Oriana found herself suddenly in great straits, hopelessly belyched once and for all. She couldn't say how it occurred exactly. Faster than thought itself, Oriana's shield was at her feet, and her feather corselet crisscrossed in layers of rusting cords. She struggled with all her might against the iron knots, but it was no use. And worse than all, she saw that her stone sceptre was now clutched firmly in the Lych's hand.

"Fool! Upstart!" he laughed triumphantly. "What is your feeble Worldsong to a Lych's might? Now you are in my power!"

Then, the grey shadow raised staff and sceptre together. It was an unholy union. Through the sceptre's golden circle, Lord Koschei thrust the enormous fang of his staff. Like a rapacious finger it was, claiming the gold and crystal ring for its own. There was a flash. The serpent fang sparked with red lightening as the golden band slid down to find its final fit. Sceptre and crosier were joined!

Out he slid the fang from the defiled ring, but the golden circle did not fall vacant in the fang's absence. The golden ring that only moments ago had been a font of cleansing rapids was now the socket of a single roving eye, yellow and cunning, its black slit narrowed in anger. Oriana could feel its scorching gaze endeavouring to unhinge her mind. It was searching for something—something it was convinced she possessed.

And so, in parallel worlds, in parallel moments, was Oriana, the fearsome swan maiden, and Oriana, the terrified Saxon girl, held at bay by a lychcraft greater and more terrible than she had ever supposed.

◇◇

Back at the Festering Fens…the Lych-priest was summoning dark incantations, whirling his staff in a wide oval above his head. With a flash of scarlet heat, an iron-spiked palanquin, hung with terrifying chains and bloodstained manacles that rattled and clanked, emerged suddenly next to Oriana where she yet sat, struggling against the biting cords round her ankles and wrists. This was the moment of dread. The Lych-priest was to be death's gaoler.

"How dare you defy me, witch! You'll pay dearly for it," he shrieked. "You will come with me. My master has been kept waiting far too long for the likes of you, and he is not patient. The time for your purification is upon you."

◇◇

Likewise, in that world Oriana had once regarded as Lord Whitethorn's sacred and private abode, in the very midst of the filth consuming the Silver Causeway, the deep but ordinary voice of the cloaked horror called:

"The time is come! Awake, master, awake! I imprecate the word of my master."

And at that same moment in the twin reality of the Festering Fens, the grey leper shrieked, "The time is come! Awake, master, awake! I imprecate the word of my master. *Perkelefa* he is!"

But then, just as the Lych-priest invoked the word of his master—that ruinous and unholy word, *Perkelefa*—something most perplexing happened to him. Something, it appeared, even he did not expect. Instantly, came a dazzling blue-green nimbus around Lord Koschei, bathing him in thin wisps of luminescence and dancing starlight. There he stood, frozen in a churning prism in parallel worlds. Not a single spidery fold of his robes was to be seen moving. It was as if he had turned to the very stone of Oriana's sceptre clutched yet in his foul grip, its yellow cat eye now gone. And similarly in the world of the Festering Fens the throng of hunched devils and helhounds likewise stood completely motionless as if turned into monstrous bronze statues.

How curious it was! So perfect and wonderfully jewel-like was the sphere enveloping the enemy in both realms that it was difficult for Oriana to accept its enchantment could have been wrought of his malicious design. After all, why would he have frozen himself at the very moment of his triumph?

Then there came a second, similar light and the sound of sweet singing from behind Oriana as she sat against her tree. A cheerful glow, dancing and singing, dappled the hawthorn's serrated leaves in soft aqua sparkles. And just as quickly as the dancing light had come, it was gone, but not the singing and not the swirling aura imprisoning the Lych; they remained.

As best she could, tied the way she was with her hands and feet fettered in tight metal knots, Oriana turned round, her eyes darting to the gay wonder above. It was a welcome sight. They had returned!

Joyous was the sound of their golden harps and flutes of pearl, silver trumpets and many-stringed fiddles of yellow wood and opal inlays. Oriana could only gasp, filled with amazement. Scores of the very same halcyon maids of the lady's hall were perched athwart the hawthorn's lower boughs, singing and caressing their instruments. As if weighing little more than the merest of winter wrens, did they bend the slender branches.

And their clothes! Oh, how splendid they were! Each was gaily adorned in a woad-dyed peplos draped diagonally over indigo hanselines, fastened at the shoulder with delicate brooches of gold and sapphire. And just as they had worn in Lady Natura's hall, the faërie maids were bedecked in the same silver chaplets, emerald scarves, and necklaces of crystal dewdrops.

Moreover, like Oriana and the enemy, whose single beings existed in two distinct worlds, so too had the faërie maids appeared in both realities. For as they sang upon their boughs at the Festering Fens, so did Oriana, the swan warrioress, behold them dancing upon the darkling causeway, clasped hand in hand, turning and swirling round the imprisoned Lych as if he were no more threat than a spring maypole.

By sight and sound was Oriana filled with a joy she had thought perished from the world.

"All hail to thee, fair lady of the blessed mortal realm," said the effervescent young ladies in one sublime chant, their words rising almost as song. "We return to aid the Dragaica Bride. We return to sing and dance and to serve—to serve thee, our lady.

We come again! As an oracle have we sung the *Lay of Dread* and protected the Dragaica Bride."

Was this another incomprehensible slip of time? What did they mean they had sung the Lay of Dread? What had they sung? She had heard no song. Had she missed something again?

"Oh thank goodness! You've come just in time," said Oriana, craning her neck to gaze up at the maids as they swayed merrily in the hawthorn. "I am most thankful, dear ladies. Please, can you tell me—what is happening?"

"That we can, but take heed, lady of Miðgard," they continued chanting. "Your strength is yet sprung to fullest blossom. Lord Koschei's necromancy is a power far beyond any you now possess. Have a care. Had we not intervened with our lay, your defiance of the enemy would have certainly meant your doom. Brave though thou art, our lady, thou must tread warily."

"But I didn't realize I was…the Silver Causeway…How? Why am I clad—" sputtered Oriana, trying to give expression to every question at once, and in consequence unable to get out a single one. She turned from the fair maids and glared in amazement at the Lych-priest frozen before her in both worlds.

"What's befallen the enemy? Why has everything come to a halt?"

"'Tis the enemy's own doing. His wroth hath blinded him to the ancient truth," they continued in one sweet voice. "He dared utter the word of their ancient master. And so have we ensnared him with that odious word. The *Lay of Dread* is the weapon of last resort and, we daresay, your only preservative from the chains of Malgorod."

"*Lay of Dread?* Oh, ladies, once again, I find myself disadvantaged to your greater wisdom," pled Oriana tensely, as she watched the faërie maids dance in circles round the imprisoned Lych atop the blackened causeway. "What is this wonder that holds the enemy?"

"'Twas the enemy himself who hath unleashed our song by invoking his master's being. Ever has it been forbidden to voice the word of their black lord."

"But … his word? I don't understand," begged Oriana, breathing heavily as she continued to stare up with a strained neck at the young maids perched atop the hawthorn. "His name, you mean? But I've already heard the name of his master spoken before now. Both Lord Whitethorn and Lady Natura so named the enemy's master. They called him the faceless foe. Is this not the name of the Lych-priests' lord?"

"A description, yes, our lady," the maids continued in twin worlds. "In all his treachery and evil, yes, he is sometimes called the faceless foe. But these words are neither his name nor the words of his being. Since time was first hatched, their master has remained nameless. Yet, though he has no name, his being may be voiced if one has strength enough to endure the torment its invocation inflicts. Now hath one among the Lych done so and survived its withering curse. Mightier still shall their power now grow in his word."

"There is so much I need learn, my ladies! What can you tell me of the faceless foe?" she asked hurriedly, still wrenching her feet and hands against the biting cords of rust. "I know so very little of these matters."

"The living daemon he was, high chancellor to the greatest of enemies."

"Not—"

"Yes, our lady, the Dark One—the ancient of ancients, lord of Hel, and purveyor of all that is evil. Of all the servants of the Dark One, the faceless foe was his greatest servant."

"How horrible!"

"Quite!" they returned in a low, collective whisper. "Yes, he was a horror without equal."

"*Was?* Lord Whitethorn told me he remains imprisoned in Malgorod. Is this your meaning?"

"'Tis a ponderous tale," they chanted in ever lower tones. "And our time is short. Behold!" they said, pointing with slender fingers. "Already doth the Lych stir beneath our enchantment. Only now will we say the spirit of their master vanished long ago. The great heorot may be right. It is possible the faceless foe passes his days in torment beneath the dead fastness of Malgorod, or so saith many."

"What of the Crystal Bulwark, my ladies? What is this?" Oriana asked urgently. " He said it's shattered—he said their master hunts again in Danuvia."

"Deception is the only answer," they replied firmly. "Wrought of the stars themselves, the Crystal Bulwark cannot be undone once cast. Of their master, they refer not to the faceless foe but his fell eme, rather—his black surrogate. There is the belief that much of the faceless foe's might passed unto his dragon steed when he departed from the living—Dread Fáfnirson he is hight, curse his scaly name—"

"Dragon steed! The visions—the cloaked rider! That was the faceless foe?" whispered Oriana in horror.

"Dread Fáfnirson is their only master now," they pressed on. "Lo! Do some fear his age-long banishment may be drawing nigh anon, but it cannot be that he now feasts freely again. Surely would we wit if his reek were once more abroad—his plundering has no like!"

"Then the light which now imprisons this Lych-priest, this Lord Koschei—it comes at your hands, I deem?"

"Verily!" affirmed the faërie maids together in a rising pitch. "The light is the residual of the *Lay of Dread*. Once the word of the faceless foe hath been proclaimed it is song alone that may cleanse the evil of that word. And so, as Lord Koschei was first to proclaim his master's being, now are we permitted to use the power of his word against him: the word of the living daemon—*Perkelefa*."

Oriana stared back at the enemy. "I am ever at your mercy, dear ladies. I shudder to think what would have become of me had you not intervened."

"Yes, we have come to sing and dance and serve our lady, though it nearly did not come to pass. But for Lord Koschei's effort to invoke the evil of his master through the Crimson Stone we could not have heard your peril and hither arrived."

"The Crimson Stone?"

"Your stag sceptre, great Lady of Miðgard. The whetstone betwixt the crimson jewels, this is the Crimson Stone—a gift from the scholars of our world to the magi of yours. O! Blessed stewards of Miðgard are they yet! Most unwise it was of the enemy to proclaim the living daemon whilst holding that mighty talisman."

But Oriana had her doubts whether the enemy had indeed erred. "I don't think he is in the habit of making mistakes," thought she, but asked instead, "Dear ladies, is this then my deliverance? Is the Lych-priest permanently immobilized in your crystal?"

"Nay, our lady," went their chant. "In attempting to use the sceptre against thee, he merely severed his own cloaking spell and alerted us to your peril. But now that our lay is ended, the enemy begins to wake. Yet some time hath thee been afforded in its song. You shall not remain defenceless."

Again, Oriana's thoughts were racing. "What do they mean, *'alerted us to your peril'?*" she asked herself. "Didn't they already know I was here? Didn't they guess I was still here? They were themselves with me in the lady's hall—the Seed of Life. They must have known. And what is this lay they keep referring to?"

Her mind was reeling!

"So is that what the enemy meant—the stag sceptre—the

Crimson Stone?" she asked the maids. "Is that what he was searching for? Is that what he wanted me to reveal to him?"

"No, 'twas not the sceptre he seeks. He guessed rightly thou wouldst attempt to wield it before him. Though why he would have attempted to summon its might against thee, our lady, is strange indeed."

"How so?"

"The enemy knows they cannot harness the beauty of Worldsong. Forever deaf have they become to its strength since the days of their black apostasy."

"But he joined them, my ladies—he united the sceptre with his staff."

"He connected tooth and ring?" asked the maids in a troubled way.

"Yes! And when he withdrew his staff a—a terrible yellow eye filled the circle."

The ladies paused, staring at one another atop the hawthorn with worried eyes. And no longer were they dancing along the blackened causeway in that parallel reality.

"Fáfnirson!" they chanted softly. "Eft of despair! Reaver of lands! He has the great heorot. The dread wyrm holds him deep in his lair." They no longer seemed so very gay. "We have no words or song for thee," they went on after a pause. "O Dragaica! You setteth us to worry afresh. Something has gone amiss. Some treacherous snare, some betrayal is afoot. Have a care, lady of Miðgard—have a care! This is our parting rede."

How frustrating it all was. For every answer she had discovered were now at least two more questions. To begin with, she still wished to know what this other part to her nature was— This courageous warrior-princess yearning still to give battle to the enemy. And why had she borne this stone sceptre with its crimson jewels? How did she come to be in Lord Whitethorn's world when he had not been there to summon her as he had done at their first meeting? There were entirely too many questions. What was to become of her? What was she to do now?

"Then what, dear ladies? If not the sceptre, then what do you suppose he meant by revealing what I've hidden?"

"We should think this obvious to thee, our lady. As do all our foes that desire dominion over all that is good and green, this Lych seeks to recast the hidden amulets—"

"The amulets?" she asked herself. "Where have I—Oh yes, Lord Whitethorn. He had once mentioned these near the elder-flower thicket."

"He sees its mark upon you as plainly as do we!"

"The mark? What mark? Please, whatever do you mean?"

"The mark of the Sun Brooch. We see it now. It breathes in every strand of thy golden tresses; like spun sunlight are your locks to our eyes. It tells us the Sun Brooch has been in your keeping ere you uttered your first word or shed your pearly swad-dling cloth."

"Pearly swaddling cloth?" thought Oriana as she too now noticed what the faërie maids had warned. The Lych-priest was beginning to stir from his bewitched slumber. From the ever-corroding causeway, her hauberk of crystal feathers wrapt still in rusting cords, and from the hollow trunk of the hawthorn, her hands and feet ruthlessly tied, Oriana watched as fine stresses began to emerge along the face of the swirling globe of light.

Oriana wished to learn all she could about this curious mark she allegedly bore and about the Sun Brooch and about the join-ing of sceptre and staff and everything else about this inconceiv-able business.

"Please, dear ladies, can you tell me? What is this Sun Brooch?"

"Of this we know: the Sun Brooch is one of the four scattered talismans," was their dire reply. "Understand, lady of Miðgard, in partaking of the pome, you have released the spirit of the Sun

Brooch from her chamber. Her spirit has joined the Dragaica Bride. By mother Danu's blessing has your transformation, your union begun, and so you see, dear swan-maiden, are you thus arrayed. It is as we've said: only the Dragaica Bride can free Ethélfleda, queen of Faërie, and it is our queen who alone may restore the hawthorn disk through her healing touch. So has it been written."

"Hawthorn disk? Ah, they mean the disk that shattered on top the mountain! They must," she told herself. "And if I had not eaten the pome?" she asked them directly, overwhelmed and still in disbelief that she could actually be the one meant to do such fantastic deeds.

"Death, our lady!" they chanted grimly. "Had you rejected it, Lord Koschei would have struck; you would have been slain. Had the Lych deceived you, had you not released Lady Natura and restored the hawthorn, the Omphalos Tree, there would have been no pome—there would have been no Dragaica Bride."

"I see."

"But you chose wisely, our lady, chusing love over fear and self," they went on with approbation in their voice. "In restoring life to the hawthorn, the Lych could not touch you, so mighty was the love of Worldsong you released. Yet, had you rejected the pome, had you refused to accept such sacrifice and consummate your nuptial, the protection of Worldsong would have sundered at once. You would have been destroyed, and your flesh stript, taken to Malgorod as feast for his black master."

"How close... how close I came to this wretched end; how so very nearly I was decieved!" she reflected in horror. "Tell me, my ladies—and do forgive my pertness, I beg—but... well, could you not have told me all this in the lady's hall?"

"O lady of Miðgard, 'tis antithetic to Worldsong," came their chant. "Such is not the way to its welling hymn. Had you not discovered these truths for yourself, there would have been no music by tree or pome."

"Just as Lord Whitethorn said, I suppose," thought Oriana. "'*It falls to us each to discover our own paths to understanding, for there exists certain knowledge that cannot be given from one to another.*'" And at this thought, Oriana similarly recalled what the great stag had said to her at their first meeting: "*'Verily the strength I have beheld in you may bear fruit of that hope.'*" The fruit of that hope! He meant the pome! That was the fruit he meant! And the hawthorn … the hawthorn is the embodiment of hope! My strength gave it fruit!"

"But alas, lady of Miðgard, the time we have awarded thee has been meager. With our lay we have done all we are able. Let us hope it will suffice. We shall know soon enough."

"Please, dear ladies, what is this lay of which you speak? Tell me, please. I feel I am at last nearing understanding."

"Why the lay we have sung to hold the enemy so! The same lay we have sung for thee, O Dragaica Bride. But our song is ended. We must bid you farewell. It is ever doubtful we shall meet again by hawthorn or silver lane or aught that is green, or silver, or fair beneath the Maker's gaze. Fare you well!"

And with blue and green sprits of light leaping skyward from both the hawthorn's leaves and poisoned cobles of the causeway, the faërie maids vanished from both worlds.

Now as time had become such an impossible entanglement of events, Oriana hadn't perceived, or at least couldn't recall having experienced, the faërie lay. It was only now, or now it seemed, that this past event was catching her up.

And so, at last Oriana heard the singing of faërie maids, as harp and flute, fiddle and horn were played as only faëries can do when spurred by the listening of tree and sun and bright moon of day.

Of course, without their music this can hardly be described as their song, yet these are at least the words Oriana finally heard that stilled Lord Koschei in his hour of triumph. It was a doleful piece with none of the gaiety one usually imagines of the bright choirs of Faërie.

> Dread Fáfnirson, Perkelefa,
> On whom death oft relies;
> Lord Fáfnirson, Perkelefa,
> Bewitched with Hel's black might.
>
> In wandering, man was content,
> With berry, nut, and game,
> At yonder ridge or distant shore,
> Borders not, but yearning for.
>
> Such faith did die, that trust was rent,
> For will, control, and might.
> Rise ye power to slay erst-age,
> From furrowed earth, not the sage.
>
> Dread Fáfnirson, Perkelefa,
> From whom despair doth flow;
> Cursed Fáfnirson, Perkelefa,
> Fell cloak is child's last night.
>
> To growth of steel shall wills be bent,
> In envy, steam, and ash.
> Behold gone crafts from smiths of yore,
> Art thou wise with art no more?
>
> Woe noble mound thy doom is sent,
> With iron, greed, and wroth.
> Thy soul be snatched from slumber deep,
> Now barren waste, willows weep.
>
> Dread Fáfnirson, Perkelefa,
> With fury, hate, and spell,
> Strong Fáfnirson, Perkelefa,
> Thy grins are knowledge fell.
>
>
> Soon gone is green, black scars are meant
> To ferry haste at will.

Caged-mindless-men are journey's bane.
Gone is one, lo! All the same.

Dread Fáfnirson, Perkelefa,
All ends are in thy voice,
In Malgorod where malice reeks,
And ruined worlds rejoice.

Progress, proceed to world's lament,
From query, truth, and thought.
With confidence in naught but seen,
Nothing's sword, falls fast, is keen.

Dread Fáfnirson, Perkelefa,
Your will shall be our end,
Lest one whose hand is sure to mend
The brooch upon death's friend.

And so, as their song ended—the faërie maids gone in a flash—
the Lych-priest burst free of his prism with unbridled hatred.
There was now no end to his wroth. High he raised his thorned
staff and smote the darkling causeway with terrible force, top-
pling Oriana to her knees amidst his terrifying howls and execra-
tions. Meanwhile, in the world of the Festering Fens, he ordered
his hunched slaves to cast Oriana into the deathly palanquin.
They rushed her at once!

Then, just then, as her end seemed certain, Oriana experienced that terrific commotion once again.

Air. Clamour. Movement. Light. Oriana waited for the worst.
She expected something dreadful.

And something did happen, something dreadful, but something wonderful too. No further harm came to her. Oriana was
not hurled from atop the causeway nor was she cast into the
shackled chamber of death.

O happy hour! For the cloaked horror, his foul servants, and
the helhounds were actually withdrawing from her and her tree.

At once, the enemy's host was beset by a mighty onslaught.
Everywhere came speeding war-wagons and winged horses. The

shrieks from slashing swords and bone-crushing axes were deafening. Glistening white arrows fell thick as winter ice into the enemy's ranks, and ever did the fireworks of faërie magic burst and whistle and singe, filling the foul host with fear and fury alike.

"I was right!" thought Oriana in that unintelligible state of time. "*I* had *seen a battle.*" Indeed was Oriana now aware that the broad hummock surrounding the smoldering blackthorn ash was filled with sights and sounds of war.

What a sight met Oriana's eyes! It was more than she could have ever hoped. All the enchanted wights Oriana had beheld crossing into the world of man in that far-off age were now arrayed before her in pitched battle with the enemy. In the distance, the Silver Causeway was reaching down from soft pearly clouds, glistening as a frozen waterfall in glorious contrast beside the hardened, black profusion stretching from the enemy's own poisonous clouds.

"To me!" Oriana heard one of the tall faërie lords cry from his winged horse, galloping at the van of his warriors and charging the enemy. High was his gilded blade held aloft, stained red from the fray. All about him a greater number of the fiends were already slain.

"Harken to me! O ye leal sons of Danuvia, silvern elves and sturdy dwarves, centaurs, sprites, and fauns—all ye sprung of noble stock! Let none say us nay! Onward! Onward! Onward I say! Honour our departed king! Honour his sacrifice. By your courage, honour him duly! Onward to trounce the enemy! Let us put these accursed hiisi to fear and flight!"

◇◇◇◇◇◇◇◇◇◇◇◇◇◇◇◇◇◇◇◇◇◇◇◇◇◇◇◇◇◇◇◇◇◇◇◇◇◇

In a world away...

Oriana found she, the warrior princess, could not budge from the glutinous pitch that had once been the Silver Causeway. Kneeling and bound, forlorn and in pain, she watched as one, then another, and then a third grey, vapour-like cocoon fell suddenly from the terrible storm clouds above. They descended directly atop the darkling causeway in answer to the Lych's call.

One by one, the Lych-priest tore at the hives of mist with the end of his staff.

"Come, Lucianus of Rucuma! Mightiest of desert sorcerers! Come, Isménor of Boyne! Most cunning of western druids! Come, Maternus of Cologne! Wisest of northern warlocks! Come, my Lych brethren! Come and commune! Come and drink of the true blood!"

Slowly, deathly, hungrily, they emerged from darkness. They were free. The four Lych-priests were at last rejoined!

Equally alike were they, alike apart from their terrible staffs. One bore a rod of knobby-jointed bone, another of greenish-black obsidian, and the third of corroding malachite, yet all were tipped with identical curved, saber-length fangs.

Creeping from their grey shells, the four Lych-priests lost not a moment. At once they touched the tips of their staffs through the ring of Oriana's stone sceptre held yet by Lord Koschei. Instantly, the terrible dragon eye returned, filling the golden circle. Slowly at first but then with increased flow, tears of blood dript dark from the unblinking eye. With mad delight, the Lych-priests thrust cupped hands under the steady flow of scarlet, and then, as if in ritual to some unholy sacrament, gulped ravenously from their blood-filled hands under the cover of deep hoods.

Finished, they turned to Oriana, blood dripping from their hoods and hands. Side by side they swept along the ever blackening causeway, their staffs tilted before them as lances.

It was horrible. The bloodied and cat-like eye filling the ring of the stone sceptre resumed its gaze, probing Oriana's mind. It was searching for something it believed she possessed—ever was it seeking the Sun Brooch.

Yet Oriana resisted—her mind was veiled still in the orb of impregnable crystal. She had strength yet to defy the enemy.

Closer and closer they pressed. They were coming for Oriana!

◇◇

"No!" shouted one of the centaurs who had taken several dark arrows to his haunches. But he was not calling out from pain of his wounds. He had cast his bright, tawny eyes skyward. "They are come!"

"The Lychgate is no more," cried a golden armoured fawn that had just gotten back to his feet after the blow from a well-aimed poleax. The sight that met his eyes high above filled him with dread. "The Lych are come! The apostates of Miðgard are here!" Down from the terrible clouds of soot swept the remaining three Lych-priests; down upon the hardened trail of black vomit into the world between worlds—the very world said to be concealed from the enemy's mind. If indeed it ever had been, it was concealed no longer.

They rode in sleighs of their own, terrible contrivances befit for none but the damned alone. And behind their lead came a vast horde of the enemy's misshapen liegemen, marching in grey columns down the hideous arc, rank upon rank, with drawn scimitars and blue-dragon shields held at the ready.

And there were the skull-speckled moths too! As an ashen cloud of locusts, they swarmed above the Lych-priests, speeding forth to shred the flesh of all faërie kind arrayed below.

In answer, up flew hundreds of nimble, pearl-armoured sprites, their deadly poniards, galails, and leather slings held stoutly. Yet for every sprite praetorian there were at least ten grey flesh-seekers. And more besides were on the way!

Whether on land or in the greying sky, the small contingent of faërie warriors had suddenly become perilously outnumbered by the hosts of Malgorod.

◇◇◇◇◇◇◇◇◇◇◇◇◇◇◇◇◇◇◇◇◇◇◇◇◇◇◇◇◇◇◇◇◇◇

Meanwhile, back in the world of Oriana's tapestry...

The four Lych-priests swept across the ever-corroding causeway, moving as a terrible grey wall of despair. They were descending upon the shackled Oriana with hatred palpable in the air itself.

And then they spoke. In a collective chant, their malice welling, they called to her in evil tones. The stone sceptre and his thorned staff were held menacingly in Lord Koschei's grip.

"The brooch! The brooch! We will have it! You will take us to the brooch!"

In answer, with all the stentorian force her great voice could muster, she proclaimed, "Were you in command of all Hel's minions, nowise should I ever consent to your bidding."

"We do have such command, witch!" they droned with one deep-throated voice. "Malgorod and Hel are joined at last!"

◇◇◇◇◇◇◇◇◇◇◇◇◇◇◇◇◇◇◇◇◇◇◇◇◇◇◇◇◇◇◇◇◇◇

The battle of the Festering Fens raged. Still was Oriana struggling to free her hands and feet of the sharp cords as the free folk of Faërie were fleshing their swords in the blood of the enemy.

Just then, Oriana suddenly felt hot breath panting over her.

"Be still, you filthy whelp!" It was the same bow-legged brigand, the very beast that had prodded her with his vile spear, tearing her clothes. Somehow he had managed to desert the battle undetected.

"Time you got your due comeuppance!" he snarled with a hateful grin.

He raised his scimitar, his intention clear and his eyes merciless. He meant to cleave Oriana's head from her shoulders in one fell swoop!

Down came his blade! Oriana screamed!

But suddenly, there came a terrible crunching sound, and he was at once lifted with a great violence off his clawed feet. Dozens of long, white points stabbed through his shredded chest and neck, dripping with the fiend's dark blood.

It was Lord Whitethorn!

With a mighty heave, he flung the devil squealing from his antlers as though he were no more substantial than the ravelings of old sack cloth. Crumpled, his body fell lifeless back onto the field of battle to join the mangled heaps of fallen hiisi.

"Oh, Sire, thank heavens you're alive! Thank you," she had wanted to say; and, "What happened? Where did you go?" she had wished to ask; and, "Oh, Sire, your poor antler," she had also wished to console when noticing the tip of one of his colossal antlers had indeed been ruthlessly hewn. But she said none of these things, so great was her fear! So short was her time!

For as soon as Lord Whitethorn returned to Oriana's aid, all four Lych-priests—those fell apostates, those dreaded cheaters of death—were upon him. As terrible grey flittermice, they flew through the air, their grey cloaks splayed wide with jagged pinions, exposing their cadaverous bodies beneath. Mighty had the enemy's power grown in their daemonic union.

In seconds they would be upon him. Ignoring them, the stag stared deep into Oriana's eyes and breathed upon and within her. Gone in an instant were the cords biting her wrists and ankles, but gone not was her fright. And with his breath, his breath of life, his breath of freedom from these desolate and ruinous Fens, came also these words:

"Abandoned daughter! You alone can find her. You alone can free her. Find Ethélfleda the faërie queen. In Malgorod, she must be freed. Now go with speed; yet have a care! Have a care— beware! For Dread is near. Dread Fáfnirson is near. Lo, I say," and he sang these staves:

> From his lair a malice flows,
> with Hel-spawn slaves the Lychcraft grows.
> Take you must that Lay of Hope, last hope Ethélfleda.
> Bring to those thy swaddling hence who wait to sing it yet—
> Lost magi guild in crimson cloaks inside their halls of oak.
> Then hasten on ere stars are met to mend fair petals new.

At these words, Oriana watched the world of the Festering Fens, that ruined realm of the Primrose Path, once a living, singing extension of the Wood of Adjoining—her personal travail through truth and deception—grow dim before her eyes. And as it faded, she was aware that she yet sat upon the causeway in her white swan mail, this world too slipping quickly away. Yet in those last moments, Oriana noticed she was no longer wrapt in the fiendish cords just as the causeway was no longer wholly black but mending its sterling radiance by slow degree with renewed silver.

For here too had her great white guide and protector returned to her in her moment of need. Ahead the four Lych-priests and Lord Whitethorn were locked in fearsome sorcery, floating up to the storms clouds above in a churning conflagration of white flame, smoke, and grey ash. Below, her stone sceptre lay at rest upon the renewing silver cobbles, the terrible dragon-eye having fled once again.

It happened, sudden and horrific! Just as Lord Whitethorn and the four Lych-priests were similarly locked in combat of flame and ash before the mighty hawthorn, a single black arrow whistled through the confusion, piercing Oriana in her right shoulder, pinning her fast to her tree!

Oriana screamed in pain. Darker and darker closed both worlds before her eyes. And exactly at that moment, as if in answer to her cry, a single horn sounded from beyond a great distance—distant but still discernible. All fell black. She heard nothing more.

CHAPTER 17

Of Lucky Breaks

"It is dark. I am hot. I am pained. It is dark."

But darkness did relent, reluctantly, did it relent. Frightened and puzzled and weary, Oriana gradually returned to the light of day. Overhead, tiny, blue patches were separated by a thick blur of green. The morning air was cool, and the lifting sun slanted long westering shadows through a dense wood. Her hinder parts were completely drenched with sitting in muddied darnels, and her neck and back stiff from the pressing of knobby bark.

Oriana was miserable. Her head was hot and throbbing something awful, her right shoulder scorching as though a sharp firebrand were piercing her flesh. Rest was all she wanted. And though she was dreadfully uncomfortable, Oriana would have been perfectly content to go on sitting with half-closed eyes, listening to the quiet splashing of a nearby brook, but for the sudden tickle wresting her attention.

Was something crawling over her? To be sure, it felt as if a gentle, velvety footfall was crossing her lap and up her chest. "Gracious! What is that?"

A wet, prickly scraping at her neck finally roused her.

Oriana opened her heavy eyes. Once again did she find herself wondering where she was and how she had come to be there.

"*No!*" she suddenly screamed, and as she wailed, a sharp jolt of pain surged from her right shoulder.

"Don't look at me!" she yelled stricken with panic. *"Not again … no!"*

It was an evil waking, the low light of early morning showing a dreadful sight. Two, tiny, yellow eyes were staring up at her, wide and unblinking. But two tiny eyes she did not behold. Instead, Oriana thought herself to be gazing yet again into the single serpentine eye once filling the circle of the stone sceptre. And in her delirium, the small licks to her neck—well, those she took to be the flickering scourge of dragon tongue.

It is likely Oriana would have gone on babbling had the winding of a single horn not interrupted her mad fit. Long the note rang in her ears. She looked again at her lap. This was no dragon at all. A grey cat with thin, black rings in his tail and tall, pointy ears (taller and pointier than cat ears generally are) was purring on her breast, stretching to lick clean the grim and dried blood from her neck.

Loud the horn sounded a second time, followed by, "Abu! Abu!"

It was a clear, familiar voice calling from somewhere near but out of sight. "Return to me at once, do you hear me? Abu Lubabah! Come back this instant."

Oriana steadied her eyes. She sighed with relief. There was no mistaking where she was.

Oriana at once recognized those telling marks, those broken crockery bits filling the clay-wheel ruts, and narrow clumps of pink lady's-smock and lavender stalks running along the low crag to the west, overhanging the wooded path. No, there could be no mistaking it. Often on her long walks, she would stop here to watch the cuckoos and rowdy warblers play amidst those tumbled, pink petals and purple flower stalks. She was sitting just beyond the wayside of the winding narrows of Feldway Lane, gazing up and round and all through the green of Selwood Forest.

Oriana's heart leapt for joy. She was home!

Oriana looked south along the road. There, little by little, with a *clappity-clap* and sharp creaking filling the air, came the horse and wagon round the bend.

Just as the tradesman's cart rattled into view, the grey cat bounded with a spring from her chest and capered back obediently toward the loud calls.

"Abu—Ah! There's a good—bless my life!" cried the stranger from his wagon. His voice sounded so familiar.

"Is it... could it be?" she muttered wearily to herself.

"Young maid," he called in a frightened way. With two quick slaps from the reins, he jolted his sorrel-coloured horse into a snappy trot.

"I say, young maid, are you in some difficulty? Hullo... Can you hear me?"

Oriana wanted to respond but found she was unable. She was shivering all over.

"Abu! Scat! Get off the road!" shouted the man, only just avoiding the grey cat as it sprang clear of the front wheel.

Oh! What was Oriana's wish to cry out to him! His voice was—was in many ways so very like … like her father's.

"Easy, Boreas! Steady now." The wagon halted where Oriana sat bruised, bloodied, and covered in vile-smelling filth.

Down jumped the short, paunchy, middle-aged man, draping the strap of his curved horn across a hook on the wagon's lamp pole. He was wrapt in a worn, hunter-green burnoose with a deep hood presently thrown back. And beneath his cloak was a long, exotic-looking sticharion, the like of which Oriana had never seen. Round his shoulder was slung an exquisite leathern satchel, burnished bright orange and studded with so great a multitude of glass-coloured beads and pearly bobbles it bore the look of a fine eastern mosaic.

The full measure of his curly, brown beard could not be seen, as it was tucked behind the green folds of his cloak, but his bushy white eyebrows were plainly seen bristling in snowy contrast to the dark brown of his hair. At first sight, Oriana thought him balding till he came and knelt in front of her. She was mistaken—the top of his pate was actually shaved in the image of a cross. How exceedingly odd. If this were indeed a monk's tonsure, it was one none too well known in Wessex, to be sure.

"My dear maid, can you hear me?" he asked, panting. He had a round, kindly face and spoke with a peculiar eastern accent. "Pray, say something!"

"Father … is that you?" muttered Oriana in a hollow voice after several gulps.

"St. Methodius be thanked! You're alive," he said with a heavy breath.

At this, Oriana began gibbering in quick undertones to herself. "Oh, Father, I'm so very glad you've come for me at last. I knew you would return. You've no idea how … I tried so desperately to … Father, oh, Father, I was never so lonely and scared in all my—"

"Easy, maid; calm yourself. You're in no fit state for wasted words."

Oriana, hot and now very thirsty, opened her dozing eyelids fully. "Are you not—No ... I—Oh, I do beg your pardon, sir, but you sound ever so like—Water ... water, if you please, sir," begged Oriana breathlessly.

"Yes, of course, one moment," he said, jumping to his feet.

In no time at all, the cleric had thrown back the tarp of his wagon, fetched a water bladder and terra-cotta goblet from one of several barrels, and was back at Oriana's side, admonishing her to take small sips only.

"Thank you, sir. You are too kind," she whispered feebly.

"Listen, I don't wish to alarm you, young maid, but you have taken fever and your pulse is low. I believe your mind may be much delusional," said the monk, removing his hand from her forehead, his eyes full of questions. "You have taken several injuries. How severely, I have not yet ascertained. Have you the presence of mind to recall how you were waylaid?"

"Waylaid?" breathed Oriana, rubbing some of the filth from her brow.

"Yes, I'm afraid so—" he said, looking round left then right through the forest with anxious eyes. "Villains ranging the woods, no doubt. Can you not remember who assaulted you?"

"I—" Oriana paused. "I'm sure I can't say, sir."

"Well," he returned pointedly, "it is well for you I came when I did. It just may have been my horn that put your assailants to flight. Prudent indeed are the laws of your Alfred.[1]

"Now tell me, what is your name? Where is your village?"

---

[1] The law the stranger is referring to actually predates Alfred's laws by more than two hundred years. West Saxon law from the seventh century stipulated that any stranger journeying through forest must shout or wind a horn upon leaving the road or nearing a village lest he be construed a bandit and put to death or ransom. Similar forest statutes outlawed felling wasteful quantities of trees, burning trees while yet filled with green life, or felling any ancient trees sufficiently large to shelter thirty swine.

"I'm—I'm the daughter of...of world's twain," spluttered Oriana, her fever worsening.

"Listen, child," he interrupted urgently, "you're in want of care. Your cheek is lacerated and not yet stanched. And your right shoulder—well...now I want you to remain calm, for I believe it could be far worse, but your shoulder has been lanced by an evil-looking arrow."

Oriana squeezed her burning eyes and, grinding her teeth, turned her head in the direction of the throbbing pain. The memory of her dark ordeal came rushing back upon her the moment her gaze fell on the bloodstained blouse and black shaft sticking out of her shoulder.

She gasped! "Oh, sir! Help me, please! I—I think I'm fading."

And well Oriana might have thought just then! Now if you've ever had a particularly nasty splinter, you know how frightful it is when you finally decide to brave a peek at it, especially if it's a large, ugly splinter and in deep. Well, just imagine if that splinter were as thick as the end of your thumb and nearly as long as your arm with terrifying, greasy black feathers glued to its end! And then try to imagine observing all this with fevered imagination. Oriana was in a fix, a terrible fix!

"You need looking after, immediately," said the monk gravely. He cleared his throat. "I ask your leave to examine your shoulder."

Oriana's vision was falling dim-grey once again. For not only was she now reflecting on all the horrors at the Festering Fens, but also in seeing the arrow piercing her dress, she suddenly noticed the tree to which she was pinned. It was a hawthorn, a completely ordinary hawthorn tree. Yet on the other hand, its gnarled shape and narrow crack running up its hollow trunk were exactly as she had seen so many times before. For the tree was identical to the one in her vision of the old man, his young pupil, and the faërie king, only much, much smaller. But it didn't make sense. It shouldn't be here. There was no hawthorn near the wide crag at Feldway Lane. If a hawthorn even remotely similar to the one in her tapestry grew anywhere within Selwood Forest, she would have long ago espied it. No, she knew this area well, indeed this very spot.

"But there should be nothing here but that wide ring of toad-stools[2] and thick root I sometimes like to sit on."

Oriana was perplexed and fading fast. Pain, fear, and puzzling drew sleep ever nearer.

"Stay with me, girl! I haven't any restoratives with me," said the monk, patting her hand. "Listen. I must tear your blouse at the shoulder. Have I your consent?"

Oriana nodded and closed her eyes. She grimaced sharply as she felt her kirtle rip.

"What extraordinary good fortune! You have the favour of the saints," he said consolingly. "It's a mercy! The arrow barely cuts your flesh." He paused. "Are you still with me?"

"Yes…I…I hear you."

"I said you are lucky," he repeated. "I am glad to report the shaft has merely grazed your shoulder. It is mostly the linen of your dress and the slightest of flesh that fixes you to the tree—but no bone, thank heavens. You are not lanced as I feared. Still, circumstanced as you are with fever, I'm not aware that I should endeavour to—"

"No…I…I suppose—"

"*Hullo, you there!*" shouted the cleric, interrupting Oriana as he got to his feet and stared ahead. "Over here! Come quickly!"

His shouts startled Oriana. She too stared, heat increasingly filling her eyes and ears.

North through the forest, Oriana saw a young boy passing

---

[2] It's likely a product of her delirium that Oriana perceived no significance in the fact that the toadstools she was recalling had grown in rings. It is of course not completely unheard of for toadstools to grow in circles, though it is rare. This pattern is commonly called a faërie ring, and toadstools are, on occasion, used as umbrellas and stools by such wee faëries as sprites and pixies.

in the distance, swinging a rush basket filled with fresh heather and chasing after a lamb that had apparently got itself lost. It darted into a briar patch, sending a cloud of thieving magpies and grey jackdaws shrieking and scolding in the air with decided annoyance.

The boy stopt abruptly. "What? Me, sir?" he piped over his shoulder, his face stunned.

"Yes, of course you, boy!" snapped the priest firmly. "I certainly am not addressing your lamb. Come quick!"

The boy reached into the thicket, struggled for several moments to free his lamb, slung it hurriedly over his shoulder, and set off toward them—

"Wait—stay, boy!" demanded the cleric suddenly. "Are those yarrows in that sunny patch yonder?" he asked, pointing.

"You mean them yellow flowers?" asked the boy simply.

"Yes. Are they your native yarrows?"

"They may be," returned the boy, putting a shading-hand to his eyes and surveying the foot of a near hill. "Course I'm no great shakes at identifyin'—"

"Never mind!" shouted the priest curtly. "Pull a handful and bring them here. You needn't bother with the roots. Be sharp now!"

A moment afterwards, the boy was staggering over to them, the lamb complaining from his shoulder and a posy of long-stemmed, daisy-like flowers thrown hastily atop the purple heather of his basket. Oriana got a good look at him as he drew near before closing her eyes once more. She knew this boy.

"If you can hear me, young maid, I'm about to break the arrow pinching your shoulder," said the monk warningly. "In a moment, you'll be free of—ah good! Stay with her for a moment."

Oriana could hear the priest scurrying back to his wagon. He was making quite a clatter as he rummaged through it.

"My lady—my lady, is it you?" asked the boy in a low whisper, setting his lamb in a patch of clover. "Lady Oriana, is that you?"

She did not respond. She might have recognized the boy's voice, only she was now too deep with fever.

"What's your name?" called the priest with heavy breath from behind his wagon.

"Offa, Your Grace, son of Alaric of Oakleigh," returned the boy, his voice trailing off inaudibly. He sounded upset. Oriana felt a light touch at the sore on her cheek.

"What? Speak up, boy!" scolded the monk irascibly. "I have old ears!"

"Offa, your servant, sir," returned the boy, his voice carrying farther this time.

"Of Oakleigh, did you say?"

"Yes, Your Grace!"

"Is that the nearest village?" he asked, still searching for something.

"'Tis, m' lord."

"How far?"

"Not two miles north on Feldway."

"Hmm, Oakleigh?" muttered the priest. "Did you say your father's name is Alaric?"

"Yes, sir."

"He isn't by chance a blacksmith, is he?"

"Yes, best in our shire," answered Offa proudly. "You may depend upon it, sir. But how—"

"Does he also display the natural aptitude for curing?"

"Why...why yes, sir, a little—"

"Splendid! This is an auspicious meeting. Tell me, Offa, son of Alaric, you seem a worthy sort of boy; do you know this maid?" he asked swiftly. Oriana could hear him returning to her side. "Does she come from your village?"

"She's all over filth, sir; so...so bedraggled I...I really

couldn't say for certain," muttered Offa with a regrettable air. "But I'd venture to guess—that is, I think she's the lost lady of our village, Lady Oriana. She went missin' nearly a month back. Folk've been searchin' all over fer 'er ever since—and not all fer the right reasons, I might add. A world of trouble, she's in, and that's a fact, or so me dad said just yesternight."

While Oriana had just enough awareness to hear what was going on about her, she could no longer speak nor open her eyes. Quickly, irresistibly, she was fading.

"Lady Oriana, if indeed that is your name, I want you to bite down on this if you can."

Suddenly a thin strip of leather was thrust between her teeth. She clenched her jaw and prepared herself.

Just then she felt something wet nuzzling her ankle—"Abu, stop that!" said the monk softly. "Get back! Don't worry, she'll be all right. Now, my lady, if you can hear me, I'm about to break the arrow—I'm afraid it's going to hurt. Bite down hard—"

And hurt it did! Oriana made a sharp whimper as the pain of tearing flesh surged from her shoulder. Instantly, what felt like a gauze of moist flower petals was being pressed into the sticky warmth at her shoulder. Then came the same feeling of moist petals to her cheek.

"It is dark. I am hot. I am pained. It is dark. Father! Bathilda! Penda!" she thought. "Help me! I need you!" It was her last thought. Some more fidgeting pressure to her shoulder and cheek, and Oriana was claimed by an uneasy darkness once more.

Solum Initium
(Only the Beginning)

Thus ends Book One of the Oriana Oakleigh series. Book Two, *Oriana Oakleigh and the Dragon Danes,* continues with Oriana's search for Britain's elusive druids amidst ever deepening dangers and political tumult between Saxons, Britons, Norse, and Danes; it further tells of Oriana's discovering that hers is but one of many fates bound to the quest of the Mundi Rediendum.